THE FAIRY TALE SERIES
CREATED BY TERRI WINDLING

ONCE UPON A TIME . . .

. . . fairy tales were written for young and old
alike. It is only in the last century that they
have been deemed fit for children
and stripped of much of their original
complexity, sensuality, and power to frighten
and delight.

⸎⸎⸎

Tor Books is proud to present the latest
offering in the Fairy Tale series—a
growing library of beautifully designed
original novels by acclaimed writers of fantasy and horror, each retelling a classic tale
such as Snow White and Rose Red, Briar
Rose, Tam Lin, and others in interesting—often startling—new ways.

Tor Books by Tanith Lee

Black Unicorn
Gold Unicorn
Red Unicorn

White as Snow

TANITH LEE

A TOM DOHERTY ASSOCIATES BOOK
NEW YORK

WHITE AS SNOW

Copyright © 2000 by Tanith Lee

Introduction © 2000 by Terri Windling, The Endicott Studio
www.Endicott-studio.com

Edited by Terri Windling

A Tor Book
Published by Tom Doherty Associates, LLC
175 Fifth Avenue
New York, NY 10010

www.tor.com

Tor® is a registered trademark of Tom Doherty Associates, LLC.

Library of Congress Cataloging-in-Publication Data

Lee, Tanith.
    White as snow / Tanith Lee.
        p. cm.
    "A Tom Doherty Associates book."
    ISBN 0-312-86993-2 (alk. paper)
    1. Snow White (Tale)—Adaptations. 2. Princesses—Fiction. 3. Fairy Tales—Adaptations. I. Title.

PR6062.E4163 W48 2000
823'.914—dc21   00-041160

First Edition: December 2000

Printed in the United States of America

0 9 8 7 6 5 4 3 2 1

ACKNOWLEDGMENTS

The author would like to extend most grateful thanks to Barbara Levick, of St. Hilda's College, Oxford, for her invaluable help and enlightenment on the Latin fringes of this book.

Nota Bene

Herbs—whether going by recognizable names or not; their preparation and dosage—as mentioned in this book, relate to old texts and methods, and are any way specified only in connection to characters. Needless to say, no prescription should ever be attempted without the guidance of a qualified herbalist or other professional dispenser.

There's a special kinship between the new and gibbous moons; fit them together and they complete a circle. Behind the full moon there's only the dark, empty sky.

—MAVIS HAUT
"Phases of the Moon"
The Necessary Virgin

Contents

INTRODUCTION
by Terri Windling

Once upon a time fairy tales were told to audiences of young and old alike. It is only in the last century that such tales were deemed fit only for small children, stripped of much of their original complexity, sensuality, and power to frighten and delight. In the Fairy Tale series, some of the finest writers working today are going back to the older versions of tales and reclaiming them for adult readers, reworking their themes into original, highly unusual fantasy novels.

This series began many years ago, when artist Thomas Canty and I asked some of our favorite writers if they would create new novels based on old tales, each one to be published with Tom's distinctive, Pre-Raphaelite-inspired cover art. The writers were free to approach the tales in any way they liked, and so some recast the stories in the modern settings, while others used historical landscapes or created enchanted imaginary worlds. The first volumes in the series (originally published by Ace Books) were *The Sun, the Moon, and the Stars* by Steven Brust; *Jack the Giant-killer* (later expanded into *Jack of Kinrowan*) by Charles de Lint; and *The Nightingale* by Kara Dalkey. The series then moved to its present home at Tor Books, where we've published *Snow White and Rose Red* by Patricia C. Wrede; *Tam Lin* by Pamela Dean; and *Briar Rose* by Jane Yolen.

Now, after a long hiatus (during which we produced six volumes of adult fairy tale short stories in the *Snow White, Blood Red* series, co-edited with Ellen Datlow), we're back to offer more fairy tale novels, beginning with a splendid retelling of Snow White by a modern master of the form: English writer Tanith Lee. We're particularly pleased to welcome Tanith into this series because she's one of the first writers in the fantasy field to work extensively with fairy tale material, in her groundbreaking collection of stories *Red as Blood: Tales from the Sisters Grimmer* (1983). Lee has been called "the Angela Carter of fantasy literature"—and like Carter, her approach to fairy tales is very dark, sensual, and thoroughly steeped in the folklore tradition. She has worked with the Snow White theme twice before, in her haunting short stories "Red as Blood" and "Snow-Drop." Now she takes a very different approach in a brutal, mystical version of the story invoking the Demeter-Persephone myth and old pagan religions of the forest.

To most people today, the name Snow White evokes visions of dwarves whistling as they work, and a wide-eyed, fluttery princess singing, "Some day my prince will come." (A friend of mine claims this song is responsible for the problems of a whole generation of American women.) Yet the Snow White theme is one of the darkest and strangest to be found in the fairy tale canon—a chilling tale of murderous rivalry, adolescent sexual ripening, poisoned gifts, blood on snow, witchcraft, and ritual cannibalism . . . in short, not a tale originally intended for children's tender ears.

Disney's well-known film version of the story, released in 1937, was ostensibly based on the German tale popularized by the Brothers Grimm. Originally titled "Snow-drop" and published in *Kinder- und Hausmärchen* in 1812, the Grimms' "Snow

White" is a darker, chillier story than the musical Disney cartoon, yet it too had been cleaned up for publication, edited to emphasize the good Protestant values held by Jacob and Wilhelm Grimm. Although legend has them roaming the countryside collecting stories from stout German peasants, in truth the Grimm brothers acquired most of their tales from a middle-class circle of friends, who in turn were recounting tales learned from nurses, governesses, and servants, not all of them German. Thus the "German folktales" published by the Grimms included those from the oral folk traditions of other countries, and were also influenced by the literary fairy tales of writers like Straparola, Basile, D'Aulnoy, and Perrault in Italy and France.

Variants of Snow White were popular around the world long before the Grimms claimed it for Germany, but their version of the story (along with Walt Disney's) is the one that most people know today. Elements from the story can be traced back to the oldest oral tales of antiquity, but the earliest known written version was published in Italy in 1634. This version was called The Young Slave, published in Giambattista Basile's *Il Pentamerone*, and is believed to have influenced subsequent retellings—including a German text published by J. K. Musaus in 1784 and the Grimms' text in 1812. In Basile's story, a baron's unmarried sister swallows a rose leaf and finds herself pregnant. She secretly gives birth to a beautiful baby girl, and names her Lisa. Fairies are summoned to bless the child, but the last one stumbles in her haste and utters an unfortunate curse instead. As a result, Lisa dies at the age of seven while her mother is combing her hair. The grieving mother has the body encased in seven caskets made of crystal, hidden in a distant room of the palace under lock and key. Some years later, lying on her deathbed, she hands the key to her brother, the baron, but makes him promise that he will never open the little locked door. More years pass, and the baron takes a wife. One day he is called to a hunting party, so he gives the key to his wife with strict instructions not to use it. Impelled by suspicion and jealousy, she heads immediately for the locked room; there she discovers a beautiful young maiden who seems to be fast asleep. (Basile explains that Lisa has grown and matured in her enchanted state.) The baroness seizes Lisa by the hair—dislodging the comb and waking her. Thinking she's found her husband's secret mistress, the jealous baroness cuts off Lisa's hair, dresses her in rags, and beats her black and blue. The baron returns and inquires after the ill-used young woman cowering in the shadows. His wife tells him that the girl is a kitchen slave, sent by her aunt. One day the baron sets off for a fair, having promised everyone in the household a gift, including even the cats and the slave. Lisa requests that he bring back a doll, a knife, and a pumice stone. After various troubles, he procures these things and gives them to the young slave. Alone by the hearth, Lisa talks to the doll as she sharpens the knife to kill herself—but the baron overhears her sad tale, and learns she's his own sister's child. The girl is then restored to beauty, health, wealth, and heritage—while the cruel baroness is cast away, sent back to her parents.

The Young Slave contains motifs we recognize not only from Snow White but also Sleeping Beauty (the fairy's curse), Bluebeard (the locked room), Beauty and the Beast (the troublesome gift), and other tales. An aunt-by-marriage plays the villain here—but a scheming stepmother is front and center in another peculiar Italian tale, titled "The Crystal Casket." In this second Snow White variant, a lovely young girl is persuaded to introduce her teacher to her widowed father. Marriage ensues, but instead of gratitude, the teacher treats her stepdaughter cruelly. An eagle helps the girl to escape and hides her in a palace of fairies. The stepmother hires a witch, who takes a basket of poisoned sweetmeats to the girl. She eats one and dies. The fairies revive her. The witch strikes again, disguised as a tailoress with a beautiful dress to sell. When the dress is laced up, the girl falls down dead, and this time the fairies will not revive her. (They're miffed that she keeps ignoring their warnings.) They place her body in a gem-encrusted casket, rope the casket to the back of a horse, and send it off to the city. Horse and casket are found by a prince, who falls in love with the beautiful "doll" and takes her home. "But my son, she's dead!" protests the queen. The prince will not be parted from his treasure; he locks himself away in a tower with the girl, "consumed by love." Soon he is called away to battle, leaving the doll in the care of his mother. His mother ignores the macabre creature—until a letter arrives warning her of the prince's impending return. Quickly she calls for her chambermaids and commands them to clean the neglected corpse. They do so, spilling water in their haste, badly staining the maiden's dress. The queen thinks quickly. "Take off the dress! We'll have another one made, and my son will never know." As they loosen the laces, the maiden returns to life, confused and alarmed. The queen hears her story with sympathy, dresses the girl in her own royal clothes, and then, oddly, hides the girl behind lock and key when the prince comes home. He immediately asks to see his "wife." (What on earth was he doing in that locked room?) "My son," says the Queen, "that girl was dead. She smelled so badly that we buried her." He rages and weeps. The queen relents. The girl is summoned, her story is told, and the two are now properly wed.

In a third Italian version of the tale, it's the girl's own mother who wishes her ill—an innkeeper named Bella Venezia who cannot stand a rival in beauty. First she imprisons her blossoming child in a lonely hut by the sea; then she seduces a kitchen boy and demands that he murder the girl. "Bring back her eyes and a bottle of her blood," she says, "and I'll marry you." The servant abandons the girl in the woods, returning with the eyes and blood of a lamb. The girl wanders through the forest and soon finds a cave where twelve robbers live. She keeps house for the burly men, who love her and deck her in jewels every night— but her mother eventually gets wind of this, and is now more jealous than ever. Disguised as an old peddler woman, she sells her daughter a poisoned hair broach. When the robbers return, they find the girl dead, so they bury her in a hollow tree. At length the fair corpse is discovered by a prince, who takes it home and fawns over it. The queen is appalled, but the prince insists upon marrying the beautiful maiden. Her body is bathed and dressed for a wedding. The royal hairdresser is summoned. As the girl's hair is combed, the broach is discovered, removed, and she comes back to life.

In a Scottish version of the story, a trout in a well takes the role we now associate with a magical mirror. Each day a queen asks, "Am I not the loveliest woman in the world?" The trout assures the queen that she is . . . until her daughter comes of age, surpassing the mother in beauty. The queen falls ill with envy, summons the king, and demands the death of their daughter. He pretends to comply, but sends the girl off to marry a foreign king. Eventually the trout informs the queen that the princess is still alive—so she crosses the sea to her daughter's kingdom, and kills her with a poisoned needle. The young king, grieving, locks his beloved's corpse away in a high tower. Eventually he takes another wife, who notes that he always seems sad. "What gift," she asks, "could I give to you, husband, so that you would know joy and laughter again?" He tells her that nothing can bring him joy but his first wife restored to life. She sends her husband up to the tower, where he finds his beloved alive and well—for his second wife had discovered the girl, and removed the poisoned needle from her finger. The lovers thus reunited, the good-hearted second wife offers to go away. "Oh! indeed you shall not go away," says the king, "but I shall have both of you now." They live happily together until (blast that trout!) the jealous queen gets wind of the fact that her daughter has come back to life. She crosses the ocean once again, bearing a poisoned drink this time. The clever second wife takes matters in hand. She greets the wicked queen on the shore, and tricks the woman into drinking from the poisoned cup herself. After this, the young king and his two wives enjoy a long, peaceful life. (I've always particularly liked this rendition, contrasting the toxic

mother-daughter relationship with the envy-free bond forged between the two wives.)

Jacob and Wilhelm Grimm collected their version of Snow
White from Jeannette and Amalie Hassenpflug, family friends in
the town of Cassel. (Ludwig Grimm, their brother, was engaged
to marry a third Hassenpflug sister.) The Hassenpflug's tale contains several elements from the earlier Italian stories, combined
with imagery distinct to the lore of northern Europe. Dwarfs do
not appear in the Italian variants, for instance, as dwarfs play
little part in the Italian folk tradition. The Nordic and Germanic
traditions, by contrast, contain a wealth of magical lore about
burly little men who toil under the earth, associated with gems,
iron ore, alchemy, and the blacksmith's craft. The Grimms' version starts, as so many fairy stories, with a barren queen who
longs for a child. It's a winter's tale in this northern clime, set in
a landscape of vast, icy forests. The queen stands sewing by an
open window. She pricks her finger. Blood falls on the snow.
"Would that I had a child," she sighs, "as white as snow, as red
as blood, and as black as the wood of the window-frame." Her
wish is granted, but the gentle queen expires as soon as her baby
is born . . . or so most readers now believe. Yet the death of the
queen, the "good mother," was a plot twist introduced by the
Grimms. In their earliest versions of the tale (the manuscript of
1810, and the first edition of 1812), it is Snow White's natural
mother whose jealousy takes a murderous bent. She was turned
into an evil stepmother in editions from 1819 onward. "The
Grimm Brothers worked on the *Kinder- und Hausmärchen* in draft
after draft after the first edition of 1812," Marina Warner explains
(in her excellent fairy tale study, *From the Beast to the Blonde*),
"Wilhelm in particular infusing the new editions with his Christian fervor, emboldening the moral strokes of the plot, meting
out penalties to the wicked and rewards to the just to conform
with prevailing Christian and social values. They also softened
the harshness—especially in family dramas. They could not

make it disappear altogether, but in Hansel and Gretel, for instance, they added the father's miserable reluctance to an earlier version in which both parents had proposed the abandonment of their children, and turned the mother into a wicked stepmother. On the whole, they tended towards sparing the father's villainy, and substituting another wife for the natural mother, who had figured as the villain in versions they were told. . . . For them, the bad mother had to disappear in order for the ideal to survive and allow Mother to flourish as symbol of the eternal feminine, the motherland, and the family itself as the highest social desideratum." It should also be noted that early Grimms' fairy tales were not published with children in mind—they were published for scholars, in editions replete with footnotes and annotations. It was later, as the tales became popular with lay readers, families, and children, that the brothers took more care to delete material they deemed inappropriate, editing, revising, and sometimes rewriting the tales altogether.

Whether mother or stepmother, the murderous queen remains one of the most vivid villains in folkloric history. She orders the death of an innocent girl, demands her heart (or liver, or tongue), then boils, salts, and eats the tender organ with a gourmand's pleasure. "The term 'narcissism' seems altogether too slippery to be the only one we want here," writes Roger Sales (in *Fairy Tales and After*). "There is, for instance, no suggestion that the queen's absorption in her beauty ever gives her pleasure, or that the desire for power through sexual attractiveness is itself a sexual feeling. What is stressed is the anger and fear that attend the queen's realization that as she and Snow White both get older, she must lose. That is why the major feeling invoked is not jealousy but envy: to make beauty that important is to reduce the world to one in which only two people count." The queen's actions are attributed to vanity-run-amok, but perhaps also fear and self-preservation. She is a woman whose power derives from her beauty; it is this, the tale implies, that provides her place in the castle's hierarchy. If the king's attention turns from his wife to another (or even his daughter, as it does in stories like Allerleirauh), what power is left to an aging woman? *Witchcraft*, the tale answers. Potions, poisons, and self-protection. In the Grimms' tale, an enchanted mirror serves not only as a clever plot device and a useful agent of information, but as a symbolic representation of the queen's insecurity, solipsism, and growing madness. Snow White, too, is a mirror—a reversed mirror of the queen, reflecting all she is not. Each day she becomes more lovely, more good—as the queen becomes the opposite. Snow White's father, the king, is notable only by his absence, his apparent indifference, and his failure to protect his own child. Yet, as Angela Carter once pointed out in a comment about Cinderella's father, the king in Snow White is also "the unmoved mover, the unseen organizing principle. Without the absent father there would have been no story because there would have been no conflict."

Blood is a recurrent image in this story, warm red blood against virgin white snow. Three drops of blood symbolize Snow White's conception. And the death of the (good) mother in childbirth. And menstruation: the beginning of both sexual maturation and the (bad) mother's hatred. The queen demands blood on the knife of the hunter as proof that her daughter is dead, as instructed. The bloody meal she then makes of the heart carries the echo of ancient pagan beliefs in which ingesting an enemy's flesh is a method of claiming their strength and their magic. Fairy tale writer Carrie Miner reflects that as children come forth from a mother's womb, "it seems as though some women feel they 'own' their child—that it's nothing but an extension of them. This theme is beautifully wrought in Toni Morrison's novel *Beloved*. The consumption of the apple by Snow White seems to mirror the stepmother's desire to consume her daughter—to take Snow White's very essence into herself." The queen in Anne Sexton's poem "Snow White and the Seven Dwarfs" (from her brilliant collection *Transformations*) cries: "Bring me her heart . . . and I will salt it and eat it. The hunter, however, let his prisoner go and brought a boar's heart back to the castle. The queen chewed it up like a cube steak. 'Now I am the fairest,' she said, lapping her slim white fingers."

Driven out of her home, out of her past, away from all that is harsh but familiar, Snow White makes her way through the wilderness to an unknown destination. This, as novelist Midori Snyder has pointed out, is often the fate of heroines in the arc of traditional folk narratives. Unlike sons who set off to win their fortune, who are journeying *toward* adventure, the daughters are outcasts, running *away*. The princes usually return at the end of the story, bringing treasure and magical brides. Princesses do not return; they must forge new lives, new alliances. Snow White's journey begins with the huntsman—who is the queen's hench-man in the Grimms' and the queen's lover in other versions of the tale. He defies his mistress and does not slay the girl, but he is no true ally, merely a coward. He declares that Snow White is too beautiful to kill, but note that he does not lead her to safety; he abandons her in the forest, aware that wolves will soon finish his job. Yet even here, the girl's blossoming beauty, the agent of all of her troubles at home, begins to assert itself as a form of power in the world of men. Beauty aids her once again when she finds the house of the dwarves and falls asleep in one of their little beds. Anger toward the unknown intruder turns to wonder as they watch her sleep; enchanted by physical perfec-tion, the dwarfs decide she may stay with them. This was later revised by the Grimms, and Snow White must consent to a long list of household duties before they'll agree to her stay. (The Disney version takes this one step further, and Snow White does the work unasked.) The change not only emphasizes the virtues of a proper work ethic, but it leads attention away from the sheer peculiarity of a ripe young girl keeping house with seven burly, earthy, and clearly unmarried men. Bruno Bettelheim, author of *The Uses of Enchantment*, who looked at fairy tales through a Freudian lens, claimed the dwarfs "were not men in any sexual sense—their way of life, their interest in material goods to the exclusion of love, suggest a pre-Oedipal existence." This reading of the tale ignores the fact that the dwarves take the place of robbers or human miners found in older renditions of the story. Some of the older narratives assure us that the robbers "loved the girl as they would a sister," while others are mute on the subject, or else intriguingly ambiguous.

Soon, the queen learns that Snow White still lives. She determines to kill her young rival herself. Here the queen stands revealed as a full-fledged witch, sorceress, or alchemist, creating potions in a "secret, lonely room where no one ever came." Disguised as an old peddler woman, she sells the girl poisoned bodice laces, then combs her hair with a poisoned comb. After each of her visits, the dwarfs return home to find their young housekeeper dead. "Why couldn't she heed our warnings?" asked "The Seventh Dwarf" in a poem by Gwen Strauss (from *Trail of Stones*). "Time and again we told her to stay inside the house, to do her tasks away from the door. We urged her daily, but she was a flitting butterfly. . . . She was driven by something." In imagery old as Adam and Eve, the disguised queen comes one last time to tempt Snow White with a crisp, red apple. "Do you think I did not know her . . . ?" writes Delia Sherman, explaining the princess's point of view in her heartbreaking poem "From Snow White to the Prince" (published in *The Armless Maiden*). "Of course I took her poisoned gifts. I wanted to feel her hands coming out of my hair, to let her lace me up, to take an apple from her hand, a smile from her lips, as when I was a child." In Sherman's poem, Snow White is every abused child who ever longed for a parent's love. "Don't curse me, Mother," echoes Olga Broumas in her poem "Snow White" (in *Beginning with O*). ". . . No salve, no ointment in a doctor's tube, no brew in a witch's kettle, no lover's mouth, no friend or god could heal me if your heart turned in anathema, grew stone against me."

In other versions of the story, taking on local coloration as it travels around the world, the princess is slain through poisoned flowers, cake, wine, pomegranate seeds, a golden ring, a corset, shoes, coins, or the ink of a letter. The dwarfs (robbers, miners, or monks) can revive her once, and even twice; but with the third act of poisoning, she seems indisputably dead. Her body (too beautiful to bury, and strangely incorruptible) is then carefully, almost fetishistically displayed in a clear glass casket—or else on a woodland bier, or a four-poster bed, or a shrine surrounded by candles. (In other variants, she is thrown into the sea, abandoned on a doorstep or windowsill, sent to the fairies, stolen by gypsies, even carried on a reindeer's antlers.) There are various ways Snow White's spell of death/sleep is broken, but generally not with a kiss. (That seems to be a modern addition.) The poisoned item must be removed, usually by pure accident. In the chaste Grimms' version of the tale, where the necrophilic imagery is strictly toned down, Snow White's body is handed over to a prince who happens to be passing by. Struck, as all men in this tale are struck, by the girl's extraordinary beauty, he swears he can't live without her. The dwarfs consent. (He's a prince, after all.) "I will prize her as my dearest possession," the prince promises the sad little men. As his servants bear the casket away, one stumbles and the fatal piece of poisoned apple flies from her mouth. "Oh heavens, where am I?" she cries as she wakes. "You're with me," he quickly assures the girl. (He is, remember, a stranger to her. Only in the Disney film do they meet at the onset of the tale.) He declares his love, offers marriage, and promptly spirits the beautiful maiden away. One dwarf protests this end to the story in Gerald Locklin's poem "The Dwarf" (in *Disenchantments*): "She went away from us upon a snow-white steed, the forest virgin scented with the rain of evergreen, to while the mythic hours in a prince's castle. Was it right of her to take away her apple innocence from seven dappled dwarfs, to arbitrarily absent us from felicity?" Even Snow White protests in Delia Sherman's "Snow White to the Prince," saying: ". . . you woke me, or your horses did, stumbling as they bore me down the path, shaking the poisoned apple from my throat. And now you say you love me, and would wed me for my beauty's sake. My cursed beauty. Will you hear now why I curse it? It should have been my mother's—it had been, until I took it from her." The prince responds to her in Polly Peterson's poem "The Prince to Snow White": "Did you think that I found you, by chance, Maiden? Did you believe I was drawn to your crystal casket, like a hummingbird to its nectar, by the allure of ruby lips, the gaze of azure eyes? . . . You are beautiful, sublime, yet not so lovely as our daughter will be: your mother's daughter's child—her immortality."

In the final scene of the Grimms' version, the queen is invited to Snow White's wedding, then forced to dance in red-hot shoes. "First your toes will smoke," writes Anne Sexton (in *Transformations*), "and then your heels will turn black and you will fry upward like a frog, she was told. And so she danced until she was dead, a subterranean figure, her tongue flicking in and out like a gas jet." It's a scene left out of the Disney film and most modern children's renditions.

Walt Disney made several other significant changes to the Grimms' fairy tale when he chose Snow White as the subject of his very first full-length animated film. At the time, no one knew whether audiences would actually sit through an eighty-four minute cartoon, and the film was called "Disney's folly" as he poured more and more time and money into it. Walt Disney was fond of fairy tales, but he was not shy of reshaping them to suit his needs, turning them into the simple, comedic tales he believed that his audiences wanted (a generation marked by economic depression and two world wars.) He emphasized the dwarfs, giving them names, distinct personalities, and a cozy cottage in a sun-dappled wood full of bluebirds, bunnies, and flowers, not snow. The role of the prince is greatly expanded, and the square-jawed fellow becomes pivotal to the story. His love for Snow White, demonstrated at the very beginning of the Disney film, becomes the spark that sets off the powderkeg of the stepmother's rage. In this singing, dancing, whistling version, only the queen retains some of the real power of the traditional tale. She's a genuinely frightening figure, and far more compelling than little Snow White (despite early notes in the making of the film in which, it's suggested, the queen should be a "vain-batty-self-satisfied, comedy type" and "verging on the ridiculous"). Snow White (who was drawn as a blonde at one point) is wide-eyed, giddy and childish, wearing rags (Cinderella-style) at the start of the film, downtrodden but plucky. This gives Disney's rendition of the tale its peculiarly American flavor, implying that what we are watching is a Horatio-Alger-type "rags to riches" story. (In fact, it's a story of "riches to rags to riches," in which privilege is lost and then restored. Snow White's pedigree beauty and class origins assure her salvation, not her housekeeping skills.) Although the film was a commercial triumph and has been beloved by generations of children, critics through the years have protested the sweeping changes Disney Studios made, and continues to make, when retelling such tales. Walt himself responded, "It's just that people now don't want fairy stories the way they were written. They were too rough. In the end they'll probably remember the story the way we film it anyway."

Regrettably, time has proved him right. Through films, books, toys, and merchandise recognized all around the world, Disney became the major disseminator of fairy tales in his century. "Disney's vision," writers Marina Warner, "has effected everybody's idea of fairy tales themselves: until writers and anthologists began looking again, passive hapless heroines and vigorous wicked older women seemed generic. Disney selected certain stories and stressed certain sides to them; the wise children, the cunning little vixens, the teeming populations of the stories were drastically purged. The disequilibrium between good and evil in these films has influenced contemporary perceptions of fairy tale, as a form where sinister and gruesome forces are magnified and prevail throughout—until the very last moment where, *ex machina*, right and goodness overcome them."

Fortunately, writers and anthologists *have* been looking again at Snow White and other fairy tales, finding that there is much more to the old material than Disney would have us believe. Prompted by writers like Tanith Lee, Jane Yolen, Angela Carter, A. S. Byatt, Margaret Atwood, Robert Coover, Emma Donoghue, Robin McKinley, Gregory Maguire, and the poets mentioned above, fairy tales are being reclaimed from Disney cartoons and from shelves marked "children only," explored and restored as a fascinating part of the world's literary heritage. If Tanith Lee's macabre new version of Snow White whets your appetite for other modern retellings, I also recommend the following: "Snow, Glass, Apples" by Neil Gaiman (published in *Smoke and Mirrors*, and in *The Year's Best Fantasy and Horror, Vol. 8*) is a gorgeous version, lush and dark, from the "evil" queen's point of view— as is Pat Murphy's affecting version, "The True Story" (in *Black Swan, White Raven*). Jane Yolen's "Snow in Summer" (in *Black Heart, Ivory Bones*) is a modern Appalachian treatment of the story. Michael Blumlein's "Snow in Dirt" (*Black Swan, White Raven*) is also a contemporary piece, satiric, clever, and strange. Donald Barthleme's acclaimed novel *Snow White* is a brash, witty, rather raunchy work of experimental fiction (first published in 1965, and somewhat dated, but still interesting). A. S. Byatt discusses the Snow White tale in her delicious essay "Ice, Snow, Glass" (published in *Mirror, Mirror on the Wall: Women Writers Explore Their Favorite Fairy Tales*); she also worked a related Grimms' tale, "The Glass Coffin," into her enchanting, award-winning novel *Possession*, and her short story "Cold" (published in *Elementals: Stories of Ice and Fire*). You'll find further information (and book recommendations) on three excellent fairy tale Web sites: Heidi Ann Heiner's "Surlalune Fairy Tale Pages" (*members.aol.com/surlalune/frytales/*), Kay E. Vandergrift's "Snow White Page" (*www.scils.rutgers.edu/special/kay/snowwhite.html*), and Christine Daae's "Introduction to Fairy Tales" (*www.darkgoddess.com/fairy/*).

We hope you'll enjoy this unusual tale of winter wolves and

blood on snow. With the help of the good folks at Tor Books, we have more Fairy Tale series novels in store for you. For information on forthcoming publications, visit the Tor Books Web site (*www.tor.com*) or my own Web site, The Endicott Studio of Mythic Arts (*www.endicott-studio.com*).

T. W.
Tucson, Arizona
and Devon, U.K.

BOOK ONE

Tam Atra Quam Ebenus
Black as Ebony

The Mirror: The Maiden

ONCE UPON A TIME, IN WINTER, there was a mirror.

It had been brought from the East, where the sun rose, and the moon; that always-rising place of curiosity and brightness.

The mirror was made of glass, which, in the lands it had been brought to, was not usual. And so, to protect it (but also because those who looked in it were sometimes very startled by the monstrous clarity of the reflections), it had a lid, which could be closed. And often then, the mirror stood shut by its silver lid, like a sleeping—or a dead—eye.

However, today the mirror had been opened.

What did the mirror see, looking in?

A young girl, slender, clear and bright herself with youth. She stared at the mirror, which she knew must be sorcerous, and then swiftly away.

But the mirror continued to mirror her as she went to a high window and, instead, looked out.

"What can you see?" asked the blind old nurse in her turn.

"The snow," said the girl, "and the black trees stretching up their arms to the sky. Nothing else."

The nurse sang in her cracked voice:

> *"Black is the wood, white is the snow,*
> *Red the roses that under it grow—"*

The girl paid no attention. She had observed something flickering, shifting through the avenues of the winter forest—was it a group of riders? A pack of wolves? Then nothing was there, only the wind thrusting by the trees. (War was bounding over the snow's book toward this castle, but the girl had not seen this. And the old nurse, witch enough once to have done so, was half blind too, now, in her psychic vision.)

"Black is the wood—"

"Hush," said the girl, irritated. She spoke to the nurse as, seven years before, the nurse would have spoken to her.

Without protest the old woman withdrew herself, a snail, into the shell of her thoughts.

And the girl went on staring at the forest. Her name was Arpazia. Her hair was black as the woods, her pale skin better than the snow. Her eyes, though, were a light, water-gray. She was fourteen years of age. She longed for change, not knowing the change of all things was almost upon her, nor what it could mean.

Draco the war-leader, soon to be a king, led his army through the forests. In his rough way, he had studied strategy, and was well aware few battles were fought by choice in winter. So, he had chosen it.

His men no longer grumbled. They were warmed by spoils from the last three stone towns, and all the villages they had sacked.

Up there, through the trees, stood the last castle on the board. But it would be easy to take. The lordling was old, and his battalions lax. Few were left to come to his help. Draco doubted if even a spy had reached this spot with the news of an army's approach.

He had dreamed of that castle. In the dream it had been iron and obdurate, but nevertheless he smashed it like an egg. Then they all acknowledged him, gave in. He rode to the palace at Belgra Demitu, a king.

As dusk began, deer roasted on the red fires. They ate them, and drank wine. Near midnight, Draco went to the priest and prayed.

"God favors you, my son."

"I know it, Father. How else could I have come so far?"

"When you are raised high, do not forget God then."

Draco thought the priest meant he must not forget the Church and his gifts which must be made to the altar, piling on the gold. But there would be plenty, and besides he was devout.

"Amen, Father."

They had dressed Arpazia in the carmine dress, braided her hair, and placed on her head a slim golden circlet with a white veil. She was being taken to see her father.

Arpazia had no memory of her mother. She had died, they told Arpazia, at the child's birth. From the beginning, too, she had not had a father, only this remote figure *called* a father, old to her even when she was an infant, who now and then acknowledged her, gave her some strange inimical present, like the emerald ring too big for her, or the Eastern mirror.

He sat in his library, and below, down the stair in the hall, there was a lot of noise, the clashing of the men in their mail, and sometimes women crying. ("What is it?" she had asked her maids, hearing these sounds at first distantly. "Has someone died?" The maids looked frightened. It was the old nurse who said, rocking herself slowly, half smiling—but without joy—"Most will.") They were at war, it seemed. A horde marched toward them. Arpazia, too, became afraid, but only a little, for it was beyond her understanding.

The library was a small room, its stone walls hung with carpets, or else shelves and great books heaped on, some large as a three-year-old child, or long tubes of wood or metal in which lay scrolls of yellowed paper.

Arpazia's father glanced up from a map he had been studying with some difficulty—his pale eyes, too, the girl had learned, were no longer much use to him.

"Is it you, Arpazia?"

"Yes, Father."

This question was not due to his eyesight, only his indifference, she suspected. He had other daughters in the castle, though none legitimate. Her own waiting-women were two of these.

"Have they informed you?"

"Yes, Father."

"I expect you're fearful. It is a terrible thing." The elderly man raised his gray face and looked at everything, the room, his books, her, with a ghastly resignation. "This one who springs down on us is barbaric. And cunning. His symbol is a black bull snorting fire, but his name's Draco—the dragon."

Arpazia felt a new, more positive fear. And yet, the gale of change blew in her face and never had she sensed her life or her youth so strongly.

"What shall we do?" she cried.

"Resist," said the remote father. "But fail. I judge there's little hope. Presently you should go to pray. Confide in the Blessed Marusa. The priest will shrive you. Wait meekly. When the hour comes, I'll find you. I will see to it you suffer nothing at their hands."

Arpazia blinked. Was this magic he spoke of? He was very clever, she had always heard, intellectual and mentally powerful, if physically a poor specimen.

"The nurse says," she blurted, "you'll give me wings to fly away—"

He laughed. It was a horrible laugh. Not cruel, but nevertheless quite pitiless. "So I shall. She spoke well, the old woman. Tell her,

I'll give her wings, too. She has been faithful, and why should they have her, these brutes, to make a slave of? Tell her, Arpazia, she too shall have wings."

But as he said this, he did something at odds with the words, a piece of bodily theater that, without instructing the girl, yet *fore-warned* her. He drew a long thin dagger and placed it, shining, on the table.

I must be shriven and then will be pure for Heaven. Angels and the souls of the dead have wings.

Arpazia backed a step away, but her father had already lost interest in her, taken up as he was with preparing his own self for death, and his castle—that no one should have the benefit of it after him.

When the girl had returned to her own apartment, she found her nurse still sitting at the fireside.

"He means to kill me!"

"Your father? Oh yes." The nurse was vague and dispassionate. Her abject fatalism might have bloomed for this moment. "He won't want the barbarians to get you. They'd rip you in bits with their dirty ways. It is a favor to you. None of the other girls will get any assistance, they'll have to see to it for themselves."

Shocked, Arpazia hissed, "He said he would kill you too."

"Good, good. That's kind of him."

The girl screamed. But all over the castle women were doing that, screaming and weeping, just as the men shouted and cursed and drank, and the priest kissed images of the Christ and moaned long prayers.

Arpazia ran to the window. There was a mark in the distance, above the forests, a sort of cloud. Something was burning, from the breath of the bull, from the fire of the dragon.

But she must get away.

She stood, irresolute. Nothing had ever happened to her. Unpracticed, she did not truly believe in this, and so, maybe, it would pass.

II.

*T*HE HORDE ARRIVED. IT WAS IN-
credible, awesome as any natural
disaster. The woods turned black
and the snow vanished beneath the darkness of many thousand
men, their horses, their fighting engines. Here and there danced a
flick or lash of flame, the fires of the encampment, for which they
felled the forest trees, or the scarlet of the evil banners.

There was no discussion, no terms were offered or asked.
Within three hours ballistas let loose huge rocks against the outer
gates, and once something snorted fire. Night fell, and then they
sent a rain of burning arrows across the castle parapets.

The castle began to stink, not only of fire but of wretched fear
and hate.

A man guarded Arpazia's door, then, near sunrise, when the lord of
the castle dispatched his force, this man, too, was gone.

The nurse slept, sitting in her chair, silent as one already dead.
Arpazia marveled she had ever run to that shriveled breast for comfort, to that idiot's face for guidance.

Instead it was her second maid (the other was also gone) who
crept close in the cold, diluted light.

She was the bastard daughter of the lord, but had a look not of
Arpazia, or her father, but of her own mother, a narrow-boned
woman with coppery hair.

"You're icy. Here's your fur. Arpazia—you won't let him *murder*
you?"

Arpazia glanced at the girl. "Oh, Lilca—what can I do?"

Years after, this foolish wail would haunt Arpazia, infuriating and
shaming her. But by then she would have lost her patience with
youth, as in youth she had no compassion for old age.

"Couldn't you run away, Arpazia? Who'd see, in the fighting? It's better to chance the snow and the forests. God says it's a sin to die, unless He allows it." Arpazia huddled in the wolf-pelt. Lilca said, "*I* don't want to die here. I'll go with you."

As they slipped across the room, the sound of fighting began beyond the walls and woke the blind nurse. She turned her head like a statue given dreadful life. "Where are you going, Arpazia?"

"To see—what they do."

"Stay here. It isn't right you watch the battle."

"Just for a moment."

"Black is the wood," sang the eyeless statue, blanched stone in the deadly ghost of dawn, "white is the snow—red the bloods that under it flow—"

"Leave the wicked old beldame," snarled Lilca, and pulled Arpazia away through the door.

There was a narrow stair, well known. In the past it had led to a little summer garden with peaches and apple trees. The door was locked, but Lilca, revealing new talents, undid the lock with a paring knife.

Outside, the garden was piled with snow and the trees were bowed white humps beneath it. Lilca drew her through a knot of these trees, and black claws reached from under the snow to scratch them. They were pressed now against the mass of the outer wall.

"Shall we hide here?" Arpazia asked—stupidly, as she ever after thought.

"There's a door," said Lilca.

It was difficult to discover, the door, hidden in bare twisted creeper and the limbs of trees. A peculiar door, very low, the height only of a child—or a dwarf. Perhaps it had been guarded, too, but again the guard had vanished. Arpazia saw with dull astonishment that Lilca had, to this door, a key.

Beyond was a devious passageway, in darkness. Above it hulked a roof of earth and roots. The path stumbled down, snowless but deathly cold. It became totally black, then a faint light returned.

Lilca reached up and began pushing at some slab above. It shifted an inch. Suddenly assistance came.

To her amazement, Arpazia saw the slab, the top of some antique cistern, dragged away, and grinning men leaned through and drew her up, and Lilca up, into white daylight.

Arpazia stood now in the forest. Glancing behind her, she could see the dim towering of the castle walls. There was no movement anywhere but for the soft drifting of smoke, yet she could hear the battle, grown thick and muddy, except when sometimes a wild shriek pierced through.

Here, there were four strangers. They wore mail like her father's soldiers, and for a moment she took them for castle men.

One of them had pushed Lilca back against a pine tree, bundling up her skirts. The others laughed, encouraged him, and as he forced her, Lilca did not struggle, only began to sob, but in a sullen, uncomplaining way. And when a second, and a third man replaced the first, still she made no protest. Obviously it was the price she had known she would have to pay in order to elude death.

The other helpful man said to Arpazia, "Don't concern yourself. That's all she's worth. We won't do you, lady. You're for a higher table."

Because Lilca had betrayed the castle, allowing Draco's army in by the secret door, Draco in fact had her hanged. He did not like faithlessness, and in those days sought always to make vivid examples of his moral stance.

But to Arpazia, seeing she had been an innocent in the matter, he subsequently gave back several of her "treasures," as he termed them, a reward for allowing him to sack the castle before her father could burn everything. He even initially forgave her attempt to escape and curse him—evidently neither had worked. He told her, her behavior was not surprising. She was a virgin and virtuous. However, all that was later, in the palace by the sea.

Arpazia knew nothing about the act a man performed with a woman, although she had sometimes heard of it. It was a sacred ritual intended to invoke pregnancy—or a dirty deed. Something delicious—or disgusting. So shrouded in mystery—and in mysterious, contrary chatter had it been—it meant nothing to her. It had no connection to any feeling she herself might ever have had, in dreams, or alone.

What she saw the men doing to Lilca that morning she had not understood, and through their hurry, and Lilca's acquiescence, Arpazia was not enlightened.

The castle, her home, fell in the hour after she left it.

Arpazia by then had been put into a tent of the war-camp, a makeshift leather thing that was full of baskets, bundles, and shed pieces of weaponry. They tied her hands together, and her feet; these quite loosely, at the ankles. And there were two old women there in the tent, sorting through the bundles and other stuff, who cackled at her, but nothing else. They were unlike the nurse, being sharp-eyed and lively. There was a brazier which kept them all quite warm.

The girl was afraid, of course, but aware she did not now have to face her father with his implacable murdering dagger. What did she think would happen to her? In the after years, when, again and again, all these scenes returned in abrupt harsh flashes, like bitter lightnings, she would strive with her younger self, asking her what she had expected. Something *nice*?

Probably nothing. The callow girl (that she would come to despise and separate from) had no imagination. Since she knew nothing, she had nothing to burn as fuel for thought. She had been taught to read and write a little but had not bothered with books, from the use of which she had been discouraged—learning was a male pursuit. Instead her head was packed with social songs of the castle, with fragmented myths, with the shadowy rhymes and chants and spells of the nurse, who had been reckoned a witch.

Arpazia fell asleep finally, sitting there in the tent, as the scavenger crones picked through the incomprehensible muddle of odds and ends.

Then mad shouting woke her, the noise of things crashing, and a wild victory paean ringing round and round.

This filled her with alarm, but also, not knowing what to do, incapable of anything, as soon as it died down she fell asleep again. *I should have chewed through the binding at my wrists. I should have done it so the women never saw. Untied the rope from my ankles. Crept away. Even if they had killed me—*

At last she woke and it was dusk. The hags were gone, and a man was pulling her to her feet. She found they had cut the tie at her ankles. They let her walk across the camp, through the churned snow.

Campfires and braziers burned, and the banners which also flickered like flames. She saw the emblem, the bull which blew fire.

Men dragged things, some of which were carts loaded with their spoils from her castle, or simply cartless spoils—carpets, furniture, chests, objects she had seen often, but never like this. Some men dragged the bodies of other men, she did not know why. Horses restlessly trampled at their pickets, shaking their heads. A few were running about riderless, calling. A woman went by in a necklace of gold, crying her eyes out. There was the smell of roasting meat, beer and death-kept-cold. And there was still some occasional screaming, from the surgeons' area. But generally the atmosphere was jolly.

The dusk changed from blue to steel to firelit red, as she crossed the camp. No one paid Arpazia much attention.

The man who escorted her was one of the four from earlier, the very one who had assaulted Lilca first. He said nothing.

Draco's tent was like a great golden bulb, and outside was planted the largest bull banner, fringed with silver, and next to it the image of a dragon in gilded iron, on a pole hung with crimson tassels.

The war-leader, soon to be a king, was sitting on a table, drinking wine. He was black with soot and splashed colorfully with a lot of fairly recent blood, but none of it was his own. This had been, for him, a lucky day.

They had to stand and wait some while until he noticed them. Arpazia was used to waiting, though, on the whim of men.

"Oh, Cirpoz—splendid. Is that the girl?"

The soldier, Cirpoz, said, "Yes, sire."

"I'm not king yet," said Draco, coyly. (Did she hear how coy he sounded? Would she have known to recognize such a thing?) Cirpoz grinned. He was apparently talented at grinning. "Well and good, then. His legal daughter." Draco shot a look at her. He did not seem interested, and at that moment was not. She was used to that, too; possibly it was reassuring. "Don't put her with the rest of the taken women. They'll hatch some plot, like that other girl, the faithless bitch. Oh, put her in the back tent."

So Arpazia was escorted out again and put into the back tent, part of Draco's traveling apartments on campaign. Here a slave woman presently came, undid the tie on her hands, and gave her a bit of greasy half-roast meat, which Arpazia did not want, and some goat's cheese crumbled in wine, which she ate and drank. She was young, a fool, and hungry.

For three days they traveled. Arpazia was in a wagon drawn not by horses but by bullocks, though their horns were gilded.

She saw only a couple of female slaves, who attended to essentials. Sometimes she looked out between the leather flaps of the wagon, but the driver unnerved her, a big man who never spoke. There were soft rugs, and she slept a great deal. Asleep, she missed Lilca's hanging.

On the fourth evening after they had stopped, a bath was arranged in the wagon. Normally indifferent to bathing, she found it refreshing and hot. After she had dried herself, and put on again her carmine gown, someone came and took her once more across the camp.

She had seen forests as they traveled, and once, miles away, a glimpse of mountains on the white sky, which she had taken for clouds, at first. Now she saw the forests had thinned. There was a

vast, white-gleaming road below, which no one explained was a frozen river. She heard wolves keening in the distance. Out of doors,
this would have upset her, but there were so many people here she
was not afraid. The fool, the poor fool.

Through its closed lid, still the mirror watched:

"I'll find you a husband," he generously said.

She looked at him blankly. He accepted her lack of response as
thrilled astoundment.

"Don't be troubled, Arpaida."

"Arpazia," she corrected him. She should not have done so, and
mumbled, "Forgive me, I'm sorry." He was a man and a lord . . .
even she had gathered that much.

But Draco was only amused.

"Try this fried cake. It's got berry juice in it."

She was too nervous to enjoy any of the dinner. If she had been
at the castle, she would have liked it. There was roast mutton, and
warm bread, and roots cooked with spices. Two or three of his captains were there with Draco, and they smiled, glancing at her, knowing something she did not.

He was dressed well, a linen shirt and velvet mantle trimmed
by sables. And many rings, even an earring of gold.

The captains started to talk and play a game with figures on a
board. He drew her aside into his arm. Despite the clothes, he had
not washed, or shaved. He was like some uncle from the past, a
brother of her father's; Draco, too, looked old to her then, she fourteen, and he in his twenties.

Arpazia made no resistance. Why should she? She had been
fondled by masculine relatives before, hugged, kissed. Even her
father had once run his remote hands across her body, alerting
her neither to excitement or unease, for she was indifferent and her
father only analytical—there had been no sinister development.

"You're young," Draco said. His voice was slurred, but she knew
all that, too, the way men became silly when their breath was fla-

vored by alcohol. "You're a pretty little thing. Don't mind it, I'll see you safe, at Belgra. Give you a dowry, why not? You can have some of your own treasures back. Maybe not that mirror over there. I might keep that. It's a fine thing. Glass. I've heard of them but never seen one like it. They say they're magic. Best to keep the lid shut. Did you look in it and speak a spell to learn who your lover would be?"

Primly, ignorantly, Arpazia said nothing.

Half an hour later, by the water clock in the tent's folded corner, he took her into another tent, which budded off from the end of the dining area.

"You're so young," he said again. "I'll swear you never had a suitor. I tell you what, little snowdrop, I'll give you this ring—do you see?—with the pearl to match your skin—if you let me take a look at your breasts."

Draco meant to be canny. He had had countless willing girls, uncountable girls who were unwilling. This one he tried to woo. A woman of any age was acquisitive, so he had learned. And the Church constantly warned that laval rages of Hell smoldered between their legs.

But this one, she stared at him as if he had gone insane.

"Come on, pretty narcissus flower. Come, come on. Just a peek. You won't mind, I promise."

And when Arpazia took a step away, just as she had from her father with the knife, Draco went after her, caught her to him, and lavished on her mouth a wet drunken kiss that had a wet drunk snake-tongue in it. And as he smothered her with his face, his free hand pulled the buttons off her dress, and felt its way in over two small full soft satin things, whose central points sprang up under his touch like startled hares.

It was more than his intrusion, his maleness, which terrified Arpazia. Then again, her body had its own instincts.

She fought him, and when she did he clasped her more closely. He was huge to her slightness, he sweated and blazed with heat and she could not breathe. If she noticed the genital dagger that pressed now, greedily, at her belly, was debatable. *All* of him was too big for her, too close, and too insistent. As well ask a girl not to run from an avalanche.

"Come now. Here, have a taste of this wine. I'd never want to hurt you, snowdrop. Don't make me do it—be my gentle girl?"

She nodded into his neck, and so he partly released her, and began to push the wine cup instead against her lips.

She struck the cup aside and jumped from him.

"God in Hell!"

She was away.

Arpazia rushed out through the little tent, and across the main tent, and the captains came to their feet, ribald with mirth, and then Draco came pounding after her.

"Shall we get up a hunt and run your rabbit down?"

"Stay where you are." His face was swollen with fury, and their laughter died.

"She's a dunce, Draco."

"*Draco?*" he said. "I'm to be your king." And then he was out of the tent.

He strode through his camp, which Arpazia bolted through.

Men and women fell back from both of them, turning from her with an oath or derisive snigger, but from him with anxious fear.

He let her run, allowing no one else to stop her. She would not get far. Let her wear herself out. He had done this before, knew it all. He put on a grim smile for those who watched, and now they began to salute him, wish him well in this latest enterprise. "There goes your fleet deer, sire!" And some girl cried, "Would it were I, Draco-king. I'd run that slow."

But *she* broke from the camp, Arpazia. She had darted up into the open edges of the woods.

The lights were behind him. Here the luminous white un-crushed spaces, the black columns of the trees, the indigo sky with its fretwork of cold stars.

"You little cunt, every step you've made me take you'll pay me for."

He wanted her.

The freezing air had fired him up more than the wine. His weapon hurt, and his whole groin, as it had not since he was a boy, and his first woman teased him.

But she, this one, would hurt worse.

In the end she stumbled and fell down, and *then* he ran. He was on her like a wolf. He flung her over and pressed her to the ground by his weight.

"Now—"

He tore her dress open and showed her white body to the heavenly stars. Her map was perfectly marked, and the dark forest citadel he must storm.

Holding her hands above her head on the snow, he tore her open like her dress, in three ramming thrusts. She screamed and her eyes were wide, but she stared at the sky as he plunged within her, until his body arched, he called her foul names, and burst in glory. She had by then stopped screaming.

"You little dolt. I would have been kind if you hadn't resisted. There, there. You'll live. And I'll have got you with a boy. I'd bet on it. Every woman I've had, she bears. Bears boys."

Arpazia dizzily, crazily searched the sky. What was she looking for? Some rescuing angel?

She did not even know what he had done. Only that he had damaged her. Only that this appalling event had definitely happened.

"Here." He hauled her up. "Take this ring. It's gold. The camp isn't far, you won't come to harm."

Draco was tired. He had had enough.

Arpazia turned, dropping the ring, and saw her own shape marked gravelike in the white snow, and her brilliant blood running over it from the hem of her broken dress, between the black trees.

"Go on now," he said. "And expect a boy."

When she saw her blood, this moment was when the rape occurred to her. She *felt* it, for it was not the pain or the fear. It was some other thing. It turned her inside out, and she fell again, and kneeling in the snow, and the blood, she cried, in a voice she heard and which was not her own: "May it be bloody on you as that blood, and black on you as the wood. May it be cold white as snow."

Draco paled. He signed himself with the cross.

"You little cunt. Shut your slit. I can have you hanged, like the other dross. What are you, some witch?"

She did not know what she had said.

She did not know where she was, or who she was.

"Black as the wood, white as the snow," she shrilled, her face white, her eyes all black, "red as your blood that under it flow—"

"You filthy bitch, shut your row." He slapped her hard across her raised face, bent and retrieved his ring, and turning, walked off toward his camp. "Stay there and let the wolves have you."

Her nurse's rhymes, heard all her years, writhed like tangled weaving in her head. But also cautionary tales of the forests— wolves. This idea must have been what eventually drew her from the ground and sent her down to safety, such as it was.

Try as she sometimes, perversely, would, she never after re-called her return journey to the camp. Only the words ringing round and round, her curse on him which came back instead to her, black as wood, white as snow, red as blood.

III.

*S*HE KNEW THE CURSE HAD MISSED him and struck her when her belly began to grow hard and round. De-spite never having had the act of reproduction detailed to her, she had often seen its result. She was terrified, of course. Yet again, ridiculously, she did not believe in this. At every waking, she would examine herself in frantic, hopeful fear, thinking the affliction must have gone.

By then, actually from the moment she found herself once more

in Draco's victorious war-camp, Arpazia was no longer being cos-
seted.

Through the winter daylight she walked with other women. Not
those from the castle, it was true, who were all by then either dead
or slaves. These free females were the followers of Draco's army.
They, with their men, had trudged for half a year up and down the
land, through the thick forests, over wild grasslands, even in mountain country among the boulders and the ice. They were hardened
women, and Arpazia unhardened. They chivvied and mocked her,
but not much else. Nor did any of the men molest her. Some edict
had apparently remained concerning her, the sole legal daughter of
a castle lord.

Her cloth shoes wore through in a day. Her feet were blistered
and bleeding when she sat down dazedly on a prone tree trunk. A
woman came and handed her, wordlessly, a pair of ugly boots that
were too big and had been stuffed with straw. Now and then she
was given a ride on a cart, among the loot, and among women tem-
porarily weakened—for a day or so—by childbirth. At these Arpazia,
as her own condition became known to her, gazed in morose, dis-
believing horror. Those sucking things clinging to their breasts, like
parasitic grubs—

The landscape altered. The forests spread away. The mountains
curved, a motionless cumulus which had dropped from the sky and
frozen into granite.

The opaque frozen rivers came and went.

Sometimes there were towns and villages where Draco had established his garrisons, crow's-nest fortresses or long houses built of
logs. Here his army was welcomed. There would be large meals,
much drinking, the camp at play, and dancing with clapped hands.
At one of these stops they celebrated Midwinter-Mass. Everyone
was happy, except for their captives. That night, Arpazia caught
sight of Draco in the distance. It was the only time she saw him
during the remainder of the march.

Probably the shock of what had happened to her kept Arpazia

in her trance. Just as she could never after remember her return to the camp, she remembered this victory march to Belgra Demitu and the sea, only in weird, isolated fragments.

Had she never thought again to attempt flight? If ever she had tried, they would have prevented it, since she was always in the midst of Draco's own people, and they seemingly highly aware of her. Conversely, the lands here were all under his banner. Even the crude inn signs had been garishly changed—there a black bull snorting sparks, there a white bull galloping through a field of flowers.

Otherwise the land was winter's. King Death, in his night palace underground, would be less kind even than Draco.

Mirrors taught: Perhaps there were always at least two sorts of reality, what you credited, and what was true.

Arpazia lived in a limbo where none of this was possible. And she lived the reality, where each day and dark she was among the army, and her belly swelled with a child only fourteen years her junior.

Did she ever consider her father—her nurse—coppery Lilca, who had betrayed her and died, for even if Arpazia had not witnessed the hanging, the camp women had carefully described the event. To Arpazia, these people, though dead, were alive still. And unimportant. They could not assist her; they never had.

In the same way, even Draco, instigator of this nightmare, became mislaid. She recalled only his heat and beard and smell and mantle, as if a violent hairy suit of clothes had raped her.

The thaw was beginning when the march reached a country above the sea, and looking down beheld the great town and the mystic ruins and palace of Belgra Demitu.

Here, it was said, at time's start, the earth had opened, and a young goddess was snatched into it in one volcanic moment, from which drama the seasons had begun. Though many other places boasted this same spot, Belgra Demitu was named for it, and for the goddess-mother of the abducted maiden.

Arpazia knew the legend, but not well. It had come to her outside its classical framework, some untidy tale of the castle.

In the wet mist of that morning, she saw the land dropping in
wide steps, and bare woods, and the always distant mountains, and
a gap which held, as the sun shed the mirage of its new light, a
filled void. The sea? All around her, shouts confirmed: The sea.

The town sprawled on and on, and on the terraces rising from
it, was a temple built in another dawn, and the ancient palace, its
columns and olive trees scorched by winter. The second palace grew
out of its toppled stones.

A thin smoke rose from the town, and from one place on the
terraces—there it was, the arcane Oracle of long ago, still fuming
up to tell its riddles. A woman tended the Oracle, although the
Christ had his church nearby. There was, too, a sacred spring. It had
been the goddess Demetra's once, or her daughter's, having leapt
from the soil at her clutching hands, when she was dragged underground. Now, the spring was sacred to Christ's Mother, the Virgin
Marusa.

Climbing the hill, the women crossed themselves, all at once
demure and pliant, wanting God to like them.

Arpazia did not notice the spring.

Her malediction had not reached him, but perhaps he felt it draw
close, then turn aside. As they approached the palace by the sea,
Draco began to think about the girl. He remembered forcing her,
and that aroused him. Then he thought of her blood on the snow
and was perturbed. He did not know why, for he had seen plenty
of blood, some quantities of which were female.

Bad dreams hovered over Draco. He could not recollect them
on waking, but he kept their feel, like a low sound in the ear. There
was no menace to them, no compunction even, it was simply that
they did not go away. He decided he had offended his own high
codes. He should have taken more care of her. She had been gently
reared, was royal, with the same watered royalty that ran through

his own veins. But then, he did not bother to seek her out, and contrasting with this laziness, his sense of wrongness waxed. Was she a witch? Had she somehow affected him? Best go to God then, take God like the bath he would have at Belgra Demitu, to scour off the muck of campaign.

Draco stood before the priest, looking angry, and the worse for a night's banqueting and drinking; miserable.

These powerful men were like little boys, the priest thought, partly to leaven his own unease. But one must be cautious.

"Father—I require a penance."

"My lord Draco, you are to have your coronation here in a month. There will need to be many cleansings—"

"No, Father." Impatient. The priest waited, covering himself with a calm skin against Draco's potential for rage. "War—is only war. I took the land for God. And I was assisted by Heaven. How else did I do so much?"

"God wills that you be king, Draco, my son."

"Yes. I believe that, Father. But something gnaws at me."

The priest still waited.

Draco walked about. A man of action, unwilling ever to be much at rest. The mind was the same. It strode from idea to idea, but the ideas of a little boy . . . A proud and brash little bully, who had been first treated harshly, then rottenly spoiled by fate.

"Let me have confession," demanded Draco.

He kneeled down, and they began.

When Draco had finished, the priest saw that his future king was now wrung-out, like a woman after tears, and malleable. You might take a certain pleasure in rubbing a king's nose in his own mess.

"She was of royal blood. Naturally what you did affects your honor. You, the king. And—she's with child by your deed, you say?"

"So they tell me. They always are, if I have them."

"Then, my lord, the teaching of the Church is clear." It was. "You must marry her."

Despite everything, the priest anticipated a vile mouthful in response. Nothing came at first. Then the kneeling bully said, quietly, "You're in the right. That's my penance then. I'll wed the girl."

She had been lying sick, the baby in her womb making her puke, when they came to tell her. The insanity of it was only at one with all the rest.

Arpazia went to the altar of the church at Belgra Demitu in her fourth month. She wore a gown of sky blue, Marusa's color, heavily embroidered with gold. Her rounding belly scarcely showed, but where it was noted, they took it for a benign omen. The naive among them even reckoned that it was only her proper womanly shape, the correct contour of a maiden made to conceive and carry to term.

The ceremonies resembled, for Arpazia, certain festivals at the castle, when she had sat crowned by a garland beside her father. She experienced the same slight nervousness, boredom, if none of the excitement she had felt as a child. The priests did put a small garland on her head—not blossom, a crown—and a dark ring on her middle finger. Bells rang, which roared inside her skull. A crowd was cheering. She wished it would end quickly. That she was getting married did not impress itself upon her, for she was in an unusual state of mind and body. She passed across the rituals and left the feast early to throw up in a bowl held by her new waiting-women.

He arrived much later.

"You're ill. I won't tax you. Do you understand you're a queen? There, little queen, you're safe. Sleep well."

He was blind drunk, and meant the sentimental words. He had realized, after all, she was only a woman and could not be much trouble to him.

So Arpazia lay alone in the wide marriage bed, with its strewing of asphodel and hyacinths, the early flowers that had been just in time. And she wondered why she had a knife, used to pare the nails, still in her hand. She let it slide out on the floor.

It reminded her of Lilca, however. So dreaming, she had to watch Lilca, dangling from a rope, her heels kicking as if in one of the clapping dances of the war-camp.

IV.

*D*RACO RETURNED TO VISIT HER about twenty days later.

"Are you well, at last?" he courteously, impatiently asked.

Arpazia was afraid, trembling, and did not know why. Could not recall why. Then she recalled. He had torn her open in order to stuff her belly with his devilish seed, this "son" the women promised her, and the physician too, as if a *son* were something she longed for, like a precious toy.

"No, I'm sick, still," Draco's queen muttered.

"What? Ah, come, no need to be nervous of me. We're as we should be, now, aren't we, little queen. Sinless in God's sight."

He was alight with lust, as before.

To Draco, this lust was his virtue. There were a hundred women he could have had, including the one he liked most often in his bed, a girl of the hills, unroyal and besotted by him—and barren.

Arpazia, for her part, had discovered she had again picked up a small knife from her cosmetics table. It was currently used to grind kohl she did not need to darken brows and lashes.

Draco had not seen. Arpazia dropped the knife in dismay. She had no notion of how to kill him, and besides incoherently knew that to kill him might only harm her worse. And she might have cut herself.

(She was of course still asleep at this time, entering the fifth month of her pregnancy, tranced. If she had not been so, probably she would have stuck the knife in him at once.)

Some supper was served them, and Draco sat graciously talking to her, telling her about the fresh fighting he would have to have, trying to pretend it irked him although in fact he had grown restless at his palace.

While they—he—ate, some gifts were brought in for her. There was a necklace, bracelets, and other such things. Then they brought her own mirror. In her trance, Arpazia had forgotten the mirror. Very likely she would have forgotten it anyway. She stared at it, thinking, *What is it?*

"You must have this frippery back," he announced. "It's no use to me. Mirrors—women's nonsense. And they're afraid of it. A witch's glass."

Arpazia got up and drifted over to the mirror, as if she must—men always gave orders, even inadvertently. She undid the clasp of the lid, and opened it out, and when she looked into the glass, did not see herself, gazed straight past herself, at the room beyond, its painted walls and long narrow windows, her bed, the carved chair with King Draco in it.

She saw Draco, the dragon-bull, as if for the first time, in the mirror. He was almost faceless, a suit of flesh with hot appetites.

But behind Draco, one door stood open, and Arpazia and the mirror saw into a part of the old palace, an ancient colonnade of pillars which ran through under a high-walled terrace, like the defile of a mountain. Antique oil-lamps hung and lit the walk, and here and there a bay tree stood in a pot. The view was an orderly compendium of dark and light, but suddenly something seemed to shift and separate.

Arpazia started—and her trance, like a pane of glass—like the glass pane of the mirror itself—seemed also for one second to tilt.

A child darted along the colonnade, on which the paint was firm and new. Her corn-colored hair streamed back—if it was able to . . .

Her eyes—if they had been real—were like new-minted coins—

Arpazia was aware the almost-child, rushing through the mirror, must not reach her. So she clapped the lid shut.

"Gently," reproved ungentle Draco. "That's a costly possession. You should be careful of it."

Then he sent the servants out and led Arpazia to the bed.

She did not struggle now, or even tremble, she was too heavy and weary, too lost, adrift, tranced. Draco had her quickly. The wall candles burned down behind his head, consumed by the minute of his panting fire. He hurt her, but not as much as before. "There," he said.

Then he got up and shook himself free of what he had spent. She was nothing to him, this sulky doll. Was she unhinged? She looked asleep. It occurred to him that one day he might wish to be rid of her, and if she was mad, that would be much easier.

Asleep . . . Of course, she did not slumber, physically, throughout all those next five or more months. Yet she did sleep a great deal, both day and night, whenever she could. It seemed she had only to let go of her body, to float miles out, to be gone. There were few dreams that she remembered, and those she recalled were mild, pleasing: childish.

Otherwise, she got up, and let herself be tended. Clothes were put on her, and her hair combed with essences and twined with ornaments. She would sometimes eat and drink, move about, along the colonnade, for example, the pillars of which were faded and pocked, to a walled garden, from where it was possible to look out at the sea.

Day would come down the hills, and the shadows of clouds. Then summer came down them.

Blushes of bronzy green over the woods, green veils, shimmering webs that wrapped the olive trees. Soon leaves thick as clusters of grapes, and the grass banded with wild flowers, lilac, milk-blue, the ruby powder of poppies, quivering with bees and the chorus of crickets. By then the mountains had blurred, losing their hard edges of white. Next the green fields were split with yellow. A tarnish of mellowness. The sea was like an Eastern turquoise.

It became the birth month of King Draco's queen. The month which belonged to the Virgin Marusa, the Virgo.

Draco was unaware of this birthday element, and anyway there had been disturbances among some of his conquered towns. He had left to skirmish through the summer, and would not return until the leaves again were gone.

"Into her eleventh month, and no sign. Is it dead inside her, do you think?"

She heard them whispering, the unkind, soulless waiting-women, as if she were deaf, or rather as if they noticed the trance she was in, and thought it *made* her deaf, which it had not.

The mirror watched, through its lid, which also reflected somewhat, like an ordinary inferior mirror of polished metal. It caught the late summer glow of sky and hills and the black ripple of a crow that sailed above the orange groves.

Draco's queen woke and sat up in her bed. She had been asleep for over ten months—almost like a girl in one of the stories her nurse had told her.

It was her fifteenth birthday. She did not know it.

Yesterday the physicians had examined Arpazia. She let them. It was never so bad as what Draco had twice done. The medicine, though, was sour, so she did not swallow it. She would do little, unless coerced, and none of these dared to force her to anything, now.

Today Arpazia was puzzled. Nothing seemed different in this day, but she had woken up, and why?

The room was softly hot; it smelled of honey and fruit. This, with the occasional whiff of sulfur from the Oracle, was the summer smell of Belgra Demitu. Even asleep, the girl had learned that. She had learned everything, asleep. And, also, that she was queen, and now the women whispered: "The physician brought her a draught to hurry the child—but she threw the draught out through the window."

The girl looked down at the round hard moon of her belly. It would never alter. Then she looked across at the mirror with its closed lid.

Leaving the bed, she walked to the mirror. Perhaps she had not undone the clasp since that last night with Draco.

The lid folded away. On the glass, the backdrop, a window of sky and flying crow . . .

But who was this?

No longer a girl or a maiden. Now a woman, a taut white moon fruit, juicily swollen to ripeness.

Arpazia stared at her belly through the thin shift. As she saw in through the linen, she saw in next through her own body—

Inside her belly was a black bowl, and in the bowl a red apple, but the heart of the apple was white. The flesh of the apple was a white serpent lying coiled there. Like herself, though taking sustenance and sometimes moving, it had been asleep. Now Arpazia saw it had woken, and this in turn had woken her—

Her first scream was of terror. Only the second scream demonstrated pain.

Then her blood poured out of her again, and as the mirror watched, with its strange, apparently callous, crystal eye, Draco's queen entered the house of agony called childbirth.

"See, lady. It lives—"

Kill it, she shrieked in her mind, *kill it as it kills me—*

But the pain had drawn off, all across the room, which now was dark and lamplit. Pain sat in the corner, folding up the instruments of the pain-trade, putting them lovingly away.

"Ah, but madam, alas—"

Arpazia opened her eyes. *Is it dead after all?* She would have killed it herself, if she could, as she had begged them to do—had she done so?

"*Not* a son, lady. And after such dreadful labor."

"A poor little girl. But she's perfect, madam. Here she is."

They put something against her heart. The mother did not take hold of it, and it rolled from her. The women caught it at once.

"She's too weak to embrace her child."

"Too *daft.* Look at her!"

From the shadows, the faces peering and leering, like masks worn in the old pagan worship Arpazia had, maybe, heard sometimes went on here. Animal masks at that, unfriendly and savage.

"I don't want it," she must have said. Something mewed, insubstantial and far off. "Take it away."

Arpazia thought, *They will throw it in a brazier, to burn it. But that will only strengthen the thing.* It was nothing to her, it belonged to pain.

Yet pain, no longer involved, had crept out of the door, and there in the mirror, which throughout the flurry no one had closed, an amber flame seemed to stand upright, almost in the shape of a gleaming woman. But this was a trick of the lamplight.

Milk was pressing from Arpazia's breasts like tears. She saw this, repelled. And then, despite what she had said, they thrust the thing again into her arms and somehow now she did hold it. It sucked on her, hurting her. A thread was drawn through her breast into its mouth, this tiny, milking grub.

She had no more stamina to resist. Oh, let it murder her then. That was all it wanted to do. To eviscerate and drain her. She could see what it was, plainly enough: The curse that she had conjured. White, with one delicate crimson silk of blood left unwiped, and the one black curl of hair on its head.

*   *   *

Arpazia dreamed she was wandering in a cavern, her only illumination a torch held high in her right hand.

Before her, a staircase of volcanic rock descended into blackness. And something tugged a thread out through her heart.

I am searching, but for what? For myself, for the child I was.

But these thoughts, which in later years would come—if without language—to overlay the dream, were not then considered. Only the awful grief of the dream, its desolate sense of robbery, and loss.

The Maiden: The Witch

I.

*N*ATURALLY, TO BEGIN WITH, SHE never knew the Woman was her mother.

What did the word "Mother" mean?

She had a nurse, who had given her milk, and next there were two attendants who—she had heard murmured—were also daughters of her father. The word *Father* she comprehended. And *Daughter*. And, *Witch*.

"There is the *witch*." "What does that *witch* say?" "Careful, the witch may hear you!"

At seven years of age, she had finally realized this narrow figure of a woman, stalking to and fro against a distant window, this briefly felt, cold, pale hand with its three large jewels, this head of hair turning away its polished darkness—this *composite*, had something to do with herself.

Soon after her birth, the child was christened in the town's great church of St. Belor. The name she received had belonged to queens in history. It had a meaning to do with fiery whiteness: Candacis.

But no one, save her father, (the king) called her by it. The name
the ordinary women in her world called her, was Coira. While the
Woman, stalking like a leopard in a cage (so the ordinary women
said), never called the child anything.

Although the Woman did, now and then, speak to her.

"Is it you?"

"Yes."

"Say, '*Yes, madam,*' " breathed the anxious nurse in the child's ear.

So the child said, "Yes—ma-madama—" stumbling not in fear,
but from unfamiliarity. She had never, until then, been required to
give anyone a title. Even the king did not, apparently, insist on it,
until his offspring were ten or eleven.

What did the Woman (the witch) say then? Nothing. She turned
her head, and the child saw the back of her, hollowly straight and
slender, and the smooth black hair that shone, held fast in a stiff
net of metallic wire and under a thin trailing veil like silver-
powdered steam. Awestruck, Coira only watched.

Yet "Who is she?" Coira presently asked, that is, she asked years
in the future, seven years old now, when they had met the Woman
(witch) as they sometimes did, in a corridor of the new palace. The
maid and the nurse had curtseyed, bowing their heads. The Woman
flowed by like water. Her mantle was edged with black bear fur
that matched her hair, for it was an icy spring. Coira knew the
Woman, knew the Woman was a ruling being in her child's life. But
never before had she thought to ask *Why?*

Had they never said once to the child, prior to that hour, "Your
mother"? Something like, for example, "Your mother will be in the
High Chamber today, with the king. You must kiss her hand, as you
do his." Possibly they *had* said this. But Coira did not understand.
Come to that, the huge gaudy man, lifting her up and laughing in
her face his wine-breath and beard, he was nothing to her either,
even if she knew his mighty part in the scheme of things. He liked
the child, however. He always did like his children, when small. He
said so. He brought her presents, toys, and so on. He felt too warm.

The hand of the woman was cold, like cold weather, stone, those things.

Yet, on the day that seven-year-old Coira had asked, "Who is she?" and the nurse exclaimed and crossed herself as if at a blasphemy, and one of the maids said, "Your *mother*—who else?"—that day Coira saw how beautiful the Woman was.

The next instant the other maid said spitefully, "Don't let the witch find out you didn't know her! She'll throw you in a spell-pot, boil you up."

The child felt a ribbon of fear rustle through her stomach. But she was not especially fearful, not then. The fear went away, and the memory of beauty flooded back. "Hush now, she's the queen," added the nurse to the maids. But she too called the queen the *witch*. It was a habit they had all got into.

The nurse was only in her twenties, the attendant girls were children themselves, ten or so, the age when the king's legal progeny were expected to address him as *sire*. Except, of course, not being legal, they had had to do that from the start. They respected him. He was a man.

The queen was a foreigner, an upland forest woman. And everyone knew she practiced witchcraft, spoke to demons and sprites when alone in her rooms. (They heard her talk to them.) She had a sorcerous mirror which no one else ever dared look into. This would show her secret things, and out of it flew evils in swarms, causing minor accidents about the palace, fevers, falls, and bad dreams.

In a way, they instinctively segregated the child from her mother for the child's own good. And the witch besides made no effort to commune with her child, and had borne no others—it was said she had refused even to suckle the baby, and that instead imps had feasted on her milk.

Coira's attendants now began to tell her such stories.

And so, to the sense of the Woman's distance, and of her beauty, the appalling allure of magic was added.

The king did not appeal to Coira, and she felt no desire to woo

him. No, the one she now wanted to win was her witch-queen
mother.

In the early summer, the ancient Oracle at Belgra Demitu was hon-
ored. This was a pagan rite, like the Midwinter festival—and like
the festival, which had become Midwinter-Mass, the Church winked,
pretending it was something else. For the smoking Oracle, and the
spring too, had been dedicated to the Blessed Virgin. Originally, they
had both belonged to the goddess Demetra, the Corn-Queen, whose
daughter was snatched underground in the myth.

Perhaps Coira had not been brought to the ceremony before.
Infants might be noisy, but she, if anything, was too quiet and still.
Certainly she did not remember the rite or the king's part in it. The
question she asked immediately was, "Will she be there?"

"Who?"

"The witch."

"Don't call her that! Do you mean the queen?"

"My mother," said the child, proudly.

Yes, said the nurse, Queen Arpazia, King Draco's wife, would
go with the rest to show her duty to the Oracle.

The child had been trying very hard these past two months, as
chill spring melted to summer and the shadows and the sun-born
green came down the hills, to see or to find her mother, the Woman-
witch-queen. But Coira, mostly, was not successful. By arrangement,
the rooms where the child lived were far away from the heart of
the palace, away from the apartment of the queen. The king never
allowed children, once out of babyhood, near his women, not wish-
ing to trip over them.

Once only, having evaded her own attendants, Coira had discovered a garden. And she had seen, not her mother, but the mantle
trimmed by bear-fur, left lying on a bench. She had meant to go
and pick up the mantle. To smell it and hold it, searching for the
Woman's magical essence. Before she was able to do so, one of her
maids ran up and dashed her away, scolding birdlike in alarm.

That morning of the rite, Coira was dressed in a little white gown. Her hair had been washed. Now the nurse combed it.

"Such a shame you're not a pretty child," said the nurse regretfully, since Coira (Princess Candacis) was currently the nurse's own property. Draco had no other lawful daughters, but some of his by-blows were charming, and all his sons were thought manly and good-looking.

Coira's skin, like her mother's, was too pale, and did not take the sun. Her eyes were changeable, never blue but sometimes a strange gray, or even black, the iris and pupil seeming all one. Her mouth was too well-shaped for her age, precocious and red, although her cheeks were always colorless. Coira looked, the younger maid had said, as if she had been eating pomegranates greedily—or had put on the salve from an adult's cosmetic jar. Her hair, though, was a splendor. Heavy silk that shone, and black as a crow's wing.

They had tried to explain about the Oracle. In the mythic past, kings had come to ask their fates from it. Though it answered in riddles, it never lied, if you could only decipher the message.

"Is it God?" asked the child, idly. Had they known, she was only being polite, for her mind was just then solely on her mother, and the chance of seeing her.

"How could it be *God*, God pardon you? God's in Heaven."

But the younger maid, Kaya, said, "Once. Once it was a god, Nursey."

Coira, her interest caught a moment, asked, "Isn't it a god now? Then why does the smoke still come?"

"It does, and there you are. And sometimes it *speaks*."

"How does it?"

"It gurgles to itself."

"Stop, you'll scare the child," rasped the nurse.

"What does the gurgle say?"

"*Feed* me. It says feed me a sweet young maiden seven years of age, gobble, gobble."

"*Stop* that. It says nothing of the sort." The nurse was firm, and this reflected in the way she roughly pulled the child's hair now with the comb. "The gurgling is right down in the rock under the hill. It's because of the spring of water. And the smoke smells bad sometimes, don't we all know that. And that's from vapors under the ground."

The maid, Kaya, said, "*He* is down there, they say."

Coira looked less sure. "Who?"

"The wicked god that dragged the goddess-girl away under the earth. He saw her playing in the ripe corn, and thought he'd like her for his own. So he opened the earth and drove out in his chariot drawn by seven black horses, each snorting fire—or they might have been seven black bulls, like the king's banner. And he seized the girl round the waist and carried her off. The poppies she'd been gathering fell on the field like blood, and her tears like diamonds, but the next moment she was gone and the earth closed over. And he wouldn't give her back, even though her mother was Demetra, the Corn-Queen. But he's *Death*, and rules the land of shadows."

"Be silent you bad girl!" cried the nurse. "These are pagan things, and you've no business to know them, let alone tell *her*."

Kaya shrugged. She had a sly face and foxy hair.

"You," she retorted, "gave her the name."

"Only in fun," whined the nurse, uneasily.

The child looked from one to the other. It was her second maid, Julah, who primly said, "*Coira* is the pet name of the corn goddess's daughter, the one the god stole."

The nurse put down the comb, turned and slapped Julah across the face. Julah screamed. Kaya stood grinning. "The Princess Candacis was born in harvest month. She belongs to the Virgin, the holy Virgo," shouted the nurse.

But Coira thought, *If I am the goddess's daughter, my mother is the goddess.* She did not think this in words, she thought it in a formless way, only the more marvelous since untrammeled by language.

Draco led the procession down the terraces.

In seven years, he had grown affluent, and thickened slightly, like a gourd. There had been minor skirmishes, a couple of raids into other territories. These had kept him occupied and assured of his manhood and power, but had not refined him at all. His brain had thickened too, becoming more hard, less flexible, and there had been little pliancy to begin with.

He walked down the hill. That was the tradition. All the kings and men of war who had once come to ask things of the Oracle, had walked, leaving their chariots, later their horses, sometimes even their attendants behind.

But two priests of the Christ walked directly after the king, and then there were boys from St. Belor with censers. The flavor of the incense mingled with the scent of ripening oranges; today, ironically, the Oracle's sulfur was scarcely to be detected.

After the priests and the church-boys came the king's noblemen and his captains, not clad in mail but in their summer linens and silks. The silken women walked behind, some with their hair un-bound and crowned with flowers.

The palace had let them out like creatures from a cave. Its stone and wood walls were turned sidelong to the morning sun, as they grew from the elder masonry, and from between the stems of faded russet pillars that had been young when other gods moved over the earth and Christ Himself was not yet born.

The way to the Oracle led by the ruined temple. The space was full only of sunlit age and lizards. Few glanced. By night trysts were kept there, and cats fought under the moon. And yet, too, occasionally after sunset, no one would go there, the temple was left alone. Even the lizards ran away. . . .

The king had reached the terrace of the Oracle.

Draco gazed earnestly at the great stone, and the small dark hole lying half under it. It was no bigger than his fist, the hole, and this morning the smoke was very faint. But that, given the smoke's foul odor, was to the good.

From her hut on the terrace side, the elderly woman had come out. She wore a fine white garment, one of which was given her new each month. Her veiled head was like the head of a tortoise. She was the kind of crone the king would have pushed from his path without thinking, but this one he superstitiously revered, since she served the smoke.

Now a priest cried, "Holy Marusa of the corn, mild Lady who smiles upon the fields and leads the bees to their work among the flowers, we come to thank you for your kindness and your intercessions."

Only crickets answered. Birds rose singing, uninvolved.

Then the crone spoke, as if the priest had not.

"Who comes here, to question the Lady?"

And her voice, unlike that of the priest's, called from another world, and the crickets and the birds fell silent.

"I am King Draco." He had learned his lesson but enunciated as he did in battle—he was too loud.

One of his gentlemen handed the king a platter and flask. Draco cast grain about the timeless stone, poured wine on its old purple veins. The smoke stirred, just a little, sleepily.

The crone raised sticklike hands against the sky. "She thanks you for your offering, Draco." The Smoke Crone of the Oracle never addressed a king by any title other than his name. "What questions would you ask?"

The court waited; on its edges the people of the town, peasants and villagers from the woods beyond. Draco thought they came to stare at him, and was quite wrong.

"Are we to be prosperous?" barked Draco.

The Oracle did not respond. That mysterious liquid rumble it sometimes gave did not come.

Draco shouted on hoarsely, "Is there more fighting to be done? Besides, will my new capital be built by winter?"

His questions hung, unimportant, on air. Then the Oracle *gurgled*. Draco started, nearly dropped the plate he still held. The noise in the rock was loud, and now suddenly the smoke gushed out, dingy and thick, and the king jumped back. So did the two priests. Only the old woman stood her ground, used to it.

Stupidly, Draco said, "Is it angry, lady? The other place—my other city—it's only to show them, there, I'm king. Belgra will still be my town."

The Crone's reptilian eyes glinted. She fed the lizards in the temple, he had heard, and fondled them like children. But that was because she was an old virgin.

"No, Draco. She isn't angry. Build where you think fit. Today, the smoke is simple to read. Your lands will be prosperous, and there will be no more wars, not in your time. But your other capital, your city, will not be ready by winter. You're never there long enough to see it properly done."

A cloud crossed the sky. There was nothing in that. Nor in a gout of strong stinking smoke from under the stone. But the court muttered and Draco scowled, feeling he had been reprimanded in public by this old nanny.

She smiled, lowering her eyes and pulling her veil across her mouth to hide it.

Knowing now her mother was a goddess, the child had understood she would see her at once in the crowd. Her mother, the queen, would shine through all the others on the terraces, as a flame shone through the side of a lamp of clay or alabaster. Nothing, no one, could really come between them.

Had Coira decided anything concerning her mother's always-coldness to her? Of course she had.

Gods must be worshipped. Even the gentle meek Christ demanded it, and his Father, Almighty God Himself, was jealous and raging if ignored. While Coira had not known to worship, what else could the goddess do but fail to notice Coira in turn?

The nurse drew her charge along just at the rear of the ranks of noblewomen, some way from the nurseries of Draco's valued sons.

Showing off in their richest best, the noblewomen had no interest in this white-faced female child the king had probably forgotten. One snapped at the nurse, "Keep back. She'll tread on the border of my gown." Humble, the nurse obeyed, hauling Coira away like a rowdy dog—for they must all descend decorously. Maids tenderly lifted the trailing trains of gowns, green as the woods, blue as the sea.

Coira looked, looked for her queen.

All that while (the nurse pushing and pulling her, the women swaying and frivolously pausing, everyone-and-thing so vastly high up, the adult world of giants), Coira had little room to behold anything else.

Then they stopped, and the sun beat down.

Trapped in the depths of this forest of dressed human forms, the child craned about. She did not ask the nurse where her mother stood. Everyone was now religiously quiet, as in the church, where Coira's penalty for speech was a sharp pinch, and afterward three or four stinging slaps across her legs.

Now one of the priests was calling something out about the Virgin Marusa.

Somehow—obviously by divine design—the mass of gleaming women separated. A gap was there, like a window.

Coira stared through, and downward.

Her father (the king) was on a lower terrace, shouting as he did at supper in the palace hall. Coira did not listen. She rarely interpreted what was said by these giants. Even when they spoke to her, it was generally a kind of nonsense.

But above the king, drawn aside among the olive trees, the queen was standing with her girls.

She was, as Coira had known she must be, totally apart.

Coira drew in her breath involuntarily. Her eyes were wide.

The queen was rather far away, and so made smaller, and somehow more absolute. She wore a dress of ivory silk, stitched with gold threads. Her hair was not unbound, but held in an openwork golden tower, which showed its glistening darkness. A veil poured from the tower like a soft red flame.

The queen's face was impassive. That is, it was empty. But so beautiful, so fair, so perfect. Less a face than an instant of revelation.

Physically unmoving, rigid as if bolted into chains and shackles, the child's spirit galvanically strained to fly out of her body, to leap and hurl itself at the feet of her queen.

And suddenly, exactly then, evidently the goddess Arpazia became fiercely aware of this intensity of worship.

She did not move, did not turn or look about. It was not that at all. She seemed merely to straighten and grow taller, and her face tilted up into the light, and her eyes, though fixed apparently on nothing, widened with a flash, just as the eyes of the child had done a moment before.

II.

*F*ALLING TO LIFE, THEY WERE BORN on the same day of the same month; they also fell in love at the exact same moment—but not with each other.

Arpazia had stayed three hundred and thirteen days in her first trance, until the violence of childbirth, in her fifteenth year, woke her up. Yet after she had given birth, she entered a second trance, unlike the first. This second trance was to last for seven years.

That night of the birth (her birthday), when she would not let the baby suckle on her any longer, the women brought a wet nurse. She was a girl not many years older than the queen.

Arpazia had lain back, not caring, and prepared to die.

But she did not die. Her traitorous body grew well, thoroughly repairing itself. A morning came when the worst of the physicians had stood over her. "Madam, you're quite yourself. The king, when he returns, may be admitted without fear. I assure you, you can give him many more healthy children." Then, leaning near to make her particularly glad, he added, "Of course, of course you were disappointed. But the little girl does very well. And I don't doubt your next will be the son you crave."

When he said this Arpazia had burst up from her bed shrieking. She had flown at him half naked, her hair like two great beating wings.

Later, to excuse his own fright, he remarked generally that some women were dangerously unstable at such times. But also he was perhaps the first to compare the queen to a sorceress. "What true woman behaves in such a fashion to her doctor? She had an uncanny look. I've suspected things. She mumbled to herself, spells, perhaps against the baby—it came very late. The women say she hates the child. And she sits talking to that vain-glass of hers. She's from out of the forests. She'll have witch blood in her."

From the bottom of her second trance, Arpazia saw how they tried, from malice, all of them, to wake her.

The women soon desisted. This second trance was different. She could reach up out of it and smite them, just as she had sprung at the physician, or pushed the baby from her breast.

In the initial months of the second trance, Arpazia became a woman and a queen, a witch and a bitch, and left her mark in scarlet blows and purple bruises, in shards of broken things and torn garments.

"She has the temper of a fiend!"

"Another would only scold—she says no word but strikes like a snake."

"Best be wary of her. Look where her biggest ring cut my cheek, when she lashed out at me."

For, too, this trance had decided on the value of armor. Each day the queen, the bitch-witch, rose and was washed, perfumed, and clad in valuable stuffs, which she chose—and which, if then disliked, she rent. Her hair was rubbed with silk, combed—God help them if they accidentally tugged, or a coil was misplaced. Collars of silver and gold rings were applied. Finery. Mask and mail. Anything disapproved of was cast on the floor or across the chamber.

Then, only then, did she go to the mirror.

She undid the lid of it, and sat before the glass. If *they* made any sound, she sent them away, usually after flinging something at them.

Them, she despised. Her enemies. Servants, slaves, nobles—all women, all men, were now that. And she despised herself, what she had been.

But in the glass, the young queen could see herself as she had become, and was. Not transparent in her flesh, the fetus—the *growth*—showing through and stirring in the cup of her breached womb. Now she was an icon. Solid, and impenetrable.

She had learned her name and title. Before, it meant nothing. Now it was a part of her armor. Queen Arpazia.

That year Draco did not return to Belgra Demitu until almost the Midwinter-Mass. He had won another fight, and found that place he would come to want for a city—his "capital," scent-marking like a wolf, not with glands, but buildings. When he came back, he was full of this, boylike and noisy in his happy humor. When the queen did not appear, and did not receive him, sending one of her females to say she was not well, he shrugged. (He did see the baby. It was not a son.) He summoned his favorite, the barren hill-girl, and lay all night with her in the king's bed.

But later he met his queen, and saw she had grown up. She was a woman. Taller, slim as a sword, with pale hands and a high white brow. Her beauty did not please him so much. Where she had been toothsome she had become gorgeous, where she had been bendable, breakable, she now seemed hard. Cold-water eyes—he did not like those, either.

In the end, two nights after the Mass feast, he went to her rooms, out of common good manners, to show he still valued her as a wife.

There had been a brief scene with his favorite. He had told the girl where he was going. Quite properly she never made a fuss if he took another. Now she only made over herself some peasantish sign.

"Don't do that, puss. You're a Christian, and in front of your king."

"Pardon me, lord. But—they say things of the queen. Go cautious, lord."

"What? What things?"

"That she casts spells. Has got an imp—"

Draco hit the girl, lightly. "Stop that."

But the memory stayed close as he went into the apartment of his wife, and saw at once—in the absence of normal feminine things—embroidery, lap dog, trinkets, cradle—Arpazia's vain-glass, that mirror, standing wide open, as if parading itself.

Arpazia had risen from her chair.

Yes, she was a beauty, but now she looked too old to him; he preferred very young women. By the Christ, he had been informed she was fourteen, a year back. She would be fifteen or so now. She looked more like twenty, thirty, and frigid as a nun.

She had been difficult from the beginning. He recalled abruptly how she had led him that prance over the snow, and then cursed him. A witch? Very likely. But God, and his own male strength, had kept him sound.

"Well, madam. Here I am."

A servant hurried to bring him a filled cup. Though he had had plenty, Draco drank it. He waved the servant out. Now they were alone, as man and wife should be.

It was a freezing night. The mountaintops had changed to marble, the sea was almost white.

Braziers and candles burned, but after the hall and his own chamber, this room was not warm. Chilled no doubt by her. He must warm her up.

Draco crossed the space and took hold of his wife by the waist and drew her in. She did not resist, but her whole body, as he held it, had become inflexible, rigid as a pole.

"Come, come on. Give me a kiss. The physician says you're in good order by now. I've been at war. It's a long while since we had a dance." He spoke coarsely, to show her he was master here; not so coarsely as he had in the forest. All that was done. She had been virtuous and afraid then—to her credit, yes, yes. Now she was lawfully his before God, and must thank him.

He did kiss her. Her teeth were closed. He drew back and took a breath. "Now, is this kind?" A second kiss. The same. All altered.

"Did I wed you for this, you sulky slut? Get a crown on you for this? Unlock your doors, or do I ram you? Is that what you like, eh? A bit of a battle? I'm used to those, I can give you a fight easily enough, if you like." And he drew back his arm, slowly, to show her its muscle.

Her expressionless face was like white eggshell.

"Have your way," she said. She did not even speak the same. "But expect nothing."

"I *expect* my way. That'll do."

So he got her to the bed, threw her over, yanked up her clothes and forced himself into that tepid, hard, ungiving body, dry to annoy him, which moved only at his thrusts.

Her face was like that of something dead. The eyes were glazed. Just like that other bed of snow—

Perhaps it was only the drink in him, he had drunk a lot, that turned the course of his energy astray. He crammed on and on, trying to rub up a spark. But he began to see he went nowhere in her lifeless body. Necrophily was not for him. He needed under him a reaction—the spurs of enjoyment, failing that, the spur of another's panic and pain. He shouted in her dead face then, in her glistening eyes. Still raised over her, still inside her, he caught sight of *himself*, across the room, in the edge of the mirror.

Quite how he did so, he was afterward unsure, for the mirror did not seem to be at the right angle to picture him. Was that some of her sorcery?

What he saw was distorted. The man-creature in the glass was swarthy with hearty meat and drink, panting and piglike. While she—she was simply a mound of velvet that might only have been one more cover on the bed. As if she were not there at all.

It put him off. That, and the drink, and the girl with her averting sign, and this one's uselessness.

He pulled away, left her. He did up his clothing, and swore so the room rang like a bell.

Then he meant to thrash her. Her face should have it first, let them all see the brand of his displeasure.

She was upright, standing there all ready, the frozen hag.

She said, "Do what you want."

"You know I can't. You cuntess, you've spoiled it. Well—you I'll spoil the next—"

"Beat me if you want. If you make another *thing* in me"—*thing*, she said, not baby, *thing*—"I'll cut it out of my inside, as I should have, with the other. And if you beat me I'll cut my throat—so you'd better see to it first, as my father wanted. But I'll scratch out your eyes. I'll tear you and then I'll cut my throat"—her voice was rising now, like a low, cold-frozen gale from the sea—"or I'll hang myself the way you hanged Lilca—they'll all see—they'll say, 'Look what she did to escape her life with King Draco.' "

And then this monster gave a laugh. It was not loud, nor dramatic. And although her voice had risen, this was soft, nearly lyrical. Yet it struck him like a shriek.

She had lost her fear, it seemed, of being cut. The voice of the forest was still in her. She said now what she should have said before; she had the strength to say it, for she had not yet realized she might be afraid to die.

Draco again raised his arm. But like his erection, the penile upthrust of anger did not sustain itself. Instead he felt queasy.

Had she put something in the wine her servant gave him? She was mad enough.

"These are fine grounds for divorcement, woman. Shall I cast you out?"

"Yes," she said. "I would like that the most."

"Be damned in Hell, you fucking sow. I'll keep you, then. You're mine, till I say so. Till *I* want. Do you hear?"

"Have what you want, king," she sang at him.

And then she threw something right at him.

He gave a cry—of abject terror—she had *terrified* him—and he was uncertain why. But the tiny knife, which all this time she must have kept clenched in one hand, nicked his cheek. ("Her ring caught me . . ." just what her women were always saying.)

Then he wished to kill her himself. He felt the cold eye of the mirror watching him.

He thought, over there, unseen now—but if he *could* see it—in the spider web of glass, two others, a man with a knife through him, and an ice-woman cackling, old as the hag of the moon.

"Beat me, hit me," she invited once more, murmuring now, almost caressing. "I'll curse you, Draco. They taught me curses. The last came back on me, but if I die, where can it go but to you?"

The blustering boy, capable of so much, was not clever enough. He rolled around and his guts heaved. He threw up on the floor. And as he spewed, he knew she laughed again, whether he heard her or not.

Finished, he wiped his lips. (Did he glance to see if he had up-thrown lizards, frogs?)

"Yes, you make me sick," he croaked. "Stew here, then. Do as you like."

He could always have her murdered, he thought as he left. But he was, this rough hooligan, also devout. He would not dare without a better excuse.

But was she a sorceress? The Church then would decide.

Rumbling, belching, and retching through the corridors, under the flaming torches, between the antique pillars, servants and guards alike sidling back from him, he heard her nagging voice go on in his head. What she might say to the priests—how she had bested him—

Better to leave it. She was only a woman.

He visualized the other place, the city he wanted there. Far off from all this, and her.

He vomited throughout the night, and otherwise had evil

dreams, but waking in the morning he was fresh again, despite all that. Then he decided he was not afraid of her—the idea did not occur to him, in the morning, that he could be. She was nothing, ugly, and growing old. Besides, she produced girls not sons. And he was busy.

Six days later, Draco rode away again, to his skirmishes and little glamorous wars. There were plenty of girls to be had, and the new capital to be seen to.

So then. The nature of Arpazia's first trance had been inertia, severance. The second trance was composed both of severance and its defense, and of her loathing of self.

Maybe she had only gone mad. That was one other answer to her riddle. She had ceased bothering about death, even when personified as a king. She *had* died, was *dead*. (This would pass, but how could she know it would pass?) The embryo, dividing her from herself on entering, had left her in two pieces. Her childhood had run out with the parturition blood, and become another being: obviously, a child. And the woman remained, crazy, in her hollow fortress.

Like other outlaws who had survived great horrors and no longer knew to fear them, Arpazia grew terrible.

They should have sent her away. Instead they kept her. But kept, too, on her kind side—for she was a queen, and a witch. The witch-queen.

The years continued. As the girl christened Candacis, and called Coira, grew from baby to child, the candle of Arpazia meanwhile burned down, melting the ordinary wax from her and leaving only the flame.

Because of all of this, others had begun to consider the queen. Others watched her. Bright eyes, as if of birds among the vines, of foxes on the hillsides. To her, they were all her enemies. Why should she take special note of any glance? She only talked to the woman she saw in her mirror, who would always answer.

"Her mirror is her tool of sorcery."
It was.
She saw things in it, and the mirror, surely, saw things in her.
"She talks to demons."
Yes, to one: herself.

At twilight, looking in the mirror, conversing with her reflection, the lamp or candle sinking, she beheld a crow which sat above the window, blinking orichalc eyes. Later, a white owl. Or two shadows stood behind her, one of whom held a spindle with white wool on it. Or a tree grew in the corner, laden with rosy fruits, while a serpent twined the trunk.

Had her women too seen such images? Did they ever risk, if she should not be there, opening the mirror and asking some question of their own? Did they get an answer?

She is a witch.

On the terrace of the Oracle: the ancient crone who cuddled lizards in the temple ruin, visited the smoke every dawn. A day came before the rite was due in summer, late in spring of that year when Coira was seven, and Arpazia twenty-two years of age.

Through the half-light, the Crone approached the Oracle and bent to the stone. If any watched, it was only what she always did.

But she too had her questions.

"Holy and holy. Is she ours, that woman in the High House?"

The Oracle smoke might be tampered with, and frequently was. Now, not interfering, the crone gave her gift of oil, and read its pattern, plain to her as language.

Though she reverenced the Christ when she must, in the church, the Smoke Crone knew quite well who He really was, the young god of joy, who must be sacrificed and rise again. There was to the compendium of any god more than one, or two—the usual number being three.

She may be ours, the smoke had said.

When the rite came, the crone would speak to Draco and send him off to his new capital. She must do it in careful, tactful words, saying the city was missing his attention, like some sickly woman or hound. But she would see him away, and so leave Belgra free of him, for her people—and for the elder powers which had always been, would always be, when all the rest was gone.

When the child looked across the hill of terraces, and saw her mother in the white dress stitched by gold, Coira fell deeply, spiritually, asexually yet physically in love. It was the adoration of the priestess for the goddess. Of the body for the vision of its soul. Great love indeed.

And in this selfsame moment, Arpazia, looking in quite a different direction, woke from her second, seven-year-long trance. And also fell into the vortex of love. But it was to her like the smashing of a vessel. As if she had been one of those many items which, through the seven years, she had flung, and which had shattered. Or as if she had been a mirror and, falling, broke into a million sparkling splinters.

What she had seen was not the daughter of her womb. It was a young man of about her own age, standing some way from her, lower down the hillside, under the terraces of Belgra Demitu.

She did not ask *Who is that?* She *thought* nothing. Flown into a million bits, still her mirror gaze was fixed.

And he, too, gazed at her. Through the crowds, across the light, the shadow, he smiled one lightning smile, blinding her.

Arpazia woke from her second trance to the noon sun in her eyes.

III.

*T*HAT VERY EVENING, THE CHANCE arrived. As such things often were, it was unlooked for. However, she had wished for it so much, considered it so repeatedly, constantly, that she seized her fate at once.

The day of the Oracle's rite was arranged oddly. No doubt the

priests had done this, in order to upset the holiday, which was a
pagan one.

After the king gave his duty to the smoke, there was a feast,
which continued through the afternoon. Then, after sunset came a
Mass at St. Belor, and everyone must go to church and sit there for
two or three hours, heavy with food and drinking, longing to sleep.
Between the banquet and the service, the prudent stole away to
rest, or to indulge other desires.

Coira's nurse had slipped off to a meeting with some lower steward. She had been tipsy, or might not have risked it. Kaya and Julah
she admonished. *They* must stay put and care for the child. But Kaya
had her own lover, a boy of twelve, a blacksmith's apprentice. And
Julah, peeved to have nobody to abscond with, pretended she had,
and also flounced away.

Coira had dozed, then made believe she did. She heard them
all go.

When the doors were shut, Coira got up. She had been un-
dressed to her shift for sleep. She herself now accurately donned
her white dress and combed her hair.

She went out barefoot on the cool stone floors of the new palace,
the colder tiles of the old. The way to the small garden remained
in Coira's mind like a map drawn in fadeless lines. In the corridors
she passed few persons. Most of the place was locked away with its
secrets, or asleep, or else still junketing in the hall. The occasional
scurrying servant or wandering lover paid no attention to a small
child in white. She was neither often seen or known.

She found the garden, which was vacant, muffled in late afternoon sun. From the garden a strange old colonnade ran along under
the wall of the elder palace. Coira went that way quietly, once or
twice touching the glossy leaves of bay trees in pots. She had at this
point a curious sensation, the child, as if she were walking down
deep underground, which must have been caused by the shade of
the high walls.

There were two doors of heavy wood, braced in bronze and with
gilded shapes on them of fruit trees. They had a pair of round

handles, like golden oranges, but these were too high up for the child to reach.

Was this the queen's door? Surely it was.

Coira raised her hand to knock or scratch, then hesitated. It was not, even now, doubt. The child felt her mortal smallness, and thought she would not be heard. She had been frequently ignored.

"Now, my pretty," said a voice, unknown yet familiar, "all alone? Have they let you get out?"

Coira turned. In a core of darkness under a single pillar, a woman seeming just as old, stood pale, slender and curved like a gibbous moon.

The child looked at her. She said nothing. Through all her peculiar childhood, she had learned this one useful trick.

But the old woman appeared amused. She was not (though she closely resembled her) the Smoke Crone. She said, "I've come to call on her majesty. And now here you are, to call on her, as well. You must go first. What better?" And she stepped forward and rapped sharply on the left-hand door. "No one else is there," said the crone, gossipy. "She's sent them out."

A voice called, "Yes, enter." The queen's voice? The child did not know.

"Go in," said the crone, bending even more to the child, "and you'll see, she'll be looking for me, up in the air over your head." And she laughed, the crone, like a goose gaggling softly.

But she turned one golden handle, and when the door opened, the child walked through, alone.

As the old woman had predicted, the queen was watching above the child's head for someone of the normal adult giant's height. Then her eyes glided downward and struck the face of the child with two glittering bright blows.

"Where is she?" said the queen. Always they were asking, this mother and daughter, these elusive enigmatic questions about or of each other.

"She said I should come in first."

"Were you with her? Are you hers?" asked the queen, apparently surprised.

"No. She was there, by the door."

"What do you want?"

The witch-queen seemed distracted. She turned away. She had, as always, no attention to spare.

Coira swallowed, her heart drumming and her eyes too large. Now she must make the goddess see her at last. Plainly it had not happened as yet.

"I am Coira," announced the child bravely.

"Yes?" said the queen, her back to the girl, not hearing her, or only partly. Not knowing the name, perhaps. (They had called her baby Candacis.)

The queen wore the gown she had had on earlier, ivory and gold, but the headdress and veil had been removed from her high-coiled, flawless hair. She paced across the wide room, as Coira had seen her do so many times, pacing across distance and windows. Then she reached what Coira took to be another window. It had an open metal shutter, like a door, but it gave on another room, identical even to the gilded water clock dripping in a corner. And next Coira became aware the queen had materialized in the other room, also, while still remaining in this one. There were two of her. She stood there, facing herself, both ways.

Coira was amazed but enchanted. This was true magic. It was miraculous.

And stealing forward, gazing only upward now to the adult height, as the queen herself had done, Coira missed her own reflection as it entered the scope of the sorcerous mirror. She saw only the witch-queen facing the witch-queen, her wonder doubled.

The child was now too moved even to need to be brave. "You're so beautiful—more beautiful—the most beautiful in all the whole world."

The fierce cry penetrated the heart of Arpazia, which today had begun to thaw and crack in pieces. She glanced over her shoulder

and down in astonishment, at the little creature, like a dwarf, on
her floor.

"Am I?"

"Yes—so beautiful. More beautiful than anyone. Like the goddess."

"Hush," said Arpazia, as she had in the past, but not to this
child. Yet Arpazia looked back into the glass. She saw her beauty
as if for the only time in her life. Her eyes darkened. "Yes. I am."

And "Yes," answered the queen in the mirror, "you are."

But then she felt something rest against her leg, as a tall dog
might do. It was this girl-child again, leaning on her, staring up.

Whose was she? *Oh, she's mine. Oh. His.*

"Where is your nurse?" said the queen. Her face became an
egg's shell. The shell peered at Coira.

Coira knew better than to say where the nurse was. She did not
want to discuss the nurse. She wanted her mother to take her hand.
Coira reached up and instead took hold of the tips of the queen's
jeweled fingers.

"Let go of me," said the queen, not loudly, not even cruelly.
"Why are you here and not with your nurse? You must go away at
once. You said an old woman was outside. Send her in to me."

Coira's heart also cracked.

It was not to let love in but to let it out, like venom from the
bite of a snake.

When Arpazia looked round again, the dwarvish child had vanished and the crone replaced her in the space of the room.

But the crone, too, was the wrong crone.

The queen tapped her foot.

The crone said, knowing the queen's mind, still amused, "*She's*
the guardian of the Oracle, she mustn't leave her spot on the terrace.
I'm her kin. She sent me."

Arpazia said, "I hear from my servants she—you, too, then—
are a sort of law in the town. They are your people, not the king's."

"Ah, lady," said the crone slyly. She denied nothing.

"Your people, then," said Arpazia, "are too bold. You must rep-

rimand them. I've heard talk here of your dancing in the woods.
Godless pagans. You make the pious priests angry." Then Arpazia
grinned, saw herself do it in the mirror. But perhaps only the queen
in the mirror grinned.

This second crone said, "Will you like to come and dance with
us, Queen?"

Years ago . . . those years came back to the queen, and the engorged face of Draco. She said, "That is a lewd term, to *dance*."

"Sometimes."

"One of your young men was insolent to me, at the ceremony
this morning. He offended me, and I asked my women, 'Who is
that man, daring to make faces at me?' They said he was one of
your people, you pagans the priests may one day burn for your
godlessness."

"Oh, we're godly," said the old woman.

The queen asked, almost shrilly, "Who is that man? Tell me his
name. The king—" She faltered, for now she had mentioned the
king twice and he was nothing to her, nothing but insane, bad
things. Her white cheeks were flushed a moment. (The little girl
had flushed in just that way, walking into this chamber, although
she had been dull white as a headstone, walking out.) *"Who is that
young man?"*

"I'll tell you a name we give him, lady. We call him Orion."

Arpazia barked—a crazy laughter—somehow she had heard the
name.

"A star!"

"A hunting star, lady."

"The king"—oh, again—"he shall hear how your *Orion* leered
at me—" But the queen was blushing. Years fell from her with the
clatter of shed armor. She stood in her expensive lovely gown, naked
before the old woman, and hid her young face in her hand.

The old woman bowed her head at this nice outcome. They
had hoped *she* might see him—and he was handsome, the young
man who had smiled at the queen. And the hand of the old gods
was on him. Those gods needed no help. They liked to play, some-

times. But for the pagan kind, in the days of the Christ, a queen's favor was worth courting. Perhaps. Always other currents moved, changeable, deep . . . the gods, liking to play . . .

Outside, in the corridors, and in the back of her skull, the crone heard the child she had met noiselessly crying, needles of her smashed heart raining from her eyes as she wandered about. Pain and weeping—the lot of human things.

"Three nights from this one, at Full Moon," said the crone, "we are going up to the wood. King Draco will be gone by then, off to his new city. And half the priests—well, lady, they kneel to the Christ one day and run with us the next. Nothing for you to fear."

"You presume—"

"To invite you? Yes, yes, fair Queen. Look in your mirror. See your beauty. See your witch's eyes. What do you say?"

"Will *he*—"

"Oh, *he'll* be there. Under the trees."

"Then I shall avoid—"

"A star in the dark. Hunting the deer. Apple grows to be bitten, lady."

Arpazia's blood, red as apples, melted to fire.

When she again looked up she was alone, and the evening was closing through amber to ash. A worrisome bell clanged. St. Belor was calling sinners to their unwanted Mass.

The sultry church, dim with incense and drunken breath. The king's head sometimes nodded, but soon he had himself in check. He feared God, and God was in this house.

Above the aisle, rising from a moonblast of candles, the frightening figure of the Christ, thin as a bone and bleached as one, hammered with gory rubies to his golden cross. The eyes harrowed down, agonized—yet watchful. *I have suffered this for you*, said these awful eyes, so some might think, *what will you give me in return?*

So it seemed tonight to the queen. She had eaten and drunk very little and she was wide, wide awake.

She saw the church of St. Belor, as if for the first time. Its
frescoes and goldleaf, the Christ, the statue of the Virgin Marusa,
with a silver star on her forehead and the single diamond tear set
under her right eye. The saint himself, Belor, waited servantlike
behind her.

Clad in Marusa's blue, Arpazia had been married here.

She had since come here every seventh day, to worship.

It had meant nothing, she was not religious, and less so now.
Yet, ironically, she heard tonight what the priest was saying as he
stood under the anchor of the enormous Bible.

"*Septem Peccata, Septem Peccata*. Against these foul Seven, at all
times you must be on guard."

He was pointing up beyond the altar, near the roof.

Arpazia, like the rest, looked there. She saw the grotesque carv-
ings, devils and monsters, such as she had once been shown in one
of her father's clever books. Had such things made her afraid then?
She did not recall. Now she found them contemptible, as she had
come to find her younger self. And as for the demanding Savior,
there smoldered in her a sort of hatred. *If ever you suffered for me,
what good has it done me? Where were you and your God when he had me
down in the snow—what return must I give you for that?*

The pointing priest was indicating a line of misshappen crouching figures. Arpazia stared at them a moment. They were men, but
crushed small—dwarves, and with curious animal attributes. One
had the paws and claws of a bear, and one a peacock's tail and lion's
ruff; one a spiked horn sticking up from his forehead.

"The seven mighty sins of the flesh," cried the priest, raging at
the crowded church, these persons redolent of transgression. "*Septem
magna peccata carnis!* See, there is Anger in his wrath, Pride in his
vainglory, and Lust puffed by his own disgusting hungers—"

Candle-flickered, the stone brutes writhed and cavorted, startling the queen. A stab of fire shot through her. The blood spangled,
rose to her face as it had done when the hag stood before her, the
weird woman with her chat of the wood.

Arpazia lowered her eyes. Inside her lids, she saw the face of the young man. And then, that he was naked. Only the shadows of leaves half covered him, his body gleamed like marble.

An elderly singsong creaked in her brain, shutting out the ranting priest.

Black is the wood, black as the night,
Hidden the roses red and white . . .

And then Arpazia heard a girl's voice, perhaps Lilca's, whisper, "I couldn't make him stop, I loved it so, what he did to me—"

The queen's eyes were fast shut. She shivered, but only once.

As he raved, the priest spat foam, and here and there a woman fainted from too much wine or remorse.

"She burns and her pillow's soaked. That's the fever-dews."

Kaya and Julah hovered meekly, as the nurse of Candacis, the king's legal daughter, gloomed above her charge.

"I didn't dare leave her," lied Kaya, glibly, "to try and find you."

"No, Kaya wouldn't leave the bedside," added Julah, squinting at Kaya to make sure her accomplicement was recognized. "But Coira didn't know us at all, she got so sick. When we patted her, she cried out we weren't there. She only wanted you."

The nurse, worn out with her own business, and the church lecture on the Septem Peccata, Pride, Anger, Lust, Envy, Covetousness, Gluttony, and Sloth—longed to lie down herself and slothfully sleep.

"It's nothing much. They take these fevers at her age. It'll be gone by morning. There, there, Coira. Sip this water. No? Then you must do without."

The Witch-Queen: The Black Wood

I.

*A*ND THE MIRROR GAZED through the night window, and met the slim white face of the three-quarters moon.

I have passed this way before, said the moon to the mirror.

I too, answered the mirror, began in the East.

Already I must go on, said the moon. Farewell, until another night.

But watching, the mirror still saw a moon, a face white as the moon, in a midnight of hair.

"Am I beautiful?" the queen asked the mirror. Someone had taught her such a question but she had forgotten who. "The most beautiful in all King Draco's rotten lands?"

Yes. Look and see. Only the moon can compare, and the moon has moved out of your mirror now.

"Will—" The queen meant to say, *Will he think me beautiful?* But the words would not come. Draco had found her beautiful, and so made her beauty vile. But that was then. Then she was that other

stupid, wretched one, and now she was a queen, and wide awake—
and still young, young as daybreak.

Three hours after sunset on the third night, someone rapped lightly
on the door of the queen's apartment.

Instead of calling to her maids—for she had sent them away—
the queen went herself to undo the door and look out.

No one was in the corridor. Then, they were.

Having pushed off her earlier girl-self, the queen was brand
new, nearly innocent again. So she, the witch, for a second took this
manifestation for sorcery.

But then she scathingly chided herself. (Her inner tongue, when
critical, had remained as harsh for herself as her outer ways were
hard on others.)

"Are you playing a game there, old woman? Leave it off. Why
are you here?"

"Don't you know, Queen? Aren't you waiting for me, fair as the
night, and King Draco gone since this morning, and you all alone."

"I should have them whip you."

"Oh, you should. But there is another king now. Another king
tonight. Come and see, Queen."

They were in the colonnade. Trees sighed from the palace terraces, and it was dark, half the lamps unlit, yet the summer stars
were blisters of white-gold. Arpazia drew the hood of her cloak over
her head, to hide from them.

A surprising turning. Had Arpazia never come this way before?
They crossed an edge of her private garden, and it looked unknown,
like a familiar scene glimpsed suddenly in a mirror. Even the sea
was visible on the *other* side, beyond a stand of pines . . .

The concealed door, which the hag unlocked, apparently without a key, reminded Arpazia of her first escape. She faltered, but
then tossed the memory aside.

Descending now a broken ancient stairway, loose small stones scattering from their feet. Between the oleanders and the olives, goats fed like blanched shadows. Out of a scabrous wall the old woman gripped in her claw a lantern.

Then they went down into the velvet dark, under the terraces, where the tangled gardens had given themselves over to the elder gods of savage things.

Above, behind them, the barely lit palace shone faintly as a ghost on the sequined sky. All of it seemed a ruin now—ancient, and barely substantial.

Tall plants brushed by, and bowed to the queen. What were they? Not garden things, nor quite things of the forest . . .

"Hemlock," the old woman muttered. "White nightshade. Moly, known to the enchantress Kirsis . . ."

Huge old white stones, and then a blurred milky statue which, as they turned from it, Arpazia saw held lightly in one hand, and smiling, its own raised phallus—

"Stop," said Arpazia. "I won't go any further with you."

"Not far now, Queen."

Above, behind, from this fresh angle of the wild ground, the temple showed. Its pillars grew like plants themselves, petrified in darkness.

And then they were on a walk, pebbled by great uneven round stones. Feather cypress trees, a scholar's rack of pens, were sentinel on either side, and then both women slipped through a little gate and were on a meadow, waist high in the dry pale summer grass, and poppies inked black, under the stars.

The land ran up into the trees there, just where a dreadful flaming face was now standing, the moon at full, a mask of beaten gold.

The queen herself became the mirror of the moon. It shone right into her.

I have passed this way before, said the moon to the mirror of the queen. *And you?*

"Never," murmured the queen.

I see you climb to meet me, said the moon. *I regret, by the time you have gone high enough up the hills, I shall have reached the summit of the sky.*

It was the hag, somehow privy to this uncanny conversation, who remarked, "Don't mind it, moon. Our way lies down into the dark."

And exactly then the first trees were there, their limbs running deep into the earth, casting the black shade of their cannopy. This church was cool and fragrant.

Arpazia had grown among enormous forests. She hung back once more. To enter here was to return into herself, her childhood, girlhood. Had that time been so occluded?

"Where have you brought me?" she demanded of the hag.

"Where have you brought yourself? Where do you think?"

The woods were black as ebony. The roots of them hooped and humped like serpents away below ground. In the boughs, unseen presences pattered, whistled, cooed, shook their wings—but these entities were not all birds.

Starlight had dripped through, and now the moonlight flung down blond carpets. A slender waterfall ran from the mossy mouth of a cave, dippered over rocks and dropped into an oval basin. The moon burned in the water, then the two narrow figures crossed against it.

They had reached a natural avenue in the wood. All around, the thick screen of the trees, the sigh and soothe of the leaves. But here the wide path was like a lawn, the grass so closely cut that perhaps it had been scythed, or else sheep were brought by day to graze.

The moon-carpet ran along the avenue, barred like the coat of an animal with shadow-stripes.

No longer delaying, the queen would have walked on. It was the hag who stayed her now. They were still then, standing there, the lantern extinguished.

Out between the trees presently, Arpazia saw beings evolve into the moon glow.

At first she thought them supernatural. Then she knew that they were human, as she was, only made bizarre—as was she?—by the night and the black wood.

Yet again, seen in the mirror of the night, despite her recognition of them, they were changed. Freed. Lawless.

Palace girls and women from the town, even some of those who had been in Draco's camps, mingled without a glance. Nobles with servants, with slaves also; and there, as the old woman had promised or warned, a priest from the church of the Christ, an old man, *altered*—made, not youthful, but *without* time.

Arpazia began to notice other matters. The unbound hair, the bare feet and legs—and there, and there, the moon in little, glimmering breasts which seemed to look back at her from their nipples—

And Arpazia experienced again, even at this allurement of her own sex, a scorching erotic thrill.

She had never felt anything for women. Nor for men. That is, she had felt only uninterest, distaste, mockery—climaxing in horror and revulsion.

There had been a slight sound as the crowd gathered in out of the wood. Though none of them acknowledged her, many turned and gaped a moment. These movements, little rufflings of garments, hair, rills of muted voices, insectile whispers, all these ended, and then there was silence again, only the rainy sound of the waterfall, the oceanic ebb and flow of the breeze among the boughs.

Like the moon, something was approaching, coming toward them. And they awaited it, Arpazia too.

She understood. Her heart raced already to meet him. For who could it be that was so anticipated—but *he*?

Soon after, there was a difference at the avenue's end. The moon had shifted further, to light that spot abruptly. Only then could you see that something stood there.

Arpazia was struck to stone in heart-sinking disappointment.

And fear. For it was not anything remotely mortal, there at the apex of the avenue.

It was a beast. Some monster of nightmare, birthed by a demon. And a glad welcoming cry rose from the people in the wood. The breeze, lifting, called too. Bells tinkled, a thin piping circled, once, twice, three times, before that overlay of silence came again.

The beast moved now, toward them, leisurely, down the avenue. Arpazia thought, *Are you a fool still? You know you can trust no one, yet here you have let them lead you. You're lost now in this wood. And they have summoned up this abomination.* But then she thought, what did she care? Was it worse than Draco, that beast in a man's hairy skin?

She thought: *Let it try me.* Her nails and teeth were sharp, now. *Look, fool, it isn't all a beast. It has to walk like a man—*

Certainly it walked on two legs. Yet it had the head of a stag, crowned round and round with four branching antlers. And its body was a freckled panther's, yet also partly a bear's—and it had the shanks of a boar.

But the bristled or hirsute skins shifted as it walked. Now one lean thigh showed an instant, the long, muscled calf of a man. And then he was nearer, quite near, and under the head of the stag, was the strong column of the young male human throat, and the massed dark hair, gilded as a carving, running out there.

A man in a panther's skin and the hide of a boar and the pelt of a bear, made king by a diadem of antlers—

Still stone, Arpazia was locked now in a panic of shame and pride, anger and desire, alone among the crowd before and about him.

For it *was* he. It was the one who had looked at her, woken her up. And beneath the plethora of the beasts, as in her waking dream, he was naked as the statue among the hemlock.

II.

SINCE, TONIGHT, SHE HAD BECOME a mirror, did she reflect this elemental creature? Did he see himself in her surface? For now he stood not three feet from her. He was taller than she, as most men were, and both of the influencing men of her life—her father, Draco. But so unlike, this beast walking upright, to those two former men whose souls ran on all fours.

He smelled of the skins he wore, yet also young and clean, and of the wood, its foliage and moss and sap, the secret crushed life of it.

From inside the wooden stag's head (like the moon, he wore a mask) she caught the dark gleam of his eyes, and it reminded her of the water she had passed, the basin under the waterfall.

No one else was near, finally. They had drawn away. The old woman had drawn away.

Arpazia stayed still as a stone.

She looked up, into the mask, at his eyes. She felt the warmth of his body, mantled only in skins and shadows.

"I know," he said, "you are the king's wife in the palace." He spoke quietly, gently, and without hurry. "But here, Lady, as you've come here, the palace means little. Here in the wood, we're not the selves we are back there, in the places of men. This is the place of the gods. Do you see?"

Her lips parted to speak. She said nothing.

He said, "Don't be afraid. We won't hurt you."

Arpazia's eyes widened and words came from her lips. "Try. See what you get."

He laughed. The wooden head tossed up, just like a stag's head, and the antlers rattled their terrible tines. But on his shoulders of panther's skin the hair coiled, thick, shining. It was somber now, but in sunlight, as she had seen on the terraces, it had the rich color of beer. His hands, though now in the gauntlets of a bear's paws, and clawed, were tanned. His throat was tanned, almost the shade of an olive under the moon. But at his chest the tan faded. He grew whiter, like marble.

A star leapt in her belly.

"Yes, Lady, they say you're fierce. That's good. Like a lioness of the goddess. But all I want is to make you my queen here, for tonight."

"Are you a king, then?"

"One king. There are other kings."

"Draco," she said.

"Oh, not Draco," said the stag's mask, coolly.

He drew the glove of fur and claws off from his left hand. She saw then the hand she remembered, and as he moved, the skins, parting, nearly down to his middle.

He was hard and spare, muscled from his work, whatever that work was. The finest rivulet of hair described the center of his chest, down to where the cord of woven grass tied in the skins at his waist.

"I'm the Hunter King," said the mask of the stag. "Those other kings gave and allow me that. The Kings of the Air and the Wood. And the King of the Lands Below. Do you see what I mean? They're gods."

"And you?" she said.

"A man. And you, a woman. But tonight, my queen."

He took her hand straight up, in his bared hand, and at the touch of his flesh, his fingers wrapping her own, she could have sunk into the grass, for she had turned from stone to molten honey.

When they walked back along the avenue, the moon was gone from it, and only shades pressed in on them, people and trees. But someone brushed off the hood of her cloak, and next her hair was loose and heavy about her, moving as if separately alive, and then a garland was on her hair, with the scent of myrtle and poppies.

She thought, *You stupid bitch, do you know what you're at? Don't you ever learn?*

But the hating inner voice was drummed away by the beating of her heart. And they were playing their music too, hollow reeds, shaken bells.

At the avenue's end, cobalt-black, a glade was shielded from the moon by massive oak trees. A primeval place it seemed to her. And on the corded trunks she saw the white gorings, the gouges of generations of boar tusks.

They were igniting a hundred little clay lamps. The smallest reddest flames perched on them, forming a crimson mist.

The altar they approached in the glade was ancient as the slab in the temple of Belgra Demitu.

Someone else had taken away her cloak. But she was accustomed to all these servantly dressings and undressings. And her hand was fast in his.

The King and Queen of the Wood were seated on two mossy boulders.

Earthernware cups were brought them. The drink was ale with a malty syrup mixed in, sprinkled by wild mint.

Arpazia saw her feet were bare.

But really she could feel only his nearness and the pressure of his hand, and all the several calluses on it, which fascinated her. And she wanted him to speak to her. His voice was like the sounds of the wood, and like music, but also the voice of a man.

Do you like men so much? jabbed the inner voice. *You know what they do in the forest and the bed.*

When she thought this, her womb spasmed inside her, twisting, like the strings on a harp.

Is this what women felt? But she knew better than to feel it.

In the dim crimson light, these people were dancing, as they might in the formal dances of the court.

Arpazia said, very low, "Do you think you can possess me?"

"Only if you allow it."

"I won't."

All she could see was the face of the stag, the rending horns. She thought of Rage, the unicorn, and Lust the stinging scorpion. She thought of Sloth, who had the paws and claws of a bear. But the Hunter King was not slothful. He was lambent with strength.

He had not answered.

She said, "It's unlawful for me to be here. The king—"

"Draco heeded the Oracle. He's taken his soldiers, his own people, and left only those who mean little to him. And some of those are here. And one of those is yourself, Lady."

Arpazia thought of Pride, a lion with a peacock's tail. Of Envy the snake and Covetousness the fox and Gluttony the boar.

Proud panther-lion, was he gluttonous in his boar's skin? Would he devour her?

He had turned his head, and his hand twitched on hers. She fell down through the chair of rock, into the wet black depths of the wood, and there she felt his weight on her, hot as the sun by night.

Arpazia tried to get up. But her legs had become very weak.

"Drink the ale-cup, Persapheh."

"Why do you call me that—?" she stammered childishly.

"That is your name, when you're queen in the wood."

"No. That isn't my name."

"In the wood it is."

It was the name of the goddess known at Belgra Demitu, who was three-in-one: Coira when a maiden, Demetra when a mother, Persapheh when, robed in hoar-frost and winter snow, she went below and became Queen Death. But Arpazia, who had heard the myth, did not recall.

She tried to pull away her hand.

But instead she found she had drunk some more of the drink, and now he stood and drew her with him, and they were in the dance, beside the prehistoric altar.

Black stains marked it, as tusk-tears marked the oaks. Things had been sacrificed on it. And so they were still, for now she saw thin little bones like slivers of new quartz, lying in the grass.

"There's no killing tonight," he said.

And then he led her away around the altar and through the ebony trees and into the black between them, where the moon surely had never found her way, not once in a hundred years, but the moon besides was gone.

"I won't go any farther."

He stopped.

"Why," she said, "have you brought me here?"

"Why have you come with me?"

"I'll give you nothing."

"I'll give you everything."

Then he let her go and she almost dropped to the ground. She caught hold of a tree and the tree supported her. She watched him as he drew off the head of the stag.

He came out laughing again, shaking back his brown lion's hair. His eyes seemed all dark, like a cat's by night, and they lighted once, as a cat's would. And then he stripped away before her (as once the rapist had stripped *her*) his garments of skin. He stood there in the faint nocturnal glim, by which, now, she seemed to see as clearly as if at noon, naked from head to foot.

He was like a column of marble, smooth and satin-slippery, yet warm, and at the center of him the warmth became another black wood, and then a great stem of flame, dark and perilous, upright as any castle tower.

"I'll kill you," she said.

But in reply he only shook his head, and putting his own bare hand upon the rod, with such grace and delicacy, he stroked it once, and twice, and three times, as a musician might an instrument of music, his eyes half closing at the pleasure, the melody it gave back.

Arpazia put her face into her hands. She slipped down the tree and lay in the feral grass.

He lay down beside her. He leaned across her and, lifting away her hands, he kissed her forehead, her fluttering eyelids. He kissed her mouth.

Then she gripped him, as she had caught hold of the tree, yet still she fell away and away. They spun together, they might have been flying, and only he could save her from the fall and from the ground.

His mouth was on her breasts, his hands stroked, making the music in her, as he had made it in himself.

"Don't do this," she said. "I forbid it."

"No," he said. "But perhaps . . ."

And it was his mouth she felt upon the dark within her thighs, and the tongue tip, also like a flame, but the agile firefly flames on the red lamps, flickering and sipping.

Arpazia lay on her back and saw the sky and stars between the arms of the wood which held them all up.

What was she looking for? An angel—

The angel had been cast out of Heaven, and was here.

The long flame rippled on and on, and she danced to its music, on her back. Then his eyes crested her body, looking at her as the moon had looked, as a beast would look, raising its pitiless and beautiful head from the thing it fed on.

"Sweet as apples," he said to her, but then he sank again and his hair furled over her belly and a burning wheel rushed through her womb, her spine, so she clutched the earth and danced on, kicking her heels. Presently her own high single cry burst from her, and it, too, flew away, without her, into the night.

III.

*A*RPAZIA WAS OBSESSED. BY him, after this act together in the dark night wood. Also obsessed by the act itself. She recreated the act, in her mind, even in sleep—and the throes of culmination overcame her. Awake, she touched herself with her fingertips, quick, light, almost as he had done. She thought of his body and his eyes gazing so savagely at her, so mercilessly, *forcing* her into the oblivion of joy.

How many days and nights passed? Three or four. Not a great

many. This was, in some sort, her third trance. But the object of her state, now, was not herself.

She knew his name. Not the pagan night-name she was given for the wood. Near morning the old woman had guided her back again to the palace, or, at any rate, *one* old woman. They all of them looked alike to Arpazia, as, really, every woman had looked alike, and every man, until now.

"Tell me his name," Arpazia had hissed, on the meadow below the palace. Subterfuge was done with. The sky was pale-sick with dawn.

The crone did not prevaricate, for a wonder.

"As a man, he's called Klymeno."

This, too, was the name of a god, but Arpazia did not realize, though she had heard it somewhere, once or twice, in this country by the sea.

"*What* is he?"

"By trade, do you mean? What do you think?"

Arpazia could not think. Part of her, despite her questions, knew he was a being of otherness, and did not exist outside his own world.

"I asked you, and you will answer."

"Will I? Oh, you're queen again, are you?"

"I am the queen, yes."

The crone said, "He hunts, that's how he makes his living. He kills things in the woods and lugs the dead carcasses to the town."

Arpazia visualized him, thick with blood. Even this enticed her. That morning in her bed, she dreamed he hunted *her*, and he was naked as he had been in the darkness. His spear brought her down and pinned her to the earth. He ate her alive, tearing off chunks of her flesh as she choked with unbearable fear and ecstasy.

This dream was repeated.

He had not been gentle. What he had perpetrated on her, woken her up to, was more ferocious than any rape.

Arpazia the queen possessed no agenda of the pagan doings of the town and palace. Because of that, she was at a loss. What would happen next? Besides, she could not wait. She had soon used her memory up.

What he had done to her he had only done two times. Then he had kissed her, got up, and left her there. Afterward she did not know if he had taken his own pleasure separately, gaining it voyeuristically from observing hers. He vanished like a phantom through the trees, as did every one of them, these Woods People, but for the escorting crone.

Arpazia found now she needed to know if he too had been pleasured. She had not seen it, and wanted to add this missing ingredient to her dreams.

Or had he been ultimately indifferent to her—unmoved to any pleasure?

How would he be, and look, suffering the pangs she had undergone? Here an image of grunting Draco intervened—she shook it off. This act had no bearing on the acts of Klymeno, performed with her.

Or, had he been indifferent, unaroused?

So the ideas superceded each other.

Somewhere during this time, one of the queen's women entered her apartments, and brought in another woman that the queen did not remember.

"She's the child's nurse, madam."

Which child? Arpazia stared, blankly.

The nurse of the Princess Candacis curtseyed, groveling.

"Excuse my presence, Lady. I thought you should know. I should ask."

Know and ask what? What did any of this have to do with the queen?

"What is it?" said Arpazia.

The nurse stumbled on her words, guilty and unsure. "She's in a fever, Lady. It doesn't break—you know, well, all mothers know—that is—children take these things—but she doesn't get well. That day of the feast—I had to go off—only an hour, I assure you, my sister was poorly—and those girls are useless—"

"What are you saying?"

"Will I get the physician, madam?"

Arpazia turned away. She was like her mirror now, which stood closed in a corner. The queen had closed herself.

"If you want."

"Thank you, Lady—yes, Lady. Oh, thank you."

Outside again, seething with humiliation, the nurse ranted to herself, "Unnatural mad bitch. She cares nothing for her own child—all left to me—whether it lives or dies."

That was true enough.

Arpazia had already forgotten. But the entry of others—the nurse—had alerted her to the possibility of sending once more for the crone.

Presently one of the attendants appeared again.

"They can't find the old woman, madam."

In a way, Arpazia seemed to have stepped out of a high window; she balanced now on the air, and might at any second crash to the ground far below. So she used no ruse. Anyone could see, she had moved beyond the limit of safe conduct. Yet she was aware of the live currents of secrets here, into which she had barely been admitted. This atmosphere she slightly heeded, and was just a *little* careful.

But with Draco gone, all the palace grew lax, and did much as it wanted. Guards dozed and diced at their posts, or abandoned them. Maids ran off to gossip. Palace washerwomen left baskets of damp clothes unheeded in the yards and passageways. It was already very warm, bees heavy in the tall, untended bushes of blue lavender, the unpruned tamarisks scratching at the walls, lizards indoors and sunning themselves in the rays from windows.

Arpazia said she would sleep. Her women were used to that. And they were always glad when she sent them away, as so often she did.

The queen wiped the cosmetics from her face, let down her hair. She pulled off her royal gown and put on the dress of one of her attendants, indifferent to its scents of skin and perfume not her own. Arpazia covered herself with a plain cloak. Unable to remove her rings, she wound a bit of cloth around them, like a bandage.

Turning then, she glanced into her just-opened mirror.

She giggled like a girl. She looked extremely young.
Who would know her, now she was disguised?

This was exhilarating, to steal out and be at large, unguarded, un-
attended, and *unwatched*. (If, inwardly, she guessed that many knew
her, *saw* her, she paid no heed. She and they were all caught in the
same pretense together.)

The town interested Arpazia fractionally. It was most bizarre,
this agglomeration of people, like a swarm, all buzzing busily about
each other, making sounds, gesticulating. Poverty and meanness,
where she noted them, seemed exotic. The occasional elegance affected her similarly. But she was not very attentive.

Did the hunter Klymeno reside in the town? The jumble of
houses and hovels, the square with its booths and animals in pens,
were not suitable habitats. There were chapels, but no church, since
the great Church of St. Belor stood on the palace terraces. But there
were many inns. She avoided their vicinity prudently, although once
a man came careering at her from an inn doorway. Her eyes, under
her hood, shot such a white look at him, he let her go and only
called a foul name after her.

Later on she paused by the shrine of a saint in a side street, a
broad, unpaved alley. A tree had been allowed to grow here, and
there was a well. Two women sat against it, their bucket and pitch-
ers set by.

"Where is Klymeno's house?" asked the queen.

It *was* the queen; she sounded royal suddenly, and ill-mannered.

One woman chuckled.

The other said, "Well, high-nose, if it's the hunter you want, he
keeps no place in the town."

Instantly, despair. Her stricken face, just visible in the cloak,
amused the amused woman further. The other seemed to think
better of her rebuff. "You might find him at the inn. He may drink
there, when he brings the meat."

"That venison goes up to the king's house," added the other.

They were quiet, looking at the queen differently.

"Which inn?" asked Arpazia. Her voice was almost frightened now.

"The inn called *Stag*, where else?"

Crippled by her lack of knowledge and education—no one had ever taught Arpazia good manners, charm, or discretion, only fear, arrogance, and paucity—she said, as if stunned, "One of you must show me the way."

"Must we?"

They did not move.

The unamused one said, "Better you find it yourself, Lady."

Arpazia went away.

In another street, soon after, now no longer adventurous, only desperate and uncertain, she could not bring herself to ask directions of the grubby children, the hurrying priest. Then a journeyman came past, tools in a bag on his shoulder. "What do you seek, woman?"

"The inn," she said. "I must find the inn called *Stag*."

"I'm for there," he said. "Come on, I'll show you."

Had she noticed him among the trees of the wood, when the full moon hammered on the earth? Perhaps not. But he guided her through the alleys, over the square again, and along a grassy run between bulging walls, to a doorway. There was no sign but for a branch of antlers. Seeing it, her heart struck her so violently she almost dropped down.

"Who is it you want here?" asked the journeyman.

"He is called—Klymeno."

"The hunter? Yes, I know him. Stay here. I'll see if he's to be found."

So the queen stood at the door of the inn like a drab, waiting for her man, or for custom. Yet no one approached her now to jeer or scare.

She began to cry, surprising herself. Unloved, uncared for, she had never been a protected child suddenly deserted in the adult world. So she did not know why she was crying, or for what comfort.

But when a new light showed in the doorway, the sun catching

the figure of a man as he came out, Arpazia knew the perfect alle-
viation of the lost child found. And then the alarm of the child
which thought it had sinned.

"Yes? What do you want of me?"

Was he as she recalled? No—yes—both of these.

He did not know her. This was the worst blow. Even disguised,
he should have known her.

Klymeno, in this daylight: in ordinary woodsman's clothes of
thin leather, bare-armed, brown. His hair, a deeper brown. His lion
eyes had kept their amber.

Did he make believe he did not know who she was, or was this
true? She had muffled her face in the cloak. She was not herself
here, either.

Then he saw her tears.

"What's the matter? Don't cry." He came right up to her and
put back the hood. His hand slipped over her hair. "You," he said,
his voice low. "Why are you here?"

She hung her head. Her tears stopped. She said nothing.

It was as if she had gone blind and dumb, deaf too, and time
had ended. He did not want her to have come here. Did not at all
want her, now.

"Do you know who I am?" he said to her.

She heard him.

But she said nothing.

Arpazia gathered herself, put up her head. Her eyes met his and
he saw they had, peculiarly, gone black, pupil and iris all one.

"How I despise you," she said, her voice lower than his, but
sharp as the edge of something broken.

He took hold of her, not roughly.

She said, "Let go, or I will rip you up with my nails."

"*Now* I know you," he said. Then he murmured softly, and
pulled her in against him, held her without effort, and she could
not struggle. "Beautiful Demetra, my darling wife." His tone was
full of love, of desire, of gladness. She turned once more molten in
the fire of it.

"That isn't my name."

"Yes. By day. When you're with me."

"I thought—" she said. She sighed.

They stood by the inn door, he holding her, and she leaning against him. The sun moved slowly over the grassy alley.

The cart was drawn by a donkey. The animal had white-lined hairy ears, like the donkey which had carried Christ on its back in one of her father's books.

Klymeno would not let her sit back in the cart. It had been stained by carcasses, and was black from old blood. She rode beside him, behind the white-eared donkey.

They left the town and took a meandering track that ran in and out of olive groves and rocky places, above the sea. The water was the color of the lavender that grew wild by the roadside. Then the track curved up and they went up with it, into the hills. Once, through cypress boughs, she saw the palace, raised on its slope yet already below. It glowed in the sun, quite unfamiliar.

The wood was not the same by day. It was deep green, *dense* green, violet in shadow, scattered with rifts of gold. She saw young does feeding, which did not run away, and later a foxlike animal trotted across the earth and tree roots which the track had now become. Her companion pointed out honeycombs like skulls, budding from some trees, frothing with bees. He and she did not talk, these were small observances of his, followed by her murmured assents. She said, always, Yes, yes. Yes, how green, yes, how gold. Yes, did a marten have her nest there? Yes.

Arpazia was insane with excitement and dread. Inside her cool exterior, she was spinning and shuddering, terrified with happiness. Nothing lay behind her, and nothing before. Her existence was this moment. She had been right to think time had ended.

She was not taken aback to find he lived in a ramshackle log hut among the trees. It did not matter where he lived, now. A stream went by the door, and he threw off his clothes and plunged in, washing away any odor of blood or sweat, which she had not even minded.

He came back to her naked, dressed in skin.

He took her in his arms. The woods soughed at the warm waves of the wind that blew in from the sea. His body had the scent of leaves and grass and maleness.

"Touch me," he said. He put her hand on him, where he had risen up. She had not expected such a texture, nor the pearl of moisture. "Listen, if you're with me here, I can't hold off. Do you understand, sweetheart? It must *be*."

"Do anything to me," she said.

"Then I will."

Her stolen clothes were removed easily. She was not shy. She paraded herself, letting him look at her, at her breasts, her belly, her sex. Then she put her hand on him again, and the stem of his lust moved in her fingers, urgent, and seeking her.

As she lay near the wall of the hut, on the cloak, she saw above her the flame green of the leaves against the sky's pulsing blue. Then she forgot such things. There was only him.

When he pierced her, it was not a penetration, but a rejoining of something sundered, so needed and desired that she seemed mended by it. Less couth and more violent than he, she tore at his hair and dragged the grass up by its roots. As she had warned him, she plowed his body with her nails. But at the last, pulling back her head, she saw the paroxysm take him as it took her, too. Now she knew. This face of agony that was delight beyond life or death.

Hurtled to earth, becoming more still than anything, she made him stay as he was, lying upon her, all his weight, crushing her. She wanted nothing else. He slept, his face turned into her neck. She loved him then, as they had told her a woman always loved her child. Nothing should harm him. She wanted only the best for him. She grew into his body, could no longer find how they were separate.

IV.

*C*ANDACIS BURNED FOR FIVE DAYS IN the fever. At night she was worse, and became incandescent like her name, so they were afraid to have contact with her for fear of scalding.

How disturbing it was, that luminously white little face, its bones showing, and the demented blackness of the eyes in circles nearly as black.

The physician regularly let her blood. Afraid the leeches were too sluggish, he employed a tiny razor. The blood was rich, healthy, he said. The child must be strong, despite her looks and condition.

Not once did he inquire why her mother, the queen, was never there.

The physician, as most of them, one way and another, had heard about Queen Arpazia. She had a lover, some artisan of the lower town, or peasant—or was he a robber from the mountains, summering in the hills? It was with him the queen spent her time, day and night, while her daughter drowned in the cauldron of fever.

The nurse called the child by an outlandish and archaic name of the region. The physician continually corrected her. Finally Kaya, the pert maid, announced, "We always call her Coira. She won't know who you mean, sir, calling her by her princess name."

Probably the child did not know anything much, he thought. He considered, analytical and dispassionate, that her small brain might be scorched out by this illness. He had seen that happen before. They lived, but were impaired, unable to walk or see, or utter proper speech.

The king would not be pleased. He liked his brats. But then, he preferred the boys.

"Fetch that tincture from my rooms—the one I mentioned, in the black bottle."

The slave ran out.

Scowling, the physician began to grind a powder of pearl in his mortar.

*   *   *

The child dreamed. She had been laid on burning wood in a brazier. The branches smelled sweet as they burned, and so, presumably, did she. There was pain, though not much; it was the relentless biting heat which frightened her the most. In the dream, her mother, the witch-goddess, bent above her. Her mother smoothed the child's forehead kindly. "There, my dear. Not much longer. Soon my spell will have burned away all your frailty, all the human dross. Then you will be very fine, most beautiful, and you'll live forever, invulnerable to hurt, surviving even death, an immortal."

This was like some story Coira had heard long ago, (even to the adult vocabulary) and as she tossed in distress in the dream, she partly knew it.

Only one question stirred on her burned lips.

"Why did you send me away?"

"Hush, my love. I would never send you away. You're my own heart born again in flesh. How I love you, Coira, best of all."

The child exhaled, and the knotting of her muscles relaxed. A vise which had seemed to hold her rigid creaked open, and let her go. Then torrents of fragrant rain burst from her pores. Of course, they put out the fire.

Coira's mother, Demetra, laughed triumphantly as she plucked her daughter up into her arms. In the dream, it did not puzzle the child that the witch-queen's hair had become blond, and her eyes like topaz. It was unimportant to Coira, providing she were loved.

"The fever's broken at last."

"Thank God for it." (The nurse, crossing herself crossly.) "Hurry and change the bed linen. It's wringing wet. She might as well have turned into a fountain. What a child! Always causing some nuisance."

*   *   *

All the months of summer came and passed, as Coira recovered. By the day she could walk, unaided, across her room, and sit in the chair to eat her bread and honey, the hills too were turning to a honey shade; the sea was streaked with gray.

Coira had not heard the talk concerning Arpazia, nor had she seen her mother since the fever. Coira had asked after her only once. Then the girl, Julah, replied, "Oh, *she* won't come in. She doesn't care at all about you."

The child thought of her other, topaz-eyed mother, in the dream.

She began to tussel with the two images: the loving, golden, kind mother; the chill, dark, uncaring mother who avoided her always.

Perhaps, after all, the dark witch-queen was not her mother. Coira had heard of such things, and she had heard too of her father's many women. He had had a previous queen, maybe, who had been cast off, or died. Perhaps Coira was that one's baby, and now the other dark queen did not like Coira—not unreasonably, since Coira was not at all her daughter.

The child said nothing of this to anyone. She took back her lesson of silence.

In silence, then, she saw time slowly move, the seasons again decline. Draco returned briefly, and a Mass was held in the great church, to honor him—or God. Her father did not bother to visit Coira, (Princess Candacis). He had mislaid her, intent only on his other capital, a city far away. They had heard its name, now: Korchlava.

Arpazia was not in the church for the Mass. Some of the townsfolk said Draco had forbidden her to be there. Others said she had declined to go—and such were the queen's uncanny skills that the king had had to concede.

The Virgo month. No one remembered Coira's birthday, except, suddenly, for the nurse, who exclaimed, "Great Lord—are you seven today?" Coira knew that she was eight. But she did not argue. The nurse gave her a quick kiss, which meant nothing, to either of them.

To Kaya the nurse remarked, thinking Coira did not hear, "That fever tweaked her brain. Be sure of it. I am. Thank God she doesn't drool or topple over when she walks. If ever the king thinks of her, she can still be a credit to him."

"Has she gone dumb?" asked Julah.

"Quiet, fool. She can speak. Didn't she just ask you for her cup of milk? It's *inside*, the damage. You mark my words. We'll all see it, one day."

"The witch's bad blood," said Kaya. "They say she lies up in the wood, dancing on her back. She goes to the old stone in the wood, where *they* go, those bad ones, and she lies down there when the blood's still wet from things they kill and lets him—"

The nurse slapped Kaya. Kaya ran off and spat into the nurse's clothes chest. Next she would insert a dead mouse there.

Coira heard without understanding, and saw it all. In silence.

V.

ONE COLD MORNING, THE WITCH-queen opened her mirror.

She looked into the glass, already touched with winter white, like the day, and her own snowy nakedness.

"Mirror, am I beautiful?"

The woman in the mirror smiled.

"Beautiful."

"Am I the most beautiful in all the lands?"

"In all the lands you are."

"In the wide world?"

"In the wide world."

The mirror had no need to speak, although it did, to the witch-queen. Turning this way and that, raising her arms, moving through the smoke of her ebony hair, pointing her pale feet, cupping her own breasts, the witch-queen saw well enough her rare loveliness, and the bloom on her now like nap on velvet.

Arpazia went from the mirror, leaving it to watch.

She chose a dress of blushing, sheer-spun wool bordered with silver, and her mantle of black fur. She no longer troubled with disguise. No one accosted her or asked her business or sent her back. Dressed as a queen, she was bowed to, and given right of way. She had even walked into the town just like this, in the autumnal fall days, and they kneeled on the street, and one woman brought her grapes and another a crimson rose.

She could do as she liked.

Even when the king had been here, rumbling through his town and palace with much noise and fuss, but absolutely no substance, even then Arpazia had more or less done as she wanted. He never came near her. He had some slut or other for his bed. He did not, this time, even send the token presents.

None of these people—no people at all—were real for Arpazia. They never had been, even when they ruled and harmed her. They had, then, been more awful for their unreality. Only one other was alive in Arpazia's world. She lived with him, inside the mirror. Indeed, now and then, she glimpsed him in the mirror, as before she had seen the raven and the owl, and the mythical hags of fate.

He would appear naked in her looking glass—a momentary vision of his strong, lean body, now pale, now bronze, or his eyes, jeweled like a beast's and, like a beast's, looking out of the shadow there, beside the chest, or from deep under the cannopy of the bed.

He lay in wait for her, too, in slumber. Sleeping or waking, ever-present. Like the god that he was.

Arpazia slipped on her dainty boots. She drew heavy bracelets onto her wrists. She liked to dress herself richly, so he might take everything from her. Even her face would be painted, if not by her women—for she hated them flagrantly and did everything now for herself, saving the most menial tasks—she gave them those—to peel fruit or tidy her couch, like slaves. But Klymeno would kiss the cosmetics from her lips, and her own tears of orgasm would wash away the kohl.

When Arpazia tried to do up the silver girdle at her waist, she found the clasp would not meet.

She attempted to do up the girdle several times.

Then she flung the girdle away in an icy blast of temper. But something else stayed with her. She had not been able to throw it away with the girdle.

Something else . . . yesterday, a dress had torn at her waist. Mended, it tore again. And another gown had pinched her.

Arpazia moved abruptly back to the mirror.

"What is it? *Show* me what it is."

The surface of the mirror dappled like water. That was all. Arpazia turned. She regarded the profile of her body. Was there some change? Could it be—

She stared deeply in at the glass and now, now—her gown became transparent, in one place, across her belly. She saw, a second time, her snow of flesh, and the black wood which flourished below, whose center was a rose. But then, straight through her belly she saw, straight through the crimson rose of her womb.

"*No.*"

The witch-queen pointed in at the little white fish which curled there, small as a seed.

The glass went black. In blackness, she heard a woman in labor screaming and screaming.

But Arpazia leaned in to the mirror. She glared down at the tiny little seed.

"*You shall be killed.*" And her breath formed on the glass like mist.

The Smoke Crone glanced up. From her hut door stretched the stone terrace, sunning itself. The weary olive trees, already bare, groped after the light. Everything old, old stones and trees, the mouth of the Oracle itself, today issuing nothing, the ancient woman. Everything old but for one thing, there.

The Smoke Crone did not rise, though she identified Draco's queen at once. It was true, Arpazia had also, a few times, been made Queen in the wood, but even so, the Crone, in the pagan hierarchy, had stayed her superior.

"Are you she?" said the queen, having gained the doorway. She was brilliant in the early winter sunlight, and another than the Crone might have been dazzled. "Are you?"

"I am."

"I've something I need from you."

"Lah-loh," sang the Crone, "lah-loh-lullah-lah."

"Attend to me, old woman. Do you know who I am?"

"Yes, a mortal. A rude one."

Arpazia flinched. Not believing in others, often they unnerved her.

"I am—"

"You are you and I am I. What do you want, Arpazia?" (The Smoke Crone never called a queen by anything other than her name.)

Arpazia said, hurrying, "Your sister used to attend me. But no longer. They can't find the old woman."

"My sister? I have no sister."

"Some kindred of yours. I was told you sent her to me, when you wouldn't come yourself."

"I am too old to come to you."

By this, and Arpazia knew it, the Crone meant she was too mighty to have done so.

Arpazia turned her head. She said to the cold sunlight, "You know what I do. That I'm Woods Queen with Orion." Despite herself, saying his holy name, her face flooded with heat. But the thought did not come to her, *This is his child in me.* She did not think of it as a child at all—as she had never thought it of the child she had borne.

"He's called Klymeno, too," said the Smoke Crone. She stroked something lying over her knee. Arpazia had believed it was an old shawl—but it was a lizard, scaled and sentient, not woven. "And Dianus is his name, too. Orion you see, was Dianus, when he became the companion of the moon goddess, but later on she killed him with her arrows of death. Then she put him in the sky, all stars. But Klymeno's the friendly aboveground name of King Death himself. Did you know?"

Arpazia was reminded of her elderly nurse in the castle. Irritated, dismayed, Arpazia said, "I'm with child. I won't bear this unlawful thing." She added—words which had no meaning at all in her mouth, less meaning than the word *child*—"It's not the king's."

"Not Draco's, no, not his."

Arpazia said, "Assist me to be rid of it."

The Smoke Crone ran her finger fondly over the lizard. She said, "If I do—for I can, of course—if I help you slay your child, what service in return?"

"What do you want?"

"Let me think."

Arpazia waited. The sun moved along the terrace, as it had in the grassy alley by the inn, five or six months before.

The Smoke Crone said, "I will give you a mixture of herbs, boar's-tongue that speaks and grows from a boar's dribblings. Other stuff."

"Will it hurt?" asked Arpazia. "Will it be quick?"

"You'll feel no more than with your usual courses. The life is smaller than a grain of sand. It has no soul in it yet, even though a soul comes to watch it through the window of your belly. I must give you heart-leaf, too, to send the soul away, or it may haunt you, after."

The old fool, thought Arpazia. *Mumbling, muttering*. She trembled.

Haughtily she said, "I am grateful to you."

"I've no need of it. This is what I'll have. In seven days, take your other child into the wood."

"Which other child?"

"Your daughter, the king's get, the one they call Candacis."

"What do you mean?"

"How long since you were in the wood at Full Moon?"

"They kill things, your pagan people, on their altar. Hares, a lamb—I don't like to see it."

The Crone laughed, a dirty coarse noise.

"Do you not, fastidious Arpazia? You were queen to Orion, but you don't like the duties of the queen, only the pleasures the queen may have. Well. Draco is that way, too. He eats the land but gives nothing back. Such a shepherd wouldn't die for his flock, even in battle. But that is the king's duty, and the queen's too. What can I tell you that you'll hear? Are you a witch? They thought so. Take your daughter at the next Full Moon, into the wood. She is a snow-child, and a fire-child, and an earth-child, but you go up through air. She was conceived as you were, under the trees. In seven days it is the first Great Orb of winter, a Scorpion Moon."

"Give me the herbal draught."

"How eager you are to drink poison."

Arpazia stood, staring away, tapping her foot.

The old woman said, "Klymeno will give you the drink, when you meet him on that night, in the wood."

"*No.*"

"No? Why do you dislike that?"

"His—it's *his*—this in me."

"Yes. You mean to kill his child. Give him the other one, then, in exchange. The little snow girl."

Arpazia's eyes sprang back, she was all attention. How exquisite, how youthful, how mad she looked, her long neck curving like a snake's.

"Why?"

"A ritual. A symbol," said the Smoke Crone. "That's all. She'll be made his daughter, she's too young to be his queen. It has no worldly purpose. But it will please the gods."

"I am Christian."

The Smoke Crone put the lizard down on the warm stones, and got up. She walked past the queen as if the queen were not there, and Arpazia felt that she had ceased to be there. The old woman bent over the smoke-hole of the god and goddess who were under the terrace, under the palace and the world. She seemed to be gazing down at someone she knew well, respected, yet had no fear of.

Arpazia gathered her cloak of fur around her and hastened away, but not to her lover, in his hut among the trees. She went to her overgrown garden in the palace, and sat there on the marble bench, and bit her fingers till they bled.

*   *   *

There was often some sort of pandemonium going on in Coira's room. Her nurse would be scolding or giving orders, and the two maids quarreling or mocking her, or pretending to obedience. Out of this evening's muffled din, words emerged. "Coira! Come here at once. You're to go to her, in her apartment."

To whom?

Julah supplied an answer. "She'll like that. To be noticed by the queen."

Coira's spirit stood up under the blows of their preparations— the wet sponge, the clean dress hauled on, the comb wrenched through her hair, and a necklace of gold-washed shells, the king's long-ago gift, put round her throat as coarsely as a noose.

The light slanted. It was intense and oddly promising.

Despite herself, Coira had quickened. But, now, she was also apprehensive. The dark queen did not like her, was not her mother. Or could it be that the queen had softened, come to be interested in this child who was not her own?

Her nurse, ridiculously self-important, bustled Coira through the corridors, where translucent shadows stole out at this hour like animals from the walls.

At the doors with handles of metallic fruit, one of the queen's own women shooed the nurse away, and took Coira in herself, holding the child's hand with dry indifference.

"Here, madam. Your daughter."

Coira waited in a pool of light at the chamber's edge.

The attendant had gone. No one else was there, but for the figure which stood, back turned, outlined before a smooth silver eye. (The lid of the closed mirror.)

Coira knew the slender obdurate back of the witch-queen. Yet, this woman was not the same. Loose black hair rivered over the russet gown. Then she turned about. Her face appeared. And the face of the witch-queen too had altered its shape, as the moon did. Though beautiful, it had become the face of a bird of prey.

Coira shrank, but there was only the wall, and as the light slid

from the window and the mirror's lid, it stayed still about her, showing her up.

"What is it they call you? Not Candacis—some pagan name."

"Coira . . . madam." Another lesson the child had learned: her
unmother's title.

"You're to come with me. You're the king's daughter and some
of your people want to see you. Do you understand?"

"Yes . . . madam."

"Behave properly. Ask me nothing. Don't talk at all, or I shall
be angry." Arpazia spoke without emphasis. She needed to employ
none. Coira was already overmastered by total horror.

Not even an unmother. A fiend.

The fiend's eyes gleamed pale. Narrow fingers with three rings
emerged from the crow-wing of hair and sleeve. "Take my hand."

Coira did as she was told.

In the past, sometimes, she had been allowed to ceremonially
touch this hand. Now it did not feel as it had before. It was hot,
bony and hard, like the talons of the dreadful bird the woman now
resembled.

The queen snatched her mantle round her. Dragging the mantle, the child, she stalked over the room, and Coira had to run to
keep up.

The shadows were drawing in now in packs. A guard leaned on
a pillar, inclining his head, glance following them only a short way.

As they crossed the queen's garden, the land grew dark. The
sea, also a shining shadow, had parted from a sky like a fading brassy
shield.

The queen opened a door.

Coira stumbled on the uneven, treacherous stair below, and the
Woman, her stepmother, tugged her on, twisting the child's arm in
its socket. But Coira had learned silence, and did not cry out.

So they went down and down together into darkness, leaving
the sky behind.

*   *   *

On the meadow, the shadows rose up and became girls. Unspeaking, they wandered behind Arpazia and the child, up the hillside and into the woods.

Coira had been run out, but the queen no longer walked so swiftly. Stumbling frequently, Coira just managed to keep up; once, when she half fell, the Woman adjusted her, as before, simply by straining on the child's arm.

The sky was now somber but still lucid against the darkness of the earth. The moon had risen early and the child stared at it, for never had she seemed to see it so round or so adamantine. In color it looked not white, more blue, but a deadly blue, like cut slate.

Then, when they entered the blackness of the woods, filtered only with thin glints of sky, Coira felt the night-trepidation common to ancient peoples, the deep tingling terror that was less fear than instinctive knowledge and awe of elder forces. These woods were full of this, alive with this, such power—but the witch seemed not to recognize it. Or if she did, it was familiar to her, and she gave no sign.

An owl called through the trees. The hair rose on Coira's scalp, and behind her a rippling whisper moved through the young women who followed them.

Much of the wood still had its leaves, though many were withered. Now and then some fell, with an eerie effect, like bats or great beetles tumbling softly through the dimness, brushing the head or wrist.

When they went by the waterfall, however, the trees there were quite bare, but for one crippled pine. The water glittered starkly in moonlight. It seemed to the child that something looked out with glittering eyes from a cave above.

Ahead, red light began to burn.

The moon was already gone from the lawned avenue under the trees. But tonight they had lit fires there, each in a circle of stones. As the witch-queen walked, holding her child by the hand, they must wend around each fire. A crowd was standing among the trees, to either side. It reminded Coira a little of a procession to Mass, or to the Oracle on the terrace. A vague chanting rose like the fire-smoke. The witch-queen took no notice of it.

Arpazia walked the length of the avenue, and suddenly a being came out from between the dark and the light.

Despite herself, Coira uttered a little noise.

"Quiet," said the witch-queen.

Coira thought the figure was not human. Then she saw that it was a man. He was clad in a belted robe of deep red, and his head was crowned, as she had seen the head of her father. But this diadem was of tangled things, branches, thorns—and because of the thorns, Coira was reminded of pictures she had been shown of the Christ. And, as the Christ before his suffering, this man was handsome.

Arpazia stopped still. Her bird's face was lifted harshly, her lips drawn thin.

The young man in the wild thorn crown looked once at her, then he knelt down by the child.

"Don't be afraid."

He reached forward and firmly undid the fettered knot of their hands, Arpazia's and her child's. Coira's hand, extricated, was bloodless and marked with the edges of rings. The young man rubbed her hand gently in both of his. "There's nothing to harm you," he said again. "You are the Maiden."

Coira regarded him. She adored him at once for his looks and his attentive gentleness to her. But she had been well taught what love was worth. She retained her silence.

Her mother-stepmother spoke, rasping and low over their heads.

"Well, I've brought the girl, as that woman told me. Now do you have something for me? A drink of herbs, she said."

"Not yet."

"When? Are you angry with me?"

Coira heard the breaking change, the abrupt note of anxiety in the witch-queen's voice.

The man rose. High into the sky above Coira he stood, facing her stepmother. "Nothing can die, kill it as you will."

"I couldn't come to you—that was my only fear—I didn't know what I should do—how can you understand—it's you I want—" Hushed, rushed now, the new frightened childish voice of the queen.

"Not—not a child—such pain—never—and if Draco learned—no—no—"

"It is your right," he said. "So, you give your child back to the wood." This was all he said. The voice conveyed little, to one who had not heard him speak before in love.

Flame-lit, more than a man, he moved ahead of them, toward the altar in the trees. Only then did Coira see the axe slung in the folds of his robe.

From inside its lid, the mirror watched. But the moon, lying down in the black sack of the wood, had closed her stony eye. Or seemed to.

The mirror saw the Hunter King invoke the night, and the spirits of the dead who were, that night, there to dance with them. He did not dance, but sat on his boulder-throne. The witch-queen sat on hers, beside him, as on other nights she had done. But the child sat between them on the turf, and sometimes the king smoothed her hair, and once, when the child turned up her face to gaze at him, for her he had a smile. No one, ever, had looked at her in this way. It had been exactly the same for Arpazia. Human, they recognized, mother and daughter both, true tenderness, goodness, even if it came too late and could not be let in.

Tears ran down the witch-queen's face—or was this an illusion of the shifting fires? She had ceased to resemble a bird, but she appeared old, in the sidelong light of the dancers' torches.

Nevertheless, when he handed her the black cup, she took it, drained it, and cast it angrily down in the grass. After that, the queen did not look at the Hunter King, nor he at her.

She said, very quietly, some while later, "Are you done with me only for *this*?"

The mirror saw that he answered, "Of course, only for that."

She whispered then. "You are unjust. So, I was nothing to you. I might denounce you and have you killed."

Her whisper-words hung in the air, and went out, leaving only some burn marks.

But this was a night of death, of the dead. And soon, through the flame-smoke dark, the King of Death was seen riding his chariot along the aisles of the woods. Perhaps not seen with the eyes, but with the mind—for the dancers described him in their chant, and the Orion King stood and saluted him, and certainly (oh yes) the mirror saw him. King Death wore the blackest mail, heavily jeweled, his black hair coiling under the helm which masked his face, that none could make it out. His chariot was bleached as bone, and the midnight horses blew fire from their nostrils—emerald fire, like elf-lights from a swamp.

Arpazia did *not* see King Death. She had turned her head, as usual. But she felt the deathly drink she had taken go seeking through her belly, finding a way into the seed in her womb. It was a frightful sensation, yet she was glad of it.

The mirror saw how the Hunter King presently led Arpazia's child to the slab of altar. He lifted her up there, and the crowd sang a whining plaint, as if she were to die. But the little girl seemed half asleep now, not taking much in. And the Hunter King only circled the axe over her head three times, to show the King of Death (who was called Hadz) that she was selected for him, betrothed to him, a living sacrifice. But this was also true of all things that lived. She was not scapegoat, but emblem.

Then the King of Death drove his chariot away, and the Hunter King picked up the child and carried her to a mound of moss and grass, where he set her down. She was fast asleep now. It was likely she had not known anything of what went on.

Soon after, both the mirror and the witch-queen saw how a young boar came stepping through the wood, heading straight through the crowd to the altar. It was glossy black, Death's animal, its tusks clean, white as milk, and the inside of its mouth a fresh red. It was evidently bewitched, and knew its hour had come. Calmly it let the women garland it with berries. The Hunter King brought it a bowl to drink from, and it bowed to him and to the god, and drank. It made no protest, showed no distress, as he clove its skull with one blow of the axe.

Arpazia knew what they would do. That they would eviscerate and portion up the dead boar, Orion the most skilfully, because of his trade. They would mix pieces of its organs with ale or wine, and eat and drink from this mess to gain vitality, and to honor the coming of winter, which was the year's night. She had seen two other sacrifices through the summer. She had not liked them, though she would eat meat in the palace without a qualm.

Now the Hunter King brought her nothing. So Arpazia got up and went among his people. She took two tiny slivers from the bowl, which tonight held the sliced lungs and liver of the healthy boar. She ate them boldly. (But later in her chamber her body would throw them back up. The Smoke Crone had lied, or been wrong. The herbs of abortion were not so mild as she had specified.)

Another woman carried the queen's daughter home in the hours before dawn. She was a woman of Draco's camp, who had her place now in the palace at Belgra. She put the little girl down in the passage which led to her own room. "Wake up, puss. That way's your bed."

"Where is—?" The child peered round her, lost in familiar things she no longer recalled, "—the King—" she finished.

The woman, who knew which king the child meant, shook her head and put her finger across her lips. "You mustn't speak of him."

Then the door of Coira's apartment was flung wide, and the nurse was there, holding up a lighted candle. "What time is this to send her back? Couldn't she have kept her till morning?" Where the light fell, hard as steel, Coira rubbed her eyes and blinked. But the other woman was gone. Her un-mother was gone, the crowned king too, and all the magic of the wood. And Coira was, as always, unwelcome.

BOOK TWO

Tam Alba Quam Nix
Shining White as Snow

The Poison Tree

*T*HAT WINTER, JUST BEFORE MID-winter-Mass, Queen Arpazia went out in her former way of the summer, to look for her lover. Draco had sent messengers: he would visit Belgra Demitu for the Mass. There was the usual uproar of preparation, which gushed round Arpazia like a swarm of ghosts. She walked from the palace on a glassy morning, when the keen wind brought the smell of snow from the mountains.

Dressed in her furs and jewels, she expected, as formerly, no one would challenge her. It shocked her therefore when they did. First guards in the palace, on the terrace walks. Then, as she crossed some open ground, a laborer gaping, and in the town itself the people scattering away from her, and soon she heard the sniggering of men. For sure they knew her, but now showed her no regard. They thought her a freak, and funny.

Naturally this would be because she had fallen out of favor with the Woods People; she grasped this, but did not care.

She had waited, in vain, for only one person, having sent him, by servants, or more naively, urchins, gifts to show her love, and three ill-written letters. Had he received any of these? Now she sought for him, Klymeno-Dianus, Orion-in-the-Wood.

At the door of the *Stag* inn, paying no attention to the men who sneered at her, she sent a loitering slave to ask for him by his daylight name. The slave went. But then one of the men called to her vulgarly, "Eh, Queen, you won't find him here. He's gone, Queen. Far away."

She did not turn or look. The slave came back and echoed, "Gone, Lady." As she moved away, the men laughed again, and another brayed, "Won't *I* do, Queenie?" But a third muttered, sounding embarrassed, "She's too old for such games."

Arpazia kept the blood from her face, kept it white and still. She went to an alley where Klymeno had once mentioned there was a man who had hunted with him, and who hired a cart.

The man came at her knock. His chin dropped two miles. "Yes—madam?"

"Where is Klymeno the hunter?"

"Gone to the west, lady. I know no more than that."

"When will he return?"

"Maybe . . . never."

"Perhaps you're lying. Do you know who I am?"

"Yes, madam."

"Then take me in your cart up to his house in the woods."

"Madam—"

She ripped the necklace off her neck and slapped it into his hand. It was one of the castle "treasures" Draco had returned to her, after their wedding.

The man took the necklace, shoving it under a filthy sack in the corner as though ashamed of it. Then he drove her in his cart behind a donkey, along the road, among the bare, seared winter olives, with the sea on their right hand gray as tears.

Arpazia could not avoid comparing this journey with another, and another man, another donkey even, those travels she had had with her lover. Now, for the very first, she felt ridiculous, seated up high on the rough cart in her queen's garments and jewels.

In the end, they reached the hut among the cold-cracked woods. A pheasant clucked over and over through the trees as Arpazia looked in at the door to where, as winter had begun, they had made their love. Nothing was there, only the blackened area that had been the hearth.

When she regained his cart, the man spoke heavily. "Some say Klymeno died in the wood. A boar gored and did for him." Then he saw her face, out of which a demon grimaced. He added hastily, "It's only a tale. But Klymeno's gone. Perhaps he will come back one day."

Arpazia wanted to walk down to the land's high edge and throw herself into the sea. But she was afraid of death, had always been very afraid of that. The carter took her back to the very spot where *he* had normally taken her. From there she climbed up an uneven path toward the palace, and black cypresses cawed in the wind.

A hole had been rammed out from the middle of her body and her soul. She had felt something at work on this, all the days since the Scorpion Moon—when she had drunk the boar's-tongue and heart-leaf, and she had eaten of a boar's liver and lungs—and sicked it all up and been rid of Klymeno's seed. She had felt it, the hole, being constructed, all that while, but now the damaged part entirely gave way.

She wished to die. She was afraid of death. A dilemma without solution.

King Draco had grown stouter. He had brought his mistress, a young, fattish, black-eyed girl, whom he treated very like a wife, and no one argued.

The bull and dragon banners blazed in the palace. There were feasts and drinking, and religious processions up and down that flashed with gold.

Arpazia paid no attention.

The king did not summon her, or call on her, or demand a single thing. But one afternoon, after Draco's departure, a man came to tell her that her apartments were to be moved. This would, apparently, be more convenient for her, the man said, bowing and beaming.

Some of the queen's women went away. Arpazia was left with three or four. What did that matter? She hated them all. The new rooms were smaller, and in another part of the palace. But her clothes came in chests, her furniture, and her ornaments, or most of them. The famous mirror was brought, carried by three men who crossed themselves when they had put it down.

Arpazia heard some chatter from her remaining women. It seemed Draco had given one of his legalized bastard sons the governance of Belgra Demitu. The man, Prince Tusaj, came to see Arpazia in the early spring.

About nineteen or twenty, to her webbed gaze he looked like Draco, when she beheld him first in the forests. But Tusaj was cleaner and not gross, and combed his tidy beard with perfume.

"Gracious madam." He was nothing if not polite. It was tact, but tact through unease. He knew her reputation and believed in sorcery.

"What do you want?"

She was never courteous now. She had forgotten how to speak to mighty men.

With her lover she had only offered total assent—yes, yes, until that last time. Or if she had been sharp, he had never heeded or minded, as he had not minded her claws in him during the sexual act. Only one thing had her lover minded. That last time. Sometimes since she had thought, *If I had put the black cup aside. If I had kept his seed, swelled up—given birth—even if Draco had had me stoned—* But then she would think, as in the past, *You wretched fool. Do you learn nothing? He valued you as a slut—as a vessel. Or less, less: some scheme of his or theirs, his people. You were nothing to him. He's gone.*

Prince Tusaj, vaguely discerned by her beyond the web of her thoughts and inner horrors, said grandly, "Although he takes the other lady as his queen, in Korchlava, you won't be deprived of your

title here. In arcane law, a king might possess more than one wife.
King Draco keeps to that, for your sake, madam."

"She's no longer young," said Tusaj, later, at wine with his new-
minted nobles. "Nor beautiful. Strange, I'd thought her dazzling
once, but then I was only a randy boy. No, she's like an icon, ivory,
jet. Hard as that, too."

"Watch out she doesn't set her imps on you."

"Oh." Prince Tusaj laughed off the very thing he mistrusted.
But he had been wary with her, just as his father Draco had. She
should have nothing definite to complain of or want a witch's ven-
geance for.

Time crossed Belgra Demitu, as all places. Sometimes time raced,
months were consumed like days. At others, time lingered, wasting
hours over a solitary minute.

The witch-queen looked at the older woman in the mirror.
"What should I have done? Tell me."

The older woman said, from the mirror, "What your nurse told
you, when you were a girl."

"What was that?"

"To take a drop of your own red menstrual blood, and mix it in
his food or drink. That would have bound Klymeno to you forever.
He could never have left you then, whatever you did."

Arpazia sat, reminiscently repeating rhymes the elderly nurse
had quavered, in the castle among the forests. How odd she should
feel this curious nostalgia.

In the mirror she saw tall black trees.

"Make a spell with your vein's blood to call him back," said the
shrouded old woman in the mirror.

Arpazia got up and took the little paring knife, the one which
had slit the skin of Draco. She nipped the skin of her palm and
caught her breath. She let the blood fall, three drops, so red, into a
tarnished silver bowl.

She plucked three hairs from her head. As she was burning

them off at a candle into the bowl, she realized the third hair was also silver. How could that be?

Arpazia went back to the mirror. She gazed at the woman there. "How old am I?"

"Not very old. Twenty-three or -seven or -eight years, no more."

"I've made this spell before," said Arpazia. "It doesn't work. Am I still beautiful?"

"The most beautiful in the world."

The queen went quite regularly to the Church of St. Belor. She sat listening with seeming patience to the angry diatribes of priests. They used as their text mortal sin and trees of poisonous fruits and suffering that made God happy. She received the sacred Host and sipped the Blood of Christ.

At other times, some ancient woman or other might go to see the queen. These were women who claimed kinship with the Smoke Crone who guarded the Oracle. Several times a year, the queen would go up into the wood. No one now invited her, nor shunned her. She did nothing there, simply stood looking on as the people danced and chanted, or when they sacrificed. Only when they coupled, she went away. There was a new King-in-the-Wood. She did not know who it was, under the stag's mask and antlers. Even when she glimpsed the young man's face, between fire and moonlight, it was nobody she had ever seen, she thought, by day. But, now and then, she noted Prince Tusaj among the people, naked even, his hairy barrel of a chest garlanded with ivy, drunk and merry. And one late summer he went off eagerly with a girl and a man, into the colonnades of the trees.

Belgra Demitu was theirs, the elder gods. A pagan country. They were easing it back from Draco and Draco was only a name there now. He never showed himself at the palace. He sent messengers. His fat girl queen had borne him five legal sons, and Korchlava was finally so great a city it was to have a cathedral.

There came a warm night in spring, when a man followed Ar-

pazia from the altar in the wood. He was not so young, but strong
and willing. She let him lie with her in the grass, which was wet
with rain. The roots of the trees hurt her back, and the man hurt
her, for she had been a long while unloved. But her body spasmed,
as it had with Klymeno. Almost like that. And later, when the man,
whose name she never learned, teased her body, rather as Klymeno
had done, in the fit of pleasure she bit him. But he did not like
this. He called her a name for it, as if she were not any sort of
queen, or any sort of lover.

A while after this Arpazia chose, for her personal confessor, a
burly priest she had occasionally seen at the dancing in the wood.

When she showed him, after the confession in her rooms, that
she would allow him to possess her, the priest hoisted up his cassock
and obliged. He was a straightforward man, who would nevertheless
do whatever she suggested. (Her suggestions were always made
with her head turned from him, and sometimes with her eyes
closed.) This priest, Brother Gaborus, announced to Arpazia that he
did not count sexual appetite as a sin. God, after all, had created it.
Arpazia scorned his words and thought him stupid. God had devised
all delight as a trap, to damn men, and in the case of carnality and
women, to enslave them by conception. But Arpazia had her herbs
now.

Sometimes, however, she would wonder at herself. How should
she like this thing so much, after Draco . . . how could such an action
have two such dissimilar faces?

She did not discuss anything except her other sins with Brother
Gaborus. She did not believe in his reality. Except as instrument,
adjunct.

It was the same with everyone.

Even with her own self, perhaps.

For who was she, the being in the glass? The lovely being, who
had two thin scars chiselled between her brows, and another two,
there and there, by her mouth? A narrow girdle of shadow had been
hollowed under her belly. The buds of her nipples had swelled, as
if to unfurl. Her shoulders were bones.

"Mirror, am I still beautiful?"

"There is none like you."

True, since no other was real.

Seven years had passed, after the night of the boar's-tongue and heart-leaf, the night of the liver and lungs. And after that, three years more.

The younger palace had aged and mellowed. Spring and summer, autumn, winter, dawn, night and the moon still came down the hills toward the sea.

But things moved to a different tempo, slower, circling over themselves, as if nothing were new anymore, nothing were old anymore. As if time had paused, stopped, lay like a snake, motionless, waiting to begin again.

II.

*W*AS A CHILD ONLY THE SUM of its parents? Her father had been the monstrous, ignorant Draco. Her mother was the mad witch-queen. No doubt, she had a thread of both of them, wound in her blood. But Candacis (Coira) was also herself. Her roots ran back, like those of a plant, to other progenitors. And she had been brought up in such a strange way, after all.

Alterations had begun when she was eight. That was, after the night of the Scorpion Moon. But Coira did not recall anything of the ceremony at the altar, except as a sort of dream she might have had, something to do with the fever and her recovery. The dream was both wonderful and frightening. She never forgot it, but neither did she take it as actual.

During the winter and spring after the dream, other events began.

Coira's nurse became friendly with another woman of the palace, who then often came to see her, in the child's room.

The other woman was more interested in Coira than in the
nurse, as Coira noted quite quickly (although her nurse did not).
There were outings then. They went to the market to watch traveling entertainers, who performed magical conjurings, or fought battles with wooden swords. Or the women, with Coira, went to the
meadows, or down to the seashore, in a rickety carriage pulled by
rams. Coira played in the sand, forming buildings from it, or hunted
for shells. Sometimes the woman-friend of the nurse, leaving the
nurse, would assist Coira.

This woman was called Ulvit. She taught Coira rhymes, and
now and then told her stories. She was not affectionate, but she
treated Coira as a live and intelligent presence, more so, perhaps,
than she treated the nurse. Ulvit knew many clever things, such as
the name and nature of a shell Coira once discovered walking sideways. When Coira's little palaces of sand were swallowed by the
returning tide, Ulvit assured her that nothing was ever lost, once it
had been constructed. Each creation had a soul, not only men and
women. The beasts had souls, and the trees, the land had a soul—
which sometimes became visible in a pale shimmering at twilight.
"And even a palace made of sand has a soul. And a song. And every
word we speak."

"Even wrong words?" asked Coira with cautious sagacity.

"Yes," said Ulvit.

Meanwhile the nurse, left on her own, started a courtship with
the driver of the ram-carriage. A decade or so before she had given
her own child away in order to tend the queen's. She did not know
where it was, but perhaps hankered after it. Though so brisk with
babies, she was now sentimentally broody. And after two years, this
developed into a marriage. With a perfect equilibrium then, Ulvit,
as the nurse abandoned Coira, assumed the role of her nurse.

It was Ulvit who forewarned of the coming of Coira's first menstrual blood. Ulvit suggested this was not to be considered fearful
or aggravating, but as a privilege given by the gods to women, because, in this instance, they had been thought the more deserving
of childbearing.

Ulvit was, of course, a pagan woman from the wood. Though she never took Coira there by day, let alone to any night ritual, still she extended to her the teachings of this primal canon.

So Coira grew now, with two distinct sides. The silent, loveless, white, light side, where everything was clear and plain and harsh. And the shadow side, softer and secretive, kind in its own elemental way, philosophical, and convinced of spirit.

But even this was not the sum of Coira. She was so young in the world, it was not possible yet to ascertain what she might be.

When Coira was thirteen, her two maids—who were seldom with her—also left her entirely. Kaya had fallen pregnant to a guard, and wed him. Julah, bitter in virginity, went inland to be a nun.

Eventually Prince Tusaj sent for Coira. That is, he sent for Candacis, King Draco's legal daughter.

"I'd heard of her, but forgot the girl. *He* seems to have forgotten her. But I'd better look her over. She must be marriagable by now."

They had told him her age. The nurse had got this wrong, clipping a year from Coira's aggregate. Coira herself had come to say she was only seven, then only nine, eleven, twelve, thirteen, although she knew, too, that she was eight, twelve, thirteen, fourteen, fifteen . . . (Perhaps Ulvit may even have assisted in this. In some occult way, was it an advantage to have two ages, as to have two names?)

The prince squinted at Candacis. He liked to collect curiosities, a lynx, a hunchback. But this girl would not be one of them. She was not, he thought, prepossessing. Overly slender, almost breastless, too white of skin and with colorless eyes. Like her mother. "But she's sound in lung and limb, and not a booby. Though she has a crazy look." Like the mother, too.

Tusaj asked Candacis politely if there was anything she lacked or might especially want. He hoped she would be modest in her desires. She was. She told him, No.

Humbleness and lack of ambition were always estimable in a woman.

Coira was not concerned with the court. Used to the palace, she accepted it, and even her royal status, when occasionally it was recognized. But she expected nothing, yearned after nothing. Wants had been excised by her mother's aversion to her. Even in the long-ago dream, she had not looked for anything from the gentle man in red, who held her so carefully and stroked her hair. The sun itself warmed, but that was its way. Why should it notice her, and why should he?

Candacis was not unhappy. Her life was almost rustic, yet she received a little tuition. She could read, she could sing. She could dance, and well, for Ulvit had taught her the formal measures of the court—later she might be called to engage in the greater feasts at Belgra. But also Ulvit had taught her dances of the wood. Coira had one gift that was always evident: she was unusually graceful. If she was not pretty, yet she drew the eyes, held them. Even Tusaj had been aware of that.

Her hair was her glory. The prince had not observed it under its net and veil, but unbound, thick yet sheer, it dropped in a curtain of black silk to her knees.

Some must have seen her, going to and fro with her companion, this slight young royal maiden. In the meadows under the palace, her hair loose and hanging round her, black as the crows in the pine trees. She was snapping off the seed-cases of poppies so they could be crushed for medicine. With a knife she cut strands of fennel and heads of lavender, and put these, too, into her basket.

On the hills, in the sinking afternoon, the woods rested like a smoke; but as the sun came and went in cloud above the sea, the smoke brightened, faded, brightened again.

Candacis had moved through all the ten years, as her mother, Arpazia, had.

Now Candacis straightened, and shaded her eyes against the brown fall sunset.

A change had happened. It was very sudden.

Ulvit, standing up from her own gathering, with her hands full of lambs-grass to ease stiffness—her back told her she would need it herself—stayed quiet, gazing at her charge. This month Coira-Candacis would be eighteen—or seventeen, according to the former nurse's timetable.

"She has come into herself, Mother," murmured Ulvit, to the goddess.

It seemed so. Candacis was not as she had been, even half an hour before. Now she was all at once a woman, mysterious where she had only been closed, profound where she had been only rather sad.

There was no plot or scheme among Ulvit's kind. Ulvit had taken on her role with Coira more from compassion than connivance. Yet—the people of the pagan wood recognized its archetypes.

They had selected no Woods Queen since Arpazia, who anyway had proved no more than a mirror-image of herself. But here another stood, the goddess-as-maiden.

"Come, Coira," Ulvit called. "The sun's that low. It'll be dark before we've climbed up to the house." As if the palace were only a cottage.

III.

*T*WO ELDERLY WOMEN BENT ABOVE a smoking bowl. One straightened. She was not old.

"What will this do?"

"I told you, Queen."

"Tell me again."

Facing each other, they were like a woman and her reflection in a mirror.

The crone said, amiably, "Whatever you want, Queen."

Arpazia hesitated a long while. She no longer knew what she wanted. It was as if her only lover were dead. And perhaps he was. Perhaps that story the cart-man had once told her was a fact. Klymeno had been a hunter, and a boar had killed him. Would she have grieved—had she done so? Had she ever properly wept, for more than a moment or two, now and then—as if she could not spare her pain, to let it do what it must? And had she ever spoken to him, or let him speak to her, other than in commonplaces, love-words, cries? She could remember nothing about him except for his looks, his voice. And all that was ten years ago. It was cold today, the first cold day, and her wrists ached, but her heart was numb.

"Let it keep me young," said the queen of the spell, glancing back at the potion.

"*You're* young. You're a girl. I can't recall what it was like, to be so young as you."

These hags, who all looked alike, were always impertinent. Arpazia summoned them only to pass the time, and because she was used to them. Sometimes they worked tricks. A bird might fly up from the smoke and vanish, or a shadow assume a face and speak, but only in some language Arpazia could not understand.

"Soon," said the hag, "is the Scorpion Moon. Do you go to the wood?"

"No." But Arpazia was undecided. She seemed driven back to the wood often. As if she might find something she had lost. In a similar way, she had taken sometimes to wandering about the palace and its terraces, going in and out of its walled gardens. She had seen the prince's menagerie on these travels, in its courtyard. They shocked her, the gray lynx fierce behind its bars, the sleeping bear in the sunlight . . . She had for a second been interested. Maybe, it was only her boredom which drove her back to the wood.

"She will be there, for the Great Orb Night. Only her second time, but the first not recalled, and perhaps not her last."

The queen did not pay attention.

"Your daughter," added the old woman, it seemed in a sinister and meaningful tone.

Arpazia cast a look at her. "What daughter? I have no child. Your hunter helped me kill it, and your crone, ten years ago."

"Oh no, Queen. You bore *this* one, and she lives."

Troubled, frowning, Arpazia tried to think of what that meant.

She had a sudden image of giving birth, herself contorted and shrieking, split by agony, and she pressed her hands to her belly to silence the memory of her womb.

"I thought it was dead."

But the born child *must* have died too. This hag lied for some pernicious reason.

"Well, come to the wood, and you will see her."

See . . . whom?

Arpazia sat in the church, expressionless, shivering a little in her black furs, which now were slightly shabby.

Her lover, Brother Gaborus, was assisting the priest at the altar. Gaborus also did not wear very well. In bed, they still performed actions which no longer had, for Arpazia, much meaning. He snored continuously when he slept; she had taken to turning him out after sex.

During her confessions to him, she had never confessed that she went to the wood. He had probably seen her there, on his own excursions.

The other priest stood up now, ready to address them all. He had that terrible glare they took on, these men of Christ, as if they longed for taloned whips to flay the congregation, and were annoyed, having to make do with their barbed tongues.

"You have heard of the Apple Tree of the Garden, the Tree of the Knowledge of Good and Evil. Know that in the world, there is another forbidden tree, and every fruit on it is poison. Yes— poison so toxic it will swiftly destroy you. What is this tree? you will ask, seeking to avoid it. Too late. Let me tell you. It is planted in your very hearts. Each fruit of it is of a differing shape, a differing hue, but the taste of them seems delicious. Ah, then, of this poison tree none of you can get enough. You reach in and pluck the fruits. You gorge on them and suck them dry. Listen, they are the apples that make you blind and deaf to all but your own selves. They corrupt you and hide from you the light of God.

But still you gobble them, the apples of the Poison Tree, hugging close your lusts and grievances, thinking only, What can I gain for myself, and keep? Only I am here, say you, these others are only shadows, and they speak in a language that means nothing to me. Oh yes, the poisoned apples assure you of this. And all the while, as it comforts you, the bane spreads itself through and through, until your soul itself shrivels up and falls to the ground, a blackened thing of rot. Then no saint or angel, nor even the Christ Himself, can save you. For he may resurrect the body, but how to revitalize a *soul* which is dead?"

The anxious faces stared, row on row. Only the face of the queen was completely pristine, stern and unmoved. She had not heard more than two or three phrases. Her mind was wandering about instead of her body. She thought of the bear sleeping in the sunlight, its fur more glossy than her mantle. She thought of the pagan altar, and of—Klymeno. But when she thought of him, she felt neither desire or sorrow, now.

On the morning of her birthday, there had been two gifts.

Candacis was eighteen—or seventeen, and, through Ulvit, had years before learned again the day of her birth, even its hour.

"Who sent these things? Not the prince?"

"The people sent them."

"Why?"

"It's thought fitting. You're the princess in the palace."

"But my mother was disgraced by the king," said Candacis. She spoke offhandedly, and even the word *mother* had become, it seemed, merely a title, as when she said *king*.

"Put them on, see what you think of them," invited Ulvit.

For the gifts were a dress and a necklace. The dress was of a shining white fabric. It might have been costly samite, from the East, so fine, so smooth to feel. The necklace was of hammered gold.

Candacis did put on the dress and the necklace.

Ulvit stood by. She had never dressed this girl, rarely touched her.

"You look very well."

There was, of course, no mirror. Ulvit had to be the looking glass. She reflected faithfully, smiling and nodding.

"*Two* gifts," said Candacis.

Ulvit said, "One for the princess. One for the maiden, Coira."

"Which for which?"

"Think, and tell me."

Candacis said, not needing to think, "The gold is for royalty. The gown—for purity? They used to dress me in white when I was a child. Must I be a child, still?"

"White may be also for virgins. You are a virgin."

Candacis blushed red. Her eyes were lowered, then lifted quickly, in defiance. "Very well, that's true. Is it right that *they* should send me a virgin's dress?"

Ulvit said, "These are the land's people, who follow the ancient ways. The goddess's daughter was a virgin, and because of her the white snow came, but later she brought back the spring and the first white flowers."

Candacis nodded. She had learned these pagan matters from Ulvit at the same time she had learned the Christian ethic of the Church. Both systems coexisted in Coira-Candacis without abrasion. And so, she accepted the dress.

Ulvit began speaking then of the first Full Moon of winter, the Scorpion Moon of the next month. Fires would be lit and vows made to the cold season the goddess sent, and to the dead, and there must be a sacrifice for the god of the Underworld, Hadz, Death's King, who at other times of the year might be called Dianus, or Klymeno.

"That is like—a dream I had once," the girl exclaimed suddenly. She had never mentioned it before; through the years it had sunk away like buried leaves. Yet now it was as if the white dress woke it up.

"What dream is this?" Ulvit, mildly folding clothes at the chest.

"Oh—black night and thick trees—and fires burning. There was a tall, slim man, lordly, and in red, with a crown of berries and thorns—I thought he was a king, I thought he was my father . . . but Draco's not like that?"

"Never. What else, in the dream?"

"I can't be sure—but—I stood on a stone and the moon rang round my head three times. There was another man. In a white chariot. He was a king too."

"And did you see *him*?" Ulvit paused, listening with every inch of her frame.

"There were bulls drawing the chariot—or boars—or horses, perhaps. I don't remember. I admired so much the man in red." She did not blush now. She had favored him as king, as father. "I thought he'd be able to keep me safe always." No wistfulness in her voice. Even in the past or the dream, she had not actually thought he would.

"And the other, in the chariot—were you afraid of him?"

"No. He was only like the night. Yet . . . I *was* afraid of him. What do I mean?"

"Never mind, it was your dream. At the Scorpion Moon, shall I take you up to the wood? It's a pagan place, as you know, but no one will harm you or try to make you do what you wouldn't like. That isn't our way."

"Yes, I know that. I'll be pleased to go with you."

Ulvit, though her rescuer and constant companion all these years, had never stirred love in Candacis. No one, in that time, had done so. To Ulvit, Candacis offered her receptivity, some loyalty, good manners, and, today, a restrained interest in fresh things. But love— Of course, love had been gouged out in early childhood. Even Ulvit's unintrusive care could not revitalize a poisoned soul. Ulvit had not expected that it would.

Yet, watching Candacis as she moved about, examining the dress, Ulvit (the mirror) added, testingly, "There are young men, and handsome ones, in the wood."

Candacis glanced round. Her face did not alter, but for a moment a dense black absence filled her eyes. She said, in a voice which startled Ulvit, who once or twice had heard Arpazia speak, "What are they to me?"

Carefully, Ulvit said, "In their manner, some of them are royal, just as you are."

"Draco's bastards?" She spoke coarsely, for her.

"No, the royal ones of the wood, known to the gods. Like the man you saw in red in your dream."

Unblushing and cool, the face, and the eyes, investigated Ulvit now, as they had sometimes done even when a child's. Well, she had grown first among betrayers.

Ulvit did not answer the eyes. As she closed the lid of the chest, the girl said, "I'm not from your kind, Ulvit."

"You're a Christian maiden, I know."

"Nor a Christian. Besides, it's all one, that. Don't you say so?"

"So it is."

Ulvit waited then, but when she turned, only the dress was there. Candacis had taken it off, casting it like a bar of white light across the chair. She had put on her ordinary garments and gone out. The necklace—how strange, could she have guessed?—she had let drop on the floor.

But there was another month to wait.

IV.

*I*F THE SORCEROUS LOOKING GLASS looked out to find the first Full Moon of winter, did it also see, that night, an image and that image's reflection, curiously moving— not toward each other—but one following the other, with the spaces of the dark between?

*   *   *

Traces of mauve winter sunset still lit the sky. Candacis saw them, and the coming nightfall, and excitement sang through her after all. She had lived nearly like a nun, domestically, routinely. But she was young, and here was change, and unknown things.

Ulvit took her through corridors, along back stairs, across a part of the elder palace. Then a broken staircase went lurching down, between terraces of orchards where, in summer, sheep and goats grazed, but now the orchards were vacant and bare. Frost sugared the boughs on which oranges had burned and lay like silver dust on the turf.

They passed through lower savage gardens. Statues glimmered with their own luminescence. The sun was down, the moon not risen. Branches and fronds dipped low.

"There's viper's root that takes off pain. And Moly, that enchantresses use at the moon's waning."

Nothing bore flowers in the winter cold. The hints of whiteness were only from phosphorous over stone. But berries grew on briars, purple-black and scarlet. Candacis heard the wind's slow scythe, and in its intervals, the sea.

Torches like summer poppies stood high in the meadow. Laughing girls gathered round Candacis, giving her their names, nodding or bobbing to her, because, Candacis assumed, they knew her to be Draco's daughter. Even in the palace, she sometimes had such courtesies. Indifferent yet gracious, Candacis acknowledged them.

They crowned her with ilex, the dark green spikes catching in her long, loose hair. Under her winter cloak: the samite gown, the necklace of gold. But these girls too had on their best, and were crowned with garlands. She made nothing of it. Besides, she quite liked the laughter, the red warmth of the torches shining on all the faces, as they ran now up the hill.

When she stared in at the window of the mirror, the mirror returned her stare, as it always did.

The mirror had heard her mumbling a chant her nurse had sung, in her father's castle.

> *Mirror, mirror, tell me true—*
> *Who is the fairest?*
> *It is you.*

Queen Arpazia had brushed the black kohl into her lashes and brows, and touched her lips with the rosy salve. Her hair hung in a raven's wing across her gown of black velvet. It was her grandest dress. Prince Tusaj had sent it to her at the summer's end. He had been honoring her birthday, having somehow learned its date. Arpazia herself had forgotten.

Torches came and went in the early dusk. Arpazia took a torch in her hand, as she had to on such dark nights since she never chose an attendant to accompany her. And by now, all Belgra Demitu was accustomed to seeing Draco's castoff queen maundering about the palace, the countryside, and the town.

She slunk through the garden by her former apartment (who lived there now?), the way she always went to the woods. She opened the garden's door and trod down the broken old stair which, with ten further years, had grown worse; whole chunks of it pushed out and rolled away, and a poplar seeded in the seventieth step.

When Arpazia moved off the stair, and got down through the wild gardens, she had a dreamlike sense of recognition. She knew the route well by now, through all four seasons, and at most times of evening and night—or dawn, when she came back. It was not that.

Among the tall plants, the bare white nightshade, the frost-limned hemlock trees, Arpazia turned and peered at the lighted palace above.

Once before she had descended like this, in darkness, a torch held high in her hand, and with just this ominous awareness of searching and loss . . . It had been a dream, the dream after child-birth, but she did not know that. She gazed about inside her brain, and not finding what she sought, turned again and went on.

Where the stones had stood, the lewd statue had long since toppled, or been overgrown. She walked along the avenue of cypresses. They pressed closer now.

Beyond, the meadow was empty.

An icy wind was blowing, and the high grass rushed like tides. Above, the stars blinked blue between thin clouds.

Mirror, mirror, tell me true—

Arpazia climbed toward the woods. The hillside drummed as if others had been running over it not long since.

In her head, she began to hear the voice of the priest she had not listened to, shouting about poisoned fruit. And then instead she heard the old castle priest of her childhood, who said, unhappily, "We are *born* clean, and white as snow, but go to our ends in garments all red and black with sin."

Then, as the ascent became more demanding, Arpazia did not hear either of the voices. She was intent on the slope, which seemed tonight far steeper than she recollected.

By the waterfall in the woods, Candacis paused a short while. The fountain shone into her eyes, so they sparkled.

As she and Ulvit continued, a badger rambled across their path, a beast of two kinds, its bundled body and striped serpentine head at odds.

Birds pattered above in the cold cages of the trees. This year, hardly any leaves had been left; only the needled pines, the larches, the flagged hemlock, the spurs of the ilex, to hold off so much sky.

The moon showed late. She was a hunter's moon, ripe like a peach.

On the lawn between the tree trunks, great bonfires blazed. The gathering there made way for Ulvit, and the maiden. Candacis saw how some bowed to her, some dipped their eyes. She was not afraid of these people, did not hate or scorn them. Others were real enough to her, and she was seldom unkind. She would hurt none, if she could help it, for she knew what being hurt entailed. Nor would she love a single thing.

But the sacred and uncanny wood, *that* did command her emotional attention. She felt again an intimation of what she had felt here in childhood, the sharp tremor of electric fear that was not fear at all.

Arpazia, passing the natural fountain, stayed a few seconds to look down into the basin of the water. She saw her own figure, but could not make out her face. Perhaps because of this, the reflection did not seem to be her own, but that of another, left behind.

A white owl skimmed high between the open boughs. As she went on, a fox screamed miles away but sounding near as her left hand.

The torch cast fire and shadow-shapes everywhere, as if she were one of a score of women. Then the fires of the avenue grew visible, and she saw the dancers were already making their patterns there. And the yellow moon stared.

Go down and dance then. Find some new rough lover, let him roll you in the grass, you slut, like his sow.

"Hush," Arpazia said aloud to the reviling voice in her head.

But, *Why else are you here? What else are you seeking? The disgusting game foul Draco taught you—was that why you never escaped him? You wanted what he did? If he were here, wouldn't you gladly welcome him? You whore. You would be better off dead.*

Dancing, the fingers of Candacis met with those of young men, and mature men, and old men. And, going another way, of women— also youthful, mature, and old. Ulvit had taught her the dances of the court and the wood. Candacis, so graceful, liked to dance.

Soon, in the hot firelight, she pushed off her cloak, as others did; and the white dress rang out like a clear bell.

"Oh, my darling sweet," a young man breathed to her as they

clasped hands for an instant. Her face was not unfriendly, only grave, and did not alter. She was not insulted, nor enthused. Another man whispered, "I'd die for one kiss, White Queen." Her face was grave. The same.

The line of dancers swung aside, Candacis with them. She turned to the women's side in the dance, and one by one they went by each other, hands and skirts brushing over and away. Maidens and matrons and grannies. Some were bare-breasted under the moon, on naked feet. It was not indecorous, here.

There was one woman—there, all in black, her cloak, her gown, which was a rich one, and her long hair.

As she drew nearer, and Candacis nearer to her, the girl saw this woman was vastly strange, beautiful and terrible like the winter wood, and the firelight found after all a tinsel-white tracery in her hair, as if the frost had scorched it.

Hands met, and parted. Candacis arrived before the woman. They were of equal height. Extraordinary eyes were fixed on her own.

Hands touched. Her hand was narrow and chill, lifeless. It had three rings that clinked together, as if grown slightly too big.

In the dance, Candacis must slide by. The woman slid away.

Two faces, both the same. The lips drawn in, the eyes wide and set like ice.

Then, both turning, to look back, and the eyes clashing against each other with a flash.

Candacis moved out of the dance, and looked up and down for Ulvit. But Ulvit was not to be seen. The Woman too had left the dance. She stood under a tree and stared on at Candacis, as Candacis stared.

The image and its reflection. But which was which?

An awful sensation, like a well of tears about to burst, but reasonless, for they felt nothing, either of them, for the other, except a confusion worse than heartbreak.

Candacis thought, *Why is the queen here? Why didn't Ulvit warn me of this?*

How could it be she had never seen her, through all these ten years, not once in the byways of the palace or the town, on the terraces, in the orchards? Not once even in the great Church of St. Belor, to which every Christian, even the pagan sort, must go?

Oh, they had seen each other. But expurgated each other, not *known* each other. Not until this hour in the wood, beneath the Scorpion Moon.

It was the moonlight. It was Time. Candacis had become herself, and Arpazia lost herself entirely.

Like two awesome planets they gleamed, ray into ray, and the dancing unraveled between them.

Just then the moon marked the end of the avenue, and a being appeared there.

It was the King of the Wood, Orion the Hunter, Dianus, Klymeno, in his winter robe of blood and diadem of bramble and berries.

Arpazia became aware of him first, and her eyes left the mirror image of her daughter. She scanned the Hunter King and knew he was no longer hers. Indeed, it was shown to her very clearly. For it was to her other self he went, the maiden in her white. And he took her hand, and Candacis was gazing up at him, for a moment overwhelmed because here was her memoried dream.

He led her away, toward the boulder thrones. King and Queen.

The Woods People followed, leaving the castoff queen to stand there by her winter tree.

How is she alive? I had her killed.

The Hunter King was bearded, good-looking enough, but nothing like her lover. This did not matter, then?

Yes, but it did.

Arpazia dragged herself after the others, to watch from the edge of the grove.

So she saw them seated on the boulders which were thrones. She saw her daughter's face had regained its gravity. If she did not mind any of this, she did not thrill to it. (Candacis had swiftly seen this king was not the one she recalled.)

Would this girl let him have her, after? As Arpazia had. As Klymeno had done. Would this one lead that girl into the depths of the trees? Tonight there would be a sacrifice. Already they were bringing the creature to their altar, this year not a boar, but a calf, black for Hadz. Drugged, it was gentle and not distressed.

When the king efficiently killed it, and made the vows and offering to the god of the dead, Arpazia saw that Candacis did not flinch or look away, though she grew incredibly pale. A true queen. A dutiful queen.

Presently the king brought her the revolting bowl of lights and blood, and the girl tasted of it—gravely, still.

Arpazia decided he would have the girl in the wood. Yes. It did not occur to her Candacis might say no.

A wolf was howling miles off, but close as Arpazia's heart. The moon pushed up out of the blood and offal, stained.

But *she*, the human moon, was beautiful, and the blood had not splashed her at all.

Gold glowed at her unlined throat. The necklace was familiar to Arpazia. Once it had been hers. Draco had taken it, given it back. Then she gave it to a carter . . . in the town. But here it was again, on her daughter's neck.

Why was she so beautiful? Why was she so young?

She is me. I am there, not here.

But the reflection answered, heard only by one, out of the glass of the night: No, Queen. You are where you find yourself. And your soul is a pebble.

Mirror, mirror, tell me true—
Who is the fairest?
Ah, not you.

Seven Sins

I.

*P*RINCE TUSAJ OFTEN HEARD OF the great feasts at Korchlava. He had become jealous, one of the great sins, and covetous, another. As Midwinter-Mass approached there were always enormous preparations now at Belgra Demitu.

This furor of planning and rehearsal, as if for some war, or other world-rocking necessity, had mostly bypassed those on the court's periphery, the ones who were not either its stars or slaves.

As the winter closed in and the mountains whitened and the sea changed to lead, Arpazia, one afternoon, saw again into the courtyard of Tusaj's menagerie. There she beheld the lynx biting at a robe of cloth-of-gold they had tried to put on it, while the bear strode up and down, clad and crowned like a king.

The prince sometimes requested Arpazia's presence at his mightier dinners. He did this to placate her. Not aware of this, always dislocated from the court, she seldom accepted.

Now he sent, too, a formal invitation to Draco's daughter, and with it a gown for Candacis and a decent woolen dress for her servant. He liked things to be aesthetically pleasing; also women, if they were before him. Besides, his spies told him the girl was going up to the woods, just as the mother did. Young sorceress and old; he wanted to make no mistakes with them, particularly as he too liked the woods, in their proper warm seasons. (Lust.)

The new gown was ilex-green, trimmed by squirrel fur. With it went a headdress for the feast, a white silk ring coiled by a gold vine, a drifting gilt-stitched veil.

Again Candacis gazed at sudden clothing which promised an event.

"He means you to be sumptuous," said Ulvit. (Pride?)

Candacis did not say to Ulvit what was in her mind: *And must I go?* Since the Scorpion Moon, she had altered to Ulvit. Prosaic, Ulvit did not remark on this.

But Ulvit said, briskly, "The queen may not be there. Generally she avoids such things."

Then Candacis spoke. "But not the wood."

"Not always the wood."

Until now, Candacis had not mentioned the meeting. Only that night, as they returned across the meadow, had Candacis asked, "Is the Woods Queen chosen again each Full Moon?" And Ulvit had said, "She may be." "Good, then," replied Candacis. "I have had my turn."

She had known of the sacrifice, of that Ulvit had warned her, and anyway, she knew about their rites. Candacis had behaved well. She had known she was given to the king only in symbol. No, none of this burdened her. Only one thing. Had Ulvit been awaiting its mention?

For Ulvit's kind, the compact between the queen and her daughter was constant and revealed as if by bright light. The waning moon and virgin crescent. Now they had adhered one moment. Such things must always be, and the psychic motivations of the gods, as of stars, were greater than men.

Yet Ulvit noted, when she put the new green gown into the

chest, that the white dress of the virgin Queen was now missing. Ulvit looked about, and did not find it. She grasped it was not virginity but the wood which had been rejected.

Candacis had taken the gown off the morning she came from the wood. Her face had still been grave and she was wan simply, perhaps, from lack of sleep. But she walked out again to an area below the palace, where gaunt trees grew and there was a weedy, stagnant pool. Into this she thrust the white dress, and when it floated like a corpse, she poked it under and down with a hazel stick.

The necklace of gold she left in the box with her child's jewelry. The necklace belonged, she thought, most probably to the prince, and he might want to claim it back.

Every time after this, however, that Candacis moved through the corridors and spaces of the palace, she was iron, and her hands were knotted, as if each were crushed in some other, larger, harder hand.

Only once, in the succeeding months, did she glimpse the Woman, the queen. Her mother.

Had they really gone by each other before, unknowing? Perhaps. Truly it was not possible now.

But Arpazia was meandering slowly along a lower walk, when Candacis, herself unseen, saw *her*.

The queen looked like a snake. Her head was held slightly forward, as if its own weight prevented her holding it quite upright any longer. But her back was straight. She wore a russet gown, good in its day, which had been ten years before.

Was she searching for something? Candacis formed the opinion that she was. Startling herself horribly, the girl whirled about and away.

She could not recall a single face from the night of the Scorpion Moon but this one. Her mother's. And she had no one to speak to now. No one at all, for Ulvit had lost her value; Ulvit also had betrayed.

Reaching her room that day, though she had breakfasted, Candacis had seized some bread and raisins, eating them ferociously.

She had the urge to fill her body. She was ashamed, yet raging. And also an imperious mockery made her jibe at Arpazia in her mind, calling her *Ugly Witch*. Then vast enervation made Candacis lie down and sleep at once. And when she woke again her shame had grown in her, unanswerable.

Gluttony, anger, pride, sloth . . .

But at that very time, the queen was copulating with Brother Gaborous after confession. And she had said to him, "You would wish me another, wouldn't you, now I'm old?"

Oh God, if only she could have that girl's youth and beauty, have them back and begin again, and be free of all this dross.

Lust. Envy. Covetousness.

II.

STORMY WAS THEIR LEADER, BUT that did not count for much. Cirpoz owned them. They were slaves—but also, they were Wonders: monsters. That was always made clear.

It was freezing weather as they rode in the wagon through the town. They sat gloomily, hidden from the public gaze, now and then exchanging dubious looks—all but Greedy, who as usual was asleep. Perhaps it was odd that it was Greedy who could sleep, while Soporo was an insomniac. But then, of course, their names only came from the thing they represented before market crowds, or lords in castles—the very thing they were due to put on here, for the prince, at the Midwinter festival. This activity was not their only talent. God had made them for the amusement and instruction of real humans, but also, because of their size, to work in small and narrow confines. They had been employed in the mountain lands, when Cirpoz saw them and bought them from the crooked overseer. Now they would ornament Prince Tusaj's pageant. After that, they were bound for Korchlava, for the mines and quarries, out of which the king's city was still being hewn.

Some seventeen years Korchlava had been in the making, and not done yet. Worse than the great city of Romus on its seven hills. They said Korchlava also covered seven hills—doubtless hillocks. "One for each of us," Greedy had remarked. But they would never properly see Korchlava, only her pits.

The wagon stopped.

All knew better than to lift the flap and look out. But Greedy gave a snort in his sleep. And Tickle combed her hair. It was lush, apricot-colored hair, newly washed, and fell softly round her crag of face. Despite her tresses, she was not the glamorous one; that was Jealous Vinka, whose face was a perfect ivory cameo, with eyes smoky green as goblet glass. But Vinka had the nasty temper Stormy was named for. She would take a fist or knife to you soon as breathe, on her bad days.

Presently the leather flap was pulled aside. Cirpoz stood there, eyeing them as if to be sure they were, all seven, still themselves.

"Come on, shift your bones, get out."

A box had been put by the wagon to make it easy. They scrambled down, Greedy last, finicking and yawning, so Cirpoz cuffed him.

On the journey there had been forests, rivers, villages. White sea fog had concealed this town. Now the wagon was in a paved, walled yard, with other wagons, carts, donkeys and a horse or two. It was so cold out here it was like being in a crystal box, the sort of crystal Stormy had been made to mine, transparent and unbreakable. Want began to snivel at once. Cirpoz raised his hand, put it down. Want was not unappealing, he would spare her face.

Of the males, Proud was the golden handsome one, and chosen for that to play the part he always did. (Stormy had looks, too, but did not think of it.)

None of them remembered their original names, except Vinka, and Stormy himself, who never bothered with that either. A mountain lord had collected and trained them first. In his house of stone rubble and logs, they had learned their other function—they already knew their nature. The lord died of red wine, out hunting, and then the overseer put them back in the mines. They only came up for the festivals, to act their mystery for yet more drunk lords. Until Cirpoz.

Cirpoz served King Draco, the conqueror. Cirpoz vaunted his closeness to the king so much, everyone knew he was a nobody, probably only in the tax-collecting business for Korchlava's coffers.

A palace servant came—they were apparently in a palace yard—haughty among the grooms, and led Cirpoz into the building. *They* were to follow. Thank the Christ. It would be warmer indoors.

The palace was nearly aged as the earth in parts, they heard. Only Stormy was at all interested. Mountains were older.

The prince had had to deal with the town's business all morning, merchants, and other things beneath him. He longed to get back to his pageant, the costumes, and training of beasts. When Cirpoz was shown in, the prince was pleased.

"Yes, a lucky find of yours. Seven of them, you said?"

"Seven, lord prince. Four males and three females. A couple are even attractive, you might say. The face, that is. Their bodies are misshapen, as with all their breed."

Cirpoz, Draco's campaign-soldier turned servant, groveled, yet he had too familiar an air. Tusaj disliked him, but as soon as he was able, he went with the man to see his dwarves, glad to stretch his legs.

When the prince entered the room, they were seated by a fire, on two long benches, from which their legs dangled. Tusaj found that comic and was at once moved to smile. Then they got down like docile children. The four males bowed with courtly precision, and the three dwarvixens curtseyed.

"Ah! Quaintly done!"

He saw no reason to stand off from them. *Obviously such creatures*

are like animals, and evidently intelligent, in their way. One of the dwarf-
vixens was fair of face, as Cirpoz had said. And one of the males
had a splendid head, maned with black hair, though the skull was
far too large, Tusaj the connoisseur decided, for the distorted, hideous trunk. Tusaj knew that some peasants still exposed such infants
in the hills. A silly reaction. They were so fascinating and potentially
hilarious.

"Ah, now, *you're* the one they call for Pride."

"No, master. That is Proud, there, who plays Pride."

Tusaj nodded amenably, though he privately considered the
black-haired dwarf handsomer than the golden-haired one.

She, meanwhile, was unnerving to Tusaj—that female with green
eyes and the face of a lascivious madonna screwed down on her goblin's body. She unsettled him in a sexual way he did not acknowl-
edge. "And what do they call *you?*" he asked her.

The green eyes sliced at him—he took it for absurd flirtatious-
ness—then humbly lowered.

"Vinka, sir master prince."

"And what Sin do you play?"

"Jealousy."

"For your eyes. You're a dainty one," he added, and stealed
himself to pat her head. But her dark hair was unpleasantly tough
and wiry, spoiling the effect.

That second female one, though, was not so comely; while the
third dwarvixen was ugly as sin itself.

"And who will *you* be, eh, my good woman?" Jovial, he liked
to talk to them as if they were normal persons in his employ.

"I am Lust, master."

"*Are* you, by the stars." Tusaj roared with mirth. A glorious jest,
this horror to represent fleshly desire.

They stood round the prince in a circle, the tallest, Pride or
Proud or however they called him, reaching only to the prince's
upper ribs. Abruptly their childish height, coupled to their haggard
ancient look, repelled him. They were brawny, both males and females, and three or four were humped. That black-haired one had

crooked feet, though he moved well enough that you did not note it at first. Tusaj brushed them aside and walked off across the room.

"Very good, Cirpoz. Find my steward. He can kit them out. You've done well. Will my father the king see them, in the city?"

"Perhaps, my lord. King Draco doesn't have much taste for their sort. They're for the mines. Their old trade."

"Perhaps *she'll* find emeralds, Jealousy there, just by looking with those eyes."

Vinka veiled her glance. She spat in the fire when they were gone.

"A prince, a provincial oaf," said Pride, proudly. He had seen another city, once. "Came all the way down to look at us rather than call us to his rooms."

"Afraid we'd piddle on his royal floor," said Greedy, who had woken up. He could fart at will, and did so with disdain.

At Belgra Demitu, they found they were not ill-treated. They were even given separate quarters, and a curtain hung up, to shield the modesty of the dwarf women. In the log-palace on the mountain, they had been rigorously segregated by order of a malign priest. Even so, they had managed carnal relations with each other, those of them that wished for it; while Soporo, who had the looks, proper men said, of a bristle-hog, had been the favorite of a kitchen maid and dallied with her all night, his insomnia proving useful.

One steward of Tusaj's sent them to tailors for their pageant clothes. Another drilled them, making them go through their performance of the Sins over and over. But they knew this act better than the act of living.

The palace food was good. Greedy, who was, stuffed himself. They all did. When this was done, life no doubt would get harder.

Only Vinka was constantly in a temper here. She tore cushions to pieces with her white teeth sharp as a cat's. Stormy stayed pragmatic, even after one of the nobles felt him over.

Cirpoz did not keep so much of an eye on them here. They

were impossible to miss, could not really make off or hide, since
everywhere they went they were, in one way or another, accosted.
Masters and servants, also the slaves, jeered at or petted them,
spoke of them over their heads as if they had either no hearing or
did not speak the same tongue.

But they were used to all that, the dwarves. Wary of men, they
expected nothing much from them, save disturbance. They, too,
kept up the fiction of their own subhuman animal cleverness, ob-
tuseness, and infantile qualities. Where they must—and as a rule
they must—they were always obedient. Even Stormy would have
let the nobleman have him, if it had been unavoidable. They were
talented survivors of the dangerous world. They feared mankind
cunningly, exploited it if they could. But God, giving them such
odds to struggle with, had thereby made them secretly arrogant, and
dismissive of any but themselves. They had been told they were
lower than humanity. They had believed it, but this depth, to them,
was like a height.

*   *   *

On that evening before Midwinter-Mass, the queen saw Cirpoz, the
king's servant.

It was twilight, and the candles were being lit in the palace, but
where she was wandering about among the ruinous byways, there
were few or no lights. So he came up a stair out of the blue smother
of the dusk, a phantom, shocking her. She shocked him, too.

Cirpoz had been prowling, seeing what was to be seen, a habit
of his. He thought himself canny and alert, able to uncover plots,
or flatter the great and trick them, bend events to his will. He was
wrong in all of that. Those he fastened on saw through him. His
prying looked suspicious and had never gained him any valuable
knowledge. Only this afternoon, an eldritch woman in the pagan
temple had made him start out of his skin, cackling suddenly at him,
then seeming to disappear in the empty space between two columns.
Now this other gaunt woman materialized. She was cranky enough,
dressed lavishly but not tidily. Nor was she young, yet her hair hung
down like a girl's. Was she deranged? How she glared at him!

Being prudent, Cirpoz bowed. He drew aside to let her go by, and by she went. Only later did he recall bits of chat he had heard and grasp she was the castoff queen Draco had left here to rot. Perhaps Cirpoz had been wise to fawn on her. He was unaware (canny, quick Cirpoz) he had ever met her before.

Arpazia took longer to identify the man on the stair.

She wandered down the terraces, went among the plants of an unruly garden—there were many of these now at Belgra Demitu. An owl floated over, and windows reddened in the palace. She always carried her little knife now. She snipped off a twig of thornapple before returning to her rooms.

No one had been there. *Her* lamps and candles had been given no life. She lit one thin wax taper, and saw the flame litter across the mirror's lid. When she had undone the lid, looking in the glass, she could see a black forest of pines and, there inside, something shining, which was the candle-flame, but then it became a bulbous golden tent. Draco's tent, far in the past, to which a Cirpoz, almost two decades younger, had conducted her. She saw the dragon standard too, with its red tassels. She saw a flickering mote, which might have been herself, trapped, strangled in trees and night and men.

Cirpoz had raped her maid, Lilca, but not Arpazia. All he had done with *her* was give her to Draco.

She remembered very vividly now. In the glass, she made him out, pushing her on between the campfires, this slight, white-faced girl of fourteen years.

Oddly and ironically, canny-quick Cirpoz himself continued not to remember any of this. Nor did he know that Draco had married that very girl taken to the tent. That very girl—who was the addled queen encountered on the stair. Women did not interest Cirpoz except in one way. In the forest she had been untouchable, meant for a powerful other. And now she was much too old.

II.

*T*HE MASS BEGAN BEFORE SUNRISE. They trooped there in the black and cold, to rejoice in the icicled church.

Reemerging, they saw the sun had risen, but the ice lay white on Belgra Demitu.

"Our winters are harsher at Korchlava," boasted Cirpoz. "And summers blaze." He had also mentioned the cathedral, whose foundations were already laid. The great Church of St. Belor would fit into it, he had told the disgruntled prince, twenty times over.

Yet never mind that, this was Christ's birthday. The feasting started an hour before noon, and would go on, with dancing and entertainments and the pageant and drinking, until midnight.

The palace hall was hot with its two broad hooded hearths, where quarterings of trees were burning. From the black beams hung garlands of evergreen and gilded kissing-balls decorated by ribbons— peasant foibles adopted for the season. On the higher tables, with their blanched cloths, vessels of silver stood about, and before Prince Tusaj's place, marked by its carved chair, a gold cup and saltcellar from Draco's own hoard.

The court warmed themselves and drank deeply. Holiday garments, which had seemed dismal in the church under God's accusing eye, shone out.

Draco's legal daughter, the Princess Candacis, escorted by her solitary attendant—the woman Ulvit—entered the room. She was remarked on, and many heads turned to see. None remembered this girl. She kept much out of sight—as she should, her mother being disgraced.

"Well—but she's a paragon."

"Would you say she was? She's very slight. So pale."

"A skin like alabaster and a heart to match."

Candacis wore the green gown trimmed by fur, the headdress of gold with its stream of veiling.

"Such grace. Like a reed in water . . ."

And she was beautiful, too. Yet it was a beauty not always seen clearly. It was too unusual, too vital—also too complete. She had not yet entirely grown into this beauty. Unlike her grace, it was not her own, had not bloomed slowly and steadily up in her, but somehow fallen suddenly over her, like a shaft of light—or some reflection.

To the spectators' gaze, she stayed mostly indifferent. She had attended other Midwinter feastings, just as she went to the church— but those times, she had not been richly dressed, and had avoided much notice. She forgot she might attract it now.

She was afraid she might have to see her mother again. This was her fear. But Arpazia had not been at the morning Mass. Candacis had, in terror, scanned every inch of the church. Now, again, Arpazia did not seem to be here.

When the time came to be seated, Candacis found herself at an outflung arm of Prince Tusaj's own table.

Wine was borne up by the pitcher and ale by the barrel, processions of roast geese with quinces, and salvers of venison, hams and pigs' heads with a creamy mash of greens, birds in their feathers. There were cakes dyed puce or yellow with saffron, and fruit painted over by edible gold.

The food and drink produced a noise which never abated. Dogs ran about the shouting, joking, gulping hall. Slaves dashed between the dogs, carrying pots and jugs, sweets and loaves baked in bizarre shapes. A riot of jollity.

Candacis had seen such festivals before, and only as a child had she marveled at them, being also frightened. Her fear was different today. Still she quested about with her eyes. Twice her heart jolted within her, once at a gown of black velvet, and once at the turn of a dark head, the sable hair in its taut silver net. But neither of these women was the queen.

And still she looked, not seeing those that looked at her.

"Who is *she*?"

Tusaj's nearest noble leaned forward helpfully. "Your sister, sir."

"My *sister*? Which sister? By God—is it her? Candacia, do they call her? I saw her a year or so back. She's improved."

"Like her mother, though, sir, would you not say?"

"Oh, very like. When the woman was young."

Even Cirpoz, far, far down the tables, where the table-goods were wood and earthenware, noticed the girl in green with such black hair. A nice piece. Perhaps she was the prince's fancy, since her clothes were costly and she was seated so high up. These great ones, damn them, they always had the best, deserving or not.

There was some music. The minstrels and a song-maker grew hoarse, trying to be heard above the din. The songs were of secular matters—love, war—Christ only mentioned in passing. Then jugglers had a turn, knives and live ducks whirled through air.

Couples strayed from the tables. They were dancing in long lines, clasping hands, waists, circling each other. Under the pagan kissing-balls they were permitted, now and then, to clasp lips. Some stole away together.

Candacis did not leave her place at the table. She sat crumbling a red pancake with a small knife. Sometimes she took a sip of the sweet spiced wine. A golden pear kept rolling about the table, batted by the prince's nobles. She wished it would keep still.

Abruptly Prince Tusaj shifted and got up. He wore a long velvet tunic of a sticky pancake red, decorated by ermine tails. Less sartorial than years ago, he had got grease onto the velvet, and one of the ermine tails was sodden from some dish.

He moved along the table to Candacis, as the court watched and watched.

"Lady sister, I hope you're well. Come down and lead a dance with me."

Quite appalled, she rose unhesitatingly, fluidly to her feet. She put her hand on his arm, amid all the watching.

They went out to the floor's center and led the dance. It was one she knew well from Ulvit's teaching. It had a sequence of skip-ping steps, and during these the prince's beard also skipped and then flopped down.

"You must be more at the court," he said. "We've neglected you. It's sixteen you are now?"

She smiled, not contradicting or confirming.

Then he was tired, the skipping was too much for him. He gave Candacis genially over to a noble who, during the next dance, drew her under a kissing-ball and meant to stick his parted lips on hers. But she turned her head. "Oh, you tease me, Princess. Come on, you can accept a lusty kiss. I hear you go up to the wood, as your mother does."

Candacis withdrew her hand quietly from his, and nodded to him, and walked away across the dancing lines, so graceful it was still as if she danced. How grave she had seemed, even smiling. Not ner-vous, not coy. People had slipped from her glassy surface, could not keep hold. And yet watching, wanting to detain, they did not do it.

The prince was thinking he was not much above thirty, and it was a pity she was such close kin, his father's daughter. But when he looked around for her again she had gone. Frowning, he gawked at his court to see who was concealing her, or who she might have left with; he could not be sure. She would miss his pageant, going off now, which was bad-mannered and foolish of her.

Beyond the windows, the short winter day was also taking its leave.

New courses of sweetmeats came, bitter oranges preserved in sugar, crystallized ginger, almond pastries, and cinnamon syrups.

The windows flushed to black. Two Eastern lamps, kept for the festivals, burned high on their stands with perfumed oil.

A dragon sidled into the hall. Its metal hide contained ten men, and from its mouth the tenth man's bellows gusted smoke. Women squealed, men swore freely, amazed by the prince's dragon. Every-one was drunk, even the dragon's crew. Bold knights came to fight it. It hiccoughed sparks and slew all but one, till, slain itself, it tottered with a crash. And the room cheered.

Then a castle of crystal was wheeled in, which being opened, let out shivering damsels nearly blue—for the castle had been sculpted from ice.

Marvel succeeded marvel.

As manned lions fought with giant black birds, both sides sustaining real injuries, and the sea-god arrived from myth in a vast shell drawn by horses masked as carp, Tusaj sat mute with satisfaction. And the court clapped and screamed and toasted him.

His bear was brought in dressed as a Persian king, and the reluctant lynx, snarling, adorned as a queen. The dignified bear, trained by honey, made the gesture of bowing. But the lynx ripped off its sequinned robe and chewed it, slavering.

"Draco and Arpazia," the playful, vicious whisper ran.

Tusaj did not hush it, or mind. Drunk, he dreaded the witch-queen not at all. (Only Cirpoz was rather insulted for Draco, made a slight fuss, and was ignored.)

The climax of the tableaux was a fire-dance, where acrobats leaped in circles of flame. At the last, rare firecrackers were ignited and sprayed violently about the hall, and there were screams in earnest. The king had sent the fireworks, but no instructions on their peril. A hanging had caught alight, a page lay felled with scorched hair. But everyone, including Cirpoz, was laughing again.

After this the priests, sozzled as any, got up and blessed the hall. Boys sang. The assembly tried to put on a solemn face, for the end of the pageant was to be religious after all, the day's last lesson in sinning, after which they might drink themselves to bed.

The story of Christ's birth was enacted, with angels, shepherds, and scholarly kings with vessels of gold, under a great star of polished tin. After the reminder of God, the Devil marched in ranting, with a train of grotesques. This culminated in the play of the Seven Deadliest Sins.

The hall by then was thick with smolders and fumes, hot as high summer. All lights swam low in this smitch; there was the Hell-smell of sulphur from the fireworks. Sluggish, the feasters rallied. They were intrigued. And even Cirpoz was struck, for the first, by how sinister they seemed, his dwarves, as they came gliding through the smoke.

Pride stalked flamboyantly, with peacock feathers on his mantle, his gold locks a lion's mane. A fox—Covetousness—followed him, pawing at his heels with ox-blood gloves, her tail trailing—dwarvixen vixen—on the ground. But then Lust approached, slinking, ugly, and unavoidable. Her half-bared breasts were creamy white, and the sting of the scorpion emerged fitfully from under her skirt. Pride was taken with Lust. They drew aside, and fumbled in the shadows. About now two others grew visible. They had stolen in, and now settled themselves to one side. The first was a pigthing, and from a leather satchel he took out a succession of foods, to the audience's amusement, and seemed to be eating them. His companion, a sort of bear, lay down at once and snored. They elicited name-calling from the hall. For they must be Gluttony and Sloth. Nor did they take any notice when presently Envy appeared. She was carried in, wrapped about a wooden tree, but from this she swiftly unfolded. In the cloud of her hair, a slim pale face and green eyes ringed with silver, so they flared. But she was in a costume of scales, like a snake. Envy met with Covetousness. They embraced, perhaps wantonly. However, Covetousness drew Envy's attention to the more ardent antics of Lust and Pride. Envy and Covetousness circled the lovers, scratching on the floor. There was a clang of thunder. Anger rushed in. He wore armor and a helm topped by a unicorn's spike. He caught Pride and Lust. Anger bellowed—his voice shook the walls—he tossed his black hair. Any laughter left in the hall blew out as Anger swung the unicorn's horn. He lunged, he gored—and howling, Pride fell dead, while Lust, mortally maimed, crawled away. Then Covetousness and Envy rejoiced. They ran to Anger, started by caressing him, then began dragging at him, nimbly tearing at him and shifting aside, before he could see what they had done. He seemed like a man beset by invisible hornets. During these moments Gluttony got up to fart and then sat down again, resuming his banquet. There was a tiny ripple of laughter and, as Sloth turned over, grunting. But they were no longer risable, more terrifying, these two. They had missed every-thing. And now they missed how Anger strode about and saw them, and again all laughter ended. The slanting horn sheered—it slashed, impaled Sloth and Gluttony, and left them rigid in death, to which sleeping and eating were superfluous. At this Covetousness and Envy sprang. They were up on Anger's shoulders, ripping at him like gulls. He held them near—even as he tried to beat them off. At last they had pulled him down. There on the ground he died in a fit, and a hemorrhage of crimson silk ribbons, uncoiling from him through the dying light, brought out one single wavering shriek from some woman of the audience. After that, hissing and spitting like the lynx, Covetousness the fox and the serpent Envy rent each other, until they fell dead among the rest.

A voice pealed through the sunken silent palace hall.

"So ends the vanity of the world." (It was the voice of Stormy—Anger. Lying facedown he had long ago learned how to pitch it out.) "For all is vanity and death claims all. Only through God shall we live. Amen."

And the crowd crossed itself, gasping, shuddering. *Amen, amen.*

But when the fearsome dwarves, under cover of shadow, had conjured themselves away, slaves replaced the candles. Light came back, the weary minstrels waxed their strings. Those that could began to eat and drink and jest and lust and argue and hate and live again.

A spider in her web, she waited for him. Staggering, sottish, to bed, he did not know it.

The water clock which dripped in the annex of the hall had shown midnight. In the torch-gloom there were still songs. "We keep later hours at Korchlava," he had said. But generally he had never been included in those.

On a narrow stair, a woman appeared. She was flinty sober, dressed as an upper servant of the house.

"You're the man Cirpoz? My lady summons you."

"*Does* she now."

"None of that. She's the queen."

"What queen? The queen's at Korchlava . . . Oh, *that* one." Unease curdled him. He had met her, last evening, in the ruins of the elder palace. That thin ghost with frost on her hair.

"Come now. What could she want with me?"

But the woman turned and he had to follow her, for a queen summoned him and he was, in fact, a nobody.

When he entered her apartment, after all the heat and noise, it seemed winter-cold to him, and dim from its two or three candles. The witch—many named her that—sat in her chair. Three dark rings stared from her hand, but not so darkly as her gemstone eyes. She made his skin creep. The servant was gone. This one and he were all alone.

"Illustrious madam." The apartment as well as dim and cold was not very luxurious. Better spread butter on his words. "This honor—"

"You know me, do you?" Her voice surprised him by its youth. It was a girl's voice.

"Why madam, you're the regal queen."

"Am I? What will you do for me?"

His gorge rose. He had heard she frolicked, this hag.

"Wh—whatever—I'm able, madam."

"Are you able," she said, "to take away from me one who harms me?"

"I—what does your ladyness mean?"

In her web, the ice-spider with the girl's voice looked at him with her five black eyes.

"There is a chit here at the palace who works against me. But she would be easy for you to lead away, out of this house. She's only young, slender—no nuisance to you."

"You mean—to kill her would be easy?"

His nerves had steadied. This task was not quite unknown to him. The other victims had been men. A woman should present no problem.

"Is she of high rank, madam?"

"No."

The hag was very definite. He wondered if she lied.

"But—"

"She's nothing. No one will miss her. Only I will notice her loss. I shall be grateful. But it must be now—tonight."

There was something in the corner, gleaming faintly. He had taken it for the glimmer of a low-slung lamp. But then instinct made him see what it was. It was the legendary witch's sorcerous mirror, standing open, reflecting all the room. And himself. Cirpoz edged from the mirror's view.

"But am I to *kill* her, madam? Sometimes that can be quite awkward. Especially since I must then go off myself—and there's my troop of dwarves to consider—"

"Do what you want. Violate her, give her to Draco. Feed her to savage beasts. Whatever you like."

Then she sighed. She looked away from him.

He fawned: "Immaculate lady, I dislike that I must ask, but I may still need . . . some funds."

"There," she said. "That's for you."

"What, madam? What am I to have?"

"Your reward. There it is. It's worth the fortune of your king. My father paid for it some hundreds of gold coins. He told me so. It was the talk of his castle."

"But—what?—Where?"

"There. Before you. *That.* It's heavy with silver, and has gold adornments. Fetch some servants to carry it, or your dwarves. Take it. I don't want it any more."

Yes, yes, she was insane. Nor did *he* want the mirror—but she was correct. It was worth a fortune. Were there even three such objects in all Draco's wide kingdom? Perhaps Draco had forgotten it was here. Perhaps his other queen would like to have it?

Cirpoz said, throatily, "Tell me where to find this pest who upsets you so."

When she described the room and the part of the palace he

would locate her in, Cirpoz was reassured. It was not an area where any important ones kept their apartments. He was glad to have been crafty.

Luckily for Cirpoz, he and his own slave were sufficiently strong that between them they shifted the glass. But by then he had closed the lid. He did not want the mirror to snag his soul on its surface.

When the servant of Draco was gone, and his slave, Arpazia paced about the empty chamber. One by one, the two or three candles died.

High in the woods wolves howled, or it might have been some last drunken noise of games from Tusaj's hall.

I want none of it any more. To go to the wild wood. To make fool's spells with old women. I don't want to see her, anywhere. Never, never again.

The girl who was Arpazia's youth, the girl they called Candacis, or Coira. Meeting her on the avenue of trees, they had clashed together, eyes and hearts and spirits. Each a blow to the other. To Arpazia, the worst blow?

But she recalled who Cirpoz was, and even though he had aged seventeen, eighteen, nineteen years, yet she knew him. How could she ever forget the one who hauled her up into the forest of war and led her through the camp to Draco? Let Cirpoz now take *this* girl, then. Let him lead *her* away to some doom. Or let him simply kill her and throw her white body, red with blood, into the black earth.

Arpazia walked round and round her chamber, now in the darkness. But if she spun her web or broke the threads of it, she did not know.

She is me. Take her away.

Take her away from me. Take her away and take the mirror away.

She thought, cruelly, *Idiotic old crone, it will do you no service. You never learn.*

But still round and round she circled, like a wheel, or the dead stars, round and round, until the night was done.

Before the night was done, Ulvit came up from her own prayers lower on the terraces. Candacis had not accompanied her. Ulvit thought that she would be sleeping, and did not try to rouse her. In the morning, when Ulvit woke, herself, she thought only that Candacis had gone out alone, and early, as sometimes she did. And so a long while passed before Ulvit knew Candacis had vanished from the palace. Perhaps others knew, who said nothing—stones in the walls, the lizards clamped by winter under the temple paving, the Oracle (which knew everything) not murmuring in the hill.

Ulvit did not make a stir, though she sought an interview with the prince—with some difficulty—and told him how the Princess Candacis was not to be found. Ulvit had already lost hold of the girl. It was not in her to be vocal with grief.

Besides, she and all her kind had known fate lay awaiting Draco's daughter, if not how, or when. She was *Coira*, the Maiden, and had been offered to the King of the Dead. They were not wicked, Ulvit's people, only, in their way, *religious*. The story had always been here: Demetra and her child who Hadz snatched and carried off. The gods might wish to reenact that story. Coira-Candacis had been shown, twice, in the wood, the second time as a queen. She was a sacrifice, perhaps. The Woods People had not connived. But they had opened the way. To hear now that Candacis, first in white, and then in green, had disappeared, would not astonish them.

As for Tusaj, like many just then, he nursed an aching head.

Surfacing from its stupor, the court at Belgra Demitu was only glad the dwarves, who had described their sins, and died for them, were no longer about.

As for Cirpoz, he was, of course, a nobody. Who would suspect him?

*   *   *

He had tapped on the door in the leaden remains of night. Tapped, until she came to see who was there. Not even a servant to protect her. And no one else near.

Cirpoz, who had watched her at the feast, envied her her place, fancied her, did not know Candacis in this slender pallid form, wrapped in night and a worn cloak, hair tied back in a plait.

He seized her at once, grinning at the facility of it, and with his big hand cut off her air until she slumped. She weighed nothing. A lot less than the bloody mirror. No one saw him take her away from that remote room and down to his wagon. Even the yard grooms were dead drunk. But the adventure and the freezing night had cleared Cirpoz's clever, canny, crafty head.

There was a ramshackle hunter's bothy along the hills, in the woods. He could store her there, tied up like a bitch-dog, till he had collected his dwarves and the mirror from his quarters.

She was young and wholesome. And perhaps she had talents; she must have, if she had enraged the queen. But that madwoman had not insisted on death. So he would not kill the girl. At least, not yet.

Under the World

I.

FOR THE DREGS OF A NIGHT, AND half a morning, she was in the hut. She did not think about whose hut it might have been—only asked herself if they might come back, discover her, and set her free. But the place was in bad repair. Even some of the roof was down, and the hearth long cold. And no one came, except for mice, and at last her captor, who returned in the sallow noon.

By then, Candacis had worked her hands free of the thick coarse rope with which he had bound them. She had reached just beyond the door, and was sawing at the cord on her ankles with a jagged stone. He had not taken many chances, but if he had been delayed, she might have got away. When she saw the wagon grinding up among the trees, a panic-stricken fury had made her go on at the cord, right up until the moment when he stood over her.

Almost petulantly Cirpoz said, "Couldn't you keep still five minutes, eh? You've made your wrists bleed. That was my best rope, and you've messed it for me. I should give you a whipping."

As a further precaution, he had sold off his slave in the town. So he would have to manage all this alone.

Then she was somehow standing, and facing him with the jagged stone. She said nothing. Her nearly expressionless face said it all. She was strange-looking—eerie. Did she have *unnatural* powers? "There, but I won't, won't whip you. That's not how I am. I'm not rough, but a king's man."

Since he was saving her, for now, he had left her some wine, and his own second cloak to keep her warm. If she had drunk any of the wine he was not certain. He finished it himself, letting her stand there, awkward from her tied ankles, weapon-stone wavering, until she lowered it.

"Throw that way. Away, or do I put out your light again?" said the unrough courtier.

It seemed she judged then if he or she would get the better of the fight, and sensibly decided it would be him. She dropped the shard on the ground. She made no protest either when he tied her hands together once more. "Just for luck," he merrily said. He picked her up and carried her to the wagon. "What's your name?"

Candacis said nothing.

"Oh, a haughty one, are you? Well, I can make a name for you, if you like. Let me think—Blackhair will do. Know who gave you to me, do you, Blackhair? A forceful female person. And I'm to take you far away from here, since you annoyed her so."

Then he opened the flap of the wagon and shoveled Candacis inside, like a bundle of yarn.

There were rugs on the floor, but the brief fall stunned her a little. She lay feeling a gray nausea for several moments, during which she was aware that the wagon had started up. Cirpoz had two horses, not of the best. She heard them trundling back down the slope, and the wheels jangled over tree roots.

Soon Candacis became conscious that there was other life, besides her own, keeping very still in the wagon's back.

She smelled it first, human flesh shut warm in heavy garments, hair washed in soap or combed with spices. Then she heard them *breathing*.

Candacis turned her head and looked.

She met two dark eyes in a great rutted face, a face young and old at once, sane and demented at once. She saw the body under the face. A small giant's head had been fixed on the physique of a big muscular child.

"Mistress, that's my bed you're lying on," said Greedy, curtly.

Candacis made a rapid, fishlike movement and pushed herself away. Hand-tied, she still struggled up, until her back rested against the side of the wagon. Greedy instantly resumed his spot on the rugs, pulled a pillow under his shaggy head, and went at once to sleep.

But by then, Candacis could see others, and their twelve gleaming wolves' eyes.

Of course she had heard there were dwarves at the palace; they had been talked of everywhere. But she had not happened to meet them, and by the hour of their play she had left Tusaj's hall.

Candacis was schooled in the malignity and probing uninterest of others. To Ulvit's care and company she had been gracious and not unreceptive—but even so she could never fully have accepted them. Finding in the wood that she could not trust Ulvit either had not appalled Candacis, if perhaps it made her unhappy. She loved none, wanted to love none, expected no love, had forgotten what love was. Enemies might find her unfathomable. Cirpoz did, but was too slow to know it.

Now she was only afraid and subdued. As she glanced at the dwarves, the dwarvixens, it was without alarm or recoil. Having noted them, and seen they were not actually about to attack her, she looked away again—and seemed to fold herself away behind some veil.

Perhaps the dwarves themselves recognized this devastating matter-of-factness. She was essentially prosaic under duress, and so were they.

Presently Tickle spoke.

"This isn't a large wagon, mistress. We keep our own space. There is a pot behind that curtain for the functions."

Want said, in her low whining chant, "Mistress couldn't help getting on Greedy's bed-rug. She was thrown on it."

"So mistress was," said Tickle.

"There's bread in that crock," said Stormy. He did not raise his eyes, put out and embarrassed by the human woman's unwanted proximity. "And water in that leather bottle, if you have a thirst, mistress."

Then the girl answered. "Thank you," she said.

But she did not stir.

"Her wrists are all bloody," whined Want, uncomfortably.

"Shut your row," said Soporo.

"When he gets angry, master lays about," Want insisted.

"Not with you, though," snarled Soporo. "It's I and Greedy-guts and Stormy gets it, and Tickle. So stitch up."

Want whined again.

Soporo suddenly began to sing in a robust baritone that rocked the bumping wagon.

Under that, Candacis heard the other dwarvixen, she with the green eyes, hiss, "Mistress is pretty. She's pretty nearly as me."

Cirpoz naturally had not discussed his plans with the dwarves. They only knew this female human superior, tossed in here, was a slave. That meant, apparently, they could not avoid her, since she had been slung almost down to their level. They would make the best of it. Greedy had needed to assert his rights, and Tickle to explain the wagon-code. Jealous Vinka was simply marveling that something properly human could aspire to her own inferior-thus-exquisite charms.

The girl kept quite still. She did not shut her eyes, or sleep, but she blinked rarely. You could just make out that she breathed. She did not utilize the pot, though once Soporo did, rattling its lid, whistling, and splashing like a dray horse. Tickle sewed a seam in the half-light. Sometimes Greedy farted odorlessly in slumber.

Stormy scowled at a wooden pipe he was shaping with a blunt knife. Want and Vinka sputtered at each other or to themselves.

Only Proud stared frequently at the girl. He was quite sorry for her—Cirpoz's slave, as they were, but without their unique stamina.

Just as Candacis (Blackhair) did not crawl to use the pot, so she did not take any water or bread and cheese.

Later, when a white sun leered through a hole in the sky, Cirpoz stopped, fed the horses and checked on his cache in the wagon.

"Don't you touch her," he now admonished the dwarves. He grinned at Vinka. "Don't you *scratch* her, you bitch. She's my property."

He seemed never to have thought they might abscond from the wagon's back, when it went as tardily as now it did. Where would they go? It was winter after all, and there were wolves about. In fact, the dwarves thought much as he did. They were indifferent to the world they must serve, being so deeply thrust beneath it.

While the wagon was at a standstill, however, the girl somehow got herself out. Her ankle cord had slightly loosened and she succeeded in hobbling behind a tree.

"What are you up to? Come back here, you curse of a girl—" But Cirpoz knew she had only gone to relieve herself. He chuckled, amused by her feminine handicap, needing to squat with tied ankles, clinging with bound hands to some low branch.

He offered her beer when she came back.

She drank a mouthful. Then she let him take the flask back. She sat down by a wheel. Once Cirpoz was ready to go on, he lifted her and pushed her in the wagon again.

"If you behave, I'll untie you tonight."

As the trek resumed, Tickle's slabby face was tucked down into her collar. It was Vinka who announced, "He'll have her. He'll fuck her."

"Stitch up," said Soporo, but idly.

Stormy shook himself and got to his feet. He was used to the difficulty of balancing, and went and stood over Candacis who was Blackhair. "Mistress, you must see to yourself. We can't help you."

When she did not respond, he said again, "We can't help."

"I didn't ask your help," Blackhair said in a voice like a thin white slap.

"Some might," said Stormy stubbornly. "Some have. But we're nothing. Can do nothing." And he wondered why he said any of this.

Want began to croon.

Surprised at himself, Stormy sat down.

It was Proud who murmured, "Poor pale thing. She can't bear it. How can she?"

But Stormy believed she could bear it. Somehow she had attracted his superfluous apology or excuse.

"Let it alone," he said. "Let her be."

Through the late afternoon as the wagon gurned on, looking out between the flaps, they saw the woods intensify to forest. It was now black-dark and dead-cold. They wrapped themselves further in their rugs and mothy furs, and Vinka went on with her wordless maledictions.

A baleful moon rose early in gaps of sky.

Greedy woke, stood, pissed out the wagon's back, leaving a starry trail for the moon to flitter on.

Candacis, behind her lowered eyes, sat thinking.

She had been shocked utterly by her abduction—she had only opened the door that night because she thought some woman had come for Ulvit's help, some herbal or other medical request. She had believed Death had her. Half aware as they descended, she thought Death carried her under the earth. And in the cold hut, she had tried to escape, but all the while known it was too late.

But he had said, had he not, that Ulvit had arranged this. The forceful "she" of the captor's tale—who else but Ulvit, and the pagan wood? Candacis had "annoyed" them. Now she thought of this, and the true shock pulled her under. Round and round she went with it, and round and round. She would have paced about, too, if she had not been tethered and the area so constricted.

II.

*D*EEP IN THE HIGH FOREST WAS an inn.

It appeared out of the darkness, glowing red like a luminous vegetable.

Cirpoz emitted a string of joyful oaths.

The wagon grumbled into the yard just before they shut the gate. "Wolves," explained the innkeeper, standing to oversee the operation, the heavy bars let down.

By now the moon had set. Yet the black trees had a vibrating sheen from the cold. The yard was slick with ice.

As the dwarves got down and filed demurely into the inn, gaped and pointed at on all sides, Cirpoz undid the girl's cords.

"Will I trust you? One hint of michief and I'll tie you up out here, I'll *chain* you—see you undo *that*—and you can freeze all night. Well?"

"I'll do what you say."

He ushered her before him. As the blast of heat hit them from the inn door, she half-missed her step. Cirpoz grabbed her arm viciously. "No games."

They ate supper in a corner of the inn hall. It was decked with a few drying evergreens left from Midwinter-Mass. The dwarves and the girl were given bread, broth, and beer. Cirpoz ate a roast and a hedgehog pie, and drank ale.

Some of the other occupants of the hall demanded to know if the dwarves would do any tricks. "There *is* a thing they do, most entertaining. Maybe tomorrow." Then Cirpoz added winningly to the landlord, "Something off your charges, maybe, if they amuse your guests? They lastly performed for the palace at Belgra. They're of some standard."

The innkeeper grunted churlishly.

Disgruntled, Cirpoz noticed the girl had wasted most of her food.

"Pernickety appetite," he said to her as they went upstairs, "you're not at the palace, here." She must, despite her threadbare cloak, have been a maid or waiting-woman of the better kind. But being refined would be no use to her now.

He had tipped one of the inn boys to keep a lookout for his wagon and the horses. His coins and small goods he had brought in with him, but the other thing, Cirpoz concluded, was well concealed and besides, far too heavy for thieves to shift without planning and noise. (Even the dwarves had not been aware of it, sat there on top of it, as it lay packed under the rugs.) In a way, Cirpoz was still not happy with the witch's mirror. If he dragged it to the city, the king might not want it after all. It could be better to attempt a sale outside Korchlava, in some partially sophisticated place where they would be impressed by the mirror but not frightened of it.

He had never meant to travel at this time of year. That madwoman had left him no choice.

Cirpoz had secured two rooms adjacent to each other. He hurried the dwarves into one, little more than a cupboard, then pushed the girl into the larger chamber, followed her, and shut the door.

"Well, now. Well, now." He had dawdled enough.

She would know what came next. Belgra was a lax, lewd place—why should she mind? He was not, he thought, such a bad bargain.

Casually he began to remove his outer garments, then he inspected the bed, an old wooden one which would creak. "Let's hope they've got no bugs in it." It did no harm to be friendly, if they were to keep each other warm.

But she had not come over to the bed. She stood by the brazier, in which the wood was almost burned through.

"Come here. It's cozier in here."

She gave him such a look it peeled his eyeballs. God's testicles, like some lord's wife.

Cirpoz glowered. "Need a smack, do you? I'm the king's man. I served him through five campaigns. I've had better than you, Blackhair, and thought nothing of it."

Something about her made him—more than angry—edgy, unsettled. Would he be able to want her? She was too thin, and carried herself (even during the time she was tied) proudly, and gracefully as a dancer.

He left the bed and veered toward her. She should have a crack across the skull. See what that did.

Candacis saw him wheeling toward her. She understood if she ran for the door, even if she reached it ahead of him, no one at the inn would assist her. And beyond the inn lay the forest, turned to black diamond, where starving wolves moved in packs and homicidal bears woke at a footfall.

A virgin, she knew what Cirpoz intended. Educated paganly, she had learned a great deal about the act of love, if nothing of love itself.

Candacis had learned spells, too, the words to say over plants when plucked and potions as she prepared them. And amuletic phrases—against snakes, beasts, men—

They slipped out along her tongue now, simply like air.

> *"Blackest wish turn white like snow,*
> *Bloodiest wish like blood outflow."*

"What? What are you mumbling?" He had stopped, irritated yet cautious. "Are you an enchantress, you black-haired strumpet?"

"No. I am King Draco's legal daughter by his first queen," said the girl slowly and clearly, as if she told herself not him.

Cirpoz roared with overdone humor. "*You?*" Then he caught hold of her and, in the way of countless million others, she readied her nails to tear at him. In that second he saw her as if never before had he done so. In Christ's mercy—she was the image of the madwoman, the queen at Belgra. Her daughter? Yes—she might be. "Who are you, you say?"

"Draco's daughter. Candacis."

"At Midwinter Feast—where did you sit in the hall?"

She sensed exactly how he crumbled to bits before her. Calm with her dying horror, she said, "The prince's table."

"In a dark red dress."

"In a dark green dress."

"Green . . . trimmed with fur," he added, "and a white ring on your hair twined by gold . . ."

Nearly lightly, to help him, she added, "And a long veil."

Cirpoz had let her go. He stumbled back, mouthing at her. "Why—why—why didn't you tell me who you are—"

She looked away from him. She had never told him because she had assumed that, like most of them, he had not known her by sight and so would not believe her.

Now, by magic perhaps, suddenly he did know.

"Ah—lady—I was treacherously misled into this—that *woman*—"

Candacis (no longer Blackhair) did not of course say what she thought now, that no one would care that he had carried her off for violence and rape.

"That—woman—a fiend—I'd heard as much, I should have guessed—"

He rambled, wringing his big, hideous hands which had caused her so much harm and had meant to give her more.

Candacis thought, stolidly, curiously, *How ever did Ulvit get money to bribe him to do this to me? She must have paid the other way, what he wanted now.*

But he was beginning to think too. Not wanting quite to name the queen to the queen's daughter, in case there might be some other blunder. "A foul and evil slut—ah, I mean no offense, lady. I didn't know you—you've seen I didn't know. But she—well, oh, well . . . What shall I do? I must take you home to Belgra."

Licking his lips as if to lick off his crime. Thinking, *The madwoman, perhaps she'll tell them I stole this royal girl away for my own ends. The prince's favorite she was, too, you could see at the feast, sister or not. I can't go back with her. And if I let the girl go, what will she tell them herself? Princess Candacis. What will she want them to do to me if they catch me up?*

Candacis saw one of the hideous hands flap down on to the hilt of his knife. She saw it before he even thought what he did. Then his hand slipped off the hilt again. *I can't kill her in here. I'll say I'll conduct her home. Then in the woods—leave the corpse for the wolves—get away, back up to the mountains—*

"The child of her own body," he muttered. "Addled, damned bitch—"

The muttering made no sense to Candacis, she did not attend. She was still considering how his hand had gone to his knife. "Oh," he was saying now, "take the bed, I beg you, madam. You must be tired out. I'll sleep with the seven deformities next door. Will I get someone to bring you something—hot water, wine—?"

Unknown to either of them, the other side of the wall beyond the bed was lined with ears.

Soporo had been the first to listen at the wall. Carnality, in almost any form, even coercive, aroused him. He had wanted to hear Cirpoz and the girl have sex, rape or not.

This disgusted Proud, who struck him. They tussled, tumbling on the floor—but all very quietly, so not to alert Cirpoz.

In the end it was Vinka, her sharpest ear at the plaster, only inquisitive, who drew their joint attention.

"He's afraid."

Then they all came to try to hear. Even Want, who had been closing off her hearing with pillows. Even Stormy, frowning, and Tickle with a bemused shake of her orange hair, and Greedy in midyawn.

"Why is he? Has he gone daft?" Want, hopeful, bothered.

"Is it witchcraft? She looks a witch." Soporo still erect.

Only Stormy and Jealous Vinka heard enough of their master's jabber to piece it together. At least, Vinka did not trouble. But Stormy moved abruptly away.

"Lie down," he told them. "He'll be coming in."

They scudded to obey. Under their coverings they lay, curled up tight or stretched rigid. Soporo played with himself, grew bored, and left off. Only Greedy fell asleep.

Cirpoz did not arrive after all.

"What's he doing now?" whispered Proud. "Has he had her or not?"

"No. She's the king's daughter," said Stormy, unaccountably angry for once, like his name.

"What king?"

"The king at Korchlava."

Kings meant little to them. Or king's daughters. Everyone stood higher and meant less than they.

In the black stillness, not a noise now from the other room, and from the night outside not even the yell of a wolf.

"He wants to kill her. I can tell from his voice."

"Why that, Stormy?" Proud, astounded.

"Think, you fool."

"I am no fool. Not I. I've thought. I'm just as foxed."

Soporo whispered, "He stole her and treated her like his dray, but she's royal. If the prince at Belgra finds out, *he'll* be for it."

"Ah."

Stormy said, "Shut up. He's coming."

The other door opened, then their door, and Cirpoz was in their cupboard.

Through the pitch dark they felt him looking round at them, hating them, loathing them. Then he was gone again.

"Where's he off to?"

"Down the stair—listen."

"To the shittery?"

"Somewhere. Anywhere but where she is."

Stormy lay on his back. In the dark he could see hallucinatory

flames, which softly coiled to and fro. He watched them, brooding.
Cirpoz, whatever he did tonight, would murder the girl tomorrow.
It was easy, out in the forest, to do things like that.

What do I care? She was not his race or kind.

Stormy thought of Cirpoz carefully. Of the horses and wagon
with its store of money and treasure-trove of stuff Cirpoz had stolen
or earned—normally under false pretenses. Stormy thought of the
forest and the wolves, and the six others lying in the dark with him,
especially intelligent Tickle and spite-full Vinka, and Soporo, with
his brazen fists. Who might also be thinking somewhat as Stormy
was.

Something tugged and teased at Stormy. But why? She was
nothing, a human. Oh, but perhaps it *was* sorcery, some spell she
had cast—with that verse she had sung out at Cirpoz. Perhaps it
was only that. By morning, Stormy decided, he would have slept it
off.

Cirpoz, having dozed by the inn fire, was up early and surly, and
soon had his wagon hitched ready. He ate his breakfast bread standing, and offered nothing to the dwarves, or to the girl. "We should
be off, Princess, get you home. There's edibles in the wagon—"
He did not mean to waste any more extra food on her. Especially
now, when she would not need it beyond midday.

Though jumpy and ill-humored, he observed nothing odd about
the dwarves. They seemed the same as always to him, misshapen,
monstrous, potentially lucrative, obedient, and uninvolved.

The inn gate had been opened.

By day, the forest was only discouraging. But in the frosted mud
by the wall, even Cirpoz made out wolf tracks.

"We'll have a stop here, Lady. Rest half an hour. Come out when
you're ready, for some air." He spoke coaxingly. Obviously he had
not tied her up this time. But she sat where she had yesterday,

speechless and quite negative. No wonder he had not recognized her, until it was almost too late. She had no spirit, less than any slave.

Disgusted by her, Cirpoz walked about in an indolent way. The dwarves meanwhile, had already got out of the wagon via the handy box. Soporo and Stormy went off into the trees to relieve themselves. The others ambled about. (Vinka was in one of her tempers, sizzling and slashing at frozen ferns with her hands.)

When he heard the shout, Cirpoz was almost unnerved. He had always been unsure, killing people; he knew it was a skilled job and he was no professional. He had been bracing himself, honing his knife—and now he dropped it and stood with his eyes out on stalks.

Soporo and Stormy pounded up to the wagon.

"Master—"

"What in Christ's name?"

"There's a man dead over there, in the trees. A rich man in furs—and gold spilled everywhere about—"

Cirpoz revived. Cupidity swamped all else.

"Dead, you say. You're sure?"

"His brain-case is stoven in."

"And gold. Show me."

They went off again, infantilely relieved to have told him, and Cirpoz went after, having picked up his knife. Vinka came wandering in their wake, and next Greedy. They were all following like lambs. "You"—Cirpoz shouted at Want and Tickle—"stay there. Look after the lady in the wagon." It would be just his luck, Cirpoz thought, to find this unexpected hoard and lose the girl because she had escaped, maybe back to the inn, and convinced someone else—

In fact, his luck took another form.

"Where is he?"

"Just over there, master."

"Here? It's a rare tangle—fucking trees—what? Here? I can't see—"

"Bend down, master, to our height. Under that dead bracken. See the blood? And there's the gold shining."

Men see sometimes only what they want to see.

Cirpoz, bending low under the boughs, his avarice striving hard for him, did make out the form of a sprawled man, a vision of spilled coins. In the less than daylight, they were really a fallen pine scattered by yellow toadstools. Two instants more, he would have known.

But before he did, Soporo had tipped him and crashed against his legs. Cirpoz plunged headlong with only a yelp, a winded grunt. It was Vinka who squirreled over him and smashed down the stone over and over on his head with all her panther's strength. Stormy, going after her, had to push her aside in order to finish the work.

Sure enough, now there was a dead man sprawled there, his brain-case stoven in. No gold though. That was kept in the wagon.

She had slept in snatches through the night, on the inn bed. Sometimes talking in her sleep, but not knowing it. She had not been certain her captor would not change his mind and return. (Once a girl had come in to see to the brazier and startled her.) Today she felt very little. Cirpoz might conduct her back to Belgra Demitu, and her enemies and un-friends there. Or he would carry her on, away to other enemies and unfriends. What did it matter? This was how the world was.

Candacis nursed her melancholy. She sat in the wagon as she had yesterday, seeing none of it. As for the dwarf people, they were like figments of a dream.

Now, in the forest clearing, a huge soundlessness gradually communicated itself to her. No wind, no movement, not even the croaking of a raven. Cirpoz and his slaves all gone somewhere. She had not . . . paid attention.

Candacis, on her knees, moved to the wagon's back. If they were gone, she might run away. That is, she might walk away, with-

out speed or intention, the world being all alike and all nothing in
its bleakness. Probably wolves would meet and devour her. At least
they would do it only in order to survive—but was this true of
everyone?

As she put her hand on the leather flap, it was pulled open. How
limber and noiseless they could be, these dwarves, like cats. She had
not heard them, even this one as he jumped onto the box.

He looked up sternly into her eyes.

A child-short, black-haired man, with a jagged beauty she
glimpsed abruptly, and half-averted herself from, as if from an old,
familiar pain.

Stormy said, "He's dead. The master. He would have cut your
throat, but it's him instead. Now the wagon's ours, and everything
in it. But we have a difficulty, being subhuman underlings." He said
these two words without rancor or hesitancy. He said them with
steely pride.

This made her glance back into his eyes.

He took this heeding for inquiry.

"Our kind can't own anything. We can only be *owned*. But you're
an ordinary woman. So, you can own us. Be the mistress. Then no
one will cause problems. Do you want to go back to your palace?"

"No," she said. It came from her without her intending to
speak. It was more an inverted gasp. (Less to her even than to him,
her status.)

"Good. Then we can go on to Korchlava, or to the mines there.
That's employment for us. We're inspired at mines. Better than at
the Sin tableau for lords."

She shook her head slightly. He saw she was shocked and not
properly in her right mind. Stormy said gently, "We won't hurt you.
You can help us out. We'll take fair care of you."

But then he, too, looked away, to hide the burning fury he felt,
saying such things to her, as if she were anything he could ever take
seriously or truly care about, like one of his own.

III.

*T*HE GREAT RIVER WHICH SWEPT below Korchlava city began in the marble hills above. The city knew it as the Chlav. In the hills, in the very depths of them, it had another name. Like the mines themselves.

"Welcome to Elusion. What's your business?"

"My lady, over there, and that I speak for, brings us to work here."

"Your *lady*, not your lord?"

"Master's dead. Her father. Wolves ate him in the forest. It upset her."

"It might." The man who leaned by the high rock gate picked his teeth, letting the dwarf wait. At length: "And that's her there, in the wagon?"

"Yes, my sir."

"With your ladylove." He meant Vinka, cuddled in close to the girl. The guard stared on for some moments. Men did become fascinated by Vinka, but not in any nice way. "Well," elaborated the gate man, "this is Elusion. If your fine lady, who scorns to come over here, wants you filthlings to work in the mines, then she must pay her tribute. We have royalty of our own, below ground. Have you heard? Speak up."

"The king," said Stormy. His voice was flat, respectful.

"The king! That king in the city—oh, he takes the stone and the gems, by Blessed Marusa. But he's not ruler, not in the hills. Not *under* the hills."

On the wagon, the girl sat with her face half-turned away. It was her usual pose. Stormy felt he could identify her better from that colorless smooth cheekbone, the wide plait of black hair, than any feature of her face. Except, maybe, her eyes. But Vinka was acting a lady's sweet pet, flicking little shy glances at the guard of the gate. The others had stayed in the wagon, unseen.

"So," said the guard, "once you're in, the prince's men will take your tribute. But here, *I* take it. You don't look wealthy. *She* doesn't, your mistress. What's her name?"

"Mistress is Coira."

"Oh, some wild name, that. What is she, a jumped-up whore? Three gold coins you can give me. Then you can go through."

Stormy looked timid, and went again to the wagon. He called up softly and Soporo, still unseen, pushed out the money. It was not gold, but a small bag of copper and silver. They had agreed beforehand, if there was this kind of demand, not to let on they possessed anything significant.

Trudging back to the guard though, Stormy prepared himself for a kick or blow. He was always the front man on such occasions. Soporo or Greedy could get careless, and Proud, tall and blond, could appear too . . . proud. As for the woman they had made their owner, God knew what she would have done. Nothing—everything—the wrong thing.

"Is this all you can offer me?"

"We regret. As you said, master my sir, we haven't much."

"Wolves eat that too? Your wagon, perhaps I'd like that."

"It's not handy. And the horses, look at them. They have the wet cough."

"They look like that, I agree. What about your lady, then. If she wants you in, what'll she give?"

Stormy crossed himself. "She's still grieving for her chewed dad."

The guard balked. He had found a larger piece of silver in the bag. "Get in, then. Go on with you. Don't waste more of my time. Remember, our own prince will require one-twentieth of any find in the mines." He meant, what Stormy would, of course, illegally keep back from his mining, stolen from King Draco. "And you'll need another coin, too. To pay the ferryman."

Stormy had heard of some of this, in towns below Korchlava they had passed through. But he blinked nervously.

"This is Elusion," repeated the guard. "And down there in the dark is Hate River. What else, in the Underworld?"

The Underworld—Elusion, the classical Hell.

These mines and quarries bored far into and below the surface of the hills, just as the wide river, turning to pour underground, carved through and through them. And here the Chlav became the River Hate—Stugus, Styx.

Beyond the gateway in the side of the hill, the track ebbed down into darkness. To the dwarves, this was an accustomed environment. If they had ever feared it, in childhood, say, no qualms remained. All mines represented a form of safety, for in them they had grown skilled, and adapted better than ordinary men. Always superior, here they realized their power.

But this girl who they must keep as protectress, who had said she would be called Coira, *she* might be afraid.

"There'll be lights presently," Tickle told Coira.

"Will there?" Coira did not sound anxious. She was always calm, deadly so. Her calm was her carapace, and this they knew.

The wagon juddered over flints and rocks. There was the smell of the white dust which descended from the upper quarries. Then, as the last daylight was sucked away, some torches appeared around the shoulder of the passage. And the scene they lit was fantastic enough.

Above, the belly of the hill rose high, and below the track ended on a shore of boulders and other debris, which in the glare of the torches was winking and glinting, as if the stone was pierced with eyes. At the shore a river moved by, sluggish, night-black, gleaming. It stretched away to either side, off into the darkness, nor was any farther shore to be seen.

Coira looked at it. She had read once of the River Styx, by which souls of the dead were conveyed into the Land of Shadows. Here it lay.

She felt cold, not on her skin, but under it. Where had she come without protest now?

There was a strange dim animal noise, indecipherable but growing louder. Just then a light began to appear out of the nothingness. It came gliding across the River Hate.

By now all the dwarves had jumped down from the wagon. Only Coira still sat above the horses, as if they were really hers.

A large, round-sided boat became visible, with two or three lanterns slung from its prow. The sounds rose from this boat. As it was rowed to the shore, Coira could see men packed on the deck, jostling and calling. One was singing.

The nose of the boat dredged itself up on the stones. The passengers sprang down. They were all types of men and a couple of women were with them, dressed alike in garments strapped round by leather. They had sacks and bags tied to their persons, each packed full. They were cheerful, going up to the world of the sun for a day, or forever.

A few jeered at the wagon and the dwarves. One man whistled shrilly at Vinka, and another grunted like a pig at the girl. But their disembarking minds were already far ahead of such things, up in the daylight. Anyone encountered down here, in the hour of holiday, was discounted.

The horde rushed by and was gone. Only the waddling boat remained.

It was not Death who was the ferryman, but three squat hulking men, one almost a dwarf himself. They threw out a ramp and roughly helped lead the unwilling horses on board. The wagon was secured on a platform bobbing at the rear. Coira, having got down, gave the crew her hands and let them pull her too up onto the deck.

She and the dwarves stood silent; the three ferrymen and their rowers were silent always. Only the water gulped against the boat.

As the shore folded back with its torches, all vestige of light seemed to die. It was indeed a kind of death, and unarguably a descent.

But then, after a time, everywhere beyond the boat's lanterns, twilight seemed to evolve.

Coira stared up. This dusk even had its impoverished stars. They must be plates or veins of metal in the cavern roof high overhead. They shone for a moment, then went out, and others shone instead.

Why have I let them bring me here?

But it did not matter where she went. All the earth was alike.

Nevertheless, Coira glanced at the faces of the dwarves. She was an alien among them, as she had always been alone among others. Yet their unspoken survivalism, their apparent sense of an aim, had caught her attention. During the grim winter journey, they had behaved toward her as adults might with some helpless child they had adopted in an indifferent charity. They gave her privacy wherever they could, brought her water, offered her food, even put it into her hands. Sometimes they talked together, apart from her. Tickle might say a word or two, usually of reassurance. Stormy informed Coira of their traveling plans, which town or village they might go into, or must avoid, as it had a chancy reputation. They were, in their own manner, very worldly-wise, while Coira knew nothing. But she could see they considered all but themselves inferior. When Proud now and then showed her some nearly sycophantic kindness, tucking a rug about her shoulders, putting a stalk of ginger into her wine at an inn, she saw these were not the gestures of an ingratiating servant, but of one who rather pitied her hopeless state.

Vinka was the only one who seemed sometimes lured by Coira. Vinka would slink against her, or into Coira's arm, like a silky affectionate cat. It seemed best not to resist these attentions. The dwarvixen would gaze at her, on and on, then shake her head, averting herself as if from an imperfect mirror.

Now their faces were all alike, set like granite with their purpose. How Coira envied them their purpose.

She herself had never found any goal—not after her first goal,

which had been to reach and be at one with the Woman, who subsequently was not to be her mother. If Coira had had a goal, would
she have been less easy prey for Ulvit, and so for Ulvit's plot to be
rid of her?

*What do I want? I too have wanted to live, to survive, I suppose, for
here I am.*

She had said she would be called Coira, not by the princess-
name of the palace. The dwarves simply accepted that. Of course
her royal name might be noticed, so near to the king's capital, if
only as unsuitable for a merchant's daughter who put her slaves into
the mine to earn bread.

Sometimes, on the journey, she missed the palace. How curious.
She missed the warm bed, but also the way the light came in at her
window, the sound of birds, and the ravens and crows in winter. She
missed gathering and preparing herbs, their aromas, the way their
colors changed—although she had never really cared for their prop-
erties of healing and harm.

What was she? Nothing, nothing. But, she was young.

Standing on the ferryboat of the River Styx, alone among the
dwarves and the silent crew, Coira felt this symbolistic death, and
lashed out desperately, suddenly against it. *No—I must have something! Oh, give me something—what can I have?*

Yet to what was she crying out? To the Christ, obdurate with
selflessness on His cross, or the gods of the savage wood?

Stormy—she had learned their remnant names—came up to
her.

Proud, when he approached, stood as tall as Coira's shoulder.
Stormy's crown was just above her elbow.

Startled, Coira looked down. The face he raised was much larger
than her own, older, and armored as if in a vizor.

"To be safe, you should cover your hair, mistress."

"All right."

There was such exasperation in his eyes. He frowned at her. Of
them all, *he* found her a burden.

"Speak to no one in Elusion Town. I'll talk. I normally speak for all of us. But you're on your own here, and a woman. The people in the mines—you saw them just now. You take my drift?"

"Yes."

"I won't—none of us will let them hurt you. That's our bargain. But you must do what I say."

"Yes. Thank you." She would not call him *Stormy*. Nor Anger. What had his name been? Had he been given a *human* name? She had not been able to intrude on him and ask. Or to say sharply, *Don't call me mistress.*

She put the plait of her hair up inside the shawl, and wound it close about her head and neck.

When the torchlit quay came in sight it was as grandiose as the awful river.

Cliffs reared up and dissolved in uncharted, smoky space. The rock of the cliffs had sinews and bulging muscles, and split in spots on seams of purest white, like skeletons. Marble was above, with quarries which opened to the sky. Marble was the core of all Korchlava's fabulous hills. And under that lay gold and copper, iron and silver, and, in sumps and grottoes whose secrets were often gained by murder, precious stones.

Unnatural tints fluttered in the air on the powder of dust. Perhaps they were the ghosts of dead rare emeralds, rubies, amethysts, malachite, and lapis lazuli.

Boats lay idle by the jetty. A shrine had been put there long ago to some saint, who raised a languid blessing hand. But his paint had rusted off and his enamel eyes had been thieved. Serves him right, the Elusians said, this Christian purveyor of poverty, for entering such a sink of riches.

Stormy had paid the crew of the boat.

They went ashore.

It was Proud who assisted Coira; Stormy and Soporo were busy with the fretting horses and the heavy awkward wagon.

Under the cliffs and up and down their shelves, and away and away inside them, rambled the miners' town. By day (and they kept rigorously to rituals of day and night down here) it was mostly quiet.

But from the galleries and chambers *inside* the rock came continuous weird ringings and mumblings, like far off bells under the sea, or giants moaning.

How terrible it is, this place, Coira wonderingly thought, as if she were coming awake at last, not out of a dark dream but into one.

A cottage on a hill—this was how Tickle described it, with a bark of laughter. It was a shack of castaway beams from the mines, and stones. However, it looked across the hills of rubble and rock to the valley where the peculiar Prince of Hell, evidently some other thief, had his mansion.

Nothing Coira had beheld was like this vista. But she had been shown very little.

Was it like Hell? If so, the classical Hell of shades and shadows, or the Christian one of flames?

For a fact, there were odors of sulphur in these caverns. But Belgra Demitu had reeked of that now and then from its Oracle. Here phosphorous flared in the dark, particularly near the river. And lanterns and torches, shallow clay lamps, fat candles—these fires, static or mobile, were everywhere.

The mansion of the prince itself blazed with red lights. From this distance, it was vivid as a dying sunset. But the architecture seemed like that of all the dwellings, an amalgamation of rubbish. Less a sunset than a bonfire.

A stream pushed through the rock valley. The Underworldians called it Woe Stream, feeding a pool they called Lethe. Trees grew there—or so it was said by those who had made the pilgrimage to visit the Prince of Hell.

Strangely, a tree of sorts grew by the dwarves' shack, which stood in an isolated position on its "hill." The tree, which hung down like a willow, consisted of the *roots* of a tree which had some-how established itself in the quarries overhead. Its tendrils were ghostly with the marble dust. When vibrations shook it, as off and

on they shook all the Underworld, puffs of white breath blew off
from it. The shack had, from this, become powdered, too. When
the torch was alight by the door, everything shone like the dull,
dire stars in the cavern's roof.

Two days before, as they had come up into the hills above Korchlava, Coira had seen her father's city below. It had been days away,
and meant nothing. But a voice had spoken in her head, chill and
precise: *Draco is king there.*

The city was indecipherable, a vague mass. It might have been
only geographical, if Soporo and Proud had not pointed it out to
each other.

But the first night below, a night timed by one of the candle-
clocks Tickle had acquired in Elusion's market, Coira dreamed she
left the shack-cottage and walked over the rocks towards the red-
windowed Hell palace in the valley. And it became instead her father's palace in Korchlava.

In the dream she presently arrived. She stood in a courtyard.
The yard was like those she remembered from Belgra Demitu, but
for the luminescent dark and dusty torchlight.

A wedding was taking place.

Quickly she understood it was her father Draco's wedding to
her mother, the bitch-queen Arpazia.

The crowd in the dream jostled and whistled and grunted.

Then Draco appeared. He was as Coira recalled him from earliest childhood, big, flushed, black-bearded. He wore a golden diadem. The woman who walked at his side, pristine in a slim white
gown, held something up before her face.

The crowd grumbled. They could not see her.

"What is that she's holding?"

"Make her take it away so we can look at her."

"It's a mirror!" a voice cried.

"A mirror! A mirror!"

"And real glass with a silvered back," said a grating and sala-cious voice almost in Coira's ear. "Worth a fortune. And we never knew."

"As well," said someone else. Coira opened her eyes and saw Proud standing between her and the light. "Robbers would have been after it."

"I'm glad we never knew it was there," trembled Want.

"We were perched on it, like God on His glass throne."

Coira sat up. A sleeping place had been made for her, unasked, by Want and Tickle, and decorated with cushions from the wagon (Vinka). The bed was in a kind of alcove at one end of the shack's large lower room. Vinka had also hung a shawl to screen it, partly concealing Coira from the dwarves or the dwarves from Coira.

None of them took any notice of Coira now.

They were all of them by the fire-pit. Something had been dragged there and laid on rugs, half-propped up by a small chest. They had been unloading the wagon, since they meant to barter the horses tomorrow, before arranging their work in the mine.

"Where did he get it?"

"Cirpoz—he'll have stolen it."

Coira could see it now, how it gave off a sharp glister every time the flames brightened. It was like a slice of water lying sideways. Like Lethe's clear pool of forgetting.

"My mother's mirror."

They craned round and looked at the stupid charity child. None of them spoke.

Then Soporo said, "Mistress said, whose?"

"My—my mother's. The queen, Draco's first wife."

Soporo hawked and spat in the fire. It spat back, green. (And the mirror was an emerald newly mined.)

"Mistress is princess-mistress. I forgot."

Stormy, kneeling the other side of the fire-pit, said, "It would be a queen's mirror. Who else could own such a thing?"

"They're magic. Dangerous," Vinka now. "Smash it!"

"That's bad luck," said Tickle. "Mirrors are full of souls . . ."

"Sell it," said Greedy. "Sell it tomorrow."

When had Coira ever heard them speak so much?

She had risen. She walked across and stood gazing down at the mirror where it lay, slantwise.

The silver lid, with its gold ornamentation, lay open like a broken wing. Soporo was crouching, fingering its costliness. Want had shrunk aside, frightened as usual.

... And the mirror *saw* ...

Coira looked down and down into the mirror's glass.

What did it show? The uneven ceiling of the shack, held by splintered beams. A wall. Firelight. And, deep in the circle, as in the pool of forgetting, a leaning woman, slender, white, great-eyed, holding back two waves of inky hair with her narrow hands.

Is that me? Is that Coira? Or—

Is it she—my mother—as I saw her that day I said, "You're so beautiful—more beautiful than anyone in the whole world."

Coira felt she would soon fall into the mirror-pool, whirl down for ever and be lost.

And then Stormy appeared beside her, bending over to tap the glass with his strong smith's hand.

And then Proud was leaning over too, admiring his golden glamour. Here and there he had been shown himself in metal mirrors. He almost knew what he looked like.

It was Proud, offended, who cried, "What are you at—?" as Stormy scooped huge handfuls of soot and dirt from the edges of the fire and smeared them across the burning surface of the glass.

IV.

*A*ND THE MIRROR GAZED through the dirt and soot, through miniscule cracks of light left unsmothered.

I am fire, said a torch beyond the door.

I am darkness, said the dark.

I, too, answered the mirror, am now both.

But the mirror watched through the cracks Stormy had inadvertently left. It had been leant on a wall, and fixed there by ropes, and bits of sack hung on it, so mostly disguised, it looked only like part of the uneven plaster of mud over stones and beams, with holes in it, not glass.

Its eyelid had been taken off. The silver and slight gold were gone, to be smelted down by Soporo and Greedy, who were skilled in this method.

Naked, the mirror. Unable to close its eye, gazing through the dirt.

Vinka passed by. She did not like or look at the mirror. She knew she was beautiful and had nothing to ask.

Want hid from the mirror, pretended it was only the wall.

The dwarves came and went, establishing themselves and their employment.

Coira stole to the mirror once, when she was alone in the shack-cottage. She touched the black muck which obscured the surface. Then Coira spoke aloud. "I still won't look at you. I may see her there. Her reflection, caught there."

For Coira had seemed to see Arpazia in the mirror, that first time when she stared in and saw herself.

Tickle's time candles marked the hours. Each one burned for a day and a night, and they were as tall as Want or Greedy.

Within a day, Soporo, Greedy, Proud, and Stormy had gained work in the gold mines which circled round inside the cliffs. Tickle went with them; she was an able miner too. Want and Vinka preferred, when they could, to be out of the workings and see to the domestic side of things. Here, since they might choose for themselves, this was what they did.

At dawn—which was signaled by the blowing of trumpets about the cavern—the five miners rose, prepared themselves and set off.

They would be gone until the hour of upperworld sunfall, or even later, because it was winter in the upper world and the sun sank early. No trumpets marked this hour, only the time candles marked it, should you look at them. In any case, the mine workers, especially the clever dwarves, were often required to labor on beyond sunfall into the hours of "night," even until midnight, which *was* signaled, by a single horn blown near the Hell-mansion in the valley.

The wages the dwarves received they brought back unfailingly to their shack-house. There they divided everything equally, even the portions of gold dust they had managed to purloin. Activity in the mines was often unsafe. The booming sounds which came from them represented engines of rock-crushing, or falls of rock. Often the dwarves returned much bruised, but by then they had revealed ancient scars to which the bruising was not comparable.

Want and Vinka ordered the shack's day. They cleaned the upper and lower rooms a little, brooming out the white dust, which instantly settled again. They fetched water from a public cistern above Elusion Town. They went marketing. Coira joined in these activities. She was reckoned to be their mistress. Supervising them publicly was sometimes needful.

The cistern stood beside a cinder track. It was fed from the stream called Woe. The story said that any who drank much of the water eventually went mad from sorrow. The Elusians compensated by drinking colossal quantities of wine and beer and other potencies brewed by stills of the Underworld.

Farther down, the town wended round the cliffs and in parts went up into them. The always-night was gaudily lit up there. Guards patroled the entrances to the mines. They would search those who came out, but randomly, and they were bribable, and tended to be drunk.

The market was on a wide flat space, illumined by torches. Everything was barter there. Even coins were barter, and had different values than they would have done above.

During market excursions, Vinka and Want clung to Coira's skirts, as if to hold her in check. Neither of her dresses, purchased haphazardly during the journey, was very sturdy. Sometimes Want's agitated clutchings tore the cloth. Then Vinka insisted Coira get herself a better gown. "You're mistress. We mustn't be ashamed of you."

Vinka, volatile, catlike, was never to be trusted—who was? Coira accepted a secondhand gown. It was of a yellowing milky silk, with heavy borders stitched with tarnished metal thread. Vinka had expressly chosen it. Vinka then bought a green dress for herself, the garment of a big child, which Tickle or Want would have to resew, for it did not quite fit Vinka's form. Want (Covetousness) gazed at this finery with fearful dislike. Want wanted nothing.

The money they spent was from dead Cirpoz's trove. Vinka assured Coira it was stolen anyway, perhaps from Coira's own kingly father.

Coira carried most of the articles back from the market. They had by then bartered the horses for various goods, and she did not like to make the dwarvixens into beasts of burden. So she became their donkey.

In the market, and going about, they were not much stared at. All types of people lived in the caverns of Elusion. There were other dwarves, too, some immensely strong, and giant men seeming nearly twice the height of an average man. There were also stone-white Elusians, whose skin had been remade by the marble dust of the higher quarries, and others with pink eyes, and blacker than charcoal from the deposits of carbon and fire. Occasionally some man might attempt to help or hinder them. It was Vinka who saw them off, snarling and yipping. Though small, her fists were like steel—Coira had seen her break a pot with one and stay unmarked herself.

By evening, indistinguishable from other times save on the candle, the two housekeeper dwarvixens were preparing a meal.

This would be porridge or soup, kept bubbling on the fire for whenever the others might return. Want baked bread, laying the flat cakes on the hot ashes. Coira's only culinary knowledge had been with herbs, of which they had few and about which they asked no advice.

Coira was the child, still. Undoubtedly something of a nuisance. As often as they felt like it, Want and Vinka spoke in an invented gabble, or slunk off to their own area, curtained by a thick sack. Only if Vinka plunged into one of her terrifying furies would Want run to Coira, getting behind the girl, even among her skirts, as Vinka thrashed about the room, smashing crocks with her fists, slinging water on the fire and fire into corners, shrieking in what seemed to be demonic tongues. By now Coira had witnessed these rages several times. Valerian might, Coira thought, have assisted Vinka, or starry-seal. None of these was available, and besides, Coira had no compassion for Vinka. She had no compassion for anyone, she believed. No, none.

Yet this was not quite true.

She shared what tasks she could, mostly to evade tedium, rolling up the sleeves of the preposterous new gown, and tying a cloth round her hair, a shawl about her waist.

With supper, a bath was also got ready to wash and ease the five miners.

When they came in, the mining dwarves were like creatures from an awesome myth. Their eyes flashed white in blackened faces pared by the stress of great toil. But they did not seem unhappy.

Tickle was always first in the bath, amused and unselfconscious, throwing off her mining garments. The men followed when she was done, in random order, although Proud was usually the next after Tickle. And Stormy usually the last of all.

Vinka and Want scrubbed at them with cloths, oil, and fat-soap, rubbing and sluicing them until the water became like liquid pitch. Stormy, when the last, would have himself sluiced again by a clean bucketful—his only affectation.

Coira had been initially horrified to see them naked. It was not nudity that perturbed her, she had been partly reared by a pagan. Nor was her inhibition due exactly to their physical appearance. She did not wish to see these beings nude. As she did not wish them to see her in such a way, and took care that they did not. They were now her constant companions. But like all companions of hers, could not be intimates. Inert, she had remained with them, but did not want to try to draw close to them. This stripping of coverings removed a barrier.

Nevertheless, she did see them. And presently, when Proud and Soporo irrelevantly called her over, she joined in, too, with this chore of washing them.

Their naked bodies were strange to her but not unattractive. They were so strong, every part of them put to use. They reminded her of trees, grown tall only in *girth*, their twisting sinews, the grain of their brown skins, the ribbed scars like a history, and the humps that rose from Soporo and Greedy like buildings carved from their wood. Tickle too was humped, but the skin of her shoulders, breasts, and of the hump itself, was an opulent creamy white. Seen in the bath, joking and friendly—most kind to Coira, sensing Coira's rebuttal and unease—she reminded the girl of the nymph who had *changed* to a tree—or, of a dryad.

Coira coped with the baths well enough. She was circumspect but quite indifferent to the maleness of Soporo, which he flaunted at her insultingly, whispering lewdness as she scrubbed his back, alternately accusing her of hurting the sensitive hump, or suggesting she might rub that other part of him, rising engorged from the water. He always called her endlessly "mistress" at such times.

But she did not *like* to wash Stormy. And mostly she avoided it, leaving him to the slavish Want and falsely lascivious Vinka. And it was, with Stormy, his maleness which distressed her, but not only that.

In the terracotta lamplight, when he stood up to be rinsed by the final bucket, his fearful scarred beauty drove away her eyes. Of all the seven tawny, twisted, and muscled dwarves, he was perfect. His chest was like a bronze shield. His short bowed legs like carved ivory. Even his male weapon, couthly quiescent at his thigh, though large was well-made, and velvet-cased. Her gaze would drop quickly down to his scar-ridged and bulging ankles, the feet which now angled, both, slightly the same way.

He, too, turned his back on her when he could.

But at night exhaustion ruled the mining dwarves. Bathed, they ate, shared their profits, and went to sleep in selected corners of the odd-shaped lower room.

As time and the candles passed, Proud and Tickle resumed sexual relations and went up the ladder after supper to the murky upper chamber.

Soporo meanwhile began an affair with a pair of mining women, "real" women who lived in one of the caves above the town, and absented himself from the communal shack. He would meet the others on the road to the mine in the un-morning, bright as gold from nights of ceaseless copulation.

Vinka and Want were more and more often off together. They eluded Coira, giggling from apparent maleficence. (She was reminded of Julah and Kaya.)

When in the shack, Greedy slept, farting melodiously from time to time, in a big crib he had made for himself out of bits of beam and straw.

They were already rich, Coira believed. They had successfully melted down the mirror's silver lid. But none of them showed any urge to leave the Underworld, even to go up and see the sun. And none of them asked Coira's opinion. Even in the matter of her mother's looking glass. Coira owned them, therefore she belonged to them, and had no say.

As ever alone among others, Coira was now alone—and *alone*.

V.

*H*IS SHADOW STRODE BEFORE
the torch ahead of him, into
the shack-house.

It was a tall, broad shadow, that of a man over six feet, and
heavy boned, and cloaked in hair.

Coira, though she knew it for a shadow, started up.

The two dwarvixens, Want, Vinka, were away as usual. Coira
was all alone, and alone.

He walked in. He moved in a limping strut, full of bravura, and
from that by itself she would have known who it was. But she only
stared at him.

Stormy looked at her, and looked aside.

"Don't get frightened, but someone came for me in the workings. We must go and visit their prince, here."

"We—"

"I, because I do the talking. And you, mistress. Since you own us.
It's because of the mirror lid, the smelting. Soporo swore no one
would tell, but someone has. This prince will want to know where we
got the silver from. And he'll expect a share of it. So, he shall have
it. It's not so bad as it sounds. All will be well. But we have to go."

She had heard, here and there in Elusion, conjecture that perhaps
Hell's prince was a bastard of King Draco's (and so another half
brother of her own.) Others said he was a bandit from across the
River Chlav, under sentence of the gallows in the city.

This prince had less importance for Coira even than Tusaj. Who
had ever been important? One. And now—now this one, limpingly
striding at her side, the crown of his dark head just above her elbow.

Once she stumbled. The track was shale and stones and uni-
dentifiable broken stuffs. Not halting his swagger-stagger gait, he

reached out and steadied her. He was strong as a horse. *Stronger* than Cirpoz's two ill-kept horses.

She wished she were not with him, and that they did not have to make this further journey together. Yet her blood leapt about. She felt alive and angry—angry as his name.

"Before you came in, I was thinking," she said. "I might as well leave you. But I suppose you won't let me. You say you need me to pretend I'm your mistress."

"How could we prevent you?" Stormy remarked flatly.

"There are seven of you. One of me. You all hate me, of course," she heard herself say, with astonishment.

He said nothing.

She added, and again the bitter grievance in her voice amazed her, "I have nowhere else to go, in any case."

"You miss the sunlight," he said.

"Do I? No. What does the sun matter? I don't miss anything. All this, all that—what does any of it mean to me?"

Shocked and dislocated, she had been—in a trance. It seemed they ran in her family. It had lasted two or three months. Above, the winter had filled the world. Down here, only cold night filled it. She was waking now. Had the stumble woken her, unlocking the choking hold on her heart? His hand had caught her arm, steadying, and rocking her like a tempest. The hand had woken her, not the stumble. Yet she had put her own hands on *him* already, in the disgusting black bath.

Two things happened to Coira. Her blood, her loins, burst into flame, melting like the silver from the mirror. And utter despair froze her, harder than an icicle.

If he guessed any of it, he did not reveal. But he did glance at her, and then away. He was scowling and his mouth had set in a grimace, as when he acted his part as the Sin of Rage.

Below the slopes were more areas of ramshackle lit-up night-town. They wove through cots built of posts, and tents of rotted leather, and under the stinking holes of caves. Then they were down in a type of trough, and walked under the columned galleries of the cliffs, where, even so, the inescapable marble dust floated down and round in drifts. Soon they passed a subground entry to the quarries, deadly pale against the firelit dark. Some pale creatures sat there, dicing, like damned figures from a warning priestly book.

"There's the boat," said Stormy.

In panic, she thought he meant the boat to return her, via the River of Hate, to the upper world, and she exclaimed *"No!"* But her voice, once more amazing her, was inaudible.

It was not the ferryboat, but a kind of raft, and she saw they had reached the stream called Woe, which was quite wide.

"Payment," said the old man who poled the raft.

"Forgo that," said Stormy. "Hadz summoned us."

"Oh, our Prince Hadz. Get on, then."

Coira said, foolishly, "Is he really named Hadz—like the god of the dead?"

"Yes," said Stormy.

They stood on the raft, which dipped and squeaked. The dark waters of the stream eddied about them, looking unnegotiable, and giddy and crazy as life itself.

But the gray old man determinedly poled them along, his back to them.

"What is your name?" Coira said to the dwarf.

His raging face did not alter.

"Mistress knows my name."

"Stop calling me *mistress*. I won't have it. Stop. Tell me your name."

"Stormy. I play Anger."

"No. Your *name*. Don't you have a name?"

"It's mine."

"Oh, keep it, then."

He grinned, but not glancing at her. "Are you having a turn, like Vinka?"

"Yes. But she has them when her courses are due or come on. They're very irregular and that makes her worse."

"Women's mysteries." He was humble, not coarse.

"I saw Hadz once. I mean, the god-king of death. When I was

a child. I thought it was a dream . . . but now I think they took me there, into the wood. And I saw him."

"You're a witch. I thought you were."

"My mother was a witch. The witch-queen."

The stream was very wide now. The shore was visible on either side, but it was far off, and looked unreachable, and the lights smoked along it garishly, or there were *no* lights, and blackness yawned. As for the raft, it was flimsy. The old man was a phantom. And they were all in Hell.

Stormy said to her, "I heard—she was a cruel woman, your mother, that queen."

"She hated me. They always hate me."

"They hate dwarves too. Anything different."

"I have no reason to be alive," she said, without any passion or complaint. Yet her blood swirled and coiled and glittered like the frightful Stream of Woe.

"I had a mother," said Stormy softly. He looked out, as she did, past the old man into the dark, where they were going. "No father, mind you. She gave me a shiny name. Then she saw what I was going to be, so she threw me off a hill."

Coira heard herself make a sound. Both of them ignored it.

"That's how my ankles were shattered. I was about two. Someone found me. The ankles mended wrongly, but they mended. Then I was put into the mines. Don't think I dislike mines. They're my home. I know where I am, there."

Coira said, "I must sit down. I'll fall off into the water." She sat down. Seated, he towered above her, but still he did not turn. She said, "It must hurt you so much—your ankle bones."

He said, "My mother called me, before she threw me off the hill, Hephaestion."

Coira put her head on her knees and cried.

The old man poled for their hidden destination.

After the raft grounded, they got off and went across the valley. He noted the skirt of her silk gown was soaking, as if she had wet herself or been monumentally fucked. But, poor thing, it was her tears.

The Christ knew what he felt.

No, he knew. But he put that aside.

It was almost the way he had felt for Vinka, once, before he *knew* Vinka, and how she was or would never be. Almost, but not the same. For Vinka was one of his own race. And this giantess, so slender he could snap her in two, she was from the other breed of cattle called Mankind.

The valley was strange but Stormy—Hephaestion—did not notice it particularly. He did note the paved road which had been made there and which they presently got onto. The stones were uneven; it was probably less helpful than the shale and litter.

Ahead lay the mansion. A conglomeration of shacks and huts that joined themselves to caves in the cliff behind, at the valley's back. It was like all the other dwellings of Elusion, save for being linked together. And there was a facade. A line of pillars had somehow been fashioned. Tree trunks, they seemed to be. There were nine of them, each one three times a man's height, and they held up the lopsided edges of the shack roofs.

A living tree grew by the mansion—at least, perhaps it was still alive. The marble dust had coated it thinly, its curving boughs and lifted, fossilized traceries. A poplar. It was whiter than snow.

The pool lay behind it, the one called Lethe, or Forgetting. The water was said to be outright fatal, worse than the stream, but some figures were there, drawing it up in buckets and jars.

Hell's prince had his own guard. One of these villains now came ambling over, bristling with knives and studs.

"What do you want?"

"I'm the dwarf Stormy, and this is my mistress. He sent for us."

"Well, if he did and you don't go to him, it will be a nasty thing for you. But he might not want you now. He's sick today," added the guard. Oddly, he marked himself with the cross. "That thing where he screams."

"I've heard of that." Stormy handed the guard a little pouch which held gold dust. "I found this on the way. Yours, I expect."

The guard took the pouch, examined it, and let them into Hell's mansion.

This was like life, too. You must even pay to be abused, as you were punished for being hurt.

But Coira did not care.

After her tears she felt cleansed and frivolous. She looked about her at the muddled interior. Lightless cells opened one into another, passages narrow as pins squeezed between. Everywhere sacking curtains hung down, but there were also curtains of sequined velvet. The braziers and fire-pits caused smoke, as elsewhere, and people came and went on slavish missions.

They were taken to an overseer or steward in one of the small rooms. By then, they had heard howls ringing through the mansion. Not some victim under torture, apparently, but Prince Hadz.

She said boldly to Hephaestion, "Why is he sick?"

"Some pain that comes in his head. He's always had it, so I've heard."

"It must be very bad," she said, careless.

Then the steward bulked in, a fat ruffian with earrings of gold.

He looked straight at Coira. "Been shedding tears? Why are you crying? Afraid we've found you out?"

Stormy said at once, "Mistress's father was killed above ground. She's always crying over that."

"What killed him?"

"Wolves," said Coira clearly. "They ate him alive."

The steward grunted and turned away.

"You've cheated on your tithes to the prince. You have silver, a lot of it, and never gave him his dues."

Another cry tore round the mansion. As if the dwarves had caused Prince Hadz's agony by their defiant act.

"How long does his pain last?" asked Coira politely.

"That yelling? A day, sometimes two. But to return to your crime."

Stormy spoke. "No crime, master. The silver was the property of mistress. Her father gave it to her. So we melted it down. And I have the prince's portion here with me."

Coira's mind wandered from this. Yet it did not let go of him, of Hephaestion. Even looking up at the ceiling of the chamber, where black rags drooped like sleeping bats, Hephaestion was there. *His hair is like black bats. No, it curls too much for that. Like coils of copper turned black. Black grapes.* She smiled at her silly thoughts, and the overseer-steward again picked on her.

"What do you laugh at, you woman?"

Coira glanced at him. He did not matter, as nothing did, so she said, "There's a herb that could assist Prince Hadz. Febrifuga."

"Ah?" said the overseer. He was interested now in the silver ingots. "There's more?"

Stormy: "No, master. It was only from a hand glass."

"Someone told it was as big as you are."

Stormy chuckled. "Someone dreamed."

Coira watched the firelight dance here and there. And in black eyes that were only stones, shadows.

She heard the overseer say, "He found out you do an act of the Great Sins."

"Sometimes, master."

"He might like to see that, some other day."

A heart-splintering cry rushed over now, beating with its wings to get free.

Coira bit her lip to stop herself laughing at the suffering of the world.

By the time they left the mansion, her tears were falling again. But many came out of that place sobbing.

According to the candles, further days and nights passed. Nothing might have happened. Even the dwarves' unease about the silver and the thief-prince faded, for there were no more challenges.

Coira had begun to walk sometimes in the Underworld. More or less known now as belonging to the seven tough dwarves, she was not attacked and seldom accosted. She had no money, had never asked for any. She sold things instead in the market, one of the two uncouth dresses, the first pair of shoes they had bought for her, since replaced. She even considered selling her long hair, which she still covered over on her walks. She did not know why she did any of this. Was she preparing to leave the dwarves and go out alone on to the winter earth? *Where* would she go? Korchlava—why? And *why* would she go?

On the journey back from the valley, she and he had not exchanged a word. Save for the intermittant courtesies—*Here, let me help you, the track's worse—Thank you for your help.*

They had ridden another raft only part of the way. He had stood by the polesman, this time a burly youth with one eye, exchanging local news. Avoiding her.

He had avoided her after, too. He did not always now come back to the shack-house. He let Soporo's two women bathe him, or found some outlet of the river to wash in, or went dirty. He went off with Greedy, drinking at a still-shop up the cliff.

He. Hephaestion.

I could go to the city and become a whore. I could live by that.

I could live in some village, making up herbs for their illnesses, and hoping not to poison them by mistake, because I never learned all Ulvit taught me.

I could go back to Belgra Demitu and slap Ulvit's face, or have her killed, as she tried to ruin me.

None of these things were believable. Such cities and villages and people no longer existed. (Did Ulvit? Did *Arpazia* exist?)

There was only the Underworld ruled by an unseen, howling arch-thief. And Hephaestion.

Alone in the shack, she said aloud to herself, "He is like *her*, like the Woman—my—perhaps my mother. He doesn't want me near him. That's why he stays away."

But the most bizarre thing had happened. Coira, who had been lessoned that she might expect nothing from anyone else, did not at last credit that. She had been an infant, now she was a woman, and Hephaestion a man. It seemed to her—so very curiously—that she need only reach out, as if to some summer tree laden with glowing fruit—to pluck what she would have and feed herself over and over.

Coira did not know why she thought this, after all her other thoughts. Nor did she ask herself why young and handsome men had sometimes in the past moved before her, and she had barely seen them.

Hephaestion was a few years older than she, but had the looks of a man of thirty. He had the body of a tree. His feet were crippled. The crown of his head reached only just above her elbow.

It did not occur to her, in her feral and innocent desire, to wonder if he would feel used or patronized by her interest. It *was* in her awareness that to the dwarves, all of them, ordinary humans were foreigners, trustless but inferior.

But not she. Not she with him. Which was her idiocy, for why should she seem any different to him?

He was the height of a tall child, but had five times her strength. Twenty times her knowledge. His limping grace stunned her. His beauty made her heart scorch so she wanted to tear herself apart before him and throw the pieces of herself against his spurning flesh. Oh, she was the child, not he.

It was night. The time-candle said so.

Above, the upper floor shifted faintly as Proud and Tickle made love on their mattress. Soporo was off with his pair of lemans. Want and Vinka were silent and motionless behind their curtain. Greedy was out drinking. Hephaestion too had not come in.

Coira had blown out her personal lamp, washed herself head to toe behind her own screen, put on her shift, in which Cirpoz had stolen her, and wrapped over that the ragged cloak.

She emerged, crossing over to heat a cup of watered wine at the fire-pit. She moved softly, not to disturb or alert the dwarves.

As she knelt there, she found she stared up at the mirror tethered to the wall. Blackened, occulted, and disregarded, she had nearly forgotten it all this while.

Coira got to her feet. She moved noiselessly to the mirror. Putting one finger on the muck, she scraped a little spot away.

She gazed into her own eyes then, that were like the eyes of the mirror itself.

Was this she? Or some sorcery . . .

To the eyes, whispering, she spoke.

"Make him come here. Make him come to me. Now. At once. Wherever he is. Make him come here. *Mirror, mirror, make it true. Make him mine by power of you.*"

How long she stood there, whisper-whispering, half-singing, without sound, her rhyme, again and again, she did not know. Miles off, she heard the wine boil over and go out harmlessly on the flames. (The pan would be spoiled.) She heard the surrealistic noises of Elusion, distant echoing shouts, filmy settlings from the mines, a baby that meowed and grew quiet.

Then, she heard—him, coming in at the door, and from her eye's edge, saw the shadow that strode before him, high as the ceiling. He was a giant.

She was too afraid to turn. Then she turned.

He stood there, glaring sadly at the fire. He smelled of the acid brews of the stills, and of the river he had bathed in. And of skin and life, of himself, and uncannily familiar, as if she had known him always.

Coira drew off the burned-out pan, and filled another with diluted wine. She let it heat, then poured it in a cup. All this while he stood there, waiting. She handed him the cup. He drank, catching his breath at the wine's temperature. Then he followed her to her alcoved wall of the shack. They moved inside the half-transparent curtain, and all the world was shut out.

"I made you come back," she said, shaking aside the crow wings of her undone hair, arrogant in humiliation.

"I thought so. I felt it pulling me here, your spell. I knew you were a witch from the start. At the inn, when you made him leave you alone. Your mother was a witch, they said."

"Perhaps not my mother. She hated me. Do you?"

"I? Hate you . . . you're another race than mine."

"Will it matter?" She drew in all her breath and said his name, "Hephaestion, will it matter?"

"Yes."

"Am I repugnant to you?" she asked. But she stared in his face, and for the first time in her life, she felt herself to be (the mirror's sorcery) beautiful. As beautiful as the queen, Arpazia—no, no, fairer far than Arpazia. Fairest in the world.

"Let's not talk," he said. "We can't talk, you and I. Sit down." She sat. He sat by her. This way, they were almost of a height. "I've had a woman, once or twice. I mean, your breed of woman. No unkindness was in it."

Then she turned and pressed her face against his, her profile to his, her nose pressed into his, her eyes blinded by his, and her lips spoke on his mouth. "But I love you."

He kissed her quickly, light, without meaning. He drew back slightly and said, "No, but you don't, Coira."

Her name. He had said her name. She put her hands around his head and locked her fingers in his hair and pulled him home again against her mouth. It was like the mirror, too, but *he* lived.

"I love you. I only ever loved *her*. But I love *you*."

"All's vanity," he said.

"Not vanity. It's *love*."

"Very well. Then—yes, you love me. I see you must do, if you cast a spell to bring me here."

They kissed now more deeply, but still with face pressed awkwardly to face, the way a face must press flat against its own self in a glass.

She felt his tongue, wine-hot in her mouth. She wrapped his tongue with hers. She drank his breath, wanting to suffocate him or to be suffocated, to drop down with him into the chasm of feeling and fear and desire that was expanding now between them.

His hands moved on her waist. It was like a dance. He lifted her up and she was lying back. He found her breasts inside the shift. She tore the thin stuff away so he must put his lips on her bare skin.

"You smell so sweet," he said. "I stink of the mines and the river—"

"You smell of metal and fire," she said.

"Your hair," he said, "as if all the bloody night fell in through the hill—"

When he tried to take her, she felt her virgin's body sealed too close. It was impossible. She was like some wall. She forced herself against him, struggling. "Lie still," he said, "be patient." He stroked her until the impossible wall melted. Then she felt him break her open like the wound of death. But she was born in him.

Connected now, as if one creature, they thrust together in a battle. The sound of their breathing filled the Underworld. Then they entered some other place through the fabric of the dark, brighter than the sun, and died in each other's grip.

"I'm sorry that I hurt you. Sometimes it has to be, the first time."

"Is that all?"

"Was it so disappointing? You seemed not to think so."

"But it ends so soon."

"It kills you otherwise. It can always be done again."

"Do it again to me."

"In a while."

"Perhaps the night won't end. Look how strong the candle is, still."

"Nights end. Days end. What are these little scars on your arm?"

"They let my blood once, when I had a fever. What are *these* scars, here?"

"The lord beat me when he was drunk."

"I hope he's dead and in Hell."

"He is. We are too, supposedly."

"Yes." She sighed. "Thank God. We're safe in Hell."

The White Snow Falls

SEVEN DAYS AFTER MIDWINTER-
Mass, snow covered Belgra Demitu.
It had come from the mountains in
the east, flying down to the sea like white swans. Perhaps, through
the years, a flurry of flakes had speckled the air. But no sooner did
they touch the earth than they were gone. This snow settled in a
cloud. Such snow had never seen there—*never*, not in a century.

"Black is the wood, white is the snow . . ."

What did the mirror see looking in? A young girl? No. There
was no young girl, and the mirror was gone.

"Snow," announced the woman, the crone. "And land, and sky.
Nothing else."

But she observed something shifting through the avenues of the
whiteness. The wind, wolves, riders. (Fate again was bounding over
the snow's book, toward her.)

Black is the wood—

"Hush," she said. She spoke to herself.

She withdrew into the shell of her thoughts.

*   *   *

Arpazia dreamed, and the wood was red as a ruby. The snow was black, and something pale flowed down—

But then, the snow was black, and the trees were white, peeled by the scorings of the tusks of beasts, and a red stream, rippling—

The white trees rose from the blood-red snow.

Arpazia saw she bled, and her blood was blacker than night.

Aggrieved, Prince Tusaj turned the letter in his hands. His father had not, of course, penned it; Draco could hardly write his own name, some scholarly scribe had seen to this, and so knew all the words.

Draco had abruptly recalled he had a legitimate daughter here. She was of marriageable age, in fact, seventeen or so, and present-able (said Draco) according to Tusaj's earlier information. Send her then to Korchlava (said Draco).

Which would be difficult, the girl having just been lost.

Tusaj had already been put out, because he had meant to pur-chase some of that fellow's dwarves, not all of them, but the three best ones, the tall blond, and the angry sable, and that minx with green eyes. But Cirpoz had taken them off before Tusaj had the chance.

And now this. Tusaj feared the king, it went without saying.

"Write—write that she's sick. Very sick, may die. Some female thing..."

Tusaj was also no scholar, and the scribe bent to his paper in the tremblous light of winter candles, unsettled as they and the prince.

"... Some female malady," repeated the scribe.

"Yes—what do they suffer from?"

"They are like us, sir, in many ways..."

"No, they're women."

At a loss, both men fumbled after secret, grisly-sounding ailments, muttered over by doxies and grannies in their boyhoods.

"Perhaps, Lord Prince, this terrible harsh winter—the cold and snow which never before—"

"That won't do."

But Tusaj looked from his window, down across the terraces and gardens, become all a desert of whiteness, to the vanished sea they said was hard as a silver mirror.

Was this some curse? Some sorcery?

Tusaj relaxed his grasp on the black wood of the windowframe.

"Wait."

"Sir, I merely—"

"Shut your noise. Let me think. What do they say of the old woman—his ugly old wife—Arpasha—Arpadzia—whatever her name is? She's a witch, isn't she?"

"They say so, my lord."

"I know she is. She goes to the wood . . . oh, some of them do that just for a bit of fun, but what fun can she get there now? No, with her it's sorcery. And she's lost her mind as well as her looks. Jealous. Green-eyed jealousy. Draco cast her off for her sourness and her devilish glamourings. Then it's her fault. She's envious and has done something against the girl. I *smell* it."

Trimming his quill with unsteady fingers, the scribe had nicked himself. A drop of blood fell on the parchment. But this would not be a problem, a new sheet would anyway need to be used.

Tusaj was almost happy now. He thought, warmly, *Draco dreads the witch. He'll be glad to blame her with the Church to back him—perhaps be rid of her once and for all.*

No one came near Arpazia. Even her waiting-women, a girl and a matron, neither intelligent, kept away as much as they could. She sent for no one. Arpazia fended for herself in her mean, cold rooms.

Rather than bother with making a fire, if no other had seen to it, she would wind herself in her mantle and some covers from the bed.

She sat thinking, thinking. Then she would get up, pace about. Thinking.

There had been a water-clock, but nobody replaced its liquid. Now her steps were the drip-drip of the mechanism.

The door was scratched upon. Arpazia believed it was mice. They had got into several of the rooms of the palace, driven there by the extremes of this winter.

When the scratching came again, Arpazia heard a human voice. It was elderly and had an edge.

"Let me in, Queen."

She took no notice.

Then the old woman undid the door and walked straight in.

A hag, as ever, one of the kindred of the Smoke Crone.

"I said," said Arpazia, sat there in her bed-covers, "you and your sisters should keep away."

"Yes, just so. You tired of us. Never mind it. I'm not here for that."

Arpazia bit at her finger absently. Like a child.

The hag approached.

"Where is your witch-glass, Queen?"

"I gave it away."

"Where is your daughter?"

Arpazia laughed. "I have no daughter."

"Yes."

"Then she's dead."

"Then you ordered her death."

"I?" asked Arpazia, ingenuous.

"Tusaj has written to Draco. Tusaj says you worked a spell on the girl that caused her to die. Either that or you spelled some hapless simpleton to murder her. Soon the priests will seek you out, Arpazia, and put you to the test for sorcery. Do you know what that means?"

"You are all witches," said Arpazia, "here." But her face had

altered, grown transparent with alarm—even if her eyes stayed vacant, not yet catching up with it.

"We are good Christian women, Queen. And besides, Tusaj
comes to dance with our girls in the wood. He'll point a finger at
none but you. It's only you they all detest, Arpazia."

"Yes, they hate me. You all hate me."

"*We* have warned you."

"Useless," said Arpazia. "What can I do?"

"Are you tied up? Are your ankles chained? Are you so old you
can't walk? Get up from your chair and take yourself away."

Arpazia thought, *I should have gnawed through the cords and escaped
Draco long ago. But I am a fool. Shall I do it now, at last?*

When she looked round, the hag had gone.

The room seemed full of hoarfrost, and the unlit braziers blue
with ice. It was much colder than the world outside.

She never heard the silent voices, telling the antique tale of the
goddess over. How Demetra, having lost her daughter, and not
knowing it was to the god of the Lands Below, went seeking her,
wandering about the earth, in the first winter of all, which was created by her own grief and desolation.

But the pagans of Belgra Demitu (whose very name meant
Ground of the Goddess Demetra), *they* heard. Maybe it was the only
reason for their warning. To help the old story along.

II.

CLIMBING UP THE HILLS IN THE
snow, Arpazia did not know her way
anymore. It was a partial memory
that led her. Already it had drawn her down from the palace, on to
the road above the sea. In summer, the hills held cedars, rocks and
stands of lavender, but all that had changed now. Everything was

changed. And only two colors were in the world. The sky and the hills and the woods in their white snow fur, drawn over and under in black.

This was the route she had traveled with her lover Orion-Klymeno-Dianus.

Yet it took a great deal longer on foot.

Not a single person had challenged her as she left the palace. She decided this was because she had aged so completely they no longer knew her. She was some thirty-three years of age. She had not seen herself in her mirror since the night of Midwinter-Mass.

On the hills, however, she began to feel young.

When she moved in under the snow-trees of the wood, and reached the log-hut where *he* had brought her, she was filled with actual terror, as she saw that half its roof had fallen in under the weight of the snow.

She stood inside the room, staring at the destruction.

But by then she was worn out.

She would have sat down and gone to sleep, there in the freezing wreck, but she heard his voice suddenly, gently saying to her, *We must make up the fire, sweetheart*. He had said this sometimes to her then, all those years ago. The fire had been for cooking on, that summer season, not for comfort; yet there had been cooler days too, as autumn came on.

She found pine-cones and some bundles of wood in the place where he had stored them, and put them on the hearth. She took his flint and tinder out from under the stone and struck sparks. And then she blew on the fire as she had seen him do, always watching him, his beauty, in fascinated astonishment, watching everything he did.

When the roof had come down, the snow had gained access. It had piled up high and impenetrable, closing off the hut-house, and making it ironically more insulated.

Arpazia sat by the fire.

She thought, and she knew—if Klymeno had lived, he would not have left the precious flint and tinder behind in the hut.

Ah, so he truly was dead, as that carter had seemed to say, lying to her...

She had forgotten how to cry.

She sat there, looking at the fire, until her eyelids slipped shut.

"These apples are baked. Eat one, and some of this cheese. The wine's hot, too. Crumble your bread into it. It will do you good."

Arpazia ate slowly, having forgotten also how to eat.

She said, "But I believed you wouldn't see me again. You were finished with me."

He did not answer. But across the flames, intently beautiful, he looked at her. The firelight gilded his long hair and his eyes were amber, like a young wolf's. But he wore bear furs, as she did, clad for winter. He was not a day older than when she had seen him last.

"Klymeno," she said.

"Oh, *that* name," he said. "Did I never tell you my human name?"

"Tell me," she said, but somehow he did not.

How could she worry over that, now that he was here with her? And he had baked the apples in the fire for her, and brought the cheese and bread and wine.

She pulled her hood across her cheek. "Don't look at me. I've grown old and foul."

"You're lovely. Just as you were."

She was filled, brimming with fiery gladness. He was alive. He had returned. And she had gone back in time and must be young as he was. All was well.

But she said, diffidently, "Why did you never—why didn't you send to me, after those letters I sent you? You were so angry—And then when I searched for you—you'd gone away—to the west, he said, that man."

Klymeno—he had no other name—looked at her between the flames. "I never received your letters, Arpazia, sweetheart. Perhaps you trusted the wrong messengers. Besides, what made you think I could read? You should have come to me sooner yourself."

"You were in a fury. You hated me."

"Did you think I did?"

"Because," she said. She stopped. She said, "Because I wouldn't bear a child again. Oh—don't you know how I suffered with the first child—Draco's rape-child—the agony and horror and that *thing* fastening itself into me—"

"Don't *you* know, Arpazia, the wise-women from the wood could have given you herbs to make you strong, so you'd carry without sickness, and at the end to take all the pain away?"

"You hate me still, then," she said, "because I wouldn't bear your child. Are you like Draco?" But the words blistered her mouth, and the cup fell from her hand, the wine sputtering out harmless on the fire.

"No woman should bear a child all against her will," he said. "The people of the wood know that, which is why they know the plants to alleviate such misery. And nothing dies, Arpazia. Even that little seed in you. You killed it, here. Its inner life you couldn't touch. But I—oh, yes I was angry. Don't you know why? Don't you know how you hurt me? I loved you, Arpazia, and you were mine. You came to me and gave yourself. But the child in you was also me, you and I, both. And you crushed it like a spark before ever it could burn. You never even told me of it, only that you would have it gone. Anger, oh, yes. But that would have passed. It would have left me. Yet you never came to me. How could I come to you, in your palace?"

"I sent you letters—presents—"

"I had nothing."

"You hated me, you told me you were done with me—"

"Arpazia, are you such a fool? Do you think that no one in this world can *feel*, save *you*?"

Amazed, she stared at him.

Klymeno, her lover, said to her quietly, "I don't accuse you of a sin, beloved. Not even of selfishness. You've never *known* that we

feel, the rest of us, as you do. Can you really believe we are all so
strong, and only you are the weakling?"

She held her breath hard within her, afraid to let it go, as if,
should she breath out and in, she would lose him again.

"I loved you," he said, "I loved our child in you. Did you love
me at all, to let me turn from you so easily?"

"Yes, yes—oh yes—" she cried.

But her breath went out on the cry.

She had none left.

She choked and woke, frantic for air, flailing with her arms. And
the fire was dying.

But he—he was not there. He was dead. And gone forever.

One of her three rings had flown off in the waking spasm. They
had grown very loose. She only realized after, and by then she was
some distance from the hut. She had risen at first light, and come
away, as if she must.

The clawing voice started up in her head at once. *They were all
you had, all you thought to bring, dolt, those rings and your necklace. What
else can you sell, to live? Not yourself, ugly old hag.*

Should she return and try to find the ring?

She could not be bothered, though the voice nagged her.

A moment later two women appeared out of the trees. Both
looked up, saw Arpazia, and started.

To her, they seemed identical. Of the same height and build,
quite young, done up in ragged gray cloaks.

The one to the left crossed herself.

The other stuck her hand down.

"It isn't a haunt!"

Arpazia stood there, in her furs black on the snow.

"She thought you'd come from the hunter's bothy—some spec-
tral thing of the elder woods. Or a beast. They said he could call
bears and deer and other animals. Even a boar. He could tame those,
they said."

"But that was wrong," said the other. "It was a boar did for him."

Arpazia watched them. They were meaningless yet horrible.

The first one said, "Where are you going, Lady?"

The black fur must appear valuable to them, but despite her solitariness and their vulgarity, they did not think of stealing from her.

Arpazia wondered. Where was she going?

They had been gathering sticks, to judge from the loads on their backs. The second one said, "The town is the other direction, Lady."

"I don't want the town."

They glanced to and fro.

They were not *of* the Wood, although perhaps they lived in the woods.

Arpazia said, "Do you know where he is?"

"Who, Lady?"

"The hunter."

"Dead, Lady. Gone to the west."

"He was a Woodsman," said the other. *"Pagan."*

"There's a grave," said the first one, taking care now. It came to Arpazia they were hoping to be of service, so she would give them something.

"A grave," she said.

"He left off the pagan rites," said the first woman. "He was the lover of the queen, in Belgra Town. But she cast him away. Then he lost heart. He didn't worship the old gods of the wood any more, but nor did he go over to the Christ. So he had nothing to help him. When he hunted the boar it ripped him up and he died."

"That was years ago," said the other. "My ma told me. Ten years or more."

The first one said, "In the end his own people, those Woods People, they put a stone over his mound, to mark it. He'd been a king among them, do you see."

"But where is it?" Arpazia asked.

She walked down, over the hard-packed, ice-locked snow, and took off another ring—it slid easily—and put it in the first woman's rag-tied hand.

"I can't take this!" But she shut the ring in her fist.

"Where—tell me where—"

They told her.

Somehow, she did find the grave, and the stone like a pillar that stood up on it.

Nothing sounded in the woods. The trees crowded into a great forest now, uphill, downhill, closing in. Evergreens and pines brought a darkness that even the white-shining snow could not erase.

Arpazia wandered round the grave, round the pillar. A dead bird, frozen, flawless, a dove pink on the snow, lay under the pillar. She could imagine he would have picked it up and warmed it in his warm hands, giving it back its life. He only slew for food, or in sacrifice.

But there was nothing for *her* there. He was gone. It began to be twilight again and she was irrationally frightened—having come into the waste of winter without a qualm.

She gazed up, and the trees were columns of a church. The stars painted themselves on the ceiling. She heard wolves, or thought she did. "Shall I die here?"

She would have to return to the camp—Draco's place. No, *no* she must not. And . . . it was not that, now, no camp at all. Yes, even Draco had gone. How strange, for a space of seconds she had forgotten that all that was over long ago.

III.

*A*RPAZIA WANDERED THE WIN-
ter earth.

To her, the time was one
nearly endless season of daylight, which eventually reached the
shore of night. It was like a year, this day.

She was very strong, in her thin, fey manner, or she could not
have borne it. Of course, though her garments were no longer of
the best, they *had* been. She was well-shod, protected by furs. And,
in her past, when she had eaten she had been well-nourished.

She walked. The ground was not so difficult, for the snow here
was thick, softer and less slippery. She saw tracks in it, little taloned
things, birds' arrow-feet, the pads of bigger animals. She did not
really know what any of them were, these writings on the snow.

The nurse's ancient rhymes went circling through her head in
various forms, on and on, yet by now, like the scolding shrewish
voice, mostly unnoticed.

White the wood . . . white the wood . . .

The trunks of the trees were black and grew near together. She
sidled between them. She had no notion where she went. She was
escaping a charge of witchcraft and the wolfish priests, who would
burn her face and cut off her fingers. Maybe she would find his
house—whose? He was dead. She had found the house; it was a
tomb.

Twilight began, and the shadows were blue. This was like
moonlight, lacking a moon.

Then, she saw the wolf.

It was moving in front of her. Under a stand of whitened ilex,
it paused and looked back.

Was Arpazia afraid of it? The wolf seemed tattered, and not
large, nor young. A she-wolf, a hag, like the queen.

She said, "If you turn on me, I'll rip you with my nails."

But she did not mean this, nor did the wolf take any notice. It went on, and she went on, and peculiarly now, she was perhaps following it.

The forest presently opened into a glen. Trees bowed from the sides and a frozen stream ran through the bottom. A man was kneeling by the ice, in which he had made a hole, pulling out silver daggers. As she came closer, Arpazia saw that they were fish, which had been lying comatose under the ice.

By then, the man had looked round, and seen the wolf, and called to it. "Here, Bully. Here, my girl." The wolf trotted up to him. It was a dog after all.

Then he spotted Arpazia.

He got up, looking her over.

"What are you?" he said.

She gazed straight at him and knew she must not tell him she was the escaping witch-queen of Belgra Demitu.

"I've lost my way."

"So you have. What do you want?"

"I'm cold," she said.

He apparently took pity on her, or on her once-fine clothes.

She found he was leading her up the glen, the she-dog trotting beside them. "Lean on me, woman," he said. "You've lost your escort. What's your name?"

She must not say she was Arpazia, the witch. She remembered another name. "Lilca."

He would rape her, inevitably, the price for shelter or assistance. That had been Lilca's fate. And something else had happened to Lilca.

The man did not rape Arpazia.

She found herself seated by a fire in a long, low room. Things hung from beams, skins, roots, bunches of wild garlic, and clinking charms.

Arpazia's hands and face burnt. Had the priests after all asaulted her?

But her mind was clearing in sudden stages.

There were some women that she thought were servants or slaves, and they were rubbing her hands with snow and then with oil from a jar, and a girl gave her a cup of barley beer.

"I'm the king here," said the man. He spoke without boasting, it was only a fact.

One of the younger servant women turned out to be the man's daughter. He called her that, she seemed to have no other name: Stir the supper, Daughter. Here's fish, Daughter. Then he went out. The women, slaves, daughters, began to chatter. Daughter explained to Lilca-Arpazia that her mother was above in the upper rooms, nursing a sick child.

Probably Arpazia slept. The women moved in and out of her awareness, and she smelled the fish frying and the rufous aroma of the stew.

Later everyone ate, and Arpazia was included, at a wooden table.

"Take some up to Mother, Daughter," instructed the king. His wife too seemed to have no other name. Indeed, *Mother* was an important title, he said it gravely, giving it due weight.

Arpazia had eaten little, but the hot ale had brought her alive, though she ached with tiredness and wanted only to sleep. Used to giving orders in her past, she had instead grown only self-reliant in isolation. Now she stood up, meaning to return to the chair by the fire and fall back as best she could into slumber.

But noting her rise, the man said, "Yes, best go up and see how she is. She'll be glad of your notice. Perhaps you know some medicine, too, a lady like yourself."

Arpazia only gazed at him. Yet now Daughter was there, leading her courteously out of the room.

It was a big wooden house, and they had made a rough stair, up which the daughter, carrying a candle, now drew Arpazia.

"You'll understand herbs," said Daughter. "Our little knowledge does no good."

Arpazia hesitated. Was the girl calling her a witch? Was this some trick? She said nothing.

The girl went on, "I think he's lost to us. I beg you not to say it to Mother. Father won't mind so much, he's two grown boys. They're off to the inn to sell our wood. King of woodcutters, that's Father. But the baby's her pet, she loves him most. Here now, mind your feet."

And they must step straight off the stair and in at a doorway.

A fire burned in a brazier—there had been a hearth below. But the window had shutters, and there were seven candles alight.

The mother was sitting on the side of a great wood bed, big enough for four or five persons. It had curtains of wool, which were roped aside.

Her face, as she bent forward to what lay on her lap, was touched golden and tender by the firelight. It was the face, almost, of the archetypal Virgin Mother, Marusa, holy with its utter absorption, its unblinking and unswerving love.

"Mother, there's the lady here, the lady father met in the woods. She may know herbs—" then the girl stopped, for her mother had lifted her face.

Arpazia saw that one of the reasons for its glistening golden quality was the streams of tears which had run, and now ran again, from her polished eyes.

"No use, my dear."

"Oh—Mother—" stumbled the girl, her pragmatism thrown away, and she hurried to her mother and caught her hard in both her arms, trying to hold her safe from the pain.

Arpazia who called herself Lilca, stood there staring.

In a way, she was trapped, and *had* been tricked, for it was not quite easy, stiff with exhaustion, to turn at once out of the stair-girt room, or even to find the door. Instead she must look and see this ecstasy of gold-lit anguish.

The woman and the girl wept together now. Arpazia saw that their tears fell like drops of diamond on to a child. He was two or three years of age, his head lolling peacefully against the woman's side, as if he only slept, just as Arpazia had longed to.

The woman spoke out of her weeping. "It's a terrible thing, to

lose your child. You'll know, madam. You will have been a mother,
too."

Arpazia nodded, separate to the scene of grief.

She heard his voice in her head.

Do you think that no one in this world can feel, save you?

And she saw this was not so.

She heard him say, her lover, his voice now canceling all the
other voices that spiked and squirmed within her brain: "I loved
our child in you."

Arpazia heard her own self saying, "My child died."

"Oh, the sorrows of the flesh," cried the mother.

Arpazia sat down on a stool by the door. She could not stand
up any longer.

Oblivious to her once more, the other two women sobbed, and
the dead male child took no note of them.

But how the daughter held her mother. As if *she* were the
mother, and the mother the crying child . . . Arpazia watched. Her
head touched the wall behind her, and she slept.

She walked through a dark tunnel of stone. Ahead there was
the lid of a cistern, which, once raised, would show her something
awful. However, there was another thing she must find, which
would prevent this catastrophe.

I killed her. I had her killed, your child and mine.

*Nothing dies, Arpazia. You killed it, here. Its inner life you couldn't
touch. Even that little seed in you.*

The woman was screaming and shouting, and there were other
voices, angry, or trying to be calm.

"No—no—*no!*"

"What else, mother? It's God's law. How can we keep off from
it? Even in this winter—the house—is warm . . . we must."

"Not in the ground! No! Not under the cold snow—"

"What then in Christ's name? *What?*"

"No, husband, not in the cold."

Did Arpazia still dream?

She saw them go out, one by one, the mother holding her dead child, and the daughter going behind her, and the man who was king of woodcutters, and some of their servants. Arpazia, too, she had gone after.

They were in a yard, standing, all of them on the blue snow under a wide sky. The forest rose around, its church columns and fretwork of stars.

"But on the Last Day," said the daughter fearfully, "when we rise up—*what will be left?*"

"Do you think all Christian souls that die in fire are doomed?"

Two of the slaves brought a brazier which blazed and caused the snow to melt in patches. From an inch of black mud which then appeared, a green flower was seen, beginning to grow.

"That is what God can do," said the mother.

The king shook his dead. He spoke some words. They seemed priestly and were to do with Christ, and resurrection. Then he carried the dead child to the brazier and laid him in on the burning wood. "We'll have to answer to the priests, in spring."

She made no protest now, the mother.

Arpazia thought, *It will come alive again through the fire.*

But the dead child did not come alive. It was burned up, and the smoke blew dense and black round the yard, and the people there coughed. The odor was atrocious but far away. Some could not bear it and slunk off.

In the end, only the mother and her daughter, and Arpazia, stood there, as the fire turned ashen and crumbled.

"Come in now, Mother."

Arpazia turned, somnambulist, toward the loving, coaxing voice. But it was not for her.

In the morning, when she woke in a small side room, not recollecting how she had come there on the pallet, she thought of the burning brazier and the dead child and believed she had dreamed it. But then, too, she had dreamed of Klymeno, and surely that had not been a dream at all.

There was dried mint in the breakfast beer. It reminded her of the ritual drinks of the wood.

"Will you want to go on somewhere, Lady?" asked the man, preoccupied and impatient. "The big inn, perhaps. You can take lodging there. My son will carry you at noon, when he goes with the wood cart."

She thought they had already taken wood to the inn, the daughter had said so. Perhaps they had, and more was wanted.

Why would she go to the inn? What would happen to her there? She slid the third ring off her hand, and hid it (belatedly) in her mantle. The inn might accept the ring in payment.

The son, a fat frowning rough boy of seventeen or so, pushed her up into the cart among the logs and branches, and they set off. There was no lamentation about the house as they left it, no keening or crying, no smell of burned meat, only the strokes of an axe, wood-smoke, and the cold-scorched pines.

IV.

*B*ECAUSE THEY ACCEPTED THE ring, and without questions, Arpazia, now Lilca, stayed most of the rest of the winter at the inn in the forest. They gave her a large room, with an old pine bed, and also use of a small adjacent room, nearly a cupboard, but this one she never needed. The inn-wife brought her clothes, of good material, that had been left to pay inn debts. "You're a lady, Mistress Lilca. I have a mirror, too. Should you like that? To see to your hair and such."

"I had a mirror," said Arpazia.

When that was all she said, the inn-wife told Arpazia, "You'll have left that behind, when you came away. Or is it sent on ahead of you, to Korchlava?"

They all assumed Korchlava would be her final destination. Or they pretended that they did.

The wife's mirror arrived and was placed in Arpazia-Lilca's chamber. It was a treasure for the forest, three hands in width, and of highly burnished bronze, in a wood frame.

Peering into its hazy depths, Arpazia could not see clearly what had become of her. But she did see that now her black hair was all woven with white and gray, as if she had brought the snow with her inside the inn.

"Poor thing," said the inn-wife to her uninterested spouse. "She's not quite right in her mind. But you can tell, a fine lady once." (The bartered ring was a black spinel of eloquent size.) "Her poor skin, all raddled and scarred with the cold. But, fair of face once."

One of the inn girls waited regularly on Arpazia. She was even awarded a chamber pot to save her nightly journeys to the unheated latrines. Mostly, she would accept no service. Half the time she sent them away, even when they brought her food and drink.

"Some great sadness in her life, poor soul."

"Oh, pin your tongue up, woman," snapped the innkeeper, who was by then sick of it all.

Guests would seldom see Mistress Lilca. They often heard her pacing about, up and down, round and round her room. But many paced this way, like cats in cages, when the winter confined them. And this was the worst winter for a century.

"Has she no kin? No son, or even a girl-child to care what comes to her?"

"I told you, wife, pin up your gob."

One night five priests stayed at the forest inn. They were bound for Belgra Demitu, for the Church of St. Belor, and had ridden through the icy days in a damp wagon. Now they sat sneezing ominously in their corner.

The inn-wife knocked on the door of her favorite guest, and was admitted.

"Mistress—have no fears. You may have heard, we've priests here. But they shan't know about you."

Arpazia started and stopped dead in the middle of her paced floor.

So, I have it, thought the inn-wife. *She was one of those who came from Belgra when the prince, as they say, turned so religious.*

"I pay my honor to the Christ," said the inn-wife now, crossing herself. Then she made an older, more secret sign. "But there's the wood, too. I live among trees, how can I forget them? I've seen things these Christians never do. Even"—and her voice fell low, an animal going down on its belly—"King Death in his chariot of bone."

But Arpazia, who for a second had risen from her own shadows, afraid, had sunk back into them. She nodded and said, "Thank you. Please close my door."

The inn-wife obeyed, and said to herself, *Yes, she was fine and high-up in the town, in her day.*

The curious thing was how Arpazia saw this woman, who was several years younger than she, and looked very *much* younger. To Arpazia, the inn-wife was her senior, and gradually from this and her attentions, Arpazia was coming to fear her—to find her important.

Although others were all at once more real to her, they were still strangers. One image clung inside her mind—the golden-faced woman, the mother and her daughter, weeping above the fire—but its meaning eluded Arpazia. She had begun to think it was herself she was seeing, as sometimes too, in memory, she saw herself with Klymeno.

When the inn woman knocked on another shivering night, some days after the priests had gone, and perhaps a month after Arpazia's advent at the inn, Arpazia allowed her to come in and add more wood to the brazier.

"Tonight, it's the Great Orb. I shall make a little offering to the Full Moon and the winter god. For spring. You'll know. Some of the girls will go with me. Shall you come with us?"

From uneasiness, Arpazia agreed that she would.

So, after midnight, when the moon was in the west, and covered with white snow from the look of it, like the earth, they went through a small side door in the wall, into the forest. Not far. There were doubtless wolves, and they were prudent.

But no wolves called. Perhaps the winter had driven even them away.

The inn-wife and her kitchen maids killed a hen and sprinkled some of the blood on the snow. Next they tasted some, and Arpazia was given some to taste. They spoke words to King Winter and King Death.

Then one girl stepped forward.

She was lank and lean and had a fox's face, but she sang in a sweet voice—a song of the goddess and her daughter that Death snatched away.

"Coira, come back to your mother!" all the inn women sang then, in the chorus. "Coira, tread up on the world with silver feet, and bring back with you the snow-drops and the asphodel and the young green corn."

> *Coira, come silver-white from the black earth,*
> *Coira, come blushing red as a rose.*

This had always been the name of the goddess's daughter— *Coira*.

Arpazia had lifted her head. She had a predatory look, like a bird listening after its prey.

She knew the name. Whose had it been?

When the song was over they shared wine from the innkeeper's cupboard. Arpazia too.

The foxy singer said, "That girl that passed through the inn, just after the Midwinter-Mass, that was *her* name."

"Which girl?" asked the inn-wife, sternly.

"The girl with such long hair. She came with that man and those dwarves, seven of them—they were to do a play for us, but then they went off in a hurry."

All of them recalled the dwarves. They began to recall the girl.

"Her hair was black as chimney soot."

"She wasn't his slave, though he treated her as if she was."

"How do you know her name? Wait, I heard him call her Black-hair."

"I went to his room in the night, to see to the fire." The fox glanced under her lids. "I thought he might fancy a turn with me, and give me a coin, they sometimes do." (The inn-wife tutted disapprovingly, resignedly.) "But only she was there, and she spoke in her sleep. She said over and over, *I'm Coira*, and then she said some other name I forget, and then she said, *Which am I?*"

"Well, which?"

"She was Coira. The Maiden. What else? She was beautiful."

"I wonder where they went?" mused the inn-wife as they trailed back to the inn.

"To the mines outside Korchlava," said the fox girl definitely. "I know those mines. Where else, with those dwarves?"

Another girl said softly, "She *was* Coira. They took her underground."

Arpazia walked with her eyes closed. And how she found her way it was impossible to tell. Then she stopped, and the inn-wife sent the others on ahead, and waited for Mistress Lilca, nervously, there in the wolfy forest.

Finally, the woman went and took Arpazia's arm.

"What's up, madam? Come on now. We'll be frozen to our bones."

Back inside, Arpazia drew away at once. She climbed up to her bed. There she lay on her back, and slept, slept exactly where Coira had slept and said, "I am Coira."

Arpazia had remembered that this had been a name of her daughter's. Arpazia had given Coira to that man who owned the dwarves.

Once, she had conceived Coira.

"My child, his and mine. Klymeno—his—his—"

Klymeno said, "I loved my child in you. That child in you was also me, you and I, both." (Coira—was Klymeno's child?)

"But I didn't kill her," declared Arpazia to Klymeno. "She escaped me. *He* kept her and took her away."

In the corner, the half-blind bronze mirror watched the witch-queen as she slept, motionless and noiseless, on her back.

In her dream, the bronze mirror spoke to her.

"She is alive, the snowdrop, under the ground."

And in the dream Arpazia clenched her fists, driving her sharp nails into her aching hands. She had confused everything now.

"How often have I tried to be rid of her. . . . It is myself, *I* am Coira. A maiden, beautiful—as I was. Let me find her and kill her and be sure, then I am myself. Let me find her, she is my daughter. She and I, in the firelight. Cold white. Golden. We touched hands. She held me in her arms—let me find my only child—"

But Arpazia lay straight as a marble woman on a tomb. Only her eyelids now and then quivering like two papers disturbed by some draught.

V.

*A*S THE THAW BEGAN TO FILL the forest with a cracking of boughs and coinlike tinkling of streams, the innkeeper started to throw unwanted guests from the inn like garbage.

"He drinks too much and doesn't pay. Gave me a painted button for his ale last night, as if that's any use. And this one is a sotten pig. This isn't his midden. Out with them."

The wife nodded, folding the inn's sheets with her girls.

"Your old crone, too, mad as a goat."

Then the inn-wife turned. "Not Mistress Lilca."

"*Mistress*—some rich slut's servant, making out she's better than she is. She's eaten up all the profit of that little ring she brought—and which she doubtless stole."

"She eats *nothing*—"

"Stitch your tongue. Out she goes."

The inn-wife went to Arpazia's room with the supper.

"Try these cakes. I made them with brown sugar for you."

Suspicious, Arpazia nibbled a cake.

The wife said this room was needed, suddenly, for a relative of her husband's.

"And we're that full. It can't be helped."

Arpazia said, "Where shall I go?" She said it drearily, in ennui not alarm.

But the wife sprang forward with her plan. Another guest had offered to take Mistress Lilca on to the city. "He'll see you safe to your kindred. There is someone, did you say, a daughter? At Korch-lava?"

Had Arpazia said this? Or had she merely given off the notion, like a scent?

The inn-wife had bribed the guest, who did not actually want to carry Arpazia in his wagon. But he had also been intrigued at the thought of a fallen lady. When he saw her, this appetite withered. He had believed her younger, having glimpsed her once from the top of the yard, but now he saw she was gray and ravaged, with ghastly weird, wild eyes.

They did not talk as the wagon moved day after day through the trees, rested night by night among them. But her demeanor irked him. She was not grateful, not even polite. And she did not offer herself. Probably he would have accepted. Though elderly, she was all that was available out here.

By the time they reached a village among the trees, in a long streaming rain, he was ready to bid Arpazia-Lilca farewell, and did so. She stood on the track, watching his vehicle rumble away, soaked with the rain, a scarecrow.

*   *   *

In the end, she walked to Korchlava, as she had once walked to Belgra Demitu, among a crowd of unfriendly others. But that was when the full flush of spring had opened up the land. Meanwhile she was "taken on" by the village. That is, she became one of their slaves.

"Granny," they called her—her face and hands seared by a feathering of frostbite, lined by the knife of her chipped mind. Hair grisaille and white, with slender threads of raven black.

"Here, gran. Take this basket. The women'll show you."

She was taught to gather fruit from the storage sheds, honeyed pears and apples, saffron or brown as nuts, and soft thick figs and ruddy apricots, tight now in coats of sugar. Autumn fruit preserved for spring, before the summer fruit began again. Raisins dried by a dead sun soon to be reborn, peaches that swam in red vinegar, quinces made jam with Eastern spice.

The village was not alone in serving Korchlava. It worked hard to keep its trade. The city was eighteen or twenty days off, on foot.

There were other old women. Jolly hags, sorting things, piles of fruit and earthernware jars. Below, hills crowded by bare orchards sparkled with rain, opened to the blanched sunlight, embryo of spring.

"Don't sit idle, Blackhair," the old women mocked old Arpazia. The nickname amused them. They were older than she, and some had guessed it, but few had lost so much color from their locks. "Blackhair's idle. Here, let her tie the necks of these sacks."

There was always plenty to do. "Keep busy, like the bees," exhorted the stern men. They sent Arpazia too among the hives. The female bees which foraged and gathered far and wide were less likely, they said, to sting a human female. Their closed-in combs had odd, musky smells from unknown grasses and flowers. Sometimes Arpazia would pick some alien leaf, a habit of her witch-queen past. Forgotten. She always let it fall.

She did it all indifferently. It was like being a small child again, ordered about, patronized and jeered at, employed in meaningless adult tasks.

I must go on. I must go down the hills.

The voice in her head had grown less harsh, as if the other voices, of the inn, the village, had blunted its point.

But Arpazia did not get up to run away. As once before, she remained where she was, among her enemies.

Besides, they had told her they would all be going on to Korchlava.

She understood (as once before) if she did not keep up, they would leave her in the forests for the savage beasts.

One morning the weather changed entirely. The sun was a different one, a new bright coin. First blossoms glittered in the orchards, almond-colored, or almost green, almost lilac. Birds crossed the washed skies, and in the woods foxes barked where the wolves had fallen dumb in despair.

The contingent from the village which would go to Korchlava set out two days after. There was one wagon, drawn by a bullock, and some donkeys laden with paniers. The men and women who walked also carried bags on their backs. Arpazia was chosen to be one of these. Despite her looks, she was a useful pack animal.

A spring market soon began in the city, but there were other makeshift markets along the hills above Korchlava. Everyone came and went there, traders, entertainers, mages—a world of wonder was to be met with, and many were excited at the prospect.

The days were quite warm, but as they came up from the trees into the hills, the nights stayed icy still. Campfires burned. The men drank and shouted. The old women crowded together, telling tales. "The king comes in white as sacrifice, green for the land. And in yellow when he's cut down, like the autumn oak. The red king is the master of the year."

"Draco's a red king," said the old women.

Arpazia listened. One of the old men shoved her. "Have you ever seen the king?"

Arpazia murmured, "I was his wife."

But they took no notice, mishearing, uncaring what she said. And the voice in her head sharpened, urging, *Be careful what you say. You are no one's wife. You're a crone selling fruit.*

Even so, she knew that when they reached the city, she must get away from them. She had a purpose, a goal. She would find her child in the city as she had almost found her once before, years back, at Belgra Demitu, after that other long walk. Then, everything might be settled. *I must find her.* Why? *To be rid of—to hold—*

How will you know her? interrupted the voice, less hectoring than restless.

I remember her. She and I are the same. Like looking in the mirror.

"She's cracked as a jar," pronounced the hags at the fire, passing a leather bottle of stale beer. "Doesn't know where she is. Fewer wits than a snail."

But another said, "Draco's a yellow king by now, well past his prime. But there's one in the Hell mines, Draco's bastard, a prince in scarlet."

Arpazia did not hear this. Her back ached now like her wrists. She turned one of the doctored fruits in her hand. It too was lined and yellow, yet rich with the syrup it had been preserved in, firm in its brittle sticky glaze.

"Look at her, you'd think it was bad, that apple, the way she plays with it. Eat that, granny, or give it here. There's none to waste."

Wisely obedient, the crone-child bit into the false succulence of the yellow apple, and ate it up.

In the warmth of a spring afternoon, the land rose, and between the rounded shapes, there was a glimpse of Korchlava City below, sun-ripened.

But the first market was that which served Elusion, the quarries and mines of the marble hills.

*   *   *

It was a sprawling place, set up with shacks and huts, booths and tents—even banners, to show in pictures what was for sale.

Jugglers threw flaming torches, or stood twelve high on each others' shoulders and necks. A girl danced with a bear. Cattle, pigs, silks, holy relics—and a man who produced a dagger from between his lips.

One of the village men cuffed her. It brought her to her senses, *helped* her; she saw better after that, and thought more coherently. She had two woven baskets of fruit. She was to go about and sell them, and put the coins—*look, here*—in the pouch at her waist. Then she must come back, where the wagon was. "Don't go wandering off, or there'll be me to see, after." He was a man. God's superior creation. She lowered her eyes and went off to do as she was told.

"Sweet pears with cinnamon," Arpazia heard herself softly calling through the lanes of the hill market, "spicy apples in honey. And berries in wine."

She was pulled at uncouthly, things grabbed from the baskets, coins or bits of metal dashed at her. She caught or picked up the payment, put it into the pouch tied to her waist.

Many of these persons were unusual. Some were black with the dark of the mines, or powder-white. They had red blinking eyes. Some had bound their eyes over with light protective gauzes, and wore wide-brimmed hats against the sun. Like bats, they spent much time underground.

"Hey, grandma—are these peaches?"

"Peaches in Heaven-spice."

"Too soft. Have you bitten them? Oh, if you have, they'll be poisonous." Laughter. How droll.

She did not tell them she was no one's grandma but rather a young girl of fourteen in a hag's old, stiff, sore body, her long hair straggling down and down under the rag on her head, her straight back slightly bowed at last from carrying the heavy bag through the forests.

Arpazia lifted her head. She looked about.

There had sometimes been fairs at her father's castle and they had been something like this, if not so vast. But the nurse had always held on to her. Shackled, held back, always.

But now, there was no one to stop her.

She glanced and saw one of her baskets was empty, so she put it down on the track. Carrying the other basket, which was still partly full, she moved off again.

As she did so, she looked up across the stalls at a sweep of hill and the faint blue sky.

Arpazia saw herself.

There she was, walking on the hill's ridge in a plain dress, her hair coiled in a shining black braid round and round her head. Such white skin, white as the snow had been, and lips red as if bitten. But eyes silver-gray as clear water.

Of course, she had an attendant. A black-haired dwarf man swaggered at her side.

Arpazia was aware it was reasonable that a dwarf, even seven of them, should be with her now. She could not recall why. But it enabled her to be utterly certain.

Her name though, was not Arpazia any more. Nor Lilca. What was her name, up there, walking along the hillside?

Coira. That was it.

The goddess three-in-one, who might be Coira the Maiden, or Demetra-Arpazia the Woman, or Persapheh (or Granny) the Crone.

Coira the Maiden was saying something. She spoke words to the dwarf and he nodded.

Arpazia-Persapheh also spoke, mouthing the words she had not heard or grasped.

Then the couple went behind a tent and were gone.

Arpazia felt great fear.

She drew herself in, all the parts of her that were constantly drifting away—mind, heart, body, concentration, soul—and hurried up the hill.

When she came to the top, for a moment she could not see them. To her own astonishment, tears ran out of her eyes. But next instant she saw herself again, wending down among the cattle-pens, and then up on to a higher path, the dwarf gallantly taking her elbow as she stepped over two large stones.

"Where are you going, bag-of-bones?"

Arpazia checked, amazed, for the burly man in studs and leathers was speaking to her.

"Sweet fruit," wheedled Arpazia, craftily.

"I don't want your rotten fruit. Get off down. This is the entry into the quarries. Wretched old booby. Get down the hill."

He blocked her path, her very life, his stinking cloak billowing across the sky.

White dust rose in a fog behind him, where a gate of sorts marked the quarries. But the girl (herself) had appeared again, above and beyond, the dwarf just visible at her side.

"That way," said Arpazia.

But the man gripped her arm and thrust her back down the track toward the market. "Be off, you bloody old fool."

Again, her eyes were wet. She had remembered how to weep. She hid it, and stumbled down.

Among the booths she waited, watching the hill path and the white mist. She had found herself. Naturally herself would return, to be found again.

Once or twice people came to her and wanted the fruit. Arpazia let them take it, not reaching for their coins, so they scoffed and did not pay, or else tossed the payment in among the apples.

Her tears dried. The ache in her back and hands turned to itching. She thought, *I must follow her, wherever she goes.*

She did not expect her younger self to know herself. Arpazia was in clever, perhaps supernatural, disguise.

It would be easy to kill her.

No, that was wrong. Easy to kiss. To hold.

What did it mean?

"White as wood," sang Arpazia under her breath, "red as snow, black as blood." So passersby now avoided her, knowing her for what she must be, a beldame speaking maledictions.

Later the sky darkened. The spring day veered. Gouts of thunder cloud herded up the sky, and rain fell in steel lines.

The market was full of rain, curses, and running figures. A man from the orchard village bumped against Arpazia. "Go on, gran. Get to the tents."

Go here, go there. Which tents?

She pretended to do as he said, but hung back.

Soon after, Coira and the dwarf came down from the higher hill, through the rain.

She had a shawl over her head, and he carried something in a bundle.

They passed Arpazia within the length of her arm, not seeing her, overwhelming her by proximity.

Again, she moved to follow them.

In the rain, gliding between its stitches, this seemed simpler than ever, and besides, she felt now, the Crone, that they were the only three real beings in that landscape. Then the dwarf too ceased to be real, and only *she* was, only herself, twice over.

So she pursued herself, now without any true fear of loss, along the hills and so to a cavelike doorway in the land's side.

She had made believe she was cunning, but now she was. She paused to let herself go in—in there to the dark beyond the dark of day. And then she went, without haste. And meeting the next man, some other guard who blocked her way, Arpazia said, "Let me through. I'm with that girl. I am her mother."

The guard stared down at her. "Yes, you look as if you are. Both damned witches. Go on, then."

And Arpazia went through into the hill, after her daughter who was her own self, through into the Underworld of Hell, armed only with a basket of dead apples.

BOOK THREE

Sanguinea
Blood-Red

The Forbidden Apple

I

*H*EPHAESTION AND COIRA HAD been lovers through the last of the winter below ground.

They were not excessively overt, but even so, it was not to be missed by the five others who shared the house.

Proud spoke first, to Hephaestion.

"Stormy, it's all well enough, but you should leave off now."

"Leave off what?"

"Come, you know what I mean."

Hephaestion did know. "That's between her and me."

"She's *human*," said Proud. All the contempt of his superior species blazed in his voice. He had never been wise.

Stormy shrugged. "Not tried such a girl?"

"Be sure, I've had my pick. But how can you go on?"

"I like it. She likes it."

"Do you want to be separate from us? Deny us?"

"Don't be a fool. What about Soporo?"

"That is never the same." It was not. "Leave her alone. Best of all, send her away. She's served her purpose—we're all right in these mines, we don't need her. Let her find someone her own *height*."

Hephaestion said, looking at the floor, "It's more than bed-dances. She and I are companions."

Proud made a speech. It concerned loyalties and un-women that might be used, but not taken up. Hephaestion left him to it, and looking round, Proud found himself orating at the air.

Soporo spoke next, on the track where they all met in the "mornings" before the mine.

"Is she good? Is she pepper-hot? Tell me, what can she do? Can she do *this—this*, then?"

When Hephaestion would not provide one explicit word, Soporo called him names, even attempted to start a fight. Greedy dragged him off.

"She's a white stick of nothing!" yelled Soporo. "Is her cunt that white? You're welcome."

None of the others said anything. Vinka hurled a pot at He-phaestion's head, meaning to damage him—but he was accustomed to her from years ago, and dodged the missile. As it smashed to bits, her eyes shot venom at Coira, who was standing by the fire. Then Vinka raised her skirt high up, displaying her belly and legs and sexual center, not to Stormy, but to the girl. Coira had occasionally seen Vinka nude, Want also. These two dwarvixens had condensed, beautiful bodies, full-breasted yet blossom-skinned, like babies, their short childish legs smooth, the pudenda hairless as if scrupu-lously shaved. But this showing was offensive, dreadful. Coira looked away, and Vinka let down her skirt with the slashing noise of a whip.

That day she and Want left the shack and did not return. Greedy too did not return that "night," nor any night after. He-phaestion learned from an insulting Soporo that these three had set up another home elsewhere in the cavern.

After that only Proud and Tickle remained on the shack's upper floor. Tickle did nothing differently, but Proud was curt, and to Coira he would never now speak.

"I'm sorry," said Coira to Hephaestion.

"Why? You didn't do it."

"Yes."

"Do you think I have no powers of my own, that I'm helpless under your witchery? Perhaps I am, but it's my choice to be so. Let them sulk."

She had learned to cook from the dwarves. She stirred the kettle of vegetables she had kept going for him, Tickle, and Proud. She did not argue, but she was very still. And when Tickle came to take the bowls for Proud and herself, Coira turned her head. That former gesture Hephaestion had memorized, and saw even in dreams.

They, too, did not discuss the severing again. They went on together. It was only a brief silence which would sometimes occur between them, dividing them for a moment like a distance of many miles.

They were lovers, but he did not love her. He knew this well. And he had never lied to her, for all the loving things he said to her, which concerned her attractions, his desire, despite the value of her presence. None of this had root in love. These feelings were the offspring of fellowship and hunger—and of their unmatchedness, too, he made no secret of that.

Sometimes they even jested together about their dissimilarities. He might call her Tiny, Child, or Little Cat. After she had told him of the phenomenon of his shadow before the torch, she sometimes flashed out at him, smiling, *Giant*.

They learned to be insolent to each other, too, in the manner of true friends.

She never stinted, however, though without demand, her murmurs of her love. He never again denied her or thrust the words away. And at certain times he relished—*loved*—her love, if he did not love her back. It was a fact which troubled him.

*   *   *

Another thing happened. After a while, sometimes he and she would leave the cavern and go up to walk on the hills.

The winter had been solid and immoveable, but then began to crack, showing it had lost heart. Light brightened and hurt their eyes.

"Look," she had said, "there's a flower." It appeared doomed to him, nearly transparent, perched on a small patch of thawed, cold mud. "I wonder if herbs grow here. They grow everywhere. I'd thought," she said, "of trying to find starry-seal in the spring, to help Vinka with her rages. Perhaps Tickle would take it to her."

He had said, awkward, "That won't bring Vinka round. She'll throw the stuff in her fire."

"Yes," said Coira, without any annoyance or sound of disappointment. She continued, as the weather and land changed, to look for the plant. This was very like her. She expected nothing, yet was dutiful, honorable. However had she *expected* he would give in to her and *dishonorably* coerced him by a spell?

He did not ask her that. Not being in love with her, it was not a question he needed to put.

To Coira, there was no mystery simply because she had fallen in love. The emotion had been so gradual, then so sudden. It had filled her and overwhelmed her, love, wanting, demand, coming in across every barrier of her barren past. In this one instance, she could not and did not think. Love itself acted, and was.

She was fundamentally uncomplex, perhaps. The complexities of her past had made her so.

But he did not necessarily think this of her. They did not speak of earlier lives. Instead they invented a present, in which they lived together. Neither spoke of any future, either, more than a few days hence.

The starry-seal eluded her, although the hills grew brown, then green.

The entries to the marble quarries and upper mines they

avoided, coming out by one of the cavern's lesser cave-doors. The
guards there did not charge them payment now, only leered and
laughed at them, the tall pale girl with her lusty dwarf. Hephaestion
was used to mockery. She seemed oblivious. Certainly she disregarded it.

Presently a sunny day set the hills in a motion of brilliance. In
the grasses only twenty steps from the cave-door, Coira saw the
shoots of something and moved spontaneously toward it. Then, hesitated.

"What's that? Is it the herb?"

"Not for Vinka," Coira said. She said, "Febrifuga. Do you see
on these twigs, the white flowers trying to come early?"

Hephaestion did not recall the significance of the herb, and
Coira said abruptly, "If he didn't suffer, would he be less a monster?"

"Who?"

"The man they call a prince in Elusion."

"Hadz? Doubtful. You mean the pains in his head?"

"Oh," she said, "let's go on."

This was her dismissive side. He had noticed, she could be also
discompassionate, *heartless*, even. She swept things from her that
could not be changed, having learned she must.

Would she do that with him, when they had parted?

Tickle and Proud had gone to the mines, and Hephaestion stayed
back, as he sometimes did now, whole days at a time. Coira sensed
in this, as in their walks aboveground, the holiday spirit of someone
who was preparing to go elsewhere.

She did not say a word about it. She hid it also from herself as
best she could. It lay deep within her, a little dull pebble scraping
against her heart.

Today he told her of the spring market and fair in Korchlava.
He did not say he would go to see it, or ask if she would like to
see it. (He had never referred again to her father, Draco.) However,

he mentioned there would be by now a market here, aboveground.

She was washing the bowls in which they had eaten the pine nut porridge, just outside their door, under the white willow-tree claws of the roots that grew over the shack-house. Something made her turn and look down, toward the valley, where the mansion of Hell's prince was.

So she saw a man climbing toward her up the cinder track. She knew him instantly.

"Hephaestion—" she said.

He came out. "What now?"

"That man who was in Hadz's house, the man who wanted the silver for Hadz. He's walking up the track."

They both glanced over at the mirror tied to the wall. More dirty sacks had been hung across it, and if you did not know, there was nothing to see.

Elsewhere the shack showed only its normal poverty. Anything from the mines which was stored there had already (mostly) been tithed by the prince.

Hephaestion stood fixedly. Coira stood by him. They waited until the man, the fat steward with earrings, came up on to their ledge. He was hot and out of breath, and behind him one of the prince's ruffianly guards hefted a club and belt of blades.

The steward glared with unliking eyes as he regained his breath.

"Get me a cup of wine," he then said to Coira.

She had it ready and held it out. The steward drank.

"Yes, I couldn't forget the pair of *you* so fast. Well. You must please yourselves, that way. Is it true though that you're a damned witch?"

"She is not," said Hephaestion.

"That's not what she told me. She was going on about her herb lore."

"I know something about herbs," said Coira quietly. "My nurse taught me."

"Good. Praise the Christ. It's for his hurts in the brain. He's had

them *three* days now. Not screaming, he's crying like a baby. You'd
better find some of your weeds, brew them for him. I tell you now,
if he dies, we'll see some pretty horrors down here. And if he gets
over it and you fail, he'll have your skin for his wall. He'll stuff his
pillows with your long hair."

Hephaestion said briskly, "Yes, master, she knows where the
plant is. We'll—"

"You will," said the steward. He sat down by the bucket with
the porridge bowls, took one out, let it fall back so carelessly they
heard it crack on the side. "This big guard will go with you, dwarfy.
So no games."

They went up by another way, the guard choosing it in case the
dwarf and the girl tried to trick him—for if she had been lying, they
might want to run off.

Hephaestion knew he had seen the herb, the Febrifuga. Yet he
pondered as they ascended the cavern steps behind the bowel of
the gold mines, which rang and moaned, if the market had since
encroached, if feet had trampled the plant or other herbalists dug
it up.

Emerging in the watery sun of day, he noted the guard blinking
and squinting at the light, and considered knifing him quickly and
rushing Coira away. But there were too many about, even if the
market was only beginning, too many who would see and give their
criminal fealty to mad Hadz.

Besides she said, almost at once, "Up there on that slope, look,
it's growing in clumps. It grows well, it's tough and versatile."

"No flowers on it," said Hephaestion as they got nearer.

"It's the leaves he'll need," she said, matter-of-fact as any nursing nun.

Then, as she bent to loosen the soil and he began to dig part
of the shrub out, she added, "But it may not help him. Some it
doesn't."

"Then we're dead. I'll take it down. You go off along the hill—
make out you're looking for a better plant—"

She shook her head.

He had seen, in other matters, how she was not to be shifted when she had made up her mind. For a second he wondered. For he had come to know her so swiftly, though he knew so little of her, too, less than he knew of anyone he had spent months with.

He took the bunch of Febrifuga. Its dark green leaves trailed over his arm. It had a pungent smell.

"How terrible," she said, as they walked back, "how terrible he should cry like a child."

Hephaestion saw her eyes were far off, looking at this image in her head. Some vicious and evil man weeping, reduced from all his mighty stature. Hephaestion did not pity Hadz at all.

"Do you care for him?" he asked lightly. The guard was behind, hanging back, not listening only watching.

Coira said nothing.

She had that faculty, too, rare in a woman—rare in all mankind, even among dwarves: silence.

Having returned below, they had to go by a raft along Woe Stream, as before.

Everyone kept quiet now. The ominous enormity of the task weighed on them. Only the steward bit his nails and spat them in the water.

As they landed, he commented, "It stinks, that plant. He'll puke."

"No," said Coira.

Hephaestion thought, *She sounds like a queen now. Or a priestess. Well, she's royal.* And then he thought, *They say Hadz is half royal— Draco's son by some hill wench, and that he took to this life to avoid the perils of the court at Korchlava—*

Hadz's Hell valley was as unpleasant as ever. The ghost poplar and stagnant Lethe pool, which today reeked like excrement, the shambles of rubbish and huts that was the mansion, made worse by its columns and the badly paved avenue.

Inside they were put into another of the cramped chambers, bare but for its sacking curtains and single smoking torch.

The steward went, returned.

"He's sleeping. They give him something, but it wears off. You, you come with me and bring your weeds." Hephaestion, too, stepped forward. "And *you* stay put."

When Hephaestion tried to ignore the command, as if too stupid to realize, one of the guards grabbed him. Then Coira spoke, cool and pure and hard as any sliver of marble from the quarry: "He must come with me and assist me."

The steward loured. After a moment he shrugged.

"Come on, then."

Hephaestion knew she had spoken to save him a beating. He had no skills with herbs.

They traversed the corridor-alleyways. All was still, everyone afraid to make a noise and wake Hadz from his drugged torpor.

At last there was a great wide room fashioned from the midst of the warren. Torches burned on spikes here. Behind a drape of black silk was some activity, not decipherable. Guards stood like gargoyles, pulling faces of repressed violence. Hephaestion considered why no one had ever seized such a chance to murder Hadz and grasp the throne of Elusion. Perhaps they had, now?

Then a thin old man came out from around the curtain. He put his finger to his lips and came to Coira. "Tell *me* what must be done. You are not to come near him." He uttered this in a whisper. His face was webby and unkind. Here then, how oddly, must be the authority which kept Hadz safe at such an hour.

Coira, too, whispered. "It's simple. Give him one leaf. He must chew and swallow it. If he keeps it down, two more at intervals, until the pain dies. After this, one leaf on waking."

"How many days?"

"While he lives," said Coira.

She was offering only the teaching of Ulvit, something she had remembered, having once seen its dramatic result.

The old man seemed to read veracity from her eyes.

He stared at and into her.

"*I* will now eat one leaf, then two more. If I die, these here will kill you, slowly. You and your goblin will stay in this room until I'm sure."

Coira retained her silence.

Hephaestion let the old man take the plant called Febrifuga.

"Is that the proper dose?" Hephaestion asked her, when they had been sent back from the curtain and again left alone, but for the guards, who had also moved off across the hall, as if to be sure no error of Coira's could rub off on them.

"It's what I recall. Perhaps it isn't right. That measure was for a woman, and Hadz is a man."

"If it fails, take to your heels. You may escape them. I can see to a few here."

But she did not reply, until she said, "You'll leave me soon, am I right, Hephaestion? When the spring is full, then?"

"Oh, maybe."

"Do the others go with you?"

"Proud and the rest? No. I'd travel alone, now."

"Is that my doing?"

"No. I've had my days with them."

"And with me."

"Not here, Coira. Wait until we're free of this."

"Very well," she said. "But if the herb doesn't help, I won't run away."

"*Why?* Not run away—to punish me, like some bitch, for going off? Coira—"

"Hush," she said softly, as if to a child she loved.

And Hephaestion did as she said.

How long they waited neither of them knew.

With no warning, an insane, loud cry burst up from behind the curtain, echoing all through the wide hall.

The guards raced forward. They made a circle around the girl and the dwarf, lined inside with drawn knives.

Hephaestion saw he had been romancing when he tried to convince her he could make any delay for death. They were in the hall of Death, in any case.

Then the old man was there, pushing the guards away with unusual strength. He poked his head forward at Coira. "Where did you get this knowledge?"

"From my nurse."

"She was a witch?"

"A Woodswoman."

"She taught you well." Impatient, he turned to the lingering guards. "Get back, you oafs. It's not poison. I took it and live. And on him it was a miracle. A great miracle."

"Is that what made him call out?" Coira said.

"Yes. I got him to eat it before he properly woke. He lay like the dead and then he cried out loud, and then he looked at me with his eyes wide, as he's not been able to open them three days. He said he felt the first leaf move in him like a snake. It found the pain and bit it in two pieces, and both flew up out of his skull and were gone. That was only the one leaf."

"Then, no more," said Coira, placid again as some nun, "no more until tomorrow, unless the pain returns."

"You shall see to it," said the old man. As if he rewarded her.

"No," Coira said. "You must do it."

They stood gaping at her, the ring of men, the guards, the sinister old one, and her lover, astounded by the sheer glass of her denial from which they slipped away.

And when she turned and walked out of the hall of King Death, only Hephaestion followed her.

Five days passed before the steward came again to the shack-house. He brought back all the mirror-lid silver that had been tithed from the dwarves. He told Coira she must gather or dig up Febrifuga from the hills. The prince would need it all.

"It won't live down here in the dark," said Coira. Careless, she added, "I'll dry the leaves so he can keep them by him. I'll show whomever you want where it grows."

By then she and Hephaestion had talked openly of his departure. Neither had raised their voice. She had not pleaded for his change of mind, as she had pleaded in her heart for him to come to her at the first.

"I'll go up with you when you gather the leaves. When it's done, you mustn't stay down here. Go with me anyway, as far as Korchlava. You're the king's daughter—"

"What is that?" she asked him, this marble priestess. "What is that worth?"

He could not tell her—for kings, and king's daughters, meant nothing also to him. And *she*—she had seen even her love did not penetrate his inmost skin.

"Forgive me, sweetheart, sweet girl."

"I made you do it," she said. "It is my fault."

"I was glad to do it. You're the best of all women—but not a woman of my kind. I made no secret of it."

"You allowed me to love you," she said. "That's all I asked. Our bargain is complete. And over."

II.

*T*HAT DAY WAS TO BE THEIR LAST, together.

They went up to see the market, and to gather one final sheaf of herbs to satisfy Hadz.

In the night, they would lie together.

Then, it would be done. He would leave her. She would make her life alone, below the ground or above. Wherever, without him.

So, they were deep in thought, each of them, and very courteous, very considerate of each other, for he was burdened by unease, and in her, rancor did not exist. She must face her loss, as ever, without rage. And her agony had become so vast, she had to turn her face from it, like a sickness of her flesh she no longer had patience with.

On the hills, the spring market was by now established. There were performances of many sorts to watch, and things to buy with the real value of coins.

He gave her a pomegranate like a rosy bulb of rock, mummified and hard. "You can't eat it, now, it's mulch inside. But it will keep its shape until the fresh ones come in summer." They had talked about pomegranates once, those she had seen grown at Belgra Demitu. They had been thought unlucky by the Woods People, but even so Ulvit had contrived to let her taste the winey pink seeds. Now he gave her this token which would not even last. As if he too tried to ensorcel her, so her painful love of him would eventually crumble and rot, like the stone fruit.

But he bought her a long piece of blue silk, too, for a gown. And then a bracelet of thin amber. So she said, "Please don't buy me anything else."

"Very well," he answered soberly.

He stored his gifts for her in the inner places of his tunic, as she requested. They would keep the aroma of his flesh for her, a short while.

For him she bought nothing. She had money now, for he had given her half of what he had, a staggering amount to any but the daughter of a king. The coins conveyed little, of course. And she had anyway given him everything, all her self, and this had not been enough. Trinkets were superfluous.

They went up and down the hills under a pale sky, looking at the market and searching for the one last fine crop of Febrifuga. She would dry its leaves over the fire, as she had done with the others, crush them into powder, which now sometimes was what she sent to Prince Hadz. She had also marked a scrap of parchment, brought her by the steward, with the spots on the hills where the plant would grow. The old man had sent someone besides. They knew the plant's places. But it seemed they valued her preparation of the herb as much as the herb. She was, after all, a witch.

"Don't linger in Elusion," Hephaestion warned her. "*He* may decide to keep you. The old fellow saw you were beautiful, and God knows how Hadz's tastes may run. The stories about his perversions are endless. Won't you come with me to Korchlava?" And be left there, he meant.

"I won't linger here."

He did not ask her where she would go. But again he said, "I'd be glad if you came on with me to the city."

They would part tonight. She said, "Let's not talk of that."

Slowly he nodded.

They turned away from the market now and once more ascended. Crossing over large stones, he assisted her like a deferential courtier.

They found a lush clump of Febrifuga easily. It was powdered by the white dust of the quarries, from which drifted the rhythm of picks. Once they had the plant free, Hephaestion wrapped it in a cloth; when visible, there were often enquiries, rude, even dangerous.

The sky was raining when they came down. Coira pulled her shawl up over her head, but they did not hurry. Everything on this last day was to be experienced, stored. (Would they ever again behold thick spring rains unmoved?)

Hephaestion failed, and Coira, to see the old woman standing by the path. Did not notice her as they passed her so closely.

The guard at the cave-entry made some remark upon them, the girl and her dwarf, the imp and his mistress. They paid no attention to that, either. This man knew what they had been at, and who needed the herb, so he was not as coarse as others. Coira was a witch. Coira was in favor with the Prince of Hell.

And when Coira was next followed by an eldritch beggar-crone with a basket, the guard was not surprised to learn she was the witch's kin, and knew to be careful of her, too.

*   *   *

She paid for her journey through Elusion with apples.

Coming in where she had, she did not need to use Hate River, but she saw it below as she wandered like a shadow in her daughter's wake. She saw all of Hell, the cliffs and great rock rafters, the descents and inner darknesses. Nothing moved her. Only her goal had meaning.

But at length she saw the torchlit, pale-glowing shack-house on the ledge above, with the pearly root-claws arching over it. To her, this was some cot in the winter wood.

She stopped still, and watched the two figures go inside.

After a while, when they did not come out again, she sat down on a spur of rock, and put her basket by her.

It was almost empty, the basket. A few copper coins were in it, and three or four fruits she had not given away to men who had come at her in the mine-caves.

No one bothered her now. She had become apparently indigenous.

Arpazia did not know it, but the day passed on. She fell asleep. She was woken by the lone mooing of the single horn from the prince's valley, which signaled midnight. Shouts went off here and there about the cavern at this note. Then died down.

She looked only at the shack-cottage. She knew the girl had not left it. Oh yes, Arpazia would now have felt such a thing, even in sleep.

And slumber came again, and took her away.

Did Arpazia dream? She thought she did. She was wandering in the Underworld, and cloudy shapes blew against her but did her no harm. She held a torch high, but it had gone out. Even so, she saw her way by all the other lights of Hell.

In the dream, the cottage was made of silver and had a golden roof. The tree was silver, too, a silver web which held the cottage fast. She sensed a snake coiled in the tree, a snake or spider, protecting something.

Arpazia knocked on a door of brackish green, polished beryl. "Let me in, let me in—"

"Who is there?" the girl called out in the dream.

"I am here."

"Is it you? But who are you?"

"Only yourself."

Arpazia thought she would go in and find a child with long black hair. She would comb the hair and dress the child in a white dress, tie a ribbon at her waist. Or the child might be a baby still, and then she must suckle it, give it the milk that flowed clear white from her breast.

In the magic beryl of the door, Arpazia seemed to foresee all this.

But then a new brassy shouting rose on all sides and woke her again. It was the trumpets of the cavern, which bellowed for dawn.

Arpazia sat bemused on her stone. What must she do?

While she worried at this, a man came down the rocks and passed her. He was a handsome, broad-skulled, cripple-footed man the height of a child. His face was melancholy and shut tight. Ambiguous as a mask.

Hephaestion did not see her, again, as he went away, nor she him, now.

Not long after this, two other dwarves came out from the cottage. (Tickle and Proud, going to their work in the mines.)

Arpazia watched, carefully.

Had all of the dwarves now left the cot?

She had lost count—had seven come out? Perhaps.

Half-closing her eyes, Arpazia fancied she saw the alchemical serpent twined in the tree roots above the house. It would be guarding the apples which grew there, forbidden to mankind.

Arpazia stood up. Her stiffness went from her instantly. She picked up the basket reflexively. How young she felt.

She went up the rock and, when she reached the torch, she looked in the shack's doorway. Something shone out—back at her.

For a second she saw herself, an old beggar-woman with a basket—

She had caught in her vision a long glass crack showing in the covered mirror on the shack's wall.

> *Mirror, mirror on the wall,*
> *Am I the fairest of them all?*

She was not.

But now—now the actuality replaced the lie.

For there she was in the flesh. A slim alabaster form, combing a veil of raven hair. Coira had come from her alcove. Alone (utterly alone), she stood naked in the shack, clad only in her hair.

Arpazia remembered and recognized the proper image.

She crept near and called, "I'm here, my love. Let me in."

III.

SHE HAD BEEN THE WOMAN, SHE had been the Witch, and the Queen, and she had even been a stepmother, which was to say a mother to a child orphaned by the maternal parent's death. She had been magnetic and unreachable as the moon. She had grown awful and phantasmal as a demoness. Her back, her turned face, these were the memory; her frozen hands.

In this new, disturbed garb, ragged garments, raddled skin, could Coira even know her?

"What do you want?" Coira said. And she drew her shawl up to cover herself, without rush or shame, more as a civility to the stranger.

But Arpazia had seen. It was herself right enough. The mirror had lessoned her in this body and this face.

"You don't know me, then," she said, rational and cool. Madness had made her again in a form of sanity. "You don't know who I am."

Always these exchanges between them: *Is it you? Who are you? You don't know me.*

Who could say they knew themselves? Who can? Even the ancient gods had reminded men of this.

Coira's brain was full only of one lost one.

As was Arpazia's brain.

"Only I'm here," said Coira. "Do you want to barter what's in the basket?" Even in her misery, she did not cast the destitute crone out.

"Delicious fruit," said Arpazia, scathingly. She realized she was hungry, so she drew out one of the yellow preserved apples and bit into it. The honey was now so saccharine it puckered her mouth. She took another bite, then held out the apple to the girl—to Coira—to her child.

But Coira did not take the apple.

There was a narrow bracelet on her wrist. Arpazia looked at it. "Let me comb your hair."

Coira said nothing. She sat down woodenly on a stool by the fire-pit, in her covering of shawl and tresses.

"Yes," said Arpazia. "I'll comb your long black hair. I'll make it smooth. That nurse-woman pulled at your hair. I saw her. She pulled it, that wretched girl, my hair, until I threw the glass bottle at her. But I can do it nicely."

Something lifted and looked up, *behind* Coira's face.

She stayed motionless, as the crone came gliding up to her. She had no comb, yet seemed to think she had one—Coira's she did not take. Instead she began to run her long, thin fingers through and through the rich, filmy skeins of hair, which grew electric at the touch, and flew up like smoke.

"Who are you?" said Coira. Her voice *was* like a child's, high and rough.

"Who am I?" said Arpazia, combing her daughter's hair, comb-

ing the hair which was hers. "Guess who I am. Who could I be?
Who would come here after you?"

There were no rings, to catch. Something so curious—the fingers silking through and through her hair—a kind of spell, an enchantment. Hypnotized, Coira leaned back upon the hands which
played her hair like the strings of harps—

How cold these hands. (She had not seen their snow-scars.)
Hands without rings . . .

Hands meeting in a wood-dance, like a blow.

Coira did not move. Her body leaned back against the hard
body of the crone—who smelled of honey and apples, of frost and
burned wood.

Within Coira something moved, darting behind her eyes.

"Are you my mother?"

"Yes, yes. I am your mother."

"Did—he send you away?"

"Hush, my love. Who could do that?"

"Why are you here?"

"Where else should I be?"

In Coira's fever dream: the shining brazier, the sweet odor of
the divine wood, the golden mother who comforted her and made
her immortal. But that had been Demetra, the goddess.

In Arpazia's waking dream: the golden faces and the diamond
tears, oh, the sorrows of the flesh, my dear, my dear. It's a terrible
thing to lose your child.

"But I've found you," said Arpazia, combing and stroking the
living hair of the young girl, which was her own, which she had
created with her own womb. "He told me you lived, even though
I tried to make you die. He said you lived and here you are. My
dear, my love—"

And Arpazia folded her arms gently around her child, cradling
her shoulders and the head which leaned on her.

Inside Coira torrents of spring rain, leaping under her eyes—

"Why did you hate me then?" she said, in her child's voice.
"Why did you—did you try—to kill me—"

"Oh, I never did. I could never do that. You're myself born again in flesh. His and mine. All made of love. How I love you, Coira, best of all."

Coira turned in her mother's arms. She clung to Arpazia, and the torrents burst from her. She wept, clinging to this woman who was her mother, and her mother held her close.

Coira thought, *What is this that I'm doing? Fool—fool—who is she?* It made no difference.

And she could hear that the woman cried too, long, hoarse sobs that were full of emptiness becoming filled, and silence finding how to make a sound.

Coira had learned to trust no one. But this was beyond trust.

The spiteful voice in Arpazia's head could discover no words.

On the hearth the fire crackled, and far off the mines boomed like the sea.

Through its cracks and eyeholes in sacking and caked dirt, the mirror looked. The mirror sensed an imminence.

The mirror gazed into the flames of the fire, on which diamonds had scattered.

I am still bright, said the fire to the mirror.

I, too, said the mirror, in parts.

But I, said the fire, shall soon go out. Is it death?

It is, the mirror said. Death is the imminence which I feel. Your death, and mine, also.

But the women were murmuring on and on, like bees. The mirror looked away, up through the dirt and the air and the rock of the cavern and the stone and marble of the hills. The mirror saw Hephaestion already walking on the road to the city. The mirror saw the sunlight, and the unwoken fields, and the bees which gathered among the first fronds of spring.

There is no death, said the mirror, only changing.

Yes, said the fire and closed its spangled eyes.

* * *

"Let me light the fire again," said Coira sleepily. "It will get cold."

But her mother would not let her go.

She's smothering me, Coira thought. *Her arms round my waist, my neck, her long dusty hair, snow-white now, all over me, in my mouth even. I can hardly breathe.*

Coira would not let Arpazia go. She held on to her, and would not let her stir, even though the fire was out and Tickle's time candle showed the day was almost gone.

Let her smother me. I want her to. What else is there for me?

And Arpazia held her as if to press her back inside her body, into the warm oven of her womb. And as if to press herself into the womb of Coira.

They had murmured fragments of the past, the dreams. They had eaten the honey-apples from the basket, sharing them. The sweet, sweet taste burned across their lips, closing their throats, gluing their tongues to the ceilings of their mouths.

Together they curled by the fire, from which a soft heat still came, though it had died an hour before.

"You're my beauty," said Arpazia, "the most beautiful in all the world. Skin like snow and hair like ebony and your lips red as a rose. Oh, you're mine." Arpazia had never known her mother, who had died, they told Arpazia, at Arpazia's birth.

Coira tried to speak, but could not. Her voice, like the dire voice in her mother's head, had gone dumb. This did not matter. Arpazia sang to her. It concerned snow and roses.

Coira's ears sang, too, like the sea. She breathed in tiny shallow gasps and her heart pounded, rattling her breast. But she was happy. So happy at last. She had not lost her love. All love was here. She did not need to trust, only give in.

She held tighter still, but now her fingers had no grip. She did not realize, for Arpazia held her so close, tighter, tight as any loving, clinging child.

Her hair tastes of the honey. Or of wood. She has the smell of apples. Why do they say not to eat the apple? Oh, because it holds the knowledge of good and evil, of living and dying. And of sleep.

Coira slept.

Arpazia slept, also.

(Tickle and Proud worked late in the mines, reluctant to come home, knowing Hephaestion was gone and the abandoned girl alone.)

The day candle glimmered down to a stump and its flame shivered to nothing. No one lit another candle.

But outside the torch burned on, and Elusion went on with its calls and thunders and blasphemies.

And the mirror looked, and saw Death standing on the threshold in the dusk, a suitor on foot, without his chariot or horses. His eyes were the eyes of night and he bowed three times to his bride, promised him so long before in the wood.

Then his shadow swung before him into the room. It was a giant. Yet when he followed, he was the greater.

The Mirror: Inside the Glass

I

WHEN THEY RETURNED, IT was after midnight. Proud and Tickle had finished their late work, and brought away a small bag of gold dust, unseen. They had begun to talk of leaving the mine, and meant soon to call on Soporo, Greedy, and the other dwarvixens, to see if they too might wish to travel elsewhere. They had all gained confidence in Elusion, for none challenged their masterless state, though many had come to realize that they were not truly owned.

They had stopped to drink at the Black Still. Proud was merry, Tickle serene.

"The house is dark," said Proud, as they climbed up to the shack. They were glad. They could slink in and not need to see Coira, either to spurn or to be kind to her. (They blamed her, too, for Stormy's going off, even Tickle did. If he had not taken up with her, surely he would have stayed.)

Just outside, under the torchlit roots, they paused. There was a savage smell, stifling, like that of certain flowers.

"What is it?"

"Some attar of the spring market, some Eastern stuff."

Into the shack they went.

"She's let the fire go out, useless mistress-slut," muttered Proud.

"No matter. We've the brazier upstairs."

"It's cold."

But Tickle found the wide room hot, and the smell of the perfume made her head swim.

"Let's go up. I don't like it here," said Proud, drunk enough to be empathic.

Tickle saw them first.

"What's there?" asked Proud, nervously.

But Tickle was already bending over them, the two women. Her eyes were more accustomed to the dark than Proud's. Besides, the torch shone in at an angle, catching the outline of two faces curiously alike, although one was scarred and fallen, the other young.

"Mistress," said Tickle, "Coira-mistress, who is this?"

Coira did not open her eyes.

It was the other eyes which opened.

Even so, they *were* the eyes of Coira, there in the undone face, pale as water.

"What do you want?" the old woman said. She was imperious. She might have been royal.

Tickle leaped back like a frog.

She pushed at Proud. "Out—out we go!"

Out they went.

"What?" said Proud, frightened, already knowing.

"She's dead. Stormy's girl. She wasn't taking any breath. That smell—it's poison. The air's full of it."

"But the other one—"

"Some market crone, her basket was there. The smell was coming out of the basket. Quick, we'll go for the others."

They scuttled down the rock and away into the lit and endless cavernal night.

And in the shack, Arpazia settled herself again, the girl clasped tight. But she did not feel so happy. She was less sure, Arpazia, of what she did. The light weight, heavier with its inertia, hung on her, giving her back nothing, now. It did not speak lovingly, *Mother, Mother, is it you?* It was no longer warm. Even the tendrils of hair were dry as torn grass. Never mind it, Arpazia would sleep again. All was well.

The next waking would be less gradual. As if she knew, she went deeply down again to nothingness.

To the dwarves all mankind—above-beneath them—was crazed, potentially lethal. Whatever they did, God's proper people, must bode no good for the dwarf kind.

Soporo, when they brought him out of his lubricious hutch, told them the situation in the shack was better left alone. But Greedy, when he joined them, exclaimed that he had left property concealed there. They must go back and take what was theirs.

Vinka, too, asserted this, nodding and sizzling, while Want hid herself in the dark.

Even Tickle assented that they could do nothing for Coira. The mad old basket-woman had killed her, perhaps even at Coira's wish. Who could gauge the minds of the God-Made, since they were all so warped?

They went back to the shack. Then crept about, and took anything that was their own.

Only Soporo leaned right over the two cuddled, unconscious women, a taper burning in his hand. He ogled Coira, storing the partial view of her slim nudity. To her life or death he was indifferent. She was of another race, and she had parted them from one of their own.

"Perhaps we may find him," whispered Proud, "now, in the city . . ."

But each of them knew they would not seek for Stormy. He was lost to them. They did not really want him any more—*she* had defiled him.

And only Jealous Vinka sniffed at the basket, and brought out of it, in her fingers, a scrap of candied apple.

"It's fruit," said Tickle, wonderingly. But the scent of it made her dizzy. She smelled it on them, and on herself, for several days after they had left the shack far behind.

The mirror had seen Death cross the threshold in the night. A pair of hours after Elusion's trumpeted dawn, he would come back, in his other, mortal shape.

But the mirror on the wall had grown cold by then. Formerly, the fire had been kept going always, and the big candles, and the torch at the door. Now the fire was long out, the candle, too, and then the torch gave up its ghost.

The hard mud and soot packed across the mirror's face chilled and grew more brittle. A piece of sacking dropped like an autumn leaf.

By then, Death's second form was already approaching. The mirror waited, which was all it could do.

Juprum had been the prince's servant in the village above Korch-lava, where his mother gave birth to him. She had boasted that the child was Draco's—King Draco's, as by then Draco was a king. In the sixteen or seventeen years which followed, the mother died. Her household declined, and the boy became a robber by trade. It was the trade of many in that area. Juprum too aged. But age did not alter his opinions, only welded them fast.

He believed the boy to be a prince, as the mother had insisted. Juprum believed this because the boy was unusual, so handsome and well-made, and capable of such extraordinary charm—as if only a king (and he had never seen Draco) could impart these qualities.

The boy's, and next the young man's alter-temperament was not enough to turn Juprum from him. He went on serving him faithfully through all the sixteen, seventeen years, and even journeyed below with him to the mine caverns. Here, through luck and chance and murder and other such things, his favorite came to be the Prince of the Underworld.

By now, Juprum had forgotten Hadz's other name.

Juprum did not lust after his lord. It was not so simple or so lively. He had only, vinelike, grown about Hadz. He would have done anything for him. And now he went with him, across Hell, with a retinue of ten of the prince's guards, to make yet one more claim.

Juprum approved of all of this. He wished his darling to be well and at his best. He preferred him to get whatever he wanted.

Strangely, Juprum also believed in God. However, he thought God was bribable, like most men, all men Juprum had seen. So it did not count what one did, providing at the end everything was repented.

Strangely too, more strangely, Juprum was not aware of how belatedly his prince entered into the history of the two white-skinned women, lying at that moment in each other's arms, both of them seeming to be dead. Juprum had had Prince Hadz at the core of all his own later life. Hadz was the crux of Juprum's story, and the two women were merely to be an added element, like another couple of silver stitches sewn on Hadz's cloak.

Also, as Juprum would have said, in many tales of women, the lord—the man—a prince or king, need only intervene during the last quarter, even the last lines. There were plenty of such recitals. A virgin would dance, the prince see her and capture her shoe as a token. Or the girl would be imprisoned by some sorcery, the prince arriving to free her in the final moment of the tale. Man was the fate of woman.

Juprum walked easily behind Hadz, admiring the tall, straight, striding figure, the cloak with its bullion fringes, the massed, cascading hair that was as black as the word *black*. There were rings on the prince's hand, a veined amethyst and a crimson ruby. His profile, shown as he turned to look about, was keen-cut and as perfect itself as a jewel.

The inhabitants of Hell peered after him. Some wisely kneeled down. A number even crossed themselves, and this amused Hadz. (He smiled—he had flawless teeth.)

He was in sound health. The witch-leaves or their powder had seen to that. Juprum had been content ever since they worked their magic. But of course, what else would Hadz want than to take that girl to him? What a treat she was to have. She did not deserve it— but then, Juprum decided reasonably, perhaps she merited *something* for her cleverness in driving off the pain.

As they came up the track through the other hovels and shambles, Hadz said, "Is that the place, up there? She has a white tree, as I do."

There was also a consumed torch by the door.

Juprum did not deal in omens.

The guard ranged themselves about, and one yelled in at the doorway, "Stir yourselves! The prince is here to visit you!"

But no one stirred.

Juprum frowned. His glorious master was all grace and unconcern.

"Leave it. I'll go in."

He ducked under the door's lintel—Hadz was tall.

Only Juprum followed, allowed such a privilege since he liked to be ever helpful and ready to hand.

"Look, Juprum. Oh, look."

The old man grimaced, trying to see in the dark. There was a heap of something—some shawls and rags The air was drowned in perfume and honey.

All at once Hadz sprang forward, leopardlike. "Christ! Marusa of the blue veil—"

Fear laid its tentacles on Juprum's spine.

"*What*, my prince?"

Hadz, like the abjects outside, was kneeling now. He snarled, the leopard, "Give me *light*."

"Light!" screeched Juprum.

Someone brought it.

Then they looked, and even Juprum saw.

After a long while, Hadz separated the women. He did this with an almost feminine delicacy, so the elder one, who had coiled the younger like a serpent, did not wake. Then Hadz tried to wake the girl. He stroked her, even kissed her forehead, cheek. Juprum stood ready to pull him back from her lips—for the old man already suspected from their stillness, from the odor, some drug or bane.

Presently Hadz slapped the girl's face, quite lightly. She did not respond. A faint whisper of blood showed from the slap, but not enough.

Hadz turned. He looked at Juprum, disappointed and almost childish. "What is it, Juprum?"

"I don't know, my prince. Something bad has been done. She was a witch, wasn't she? And from the look of it, she consorted with other witches."

"But she's beautiful. She's as beautiful as I am," said Hadz, logically. Somehow he had never learned beauty did not necessarily protect.

He went on idly smoothing her breasts that a loose shawl did not much conceal, her hip and thigh, the slender hands with nails so bloodless now they were like crystal, her flowing hair which was, Juprum grudgingly thought, as black as Hadz's own.

She might have been a fitting consort. But Juprum could see she did not breathe. The other one did.

"She's dead, sir. But the old beldame's alive. Shall I wake her up?"

"*I* will," said Hadz.

And then, in one of his graceful, superlative movements, he took the older woman in his arm, and rose straight up with her. And for a moment then, he stood looking in her ruined face, and her eyes began to open and to see him. Hadz smiled. "What have you done, you bitch?" said Hadz gently, "What have you done to my lovely girl?" And then he flung the old woman from him, with all his considerable young strength, straight at the wall.

And the mirror waited, and saw the black star flung and rushing toward it. The mirror felt the meeting with the star. Then the mirror was shattered, and became also stars, black stars and white, and scarlet.

The packed soot, the sacking, the shards of glass that broke free and clean, and the splinters that were suddenly edged with blood, they burst around the body of Arpazia. They fell like thick snow upon the floor. They covered over the motionless body of the girl, leaving only her face quite alone, filling her night of hair with glittering constellations.

I am dead, said the mirror, in its thousand severed voices.

But then it found its soul still stood upright in the smoking air, whole and reflecting—but invisible to the creatures in the room.

"Has she been cut, my lovely one?"

Hadz pulled the glass away from Coira. He took no notice of its rarity, nor its teeth. Juprum pulled him back, and got Hadz's fist in his face as recompense. But Juprum was used to that.

"No, no, Prince—you'll damage your hands. Let me do it."

So Hadz stood away, and the guards and Juprum gingerly picked off the glass.

She had not been cut—oh, just two or three little red kisses, on her shoulder, and on her foot, and her palm. They scarcely bled.

But over there, the other woman had sat down, and she had been cut rather more—her cheek, her arms, her knees, the length of her back. Her grimy dark and pallor was brightly dyed.

Her eyes were wide now, like those of a half blind, uncanny owl. But she did not speak. She seemed to be searching round after something she had no vitality to get up and look for.

When Hadz towered over her again and screamed at her in his fury, she only shook her head. Perhaps she was dazed.

So he turned from her.

"Who is she?"

"Some old witch—"

"Find out who she is."

What would that be worth? But they never protested the orders of Hadz, Hell's Prince.

Some of his scum of guards went out at once to inquire, glad enough to go.

They found out, too. A few of Elusion's inhabitants had belly-aches from her wares, and were cursing her. There had been something in her fruit which did not agree with everyone, though others who had eaten it had nothing to report. But then the man spoke up who had witnessed her come into Hell from the hill, following the one now known as the witch who served Hadz.

"Her mother she said she was. I could see it, too. They had the same face, though one was a hag."

Then Hadz, in another place of darkness, bent to Arpazia again. "Your daughter? You were her *mother*? Mothers love their children. Why did you poison her?"

Arpazia heard his voice, and the other voice that spoke beneath: *"You killed . . . don't you know how you hurt me? The child in you—you and I both . . . you crushed it out . . ."*

"Yes, I killed her," Arpazia murmured. "I came to find her and do it. I didn't want the child, I never did. It was with herbs I had, in a black cup. She's dead now. Now there's only me."

The mirror, standing in the air, closed its single huge eye.

Dwarves constructed the girl's coffin, an irony of which Hadz was unaware. For they were not the seven who had entered Elusion with her, of course. Those seven were gone. But these other dwarves had a reputation for being talented artisans. One of them had already made for Hadz his exquisite ruby ring.

The coffin was unusual. Hadz had wanted it to be as it was, something rare, unlike all other things. And, he had come to understand, such mirror-glass was fabulous, a sorcerous artifact from the East.

"She's so beautiful," he said, on the third day, lamenting, weeping even, cheated. Juprum was not so afraid of these tears; they did not denote pain. "She's not gone rotten, she doesn't reek. Look—she's pliable still."

"It's curious, my prince. But it can't last. She doesn't breathe; I can find no pulse-beat. Better to put her away while she's fresh, and not spoil your memory of her."

Juprum did not know if Hadz, during these days when he kept the corpse in the High Chamber of his palace, took advantage of her state to copulate with the dead witch. Juprum hoped not.

The coffin was made of the broken mirror. A coffin of glass. Each piece of any size had been set into a frame of heavy iron, then all was decorated by leaves of gold and flowers of silver, with jewels from Hadz's treasury. Hadz loved the result dearly. It was the most bizarre object imaginable.

Gazing at it, once it was sealed, Hadz at last noted that he could see himself reflected there over and over. Which was almost better than being able to see straight in at the coffin and observe the wonderful dead girl.

"She and I were equals in beauty. What was her name?"

Juprum had already told him he did not know. Hadz tended to forget.

"I never heard it, sir."

"A witch's name?"

"Perhaps, my prince."

Juprum had seen that the coffin, fashioned so elaborately and in such a hurried, short space of time, had many little portions that were not properly joined or closed. With the days, the months, the stink of death would issue from this coffin (then God help the dwarvish artisans). Then it would need to be moved out of the mansion's hall. Juprum would prefer that, and said nothing about having the cask more tightly corked.

Soon, with luck, Hadz, who was currently obsessed, must lose interest in it.

He had already forgotten the mother—if so she was. Juprum, aware that Hadz might recall her eventually, had seen to it that her cuts were dressed, and that she was fed. Once he went himself to look at her, where she paced about in the hut, one of several kept as the prince's dungeons. Outside the metal wall, you could hear Lethe Pond wiggling on its stones.

"How are you today?"

"I am well enough," said the old witch in the queenly voice she sometimes assumed.

"Are you still pleased you killed her?"

"Killed whom?"

"Your child, you old beast. Your daughter."

But then she did not reply. She went up and down, round and about, pacing out the hut. Her face was gravely marked. A bandage on her wrist had come away. The dried blood was black.

Juprum was offended, despised her. Whatever other crimes were committed, mothers must not kill their own children. Even a bribable God would never forgive that.

II.

*T*HE MIRROR'S SOUL SAW COIRA, walking across the sky. It was that time between day and dusk. Traces of the sun still lingered below, but here and there stars were piercing through. The land was like a shadow, miles down. Coira looked at it, holding back her blowing hair. She walked on small banks of cloud, like steppingstones or ice-floes in a transparent river.

She was puzzled, thinking she should descend, but not knowing how. Then she saw Hephaestion in the distance, walking toward her.

Coira straightened. At first he seemed as he had always been, and delight suffused her. But then, as he came nearer, she saw he was the same height as herself. Then she drew herself together, unsure.

He paused, across a floe of cloud. He gazed back at her. Soon, by some unknown process, he was no longer her height, but his own, as she remembered him.

While this happened, more stars appeared, but the sky did not lose any of its clarity.

"Have you come back?" she said.

"I don't know. I'm dreaming of you," he said. "I'm convinced I'm dreaming. Why are you here?"

"I died," said Coira, but hearing the words, she checked and grew still. "How can I be dead?"

"Coira, don't be dead. Why would you die?"

"My mother—my mother came to me, and I was somehow drunk—and like a child. And then I fell asleep. But all I can taste is honey, only it's so bitter. Oh, I know what it is—yes, Ulvit once warned me. Sometimes the bees gather from the wrong plants. Not everyone is harmed—but some—sometimes whole families. The honey from the flowers will be like deadly venom to one, and like nothing to another. Poppies can be the worst, she said. Perhaps— but I can't recall any remedy. Besides, it's too late. It must have been the fruit we ate. We shared apples. The smell—perhaps that made me drunk. She ate it too. We slept. But I'm dead. Oh, what shall I do—where shall I go?"

He stood across from her on the cloud. The space of open sky between them was too broad to jump, too deep to wade across.

"If you were dead, Coira girl, you wouldn't be here, but in the other life."

"Yes. What is it, then? What am I to do?"

She began to cry.

He could not reach her, and this broke her heart, but he had left her anyway. He had left her and her mother had wished her to die, and brought the baleful honey-apple to see to it.

As she wept she became totally a child. She shrank as he had done, and now she was as short as Hephaestion. Her hair poured all round her, heaped over the cloud as it had never heaped round her when she was a little girl.

"I'm in a tomb, I know that I am," she sobbed. A voice in her head upbraided her: *Don't speak. Trust no one. Trust has brought you to this, you fool. Be silent.*

Then he sprang across the cloud and caught her to him. The same height again, he seized hold of her, more tightly than the wicked stepmother who had stifled and poisoned her.

"Try to see where you are," he said. "Where they've put you. Then show me."

She looked, but not with her eyes. Deep down in her mind, or the mind of her wandering spirit, she saw an iron hull with gold and silver briars that clambered over it, and set in these, luminous gems of emerald and violet. But there was water on the iron, too, sheets of it, gleaming.

"Do you see?" she asked. How could he? But he did. "Yes, Coira. It isn't water. It's the witch-glass we fixed to the wall. It's the mirror. *Hers.*"

"I'm shut inside the mirror," she whispered.

"Break out," he said.

"How?" she implored.

"I'll go across and wake myself up. Then I'll come back for you. I'll find you, Coira, wherever you are. I'll set you free. Sweetheart—don't be afraid."

He was gone. She spun about in terror and her foot slipped from the shining icy cloud.

How much the stumble had cost her. She fell with one shriek, from sky to earth.

It was done in a second. She struck the ground with a blow that shook her into bits, and at its impact, the thump of it between her shoulders, she choked.

Still half-detached, she heard herself crowing for her breath, heard and vaguely felt an acid vomit fly from her throat, rolled side-long, striking her body now against the hard shell which contained her.

Her voice was pushed away from her. It called piteously, even though she knew she must stay silent. "*Help me—help me—*"

Who would help her?

She was hated.

Darkness closed her eyes.

The howling of Hadz brought his faithful old servant running, as always it did. In abject fear for him, Juprum rushed into the High Chamber among the bright torches. Behind the drape of black silk, where Hadz had insisted the coffin be placed, Juprum found his prince lying full-length on top of it, beating with his fists.

"My prince—my dear one—"

"Be quiet, you cunt. *Listen!*"

"To what—to what, my best angel?"

But Hadz had grasped him; he pulled Juprum forward, twisted him and ground his ear against the adorned sarcophagus.

So, in this position, pinned against shards of glass, Juprum too heard. He heard the little struggling moth-voice flittering about in the coffin.

And Juprum crossed himself. For he was always respectful in the chancy presence of an ultimate master. (God.)

That day, King Draco rode through his spring city wearing a ver-milion mantle trimmed by panther-skin and gold, with his queen beside him. On her knee was the latest child, a fat, heavy boy who grinned his first teeth like a wolf. He resembled his father. The boy waved a rattle of silver; and the wide neck of the queen had em-bedded in it a necklace of fifty pearls.

The city saw them. Korchlava called acclaim. Canopied carriage

followed carriage. Horses nodded burnished heads, manes and tails
plaited by bells. Asphodel was tied on bridles, and hyacinths. They
had grown just in time.

Draco was still a king in red, at his prime. And she, his queen.
Her belly might already be rounding again. She was the moon at
full, the Nubile Woman.

Hephaestion watched them all go by, pushed though he was
this way and that by the holiday crowd. As by his thoughts.

It was a festival of the Christ. The city people were exchanging
red-painted eggs which symbolized Christ's blood, expected to be
spilled for them in due course.

But it was not the season of poppies, yet somehow he thought
of them. The poppies were in a girl's hand, as she was pulled
screaming down into the earth, which covered her over, swallowed
her.

Only the dead went into the earth.

And the physicians brewed a drug from poppies, which, in the
correct amount, made men glad and drew away their hurts. He had
seen that in the mines. But the draught could also suppress
breathing and induce death, if made too strong.

Why keep thinking of it? A dream he had had . . . He could not
recollect it, only Coira crying, as she had not done, when he left
her. No, she had been composed and stony-eyed. What would he
have done then, if she had wept? In the dream, he had wanted only
to hold her.

In God's name, why think of her now? She was behind him.
There was only this bloody world, this land of giants shoving him
about, jeering, all these subhuman superiors. He would have to do
tricks, clown, stupid things, to earn his living. And that must come
to be, when his valuables ran out. Look forward then, there would
be enough dross there. Let *her* alone. She had not tried to hinder
his leaving. "Farewell," she had said. Why then did he hear her
calling him now, *Help me—what shall I do?* She would never have
gone on like that. She had learned silence.

Yet that night, after seeing King Draco, he dreamed again of

the mirror they had tied on the wall. Someone was trapped inside—
he heard them calling. Then it shattered, and seven pieces jumped
from it, and each piece of glass was a woman, perfect and entire,
her black hair furled around her and her eyes flaming.

After which there flew out of the glass a white owl, then a raven
black as the soot, and last a nacreous dove, mourning, calling, *Help
me,* calling, *Where shall I go?* Which clung to his shoulder with its
coral claws, beating with its snow-white wings. *Don't leave me! Never
leave me!* So he took hold of it in his hands to save it from itself—
but it broke in fragments, since it, too, was made of glass.

Blood-Red

I

IN THE UNDERWORLD EVENING he returned to visit her. "Are you well at last?" he ardently demanded. Coira felt weak and weightless. She gazed at him. Somehow, it seemed he knew her familiarly. Obviously, he had had time to look at her, to study her while she lay in her stupor, her sham death. To her, he was a stranger.

"Perhaps I'm rather sick, still," she said, carefully.

"What? Oh, don't be, my beloved. I want to see you in health at once. We're meant to be together, you and I. God made us for each other."

He was alight with concupiscence. When he had been with her before, had this also been so?

She could see, for him, it was a welcomed, rational state, and that he enjoyed it, and was almost impatient with her. She had come back to life. They had revived her and let her out of the coffin. She had had all that night, and all this day, to recuperate, to bathe and use the scented unguents, to make herself ready, to grow hale, en-

amored and willing. For it was Hadz who was her prince, and she
had been made for him by God.

Coira accepted there was little she could do. Hadz was insane.
The whole of Elusion had always said so. Insane and liable to inflict
harm. He would not be open to reason or denial. She must give in
to whatever he wished with the best show of approval she could
summon.

But beyond his ghastly lust, still she felt mostly dead.

She had not properly known what happened. The first awak-
ening, the brief vomiting, and her agonizing first breaths, fading
away once more, with her pleading cry left hanging in the void
behind her. Before, there had been a sort of dream, but she could
not recapture it. After her initial return, there was a murky nothingness, and in it horrible clanging blows came and went, burning
the inside of her skull, roaring like church bells, so she thought she
lay in St. Belor, under the floor of the church. But that, too, passed.
And then she had been pulled out of the coffin, which axes had
shattered.

She thought later she had seen Prince Hadz staring down at
her, and for a moment she had seemed to recognize his face. There
was something in its pale-skinned glamour, its wildness of black
hair, that was like—her mother, then like *herself*. But then she
thought he was her lover, Hephaestion—but as they lifted her, and
carried her away, she knew that he was not. He was taller than any
of them. And at the back of his eyes skulked a bright something,
half animal, half phantom, which she did not know, but which made
her afraid.

Despite all the ministrations of Hadz's slaves, Coira lay very ill,
and leaden with despair. Her return to life was worse, it seemed to
her, than the onset of death.

Besides, she could not remember why she had died. It had been
a deliberate act, someone said. Who had slain her? Who? Ulvit—
no, not now—then who had it been? Was it Proud? Or had Vinka
done it in one of her fits?

Yes, it had been Vinka. It had been a woman . . .

As the awful night and day dragged on, the truth began to play a game with her mind, emerging, running to cover before she could quite see. In the end she did see it, the being of truth. It had the face of an elderly woman, scarred and sewn to its skull.

"Who is she?"

Your mother. Who else?

Coira was so fragile, she lay there weeping, weeping, and weeping. Until she made herself stop. She was in Hell. No one could assist her. By some fluke, and because Prince Hadz itched for her, she had lived.

Better get up then, use the hot bath full of scents which the memory of the apple infused. So, she made herself forget her mother. As every night, she would remember again.

A girl came and washed Coira's hair.

Cleansed by such things, the Miasma seemed to leave her. Dry-eyed she let his minions tend her.

Coira pulled round her a cover from the bed. They had not brought her any garments.

She knew he would come in. She knew that maybe—doubt-less—he had already seen her bare.

Once an old man appeared, went round her, making sure that she was wholesome enough for Hadz. This old man reminded Coira very oddly of a maiden's nurse—some male crone set to wait on the prince. At last she recollected she had met the old man before, when she had brought the Febrifuga leaves.

The old man spoke to Coira. "You've had a stroke of good for-tune. Be cheerful. Put this red salve on your lips. This kohl is for your lashes—they should have given you all this before. Yes, that's better. You must be tempting for him. Don't dare disappoint. I'll flog you myself if he regrets you."

Too ill to rally to her own horror, Coira said nothing.

And then, in the evening, Hadz arrived.

She could no longer pay much attention to his looks. For her, it was as if she sat in this little chamber with a mountain cat. She could see its talons and the long teeth, tipped by blood. No jot of its prettiness.

But the leopard sat down beside Coira on the couch.

"You're my lady in Hell," he said, musingly. "They told you your name? Let me tell you. You are Persapheh."

Coira knew the name, which belonged to the stolen goddess-daughter when she was the bride of Death.

She made no remonstrance, of course.

While they sat there, and he drank wine from a gold goblet, some gifts were brought in for her. There was a necklace of glaucous stones, and her own amber bracelet, which he slipped on to her wrist, it and his fingers like the shiver of a worm. But Hephaestion had given her the bracelet. She had been lucky to get it back.

Then they brought in another thing. A monstrous and unbelievable thing. She stared at it, partly losing her breath again, thinking, *What is it—what is it?* Knowing.

"She must have this back, my princess in Hell, my Persapheh," he announced. He seemed amused, but also vaunting—avaricious, lusting again—wanting her body but also this other *entity*—which was nearly a body, too. "They're afraid of it, those crawling vermin, those dung-fleas. The glass. Witch's glass. But you are my witch, Persapheh-Hekatis, Lady of Hell. Well, beloved. Get up. Go and put it on."

Naturally, she did what he said.

She got to her feet and drifted deathly to the nightmare thing.

As she did so, she saw herself, over and over, in fragments. She had fallen to the earth from the sky, and been smashed in bits. But her reflections were not all herself. She had become her mother as well, both old and young. She had become her father, King Draco. She had become Hephaestion. Hadz. And she had become the real Coira, the daughter of Demetra, whose corn-yellow hair hung round her, whose eyes were topaz. There was no means to shut these images away, for now the mirror was broken and had no lid. Instead it had been hung in segments upon this elemental object, tied there by gold wires, as were the silver and gold leaves and flowers, and strung between, the violet gems and the green emeralds. The tent-like structure which carried all this was itself some stiff velvet, the color of blood. It seemed it might have stood up by itself, so laden and immobile it had been made. Like armor.

Her coffin of glass and metals and jewels was given back to her—as a gown.

They had been putting it together, stitching and maneuvering in fear of his tortures, all this while. The mirror had mended, though it was in pieces; as she had, also in pieces.

A red queen. Hekatis, the witch of the Death Lands.

"Yes, yes. Help her into her robe!"

How insistent he was, the young and handsome prince.

"Gently," he added, and they quailed, the attendants, removing her bed-cover, passing her naked into the velvet sheathe.

Her coffin. It weighed on her like a robe of sins, the crimes of all her life. Of the lives of sinful others. Too heavy to bear. But Coira bore it, now she was Persapheh. She stood straight in the robe, and they combed her silken hair over it, while Hadz watched, torch-eyed.

When everything was done, he sent the servants out. He came up close. He slipped his hands inside the robe and felt of her, and now only the armor and weight of the coffinrobe kept her standing or alive.

"Do you like my gift? Was I clever? It was too lovely to waste. Now it's still yours. Ah, your skin, better than the velvet. No need to be modest. I've had you already, my beloved, my lovely one. When you were asleep. Twice, thrice. And I felt you breathing—it was light as a smoke. No one else could see. Only I could feel your pure breath against my ear as I rocked your body with my hunger. It was *I* who woke you, wasn't it, Persapheh?"

The broken mirror was dead, and did not look.

Coira was dead, as befitted her now. Her eyes, closed.

She allowed the robe to hold her in position as the madman pierced her. She let him thrust inside her, groaning and flaming upon and in her body, until in orgasm he reared and shouted his own name, *Hadz! Hadz!*

He sank down and lay against her feet on the floor. This was the quiescence of victory and power.

She thought, it was nothing. He had done it already, twice, thrice.

And he needed no reaction under or against him. He had raped women, boys of seven, locked in chains; he had copulated with caskets of polished gems. Basically he needed only himself, but he had been there, too, reflected back at himself from her gown of glass.

Even lying on her feet, which were very cold, he saw himself, lazy and smiling. There—and there and there, in the mirror bits at the robe's edge. He, too, was beautiful. How beautiful.

"My love," he said, her prince.

II.

*I*T WAS WHEN HE STOPPED DREAMing of her every night that he began to think he might have to go back. That is, return to the cavern and make sure. While the dreams came, he could simply tell himself that he missed her somewhat, her sexual company if nothing else. Also that he was only guilty at leaving her. Then, this gap appeared between them. As if she had been sending him letters, although he could not read more than a word or two; messages, then. And suddenly they did not reach him any more. Why not? What had happened? Had anything happened at all? If so, were those vaguely remembered visions of her lying in the earth, drifting in the air, the breaking mirror, pieces of mirror-women moving about, white owls, black ravens, crying doves—were these dream pictures in some way true? Had there been a moment in the dreams when she told him she was dead—worse, buried

alive? Or that she was walking about inside a coffin, unable to
get out?

That day something else was going on in Korchlava. Noises, up-
heavals.

The city was like all such human heaps, towns, even large villages, Hephaestion thought. There was a hub of better buildings, a
well-built house of palace, gardens, a gilded church or this cathedral,
which seemed likely never to be finished, but which was towered
and faced with marble and goldwork. The appetizing kernal was
then surrounded by a debris of houses, markets, shops, and inns,
quickly degenerating into slums.

Today some of the citizens were burning effigies of a witch. At
first he paid no heed. He only avoided the loud, jolly, foul-mouthed
groups where he was able. Then he heard a name they were giving
the straw-stuffed sacks. It was Draco's first queen they were ritually
disposing of.

Then, in a lightless wine-shop, he let himself overhear the story.
The first queen had always been a sorceress, seeming young and
fair but in fact kept young only by her devilish arts. In reality she
was an ancient hag. Draco had left her and come away here, and
made a new marriage through a special Church dispensation. Then
the witch-hag practiced against her only daughter, or some daughter
of Draco's by another. The witch succeeded in murdering the girl
at Belgra by the sea. But when the authority there, Draco's own
son, sent for the witch, she vanished into thin air.

Some said she had changed into a serpent and slithered off, or
a winged one that flew. Others said she made herself into a woman
either so gorgeous or so loathesome that she was unrecognizable.
Whatever she had done, she was never found, or Draco would have
put her to death. His loyal subjects therefore, at Korchlava, burned
her as a doll, sympathetic magic.

Hephaestion sat in his corner, even after the chatterers slob-
bered off to other things.

Did any of this penetrate to Elusion? Had Coira heard of it, and what had she thought? He recalled how she had said to him, the first time he lay with her, *"She hated me,"* and then, "Do you?" and later, "I only ever loved *her*. But I love *you*."

"Christ, oh, Christ," he said very softly.

What had happened, what had gone on? Was this idiot's ugly story here some garbled version of a fact?

I love you, she said, inside his ear.

I know. I know it. You were a joy to me, Coira.

You allowed me to love you. That's all I asked, she said.

Christ—why didn't you ask me for more? Why—why didn't you, Coira? Why didn't you shriek at me and stick your nails into my arms and make me stay with you?

Astounded at himself, the inner voices fell silent.

But then he saw himself holding her to him, up in the air. She was a child's height, so they matched.

"I'll come back for you," he had said.

That must have been in one of the dreams. How long had gone by? Days, months—the spring was full, it was quite warm today.

"Hey, you, mistake-of-God, do you want work?" Hephaestion looked, and saw a carter hulking near. "Your keep and a copper coin, two days hefting loads for me—donkey's sick."

"You're kind, master," said the dwarf, doubling down, grateful and inferior. "But I've got to get back to my mistress."

"Work-shy cur. Drinking here when you should be laboring."

They sent him off with oaths and a flung clod, which struck him in the back. He barely noticed.

Hephaestion turned for the city gate.

What am I doing?

He was on the road above the galloping river, striding unevenly back toward the mines, before he answered himself.

Coira.

*   *   *

How many days had it taken him to reach the city? Four, five, more. Walking back, up the hills, not pausing often, sleeping only an hour or so, here, there, in the nights. Two days. The days he might have been earning his keep and a copper coin as a donkey.

He needed to earn no money. He had plenty saved from the mine. Besides, it was possible to live as the Christ advocated, accepting what came, relying on fate—or God.

There were flowers all over the hills. The river, when he saw it carving between the rocks and the finely budding trees, was blue as the silk he had bought her, that day before he left.

"So, it's you back. Liked it here so well? Or not done so well up above? Your kin were off, don't expect to find *them*. But it's all one to you. There are plenty of your sort still here."

Hephaestion was startled the guard at the hill gate recalled him. As he said, there were so many dwarves who worked the mines. Hephaestion was *not* surprised Proud, Tickle and the rest had also gone away, surprised only at how little the thought of them tugged at him. He had known them most of his adult life. And he had been crazy for Vinka, once. But then he heard himself saying, "Did they go with my mistress?"

"What mistress? You had none. Oh—that girl with the hair— that witch-girl, do you mean? Marusa's tits, she's *queen* here now. She's Hadz's darling."

Hephaestion waited humbly, being slow-witted, listening, his bowel churning with dismay, and stormy rage.

The guard was examining the payment Hephaestion had offered him. Now he became off-hand. "Go on, then. Get down, if you want."

Hephaestion would rather have questioned him, but thought he could not. Let the man forget again the dwarf had any link to her. The girl with the hair—the times he had told her to hide it—the witch-girl, queen's daughter, Queen of Hell. He might have guessed, she would go with some proper man—but not Hadz. She never would, would she?

The guard certainly had said nothing about death, or burial.

Hephaestion went back along the River of Hate, and all the time he thought of her, now. He thought how she had been with him on Woe Stream. Of how she had drawn him to her in the night. He thought of sex with her and grew hard, he thought of her loving Hadz, and then of dreams of death, and saw his hand begin to shake where it rested on the boat's side.

You simpleton, you like her so much.

But fear only took hold of him when they came to the cliff under the metallic-starred rock roof, and he saw the insipid icon of the saint, holding up his ineffectual hand to bless.

Hate, yes. He hated this place. He would never have come here again, if not for Coira. He had told her how he was comfortable with mines, but that was a lie. They were asphyxiating pits of danger and death. Like graves. Coffins set with veins of iron, gold and silver, and glimmering gems.

She had not loved anyone else. God knew, he had seen she was not to be moved, when once she had decided. It was not the prince, then, but the king . . . King Death . . .

It seemed to take him more days and nights to get up the wending rockery, through the rubble of dwellings, and find the shack on the cliffside which overlooked Prince Hadz's mansion in the valley.

The powdered lunar roots still hung over the shack Tickle had called a cottage. The torch was alight. A fat woman sat tending a pot on a fire now outside the door, and she was wrapped in an achingly sky blue mantle. It was the silk he had left for Coira.

"I like your gown, Lady," he said, fawning, joking courteously.

The woman glanced up. She had a face unsightly from the brain behind it.

"Get away, you shit-thing. All this is mine!" And out of the cauldron she shot a ladleful of boiling watery soup. It just missed his eyes, his cheek. One drop bit scald-cold against his ear.

She was only the world. He was quite used to her. He turned and swagger-strode away, down among the tracks and rubbish, toward the valley.

But a voice sang low in his scalded ear. *She did not take your gift. Cared nothing for you once Hadz wanted her.*

And a second voice said below the first, *Or she's dead.*

But he knew voices. In the clefts of workings they would call and whimper. In empty spots they would treacherously sing. At last now he pushed them away. Whatever had happened he was nearly up to it.

On Woe Stream, the same gossipy, one-eyed youth appeared, to pole the raft. *He* did not remember the dwarf at all, or rather remembered him as another dwarf, known as Pack.

"How are you, Pack? Spend your wage already? That's the silliness with you, Pack, you drink it all away."

"So I do," assented Hephaestion. He stood up to the front with the boy. The river crinkled and gleamed, and Hephaestion thought of Coira, standing at his back, burning there like the scald of cold on his ear, fire and ice.

"What's all this about the Hell Prince?" asked Pack.

"What?"

"Some tale I heard. Some girl he's got."

"He's always got a girl. Or a lad. No, it is a girl, that's true. She can charm his headaches off. But she got ill. She died, now I think of it, and he had to make a box for her. It was a rare old sight, I heard. Jewels in it and hammered gold and iron. Hadz's notion."

"She's dead."

"Last I heard."

Hephaestion knelt down. He threw up in two fast heaves, in the leaden Stream of Woe.

"There, Pack, that's all your drinking gets you. A belly-quake and a sore head."

"Yes, you're right," said Pack. Hephaestion wiped his mouth. When he could, after a minute, he stood up again.

There was no point in continuing to the prince's mansion.

Then the boy said, "Wait though. Now I think—she got better, the girl, she got over it. Some old witch poisoned her, jealous of her. But she came to herself. I think she did."

Hephaestion said, "Stop this. Stop playing with me, or I'll break your fucking back."

"Eh?" said the boy.

Hephaestion had spoken too low for any but the stream, the ghosts in the air, to hear him.

"I said, who was it?"

"Oh. Some slut."

"Yes, some slut. They always are."

"Praise Marusa for the sluts."

The raft bumped in against the shore.

When he was clear of the stream, Hephaestion strode on toward the mansion.

He stumbled twice on the unevenly paved track where he had once helped Coira. Then he reached the untidy roil of the mansion, the facade of trunk-pillars, and the white poplar by Lethe Pool.

Drink the pool and forget.

It would be best. But first, be sure. For if she needed him, he must offer his help. What help he could give. "See to yourself . . . can't help you . . ." Yes, he had said that to her once. In the wagon, when Cirpoz was set to rape her.

She was of the giant and obnoxious race. Nothing to him. Yet, until he knew she was safe and did not wish for him, he would, he would go on.

"What do you want, half-man?"

Hephaestion looked up at the new giant.

Oh God, she was not of this kind at all.

She was of another race, the same race as himself. Not anything to do with Man or dwarves, or with God.

His.

She was his.

I own her. And she me.

"Mistress told me to come back, to the prince's house."

"Mistress? Whose is it you are?"

"Coira's." (Oh, and I am.)

"That one. She's a queen now. She's called Persapheh. Get it right."

"Thanks, sir master. *Persa-pheh*."

She was alive.

He prevented himself from laughing, since the ruffian would misunderstand it. It was only savage relief and Heaven-sent happiness, breaking him and making him mad.

Hephaestion trudged forward slavishly, and the ruffian kept pace with him.

If Coira disowned him now, then certainly they would have some sport with him. Hurt him, kill him.

They went into the palace of Prince Hadz.

Whenever Hadz desired her, he took her. He would come in and send the others out. He would lead her to the couch or the floor, or lean her on a wall. Then he would slide his hands inside the exotic coffin she must always wear, caress her, taste her and, cramming within her, achieve the pinnacle.

Sometimes, when they sat in the High Chamber, the large hall of torches, with his court (such as it was) around him, he would stand up and draw her quietly by the hand, guiding her behind the black drape, then rushing his body into hers. Recently he cried out less at their unions. She did not think this was from rectitude.

Now and then, he wished to take longer. Then she must do things to him. His body was fine, young, clean, even wholesome. He liked little games. Feathers, and things which clawed. He never did any of this to her. She must do it. Once he had her bugger him with an ivory thumb. Once she must whip him with a quill.

He was capable of having her, in one way or another, many times over during the torchlit days, and up to seven times during a single lamp-lit night.

Never did he anticipate any need from her, save to serve him. At least she was spared one lie.

Her glassy surface he liked. He did not slip from it. He fastened himself in with hooks of adamantine, until each climax shook him away.

She was functional. A chair of orgasm. A paroxysm-making apparatus in a robe of blood and crystal, and silken hair and skin.

III.

*H*ER NAME WAS PERSAPHEH, and occasionally Hadz spoke it. No other name or title.

In the beginning she had turned to him when he uttered the name. Finally she saw she did not need to. It was only that he liked the sound of the name, its nature. King Hadz, Queen Persapheh.

The old man—Juprum—had quickly informed her there had been other Persaphehs in the past. Two of them had even been male. They had all . . . died. Or gone somewhere, where no one saw them again.

Juprum wanted to frighten her, Coira believed, as this must make her more grateful for Hadz's appreciation. Or maybe Juprum simply preferred to know her condition (fear), finding that more efficient.

Every morning she plucked a leaf from the Febrifuga which now grew, sallow and wilting, under the lamps. Hadz took the leaf and ate it, and once, once only, he remarked, "Eve gives me her apple of sin."

Did he think a transgression was involved in release from pain? She did not care what he thought.

Bitter honey, black as hair.

Today she had not seen him, not since he got up and left the couch he had that night shared with her. The day passed as always, the hours so slow Coira knew that by now she had lost her mind and become a water-clock, her movements its dead drip-drip.

She was, after all, still confined in her tomb. After the bath they would scent her, the cringing female slaves who never spoke, either. Then they hauled the coffin back on to her shoulders, over her breasts and arms, and closed and belted it bulkily at her waist with a snakelike cord of silver and gold. The robe's weight soon pushed the girdle to her hips.

Coira sat in a chair, and she thought, *I must leave. It doesn't matter if I die. I must only go away as far as I can until someone catches me and cuts my throat.*

But death had tired her so the first time, she could not decide where else to go, or even when to go, or what to wear for travelling—there was nothing to put on but the coffin.

Soon it was the hour of the night meal Hadz maintained in his hall. This was in essence like the feasts and dinners of her father, Draco, or of Tusaj, which she had not frequently attended. Belgra's court had not really been so much less rowdy or obscene than this one, although there had generally been more women present. Coira took her place here on the bench by the prince's chair, which tonight he had not yet filled.

Was Hadz her father's son, as they said? Then he would be her brother. That might account for the physical likeness between them.

She turned this idea in her mind as if it were a colorless stone, looking at it. In fact, she was waiting for Hephaestion to enter the hall, and her life, once more. She did not know it; how could she? She had been doing the same thing at Belgra Demitu and not known. And only her mother's dementia, and the witless Cirpoz, had caused the meeting to occur. (Her mother? Something about her mother? She could not think what. Let go.)

Just then, a black-haired dwarf stalked into the hall, one of the guards trailing behind him, seeming too tall and all out of proportion. The dwarf looked about, his head lifted keenly, scenting the air, a black wolf.

Coira saw him.

It was as if she saw only what she anticipated. Having been waiting intently, she could not be amazed. But then the shock smote her. No one detected it. She shut her eyes for half an instant. And for an instant longer she was like a bloodless, frozen corpse. Then she blushed—but it might have been some glow of the torches, warming her face and neck. For she was so composed, and did not move.

He met her eyes. One flaring second.

Then he cast his own down. Frowning, lurching, reluctant, he came round the hall, and the guard gave him a push to hasten him, for apparently he was scared now, the halfling, of what his "mistress" would say and do.

If he had had doubts still, which he had not, seeing her, he would have had to dismiss them.

She was like some hallucinatory winter flower. The robe—and she, growing in it, from it, an opalescent stem and bud from the bloody calyx.

And she was herself. The only one he had ever known.

A lifetime (nineteen or twenty years) of cunning and disembling was ingrained in Stormy Hephaestion.

He jumbled around the hall, cringing, looking under doglike brows and lids.

In front of her, he threw himself flat. But in the moment before he did so, he grinned—too fast for any but her, his girl, his Coira, to make it out.

"Is this yours?" asked the guard.

"Oh," she said. She sounded unenthusiastic.

"I mean, it says it's your property."

"Yes," said Coira, Princess-Queen Persapheh.

"Do you want him tumbled about a little? Reshaped?"

"Oh no." After another lingering second, Coira said, "He's not quite right in his head. He means no harm."

Somewhere in another world, everyone rushed and made sounds, for Prince Hadz was coming in.

In the only real world there was, Coira gazed at Hephaestion.

"Why—"

"Not now, my girl. Shut up your mouth."

"Yes."

Then Hephaestion kneeled down there, by her ankles, and bowed low to the prince of the dead and Hell.

But Hadz did not notice him. Hadz stared at Coira.

She rose and Hadz took hold of her.

Coira thought, *Now he will lead me out and have me.* And she smiled to welcome this. For anything was now welcome to her, even death again, perhaps.

But Hadz only kissed her forehead and they sat down. And *he* was there, sitting cross-legged, unseen, at her feet. She felt his weight and strength and heat soak through the coffin-gown and her blood.

"I have a quintessential pleasure for you tonight," said Hadz.

Yes, he seemed more than ever enthralled, and satisfied.

But *she* had been given the earth. She said, concentrating, her voice trembling with love, "Thank you, my lord."

Hadz still did not notice. He expected everything, only becoming startled when not quite everything was there for him. Even pain had been greater for him than for ordinary men. He was among the Chosen of God.

"I'd overlooked her. Then Juprum reminded me. Once, one of *these* tried to kill me. He isn't here now. He lasted days. I was inventive. But for her, this is more apt."

Turning, Hadz reviewed his queen in Hell. She was not the same. She seemed all full of lights. Hadz put his head to one side, measuring her and what he thought of this.

Then Juprum appeared.

"Shall they bring her in, my prince?"

"Yes. Now. Persapheh, who do you think this is?"

Cloudy with love, adrift with love, not really in the hall with him, she said, meekly, "Who, my lord?"

But there were only two people in the world.

She had forgotten, there were three.

IV.

*T*IME HAD SLIPPED ITS MOORINGS, but most of all for Arpazia. She had passed it, or through it, anyway. She paced round and about. Or she sat on the hard floor, her back against the wall which sounded with the wrinkling pool of forgetting. Eventually, this seemed to be all there was.

She was not ambitious and had nowhere to go, and knew herself ill-equipped either to get out, or to travel anywhere.

Her pain—the slowly healing cuts of the mirror, her inflamed joints—she mostly ignored, as if it had nothing to do with her at all. Yet there was the sense of loss. This seemed familiar as the pain, but far more urgent. She rumaged in her mind, searching for the cause, and how to alleviate it. But it was like a dream. Sometimes she knew her lover was dead and it was this which hurt her worse than any physical distress. Then again, he had been dead for many years. She was accustomed to the agony—which duly faded.

Othertimes, she thought she had lost her child. It had died in her arms, rolling away from her body as she tried to suckle it. This hurt was worse, for although she felt it less keenly, yet she felt it over every surface of her heart and brain. It was not so much loss as an omission. Through it, she mislaid her self.

She knew it was her fault. She had poisoned her child by sorcery. Why, she could not remember.

Once a day, in the dark, some person or other put a dish of food (slops) into the hut. Arpazia ate a little of this muck, sometimes. And twice a woman had come to redress her wounds. But in the beginning they had stitched her back, holding her fast, and at this second visit Arpazia thrust the woman off, slapping her face. Arpazia was the queen, and this maid exacerbated her discomfort. The slave ran away, and Arpazia forgot her. No one bothered after that.

They hate me. Let them beware of me, then.

She bit her nails to points, but they broke.

When the prison door was opened for the last time, she did not guess.

She stood, eyes watering in the torchlight.

There was a knotting in her face, and she did not know, either, it was one more cut from the shattering glass. The light seemed to irritate the seam, and she laid her palm over the area, feeling the swollen, ridged skin with a removed revulsion.

"See, she's vain, wants to hide her blemishes. Cheer up, old girl. You're off to a wedding."

This was what they called such an event, Hadz's mansion guards. A wedding—the sentence of execution.

None of them touched her. They too found her repellant. She walked in the midst of them, her back almost straight, her head slightly thrust forward.

"Should we cut off that hair? It's long—may get in the way."

"No, he'll like to see it flapping."

They went through the crooked passageways of the Prince of Hell's house, and she heard shouting, and blinked again at a flush of stronger light. The wide hall expanded before her and Arpazia walked into it. A memory of Draco's palace made her lift her head.

There were diners at their meat and drink. But no, this was not Belgra Demitu. Nor her father's castle in the forest. It was a very black place, fiercely lit.

All the guards had drawn away, and a general silence was settling.

Arpazia stood out on the floor.

She was like a girl; as they had called her, an *old* girl. She had been Maiden, now she was Crone. The two ends of her existence met in a ring. There was nothing, surely, in between. Her gray hair, thick with filth, trailed all round her. Her scarred face was unrecognizable to anyone who had not, once, known her well.

A man came sauntering up. His garments rained silver and gold, and his black curling mane shone with health. She had seen him before, but where? He was hideous. Arpazia could tell this plainly. He must be some extra Sin, invented by God, to threaten mankind.

"Here you are," he said. With one finger he tapped her shoulder. "Christ, how she stinks, the old fright. Look at her disgustingness. She's a witch. And she's a mother. But an unnatural mother." His voice grew darker and more full. "Do you speak?"

"Yes," said Arpazia, the witch-queen.

"Why did you do it? I mean, why try to kill your own child? You will be damned to everlasting night."

Arpazia glanced about. She said, "Very well." It was how she had made the unavoidable responses in church.

"What do you think you deserve first?" said Prince Hadz. But he had already decided. "I want to see you dance," said Hadz. It was a lewd term. She looked at him scornfully. "But even that isn't enough. Listen to me. I gave her the loveliest parts of her coffin, but I saved the frame for you. You shall have that."

Arpazia heard the creaking nurse-voice singing in her head.

Aloud, Arpazia murmured, "Snow, wood, blood."

Hadz struck her lightly across the temple and she fell to the floor. With no alarm he told her, "Don't try to curse me. I'm God's. The curse will miss me and go back on you."

And then Juprum called something, and a couple of the less fastidious ruffians came, and clasped the crone. Another door was flung open. At the end of another walk, rabid with torchlight, an open space was revealed, like a sort of hole.

They were going out of the High Chamber.

As Coira stood up, Hephaestion too got to his feet.

Everyone had heard what Hadz had said, and most had not grasped its significance. They would do what he said, laugh when he did, applaud and obeyse themselves when required. But Hephaestion knew what was going on. He did not need to say to Coira, his girl, *That is your mother? She poisoned you? He means to chastize her?*

With the reserve of his life of self-control, he had not glanced up into her face.

But then, as they with the rest moved forward after Hadz, the guards and the old woman, Coira's fingers pressed into Hephaestion's shoulder.

"Walk, but inside you, keep very still," he said quietly. "You can't do a thing for her."

"I must," was all she said.

"*No.* Best love, no. She'll still be hurt by him, and so will you."

Coira said, in that remote white voice above his head, so that for one of only a few times he uselessly raged at God, who had built him too low down, "I must."

Hadz was away with his captive. The others were streaming out into an open yard, with only the mansion walls and the night sky of the cavern roof above. No one paid any real attention to Coira and her dwarf.

Hephaestion knew how she was, once she had decided. What she said, she meant.

He stopped, and for a moment they were stationary, the last of Hadz's court moving around them and on.

"Then," Hephaestion said, "*I'll* do it. I'll see to him. I'm practiced, it will be a treat. Then as many others as I'm able. Try to get her away. There must be plenty of nooks to hide in, here." But he did not believe that, of course.

And Coira said in her turn, "No. *No,* they'll kill you. *I* must do it alone."

"You'll die at once. Leave it to me. *I'll* do it."

"No. *I.*"

The crowd was gone, had left them there, hissing at each other, bent together, she leaning to him and he arching his back, leaning up toward her. (One or two who saw had found it amusing, this cranky little altercation. If she did not hurry, Hadz's stupid whore would miss the witch's sentence, and serve her right.)

"I won't endanger you," she said. "It isn't your quarrel."

"Yes, if it's yours. My way of it, you and she have some chance."

"And you have none."

"If you lose your life, Coira, what do I care what happens to me?"

Her face was like a slender moon. How had he ever thought he did not love her?

"You came back," she said, as if suddenly understanding.

"Yes. I kept dreaming about you. I knew you were dead—how did I? But then, you lived—"

"Hephaestion—" she said.

A sound rose from the courtyard under the open rock. Rose, rose again and again.

Hephaestion had heard something similar, in the woods, the countryside, and for a moment, though his heart jolted, his attention did not properly respond. But Coira seemed to fly up and away from him into the roof. Then she dashed by him toward the court, her own mouth stretched on noiseless screaming.

Lilca had been hanged. In Draco's war-camp, they had told the fourteen-year-old Arpazia, making sure she was given the details. She had forgotten them, had named herself Lilca. Now, she recollected.

This was the other dance, not the sexual act, but the kicking act of death at the end of a rope.

Up there, that strut which protruded from the wall, the iron hook, and from it, the iron chain. If the metal had come from the coffin, even Hadz was not certain. Probably not. But *some* metal had come from it which he would award the poisonous witch.

Juprum had spoken to Hadz, yesterday. "If you hang the old bag, my prince, she's very lightweight. You'll need to weigh her down a little, or she'll scarcely even strangle." He was often invaluable, Juprum, in such matters.

But it was Hadz who had then announced, "They can tie two

pieces of iron off my Persapheh's coffin, tie them on the hag's feet. That will anchor her."

Then he circled about, thinking.

"It's not sufficient," he said, discontented.

Juprum said, "Perhaps you mean to be merciful, sir. Like the Church, with such a sinner."

"Eh? What do you mean—merciful—?"

"She will spend many ages in Hell, but you might ease her time there, in this Hell we have, seeing you are Hell's Prince. A priest, sir, would try to do that for her. He would cauterize her soul." Hadz smiled a little. Juprum made all plain, "Attach the metal. Heat it first."

As she stood in the courtyard, Arpazia might have been rooted to the spot. But she was not, and next a man lifted her right off her feet, and on to a wooden stool. They arranged the noose of iron chain about her throat, and Arpazia put up her hands, which they had not bothered to bind, and felt the noose. She now remembered everything concerning Lilca. And a torrent of fear blanched through her, so all her body changed to liquid and liquid ran from it.

But strengthless with terror, mindless and uncomprehending how she had come to this, she could not even cry out. Not yet.

"Hold her now," someone said.

She was held. More firmly than before, when they tried to heal her. More firmly than any binding.

The stench of her own loosened bladder and bowels confounded her. She had not a single thought. Already she was only fear.

And through the fog of panic, they were bringing, from a brazier, two red roses.

Used to Juprum's suggestions and Hadz's performances, the guards grappled the bony hag effortlessly as she jumped and spasmed in their grip.

Red-hot, held in tongs, the iron plates were thrust against her feet, bent round, and from their own malleable state, adhered.

Then the men let her go. The chain about her throat pulled taut, and sliced and jammed her shrieking, which had been that of a fox in a trap, into retching grunts.

Up high they hoisted her then. She had herself already kicked away the stool. But as Juprum predicted, she was not heavy enough to break her spine, or strangle instantly.

She hung in the black air, jerking and dancing, while Hadz, and so his court, congratulated and toasted her.

And it was to this that Coira ran out. This which Coira saw, there before her, hoisted high on blackness, the red and white flailing of her grunting dying mother, dancing to death in her gown of urine and dirt and her shoes of cooking red-hot iron.

"*Take my hand.* Take it. There. I've got you now."

"It hurts me"—she screamed—"hurts me—hurts—"

"No, now you're safe. Let the pain go out of you. It will."

And the anguish whistled down and away, it fell from her, she saw it fall, a white and black thing, dying red.

He held her in his arms.

Oh, she remembered his arms. Of all the things kept in her thoughts, or forgotten, this, *this* she knew.

"It's done. It's over. Trust me, sweetest love."

She wept.

But he spoke a fact. The pain was gone completely. She was cool and clean, and could smell perfume on her skin, and the warm scents of him, the aroma of the summer wood, the robe of skins, his gilded hair that had dried her tears.

"Now, look at me," he said. And she raised her face and there he was, as she had always known him. Her only lord and husband. Her lover. Her only love.

Then she hid her face. "Don't look at me. I've grown old and foul."

"You're lovely. Just as you were. My Queen-in-the-Wood. My Demetra by day, my Persapheh by night."

"No—no . . ."

"Come then," he said, "I'll show you."

The wood was closing to the wave of night. Stars gemmed between the boughs where birds and spirits rustled. The waterfall rippled like glass. The grass was soft beneath her flawless feet.

They looked down into the mirror of the collected water, and Arpazia saw herself as she had been at fourteen, at twenty, in the beauty of her flesh. And Klymeno, handsome and a god, standing by her.

"What fell from me?" she said.

"Everything."

"Now can I be with you?"

"Where else?"

"Forgive me," she said.

"For what?"

"God's law," she ventured, "my sins—His Hell—"

"Ah," he said. "Let that fall, too."

"But are we real?"

"More real," he said. He held her. It was so.

Hadz stared down at the girl. She lay stretched on his yard. In her wonderful blood-red artifact of robe, which seemed to have pulled her right over.

He was displeased.

"What is wrong with her?"

Juprum said, "She swooned. She didn't like your show, though devised for her."

Hadz spat on the ground. For a second he looked like what he was.

"I am disappointed in you, Persapheh. No, she doesn't deserve that name." Scowling, he walked away from her, and back again. (Dimly Hadz noted that dwarf servant of hers, that he had been told of, squatting there beside her, like some dog.) "She wasn't worthy of this gown I gave her. No. The wonderful coffin was spoiled, and that was her fault. She was meant to be dead but she revived; such a fuss, I had to tell them to let her out. It was ruined, the coffin. And now, see here, the mirror's cracked." He toed Coira's prone body. A jewel rolled from the mantle, deep violet-purple, like another kind of blood.

Jurpum waited, eager, but too wise to prompt.

Hadz said, "Do you know, she isn't perfect. Her arm is scarred. Little white scars. Most ugly. She was never worthy of me. *Not* Persapheh, I think."

Juprum undid his lips to speak.

Hephaestion moved first. He went cartwheeling across the courtyard, stood on his hands, brought one leg, then another, over his head. Leapt upright and bowed low before Hadz in exact equilibrium.

"How quaint," said Hadz, smiling again.

"Give her to *me*, lord master prince, prince of all princes, fairest in the world."

Hadz, intrigued (childlike, fearsome) smiled more. "To *you*?"

"I'll make her pay, master prince. She owes me a few blows—but it's worse, to have been annoying *yourself*. Think of her degradation, Lord, Me, after *you*."

"Oh," said Hadz. "But you're a pretty fellow, now I look at you. Not like most of your kind."

"Am I, master?" Hephaestion crept near. He put his hand upon Hadz's thigh. "You are the most beautiful," he murmured, "in the world. Who can compare to you? I'll make her suffer for offending you, trust me. You should have only the loveliest things."

Hadz considered. He said, reasonably, "You must earn her from me, then."

Hephaestion, too, smiled, and midway became all one miraculous somersault. Hadz chuckled, delighted. "Are you cunning at other matters, half-man?"

Juprum drew in a noisy breath to remonstrate. Turning idly, Hadz smacked his faithful old servant in the mouth, hard enough, for once, to extract a tooth.

None of them attended the crone, still swinging from her chain. Or the girl lying on the yard, her hands folded in against her womb. Both seemed dead. Even Hadz's scum of guards did not touch them, in case the prince might still have some use for them, when he was done screwing the dwarf.

V.

$\mathcal{B}$EYOND KORCHLAVA, GREAT plains moved away, and then there were once more the mountains, like clouds which, while resting on the land, had been changed to granite.

Concealed in glassy air, the soul of the mirror watched.

What did the mirror see?

A young girl, a young woman, slender, clear and bright. Her companion, a black-haired man of the race of dwarves.

"How wide the plains are. Where do they end?"

"At the mountains. And then they say there's another land."

Both of them were on foot, but they were not quite unprosperous, for they had a donkey, which moved placidly behind them, with their meager goods on its back.

"You're sad," Hephaestion said, an hour later.

"Forgive me."

"For what?"

"For—what was done to you."

"Coira," he said, "what he did was nothing. He wasn't the first and may not be the last. It got me *you*. He was easy to deal with, in his happy mood."

Coira said, "She'll feel nothing now. She's safe. The fire was—it was warm, quick. Perhaps she's an angel, now."

"Perhaps."

"She meant no harm. No, she meant harm. But she was mine."

"I'm yours."

Coira smiled.

Later still, the evening began to come, blowing softly over the plains, on wings of damson cloud which might, if not careful, be changed too into mountains during the night.

They camped by a stream. The moon stole over a slope and shone in the stream like a face in a mirror.

"I have something to tell you," said Coira.

"I thought so."

She stared at him, then looked far off. "You can't know it yet. I'm carrying a child."

"I did know. I know you, my girl."

"Then you must see—I've no means to know if it's yours, or his."

Hephaestion fed sticks into the fire. He was always so glad fire did not seem to remind her of the corpse's cremation.

He said, "His or mine. Well, it's yours."

She sighed. "I know the proper herbs to be rid of it."

"Then if you want that, you must take them."

"Would you despise me for it?"

"Only if you did it for me. No woman should carry if she doesn't want, can't bear to. What's the use of that?" Hephaestion said, "I heard this, in a church once. We come into the world blameless, whoever is father or mother. Even Eve and the Apple, this priest said, can't mark first innocence. I remember the words—*Vestis pura niveo candore*. The sinless robe, brilliantly white as snow. So if it's Hadz's child, even then, it's—new. New, unmarked snow."

And later still, when they lay close in their bed of grass, with only the sounds of the donkey grazing and the night moths dusting over the plain, she said this:

"If the child's his, yet it *is* mine. The poison almost killed me. It made my breathing invisible, and the beat of my heart—only someone who cared for me could have seen it. You would have done. In a way, you did, in your dreams. But they never knew. They shut me in a box of gems and glass. Yet here I am. And when he did that—to—my mother—I *felt* the child's life in me, its breath, its heartbeat. It's curled up inside me—it's *mine*—it's me—another me, myself born again in flesh, yet new and unlike and changed— I'm not a grave—I can give it the world. And I want my child. My motherhood. I want that."

"Then have that," he said again. Then: "Coira, will you let it be my child too?"

He knew, he thought, it could not actually be his. He had never sired an infant. But then, according to the talk of Elusion, neither had the tyrant Hadz.

They slept. Stars flew over. The sky grew thin.

Blood, that dye of war and butchery, announced it was also the color of life. It bloomed in Coira's lips. It dazzled in flowers along the wide, adventurous plain.

Soon the watching mirror saw in the East, that always-rising place of renewals, advents, a brightness like itself. The mirror offered neither question nor reply. The mirror's dialogues were done.

And when the sun rose, it rose blood-red.